Henry James

Henry James OM (15 April 1843 – 28 February 1916) was an American-British author regarded as a key transitional figure between literary realism and literary modernism, and is considered by many to be among the greatest novelists in the English language. He was the son of Henry James Sr. and the brother of renowned philosopher and psychologist William James and diarist Alice James.

He is best known for a number of novels dealing with the social and marital interplay between émigré Americans, English people, and continental Europeans. Examples of such novels include The Portrait of a Lady, The Ambassadors, and The Wings of the Dove. His later works were increasingly experimental. In describing the internal states of mind and social dynamics of his characters, James often made use of a style in which ambiguous or contradictory motives and impressions were overlaid or juxtaposed in the discussion of a character's psyche.(Source: Wikipedia)

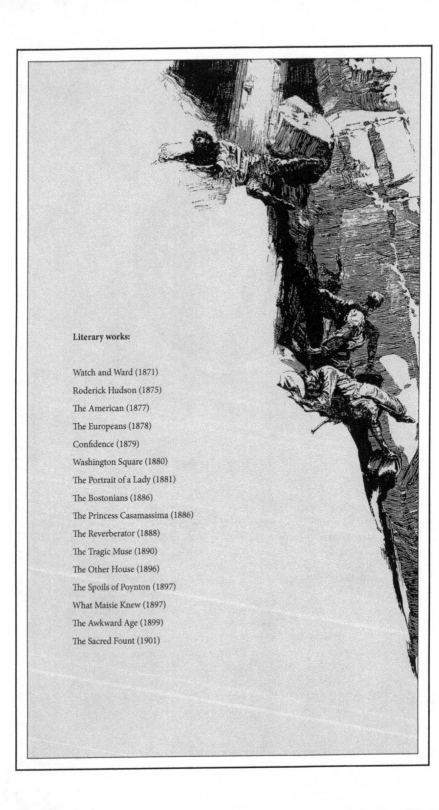

Literary works:

Watch and Ward (1871)

Roderick Hudson (1875)

The American (1877)

The Europeans (1878)

Confidence (1879)

Washington Square (1880)

The Portrait of a Lady (1881)

The Bostonians (1886)

The Princess Casamassima (1886)

The Reverberator (1888)

The Tragic Muse (1890)

The Other House (1896)

The Spoils of Poynton (1897)

What Maisie Knew (1897)

The Awkward Age (1899)

The Sacred Fount (1901)

THE
WORKS OF HENRY JAMES

VOL. 02 (OF 24)

A PASSIONATE PILGRIM
A SMALL BOY AND OTHERS
AN INTERNATIONAL EPISODE

An Imprint of Moon Classics LLC

A Wholly Owned Subsidiary of Queenior LLC

A Melodragon Company

First Printing: 2020

ISBN 978-1-6627-1622-5 (Paperback)

ISBN 978-1-6627-1623-2 (Hardcover)

Published by Moon Classics

www.moonclassics.com

Contents

A PASSIONATE PILGRIM   **11**

I   13

II   32

III   47

IV   70

A SMALL BOY AND OTHERS 87

I 89

II 97

III 103

IV 110

V 117

VI 124

VII 131

VIII 139

IX 145

X 159

XI 165

XII 174

XIII 184

XIV 192

XV 197

XVI 205

XVII 215

XVIII 222

XIX 231

XX 238

XXI 245

XXII 251

XXIII 259

XXIV 266

XXV 274

XXVI 284

XXVII 289

XXVIII 294

XXIX 308

AN INTERNATIONAL EPISODE 323

PART I 325

PART II 363

About Author 407

NOTABLE WORKS 425

THE
WORKS
OF
HENRY JAMES
VOL. 02 (OF 24)

A PASSIONATE PILGRIM

I

Intending to sail for America in the early part of June, I determined to spend the interval of six weeks in England, to which country my mind's eye only had as yet been introduced. I had formed in Italy and France a resolute preference for old inns, considering that what they sometimes cost the ungratified body they repay the delighted mind. On my arrival in London, therefore, I lodged at a certain antique hostelry, much to the east of Temple Bar, deep in the quarter that I had inevitably figured as the Johnsonian. Here, on the first evening of my stay, I descended to the little coffee-room and bespoke my dinner of the genius of "attendance" in the person of the solitary waiter. No sooner had I crossed the threshold of this retreat than I felt I had cut a golden-ripe crop of English "impressions." The coffee-room of the Red Lion, like so many other places and things I was destined to see in the motherland, seemed to have been waiting for long years, with just that sturdy sufferance of time written on its visage, for me to come and extract the romantic essence of it.

The latent preparedness of the American mind even for the most characteristic features of English life was a matter I meanwhile failed to get to the bottom of. The roots of it are indeed so deeply buried in the soil of our early culture that, without some great upheaval of feeling, we are at a loss to say exactly when and where and how it begins. It makes an American's enjoyment of England an emotion more searching than anything Continental. I had seen the coffee-room of the Red Lion years ago, at home—at Saragossa Illinois—in books, in visions, in dreams, in Dickens, in Smollett, in Boswell. It was small and subdivided into six narrow compartments by a series of perpendicular screens of mahogany, something higher than a man's stature, furnished on either side with a meagre uncushioned ledge, denominated in ancient Britain a seat. In each of these rigid receptacles was a narrow table—a table expected under stress to accommodate no less than four pairs of active British elbows. High pressure indeed had passed away from the Red Lion for ever. It now knew only that of memories and ghosts and atmosphere. Round the room there marched, breast-high, a magnificent panelling of mahogany, so dark with time and so polished with unremitted friction that by gazing a while into its lucid blackness I made out the dim reflexion of a party of wigged gentlemen in knee-breeches just arrived from York by the coach. On the dark yellow walls, coated by the fumes of English coal, of English mutton, of Scotch whiskey, were a dozen melancholy prints, sallow-toned with age—the Derby favourite of the year 1807, the Bank of England, her Majesty the Queen. On the floor was a Turkey carpet—as old as the mahogany almost, as the Bank of England, as the Queen—into which the waiter had in his lonely revolutions trodden so many massive soot-flakes and drops of overflowing beer that the glowing looms of Smyrna would certainly not have recognised it. To say that I ordered my dinner of this archaic type would be altogether to misrepresent the process owing to which, having dreamed of lamb and spinach and a salade de saison, I sat down in penitence to a mutton-chop and a rice pudding. Bracing my feet against the cross-beam of my little oaken table, I opposed to the mahogany partition behind me the vigorous dorsal resistance that must have expressed the old-English idea of repose. The sturdy screen refused even to creak, but my poor Yankee joints made up the deficiency.

While I was waiting there for my chop there came into the room a person whom, after I had looked at him a moment, I supposed to be a fellow lodger and probably the only one. He seemed, like myself, to have submitted to proposals for dinner; the table on the other side of my partition had been prepared to receive him. He walked up to the fire, exposed his back to it and, after consulting his watch, looked directly out of the window and indirectly at me. He was a man of something less than middle age and more than middle stature, though indeed you would have called him neither young nor tall. He was chiefly remarkable for his emphasised leanness. His hair, very thin on the summit of his head, was dark short and fine. His eye was of a pale turbid grey, unsuited, perhaps, to his dark hair and well-drawn brows, but not altogether out of harmony with his colourless bilious complexion. His nose was aquiline and delicate; beneath it his moustache languished much rather than bristled. His mouth and chin were negative, or at the most provisional; not vulgar, doubtless, but ineffectually refined. A cold fatal gentlemanly weakness was expressed indeed in his attenuated person. His eye was restless and deprecating; his whole physiognomy, his manner of shifting his weight from foot to foot, the spiritless droop of his head, told of exhausted intentions, of a will relaxed. His dress was neat and "toned down"—he might have been in mourning. I made up my mind on three points: he was a bachelor, he was out of health, he was not indigenous to the soil. The waiter approached him, and they conversed in accents barely audible. I heard the words "claret," "sherry" with a tentative inflexion, and finally "beer" with its last letter changed to "ah." Perhaps he was a Russian in reduced circumstances; he reminded me slightly of certain sceptical cosmopolite Russians whom I had met on the Continent. While in my extravagant way I followed this train—for you see I was interested—there appeared a short brisk man with reddish-brown hair, with a vulgar nose, a sharp blue eye and a red beard confined to his lower jaw and chin. My putative Russian, still in possession of the rug, let his mild gaze stray over the dingy ornaments of the room. The other drew near, and his umbrella dealt a playful poke at the concave melancholy waistcoat. "A penny ha'penny for your thoughts!"

My friend, as I call him, uttered an exclamation, stared, then laid his two hands on the other's shoulders. The latter looked round at me keenly, compassing me in a momentary glance. I read in its own vague light that this was a transatlantic eyebeam; and with such confidence that I hardly needed to see its owner, as he prepared, with his companion, to seat himself at the table adjoining my own, take from his overcoat-pocket three New York newspapers and lay them beside his plate. As my neighbours proceeded to dine I felt the crumbs of their conversation scattered pretty freely abroad. I could hear almost all they said, without straining to catch it, over the top of the partition that divided us. Occasionally their voices dropped to recovery of discretion, but the mystery pieced itself together as if on purpose to entertain me. Their speech was pitched in the key that may in English air be called alien in spite of a few coincidences. The voices were American, however, with a difference; and I had no hesitation in assigning the softer and clearer sound to the pale thin gentleman, whom I decidedly preferred to his comrade. The latter began to question him about his voyage.

15

"Horrible, horrible! I was deadly sick from the hour we left New York."

"Well, you do look considerably reduced," said the second-comer.

"Reduced! I've been on the verge of the grave. I haven't slept six hours for three weeks." This was said with great gravity.

"Well, I've made the voyage for the last time."

"The plague you have! You mean to locate here permanently?"

"Oh it won't be so very permanent!"

There was a pause; after which: "You're the same merry old boy, Searle. Going to give up the ghost to-morrow, eh?"

"I almost wish I were."

"You're not so sweet on England then? I've heard people say at home that you dress and talk and act like an Englishman. But I know these people here and I know you. You're not one of this crowd, Clement Searle, not you. You'll go under here, sir; you'll go under as sure as my name's Simmons."

Following this I heard a sudden clatter as of the drop of a knife and fork. "Well, you're a delicate sort of creature, if it IS your ugly name! I've been wandering about all day in this accursed city, ready to cry with homesickness and heartsickness and every possible sort of sickness, and thinking, in the absence of anything better, of meeting you here this evening and of your uttering some sound of cheer and comfort and giving me some glimmer of hope. Go under? Ain't I under now? I can't do more than get under the ground!"

Mr. Simmons's superior brightness appeared to flicker a moment in this gust of despair, but the next it was burning steady again. "DON'T 'cry,' Searle," I heard him say. "Remember the waiter. I've grown Englishman enough for that. For heaven's sake don't let's have any nerves. Nerves won't do anything for you here. It's best to come to the point. Tell me in three words what you expect of me."

I heard another movement, as if poor Searle had collapsed in his chair. "Upon my word, sir, you're quite inconceivable. You never got my letter?"

"Yes, I got your letter. I was never sorrier to get anything in my life."

At this declaration Mr. Searle rattled out an oath, which it was well perhaps that I but partially heard. "Abijah Simmons," he then cried, "what demon of perversity possesses you? Are you going to betray me here in a foreign land, to turn out a false friend, a heartless rogue?"

"Go on, sir," said sturdy Simmons. "Pour it all out. I'll wait till you've done. Your beer's lovely," he observed independently to the waiter. "I'll have some more."

"For God's sake explain yourself!" his companion appealed.

There was a pause, at the end of which I heard Mr. Simmons set down his empty tankard with emphasis. "You poor morbid mooning man," he resumed, "I don't want to say anything to make you feel sore. I regularly pity you. But you must allow that you've acted more like a confirmed crank than a member of our best society—in which every one's so sensible."

Mr. Searle seemed to have made an effort to compose himself. "Be so good as to tell me then what was the meaning of your letter."

"Well, you had got on MY nerves, if you want to know, when I wrote it. It came of my always wishing so to please folks. I had much better have let you alone. To tell you the plain truth I never was so horrified in my life as when I found that on the strength of my few kind words you had come out here to seek your fortune."

"What then did you expect me to do?"

"I expected you to wait patiently till I had made further enquiries and had written you again."

"And you've made further enquiries now?"

"Enquiries! I've committed assaults."

"And you find I've no claim?"

"No claim that one of THESE big bugs will look at. It struck me at first that you had rather a neat little case. I confess the look of it took hold of me—"

"Thanks to your liking so to please folks!" Mr. Simmons appeared for a moment at odds with something; it proved to be with his liquor. "I rather think your beer's too good to be true," he said to the waiter. "I guess I'll take water. Come, old man," he resumed, "don't challenge me to the arts of debate, or you'll have me right down on you, and then you WILL feel me. My native sweetness, as I say, was part of it. The idea that if I put the thing through it would be a very pretty feather in my cap and a very pretty penny in my purse was part of it. And the satisfaction of seeing a horrid low American walk right into an old English estate was a good deal of it. Upon my word, Searle, when I think of it I wish with all my heart that, extravagant vain man as you are, I COULD, for the charm of it, put you through! I should hardly care what you did with the blamed place when you got it. I could leave you alone to turn it into Yankee notions—into ducks and drakes as they call 'em here. I should like to see you tearing round over it and kicking up its sacred dust in their very faces!"

"You don't know me one little bit," said Mr. Searle, rather shirking, I thought, the burden of this tribute and for all response to the ambiguity of the compliment.

"I should be very glad to think I didn't, sir. I've been to no small amount of personal inconvenience for you. I've pushed my way right up to the headspring. I've got the best opinion that's to be had. The best opinion that's to be had just gives you one leer over its spectacles. I guess that look will fix you if you ever get it straight. I've been able to tap, indirectly," Mr. Simmons went on, "the solicitor of your usurping cousin, and he evidently knows something to be in the wind. It seems your elder brother twenty years ago put out a feeler. So you're not to have the glory of even making them sit up."

"I never made any one sit up," I heard Mr. Searle plead. "I shouldn't begin at this time of day. I should approach the subject like a gentleman."

"Well, if you want very much to do something like a gentleman you've got a capital chance. Take your disappointment like a gentleman."

I had finished my dinner and had become keenly interested in poor Mr. Searle's unencouraging—or unencouraged—claim; so interested that I at last hated to hear his trouble reflected in his voice without being able—all respectfully!—to follow it in his face. I left my place, went over to the fire, took up the evening paper and established a post of observation behind it.

His cold counsellor was in the act of choosing a soft chop from the dish—an act accompanied by a great deal of prying and poking with that gentleman's own fork. My disillusioned compatriot had pushed away his plate; he sat with his elbows on the table, gloomily nursing his head with his hands. His companion watched him and then seemed to wonder—to do Mr. Simmons justice—how he could least ungracefully give him up. "I say, Searle,"—and for my benefit, I think, taking me for a native ingenuous enough to be dazzled by his wit, he lifted his voice a little and gave it an ironical ring—"in this country it's the inestimable privilege of a loyal citizen, under whatsoever stress of pleasure or of pain, to make a point of eating his dinner."

Mr. Searle gave his plate another push. "Anything may happen now. I don't care a straw."

"You ought to care. Have another chop and you WILL care. Have some better tipple. Take my advice!" Mr. Simmons went on.

My friend—I adopt that name for him—gazed from between his two hands coldly before him. "I've had enough of your advice."

"A little more," said Simmons mildly; "I shan't trouble you again. What do you mean to do?"

"Nothing."

"Oh come!"

"Nothing, nothing, nothing!"

"Nothing but starve. How about meeting expenses?"

"Why do you ask?" said my friend. "You don't care."

"My dear fellow, if you want to make me offer you twenty pounds you set most clumsily about it. You said just now I don't know you," Mr. Simmons went on. "Possibly. Come back with me then," he said kindly enough, "and let's improve our acquaintance."

"I won't go back. I shall never go back."

"Never?"

"Never."

Mr. Simmons thought it shrewdly over. "Well, you ARE sick!" he exclaimed presently. "All I can say is that if you're working out a plan for cold poison, or for any other act of desperation, you had better give it right up. You can't get a dose of the commonest kind of cold poison for nothing, you know. Look here, Searle"—and the worthy man made what struck me as a very decent appeal. "If you'll consent to return home with me by the steamer of the twenty-third I'll pay your passage down. More than that, I'll pay for your beer."

My poor gentleman met it. "I believe I never made up my mind to anything before, but I think it's made up now. I shall stay here till I take my departure for a newer world than any patched-up newness of ours. It's an odd feeling—I rather like it! What should I do at home?"

"You said just now you were homesick."

"I meant I was sick for a home. Don't I belong here? Haven't I longed to get here all my life? Haven't I counted the months and the years till I should be able to 'go' as we say? And now that I've 'gone,' that is that I've come, must I just back out? No, no, I'll move on. I'm much obliged to you for your offer. I've enough money for the present. I've about my person some forty pounds' worth of British gold, and the same amount, say, of the toughness of the heaven-sent idiot. They'll see me through together! After they're gone I shall lay my head in some English churchyard, beside some ivied tower, beneath an old gnarled black yew."

I had so far distinctly followed the dialogue; but at this point the landlord entered and, begging my pardon, would suggest that number 12, a most superior apartment, having now been vacated, it would give him pleasure if I would look in. I declined to look in, but agreed for number 12 at a venture and gave myself again, with dissimulation, to my friends. They had got up; Simmons had put on his overcoat; he stood polishing his rusty black hat with his napkin. "Do you mean to go down to the place?" he asked.

"Possibly. I've thought of it so often that I should like to see it."

"Shall you call on Mr. Searle?"

"Heaven forbid!"

"Something has just occurred to me," Simmons pursued with a grin that made his upper lip look more than ever denuded by the razor and jerked the ugly ornament of his chin into the air. "There's a certain Miss Searle, the old man's sister."

"Well?" my gentleman quavered.

"Well, sir!—you talk of moving on. You might move on the damsel."

Mr. Searle frowned in silence and his companion gave him a tap on the stomach. "Line those ribs a bit first!" He blushed crimson; his eyes filled with tears. "You ARE a coarse brute," he said. The scene quite harrowed me, but I was prevented from seeing it through by the reappearance of the landlord on behalf of number 12. He represented to me that I ought in justice to him to come and see how tidy they HAD made it. Half an hour afterwards I was rattling along in a hansom toward Covent Garden, where I heard Madame Bosio in The Barber of Seville. On my return from the opera I went into the coffee-room; it had occurred to me I might catch there another glimpse of Mr. Searle. I was not disappointed. I found him seated before the fire with his head sunk on his breast: he slept, dreaming perhaps of Abijah Simmons. I watched him for some moments. His closed eyes, in the dim lamplight, looked even more helpless and resigned, and I seemed to see the fine grain of his nature in his unconscious mask. They say fortune comes while we sleep, and, standing there, I felt really tender enough—though otherwise

21

most unqualified—to be poor Mr. Searle's fortune. As I walked away I noted in one of the little prandial pews I have described the melancholy waiter, whose whiskered chin also reposed on the bulge of his shirt-front. I lingered a moment beside the old inn-yard in which, upon a time, the coaches and post-chaises found space to turn and disgorge. Above the dusky shaft of the enclosing galleries, where lounging lodgers and crumpled chambermaids and all the picturesque domesticity of a rattling tavern must have leaned on their elbows for many a year, I made out the far-off lurid twinkle of the London constellations. At the foot of the stairs, enshrined in the glittering niche of her well-appointed bar, the landlady sat napping like some solemn idol amid votive brass and plate.

The next morning, not finding the subject of my benevolent curiosity in the coffee-room, I learned from the waiter that he had ordered breakfast in bed. Into this asylum I was not yet prepared to pursue him. I spent the morning in the streets, partly under pressure of business, but catching all kinds of romantic impressions by the way. To the searching American eye there is no tint of association with which the great grimy face of London doesn't flush. As the afternoon approached, however, I began to yearn for some site more gracefully classic than what surrounded me, and, thinking over the excursions recommended to the ingenuous stranger, decided to take the train to Hampton Court. The day was the more propitious that it yielded just that dim subaqueous light which sleeps so fondly upon the English landscape.

At the end of an hour I found myself wandering through the apartments of the great palace. They follow each other in infinite succession, with no great variety of interest or aspect, but with persistent pomp and a fine specific effect. They are exactly of their various times. You pass from painted and panelled bedchambers and closets, anterooms, drawing-rooms, council-rooms, through king's suite, queen's suite, prince's suite, until you feel yourself move through the appointed hours and stages of some rigid monarchical day. On one side are the old monumental upholsteries, the big cold tarnished beds and canopies, with the circumference of disapparelled royalty symbolised by a gilded balustrade, and the great carved and yawning chimney-places where dukes-in-waiting may have warmed their weary heels; on the other, in deep recesses, rise the immense windows, the framed and draped embrasures where the sovereign whispered and favourites smiled, looking out on terraced gardens and misty park. The brown walls are dimly illumined by innumerable portraits of courtiers and captains, more especially with various members of the Batavian entourage of William of Orange, the restorer of the palace; with good store too of the lily-bosomed models of Lely and Kneller. The whole tone of this processional interior is singularly stale and sad. The tints of all things have both faded and darkened—you taste the chill of the place as you walk from room to room. It was still early in the day and in the season, and I flattered myself that I was the only visitor. This complacency, however, dropped at sight of a person standing motionless before a simpering countess of Sir Peter Lely's creation. On hearing my footstep this victim of an evaporated spell turned his head and I recognised my fellow lodger of the Red Lion. I was apparently recognised as well; he looked as if he could scarce wait for me to be kind to him, and in fact didn't wait. Seeing I had a catalogue he asked the name of the portrait. On my satisfying him he appealed, rather timidly, as to my opinion of the lady.

"Well," said I, not quite timidly enough perhaps, "I confess she strikes me as no great matter."

He remained silent and was evidently a little abashed. As we strolled away he stole a sidelong glance of farewell at his leering shepherdess. To speak with him face to face was to feel keenly that he was no less interesting than infirm. We talked of our inn, of London, of the palace; he uttered his mind freely, but seemed to struggle with a weight of depression. It was an honest mind enough, with no great cultivation but with a certain natural love of excellent things. I foresaw that I should find him quite to the manner born—to ours; full of glimpses and responses, of deserts and desolations. His perceptions would be fine and his opinions pathetic; I should moreover take refuge from his sense of proportion in his sense of humour, and then refuge from THAT, ah me!—in what? On my telling him that I was a fellow citizen he stopped short, deeply touched, and, silently passing his arm into my own, suffered me to lead him through the other apartments and down into the gardens.

A large gravelled platform stretches itself before the basement of the palace, taking the afternoon sun. Parts of the great structure are reserved for private use and habitation, occupied by state-pensioners, reduced gentlewomen in receipt of the Queen's bounty and other deserving persons. Many of the apartments have their dependent gardens, and here and there, between the verdure-coated walls, you catch a glimpse of these somewhat stuffy bowers. My companion and I measured more than once this long expanse, looking down on the floral figures of the rest of the affair and on the stoutly-woven tapestry of creeping plants that muffle the foundations of the huge red pile. I thought of the various images of old-world gentility which, early and late, must have strolled in front of it and felt the protection and security of the place. We peeped through an antique grating into one of the mossy cages and saw an old lady with a black mantilla on her head, a decanter of water in one hand and a crutch in the other, come forth, followed by three little dogs and a cat, to sprinkle a plant. She would probably have had an opinion on the virtue of Queen Caroline. Feeling these things together made us quickly, made us extraordinarily, intimate. My companion seemed to ache with his impression; he scowled, all gently, as if it gave him pain. I proposed at last that we should dine somewhere on the spot and take a late train to town. We made our way out of the gardens into the adjoining village, where we entered an inn which I pronounced, very sincerely, exactly what we wanted. Mr. Searle had approached our board as shyly as if it had been a cold bath; but, gradually warming to his work, he declared at the end of half an hour that for the first time in a month he enjoyed his victuals.

"I'm afraid you're rather out of health," I risked.

"Yes, sir—I'm an incurable."

The little village of Hampton Court stands clustered about the entrance of Bushey Park, and after we had dined we lounged along into the celebrated avenue of horse-chestnuts. There is a rare emotion, familiar to every intelligent traveller, in which the mind seems to swallow the sum total of its impressions at a gulp. You take in the whole place, whatever it be. You feel England, you feel Italy, and the sensation involves for the moment a kind of thrill. I had known it from time to time in Italy and had opened my soul to it as to the spirit of the Lord. Since my landing in England I had been waiting for it to arrive. A bottle of tolerable Burgundy, at dinner, had perhaps unlocked to it the gates of sense; it arrived now with irresistible force. Just the scene around me was the England of one's early reveries. Over against us, amid the ripeness of its gardens, the dark red residence, with its formal facings and its vacant windows, seemed to make the past definite and massive; the little village, nestling between park and palace, around a patch of turfy common, with its taverns of figurative names, its ivy-towered church, its mossy roofs, looked like the property of a feudal lord. It was in this dark composite light that I had read the British classics; it was this mild moist air that had blown from the pages of the poets; while I seemed to feel the buried generations in the dense and elastic sod. And that I must have testified in some form or other to what I have called my thrill I gather, remembering it, from a remark of my companion's.

"You've the advantage over me in coming to all this with an educated eye. You already know what old things can be. I've never known it but by report. I've always fancied I should like it. In a small way at home, of course, I did try to stand by my idea of it. I must be a conservative by nature. People at home used to call me a cockney and a fribble. But it wasn't true," he went on; "if it had been I should have made my way over here long ago: before—before—" He paused, and his head dropped sadly on his breast.

The bottle of Burgundy had loosened his tongue; I had but to choose my time for learning his story. Something told me that I had gained his confidence and that, so far as attention and attitude might go, I was "in" for responsibilities. But somehow I didn't dread them. "Before you lost your health," I suggested.

"Before I lost my health," he answered. "And my property—the little I had. And my ambition. And any power to take myself seriously."

"Come!" I cried. "You shall recover everything. This tonic English climate will wind you up in a month. And THEN see how you'll take yourself—and how I shall take you!"

"Oh," he gratefully smiled, "I may turn to dust in your hands! I should like," he presently pursued, "to be an old genteel pensioner, lodged over there in the palace and spending my days in maundering about these vistas. I should go every morning, at the hour when it gets the sun, into that long gallery where all those pretty women of Lely's are hung—I know you despise them!—and stroll up and down and say something kind to them. Poor precious forsaken creatures! So flattered and courted in their day, so neglected now! Offering up their shoulders and ringlets and smiles to that musty deadly silence!"

I laid my hand on my friend's shoulder. "Oh sir, you're all right!"

Just at this moment there came cantering down the shallow glade of the avenue a young girl on a fine black horse—one of those little budding gentlewomen, perfectly mounted and equipped, who form to alien eyes one of the prettiest incidents of English scenery. She had distanced her servant and, as she came abreast of us, turned slightly in her saddle and glanced back at him. In the movement she dropped the hunting-crop with which she was armed; whereupon she reined up and looked shyly at us and at the implement. "This is something better than a Lely," I said. Searle hastened forward, picked up the crop and, with a particular courtesy that became him, handed it back to the rider. Fluttered and blushing she reached forward, took it with a quick sweet sound, and the next moment was bounding over the quiet turf. Searle stood watching her; the servant, as he passed us, touched his hat. When my friend turned toward me again I saw that he too was blushing. "Oh sir, you're all right," I repeated.

At a short distance from where we had stopped was an old stone bench. We went and sat down on it and, as the sun began to sink, watched the light mist powder itself with gold. "We ought to be thinking of the train back to London, I suppose," I at last said.

"Oh hang the train!" sighed my companion.

"Willingly. There could be no better spot than this to feel the English evening stand still." So we lingered, and the twilight hung about us, strangely clear in spite of the thickness of the air. As we sat there came into view an apparition unmistakeable from afar as an immemorial vagrant—the disowned, in his own rich way, of all the English ages. As he approached us he slackened pace and finally halted, touching his cap. He was a man of middle age, clad in a greasy bonnet with false-looking ear-locks depending from its sides. Round his neck was a grimy red scarf, tucked into his waistcoat; his coat and trousers had a remote affinity with those of a reduced hostler. In one hand he had a stick; on his arm he bore a tattered basket, with a handful of withered vegetables at the bottom. His face was pale haggard and degraded beyond description—as base as a counterfeit coin, yet as modelled somehow as a tragic mask. He too, like everything else, had a history. From what height had he fallen, from what depth had he risen? He was the perfect symbol of generated constituted baseness; and I felt before him in presence of a great artist or actor.

"For God's sake, gentlemen," he said in the raucous tone of weather-beaten poverty, the tone of chronic sore-throat exacerbated by perpetual gin, "for God's sake, gentlemen, have pity on a poor fern-collector!"—turning up his stale daisies. "Food hasn't passed my lips, gentlemen, for the last three days." We gaped at him and at each other, and to our imagination his appeal had almost the force of a command. "I wonder if half-a-crown would help?" I privately wailed. And our fasting botanist went limping away through the park with the grace of controlled stupefaction still further enriching his outline.

"I feel as if I had seen my Doppelganger," said Searle. "He reminds me of myself. What am I but a mere figure in the landscape, a wandering minstrel or picker of daisies?"

"What are you 'anyway,' my friend?" I thereupon took occasion to ask. "Who are you? kindly tell me."

The colour rose again to his pale face and I feared I had offended him. He poked a moment at the sod with the point of his umbrella before answering. "Who am I?" he said at last. "My name is Clement Searle. I was born in New York, and that's the beginning and the end of me."

"Ah not the end!" I made bold to plead.

27

"Then it's because I HAVE no end—any more than an ill-written book. I just stop anywhere; which means I'm a failure," the poor man all lucidly and unreservedly pursued: "a failure, as hopeless and helpless, sir, as any that ever swallowed up the slender investments of the widow and the orphan. I don't pay five cents on the dollar. What I might have been—once!—there's nothing left to show. I was rotten before I was ripe. To begin with, certainly, I wasn't a fountain of wisdom. All the more reason for a definite channel—for having a little character and purpose. But I hadn't even a little. I had nothing but nice tastes, as they call them, and fine sympathies and sentiments. Take a turn through New York to-day and you'll find the tattered remnants of these things dangling on every bush and fluttering in every breeze; the men to whom I lent money, the women to whom I made love, the friends I trusted, the follies I invented, the poisonous fumes of pleasure amid which nothing was worth a thought but the manhood they stifled! It was my fault that I believed in pleasure here below. I believe in it still, but as I believe in the immortality of the soul. The soul is immortal, certainly—if you've got one; but most people haven't. Pleasure would be right if it were pleasure straight through; but it never is. My taste was to be the best in the world; well, perhaps it was. I had a little money; it went the way of my little wit. Here in my pocket I have the scant dregs of it. I should tell you I was the biggest kind of ass. Just now that description would flatter me; it would assume there's something left of me. But the ghost of a donkey—what's that? I think," he went on with a charming turn and as if striking off his real explanation, "I should have been all right in a world arranged on different lines. Before heaven, sir—whoever you are—I'm in practice so absurdly tender-hearted that I can afford to say it: I entered upon life a perfect gentleman. I had the love of old forms and pleasant rites, and I found them nowhere—found a world all hard lines and harsh lights, without shade, without composition, as they say of pictures, without the lovely mystery of colour. To furnish colour I melted down the very substance of my own soul. I went about with my brush, touching up and toning down; a very pretty chiaroscuro you'll find in my track! Sitting here in this old park, in this old country, I feel that I hover on the misty verge of what might have been! I should have been born here and not there; here my makeshift distinctions would have found things they'd have been true of.

How it was I never got free is more than I can say. It might have cut the knot, but the knot was too tight. I was always out of health or in debt or somehow desperately dangling. Besides, I had a horror of the great black sickening sea. A year ago I was reminded of the existence of an old claim to an English estate, which has danced before the eyes of my family, at odd moments, any time these eighty years. I confess it's a bit of a muddle and a tangle, and am by no means sure that to this hour I've got the hang of it. You look as if you had a clear head: some other time, if you consent, we'll have a go at it, such as it is, together. Poverty was staring me in the face; I sat down and tried to commit the 'points' of our case to memory, as I used to get nine-times-nine by heart as a boy. I dreamed of it for six months, half-expecting to wake up some fine morning and hear through a latticed casement the cawing of an English rookery. A couple of months ago there came out to England on business of his own a man who once got me out of a dreadful mess (not that I had hurt anyone but myself), a legal practitioner in our courts, a very rough diamond, but with a great deal of FLAIR, as they say in New York. It was with him yesterday you saw me dining. He undertook, as he called it, to 'nose round' and see if anything could be made of our questionable but possible show. The matter had never seriously been taken up. A month later I got a letter from Simmons assuring me that it seemed a very good show indeed and that he should be greatly surprised if I were unable to do something. This was the greatest push I had ever got in my life; I took a deliberate step, for the first time; I sailed for England. I've been here three days: they've seemed three months. After keeping me waiting for thirty-six hours my legal adviser makes his appearance last night and states to me, with his mouth full of mutton, that I haven't a leg to stand on, that my claim is moonshine, and that I must do penance and take a ticket for six more days of purgatory with his presence thrown in. My friend, my friend—shall I say I was disappointed? I'm already resigned. I didn't really believe I had any case. I felt in my deeper consciousness that it was the crowning illusion of a life of illusions. Well, it was a pretty one. Poor legal adviser!—I forgive him with all my heart. But for him I shouldn't be sitting in this place, in this air, under these impressions. This is a world I could have got on with beautifully. There's an immense charm in its having been kept for the last. After it nothing else would have been tolerable. I shall now have a month of it, I hope, which won't be long enough for it to "go back on me. There's one thing!"—and here, pausing, he laid his hand on mine; I rose and stood before him—"I wish it were possible you should be with me to the end."

"I promise you to leave you only when you kick me downstairs." But I suggested my terms. "It must be on condition of your omitting from your conversation this intolerable flavour of mortality. I know nothing of 'ends.' I'm all for beginnings."

He kept on me his sad weak eyes. Then with a faint smile: "Don't cut down a man you find hanging. He has had a reason for it. I'm bankrupt."

"Oh health's money!" I said. "Get well, and the rest will take care of itself. I'm interested in your questionable claim—it's the question that's the charm; and pretenders, to anything big enough, have always been, for me, an attractive class. Only their first duty's to be gallant."

"Their first duty's to understand their own points and to know their own mind," he returned with hopeless lucidity. "Don't ask me to climb our family tree now," he added; "I fear I haven't the head for it. I'll try some day—if it will bear my weight; or yours added to mine. There's no doubt, however, that we, as they say, go back. But I know nothing of business. If I were to take the matter in hand I should break in two the poor little silken thread from which everything hangs. In a better world than this I think I should be listened to. But the wind doesn't set to ideal justice. There's no doubt that a hundred years ago we suffered a palpable wrong. Yet we made no appeal at the time, and the dust of a century now lies heaped upon our silence. Let it rest!"

"What then," I asked, "is the estimated value of your interest?"

"We were instructed from the first to accept a compromise. Compared with the whole property our ideas have been small. We were once advised in the sense of a hundred and thirty thousand dollars. Why a hundred and thirty I'm sure I don't know. Don't beguile me into figures."

"Allow me one more question," I said. "Who's actually in possession?"

"A certain Mr. Richard Searle. I know nothing about him."

"He's in some way related to you?"

"Our great-grandfathers were half-brothers. What does that make us?"

"Twentieth cousins, say. And where does your twentieth cousin live?"

"At a place called Lackley—in Middleshire."

I thought it over. "Well, suppose we look up Lackley in Middleshire!"

He got straight up. "Go and see it?"

"Go and see it."

"Well," he said, "with you I'll go anywhere."

On our return to town we determined to spend three days there together and then proceed to our errand. We were as conscious one as the other of that deeper mystic appeal made by London to those superstitious pilgrims who feel it the mother-city of their race, the distributing heart of their traditional life. Certain characteristics of the dusky Babylon, certain aspects, phases, features, "say" more to the American spiritual ear than anything else in Europe. The influence of these things on Searle it charmed me to note. His observation I soon saw to be, as I pronounced it to him, searching and caressing. His almost morbid appetite for any over-scoring of time, well-nigh extinct from long inanition, threw the flush of its revival into his face and his talk.

II

We looked out the topography of Middleshire in a county-guide, which spoke highly, as the phrase is, of Lackley Park, and took up our abode, our journey ended, at a wayside inn where, in the days of leisure, the coach must have stopped for luncheon and burnished pewters of rustic ale been handed up as straight as possible to outsiders athirst with the sense of speed. We stopped here for mere gaping joy of its steep-thatched roof, its latticed windows, its hospitable porch, and allowed a couple of days to elapse in vague undirected strolls and sweet sentimental observance of the land before approaching the particular business that had drawn us on. The region I allude to is a compendium of the general physiognomy of England. The noble friendliness of the scenery, its latent old-friendliness, the way we scarcely knew whether we were looking at it for the first or the last time, made it arrest us at every step. The countryside, in the full warm rains of the last of April, had burst into sudden perfect spring. The dark walls of the hedgerows had turned into blooming screens, the sodden verdure of lawn and meadow been washed over with a lighter brush. We went forth without loss of time for a long walk on the great grassy hills, smooth arrested central billows of some primitive upheaval, from the summits of which you find half England unrolled at your feet. A dozen broad counties, within the scope of your vision, commingle their green exhalations. Closely beneath us lay the dark rich hedgy flats and the copse-chequered slopes, white with the blossom of apples. At widely opposite points of the expanse two great towers of cathedrals rose sharply out of a reddish blur of habitation, taking the mild English light.

We gave an irrepressible attention to this same solar reserve, and found in it only a refinement of art. The sky never was empty and never idle; the clouds were continually at play for our benefit. Over against us, from our station on the hills, we saw them piled and dissolved, condensed and shifted, blotting the blue with sullen rain-spots, stretching, breeze-fretted, into dappled fields of grey, bursting into an explosion of light or melting into a drizzle of silver. We made our way along the rounded ridge of the downs and reached, by a descent, through slanting angular fields, green to cottage-doors, a russet village that beckoned us from the heart of the maze in which the hedges wrapped it up. Close beside it, I admit, the roaring train bounces out of a hole in the hills; yet there broods upon this charming hamlet an old-time quietude that makes a violation of confidence of naming it so far away. We struck through a narrow lane, a green lane, dim with its barriers of hawthorn; it led us to a superb old farmhouse, now rather rudely jostled by the multiplied roads and by-ways that have reduced its ancient appanage. It stands there in stubborn picturesqueness, doggedly submitting to be pointed out and sketched. It is a wonderful image of the domiciliary conditions of the past—cruelly complete; with bended beams and joists, beneath the burden of gables, that seem to ache and groan with memories and regrets. The short low windows, where lead and glass combine equally to create an inward gloom, retain their opacity as a part of the primitive idea of defence. Such an old house provokes on the part of an American a luxury of respect. So propped and patched, so tinkered with clumsy tenderness, clustered so richly about its central English sturdiness, its oaken vertebrations, so humanised with ages of use and touches of beneficent affection, it seemed to offer to our grateful eyes a small rude symbol of the great English social order. Passing out upon the highroad, we came to the common browsing-patch, the "village-green" of the tales of our youth. Nothing was absent: the shaggy mouse-coloured donkey, nosing the turf with his mild and huge proboscis, the geese, the old woman—THE old woman, in person, with her red cloak and her black bonnet, frilled about the face and double-frilled beside her decent placid cheeks—the towering ploughman with his white smock-frock puckered on chest and back, his short corduroys, his mighty calves, his big red rural face. We greeted these things as children greet the loved pictures in a storybook lost and mourned and found again. We recognised them as one recognises the handwriting on letter-backs. Beside the road we saw a ploughboy straddle whistling on a stile, and he had the merit of being not only a ploughboy but a Gainsborough. Beyond the stile, across the level velvet of a meadow, a footpath wandered like a streak drawn by a finger over a surface of fine plush. We followed it from field to field and from stile to stile; it was all adorably the way to church. At the church we finally arrived, lost in its rook-haunted churchyard, hidden from the workday world by the broad stillness of pastures—a grey, grey tower, a huge black yew, a cluster of village-graves with crooked headstones and protrusions that had settled and sunk. The place seemed so to ache with consecration that my sensitive companion gave way to the force of it.

"You must bury me here, you know"—he caught at my arm. "It's the first place of worship I've seen in my life. How it makes a Sunday where it stands!"

It took the Church, we agreed, to make churches, but we had the sense the next day of seeing still better why. We walked over some seven miles, to the nearer of the two neighbouring seats of that lesson; and all through such a mist of local colour that we felt ourselves a pair of Smollett's pedestrian heroes faring tavernward for a night of adventures. As we neared the provincial city we saw the steepled mass of the cathedral, long and high, rise far into the cloud-freckled blue; and as we got closer stopped on a bridge and looked down at the reflexion of the solid minster in a yellow stream. Going further yet we entered the russet town—where surely Miss Austen's heroines, in chariots and curricles, must often have come a-shopping for their sandals and mittens; we lounged in the grassed and gravelled precinct and gazed insatiably at that most soul-soothing sight, the waning wasting afternoon light, the visible ether that feels the voices of the chimes cling far aloft to the quiet sides of the cathedral-tower; saw it linger and nestle and abide, as it loves to do on all perpendicular spaces, converting them irresistibly into registers and dials; tasted too, as deeply, of the peculiar stillness of this place of priests; saw a rosy English lad come forth and lock the door of the old foundation-school that dovetailed with cloister and choir, and carry his big responsible key into one of the quiet canonical houses: and then stood musing together on the effect on one's mind of having in one's boyhood gone and come through cathedral-shades as a King's scholar, and yet kept ruddy with much cricket in misty river meadows. On the third morning we betook ourselves to Lackley, having learned that parts of the "grounds" were open to visitors, and that indeed on application the house was sometimes shown.

Within the range of these numerous acres the declining spurs of the hills continued to undulate and subside. A long avenue wound and circled from the outermost gate through an untrimmed woodland, whence you glanced at further slopes and glades and copses and bosky recesses—at everything except the limits of the place. It was as free and untended as I had found a few of the large loose villas of old Italy, and I was still never to see the angular fact of English landlordism muffle itself in so many concessions. The weather had just become perfect; it was one of the dozen exquisite days of the English year—days stamped with a purity unknown in climates where fine weather is cheap. It was as if the mellow brightness, as tender as that of the primroses which starred the dark waysides like petals wind-scattered over beds of moss, had been meted out to us by the cubic foot—distilled from an alchemist's crucible. From this pastoral abundance we moved upon the more composed scene, the park proper—passed through a second lodge-gate, with weather-worn gilding on its twisted bars, to the smooth slopes where the great trees stood singly and the tame deer browsed along the bed of a woodland stream. Here before us rose the gabled grey front of the Tudor-time, developed and terraced and gardened to some later loss, as we were afterwards to know, of type.

"Here you can wander all day," I said to Searle, "like an exiled prince who has come back on tiptoe and hovers about the dominion of the usurper."

"To think of 'others' having hugged this all these years!" he answered. "I know what I am, but what might I have been? What do such places make of a man?"

"I dare say he gets stupidly used to them," I said. "But I dare say too, even then, that when you scratch the mere owner you find the perfect lover."

"What a perfect scene and background it forms!" my friend, however, had meanwhile gone on. "What legends, what histories it knows! My heart really breaks with all I seem to guess. There's Tennyson's Talking Oak! What summer days one could spend here! How I could lounge the rest of my life away on this turf of the middle ages! Haven't I some maiden-cousin in that old hall, or grange, or court—what in the name of enchantment do you call the thing?—who would give me kind leave?" And then he turned almost fiercely upon me. "Why did you bring me here? Why did you drag me into this distraction of vain regrets?"

At this moment there passed within call a decent lad who had emerged from the gardens and who might have been an underling in the stables. I hailed him and put the question of our possible admittance to the house. He answered that the master was away from home, but that he thought it probable the housekeeper would consent to do the honours. I passed my arm into Searle's. "Come," I said; "drain the cup, bitter-sweet though it be. We must go in." We hastened slowly and approached the fine front. The house was one of the happiest fruits of its freshly-feeling era, a multitudinous cluster of fair gables and intricate chimneys, brave projections and quiet recesses, brown old surfaces weathered to silver and mottled roofs that testified not to seasons but to centuries. Two broad terraces commanded the wooded horizon. Our appeal was answered by a butler who condescended to our weakness. He renewed the assertion that Mr. Searle was away from home, but he would himself lay our case before the housekeeper. We would be so good, however, as to give him our cards. This request, following so directly on the assertion that Mr. Searle was absent, was rather resented by my companion. "Surely not for the housekeeper."

The butler gave a diplomatic cough. "Miss Searle is at home, sir."

"Yours alone will have to serve," said my friend. I took out a card and pencil and wrote beneath my name NEW YORK. As I stood with the pencil poised a temptation entered into it. Without in the least considering proprieties or results I let my implement yield—I added above my name that of Mr. Clement Searle. What would come of it?

Before many minutes the housekeeper waited upon us—a fresh rosy little old woman in a clean dowdy cap and a scanty sprigged gown; a quaint careful person, but accessible to the tribute of our pleasure, to say nothing of any other. She had the accent of the country, but the manners of the house. Under her guidance we passed through a dozen apartments, duly stocked with old pictures, old tapestry, old carvings, old armour, with a hundred ornaments and treasures. The pictures were especially valuable. The two Vandykes, the trio of rosy Rubenses, the sole and sombre Rembrandt, glowed with conscious authenticity. A Claude, a Murillo, a Greuze, a couple of Gainsboroughs, hung there with high complacency. Searle strolled about, scarcely speaking, pale and grave, with bloodshot eyes and lips compressed. He uttered no comment on what we saw—he asked but a question or two. Missing him at last from my side I retraced my steps and found him in a room we had just left, on a faded old ottoman and with his elbows on his knees and his face buried in his hands. Before him, ranged on a great credence, was a magnificent collection of old Italian majolica; plates of every shape, with their glaze of happy colour, jugs and vases nobly bellied and embossed. There seemed to rise before me, as I looked, a sudden vision of the young English gentleman who, eighty years ago, had travelled by slow stages to Italy and been waited on at his inn by persuasive toymen. "What is it, my dear man?" I asked. "Are you unwell?"

He uncovered his haggard face and showed me the flush of a consciousness sharper, I think, to myself than to him. "A memory of the past! There comes back to me a china vase that used to stand on the parlour mantel-shelf when I was a boy, with a portrait of General Jackson painted on one side and a bunch of flowers on the other. How long do you suppose that majolica has been in the family?"

"A long time probably. It was brought hither in the last century, into old, old England, out of old, old Italy, by some contemporary dandy with a taste for foreign gimcracks. Here it has stood for a hundred years, keeping its clear firm hues in this quiet light that has never sought to advertise it."

Searle sprang to his feet. "I say, for mercy's sake, take me away! I can't stand this sort of thing. Before I know it I shall do something scandalous. I shall steal some of their infernal crockery. I shall proclaim my identity and assert my rights. I shall go blubbering to Miss Searle and ask her in pity's name to 'put me up.'"

If he could ever have been said to threaten complications he rather visibly did so now. I began to regret my officious presentation of his name and prepared without delay to lead him out of the house. We overtook the housekeeper in the last room of the series, a small unused boudoir over whose chimney-piece hung a portrait of a young man in a powdered wig and a brocaded waistcoat. I was struck with his resemblance to my companion while our guide introduced him. "This is Mr. Clement Searle, Mr. Searle's great-uncle, by Sir Joshua Reynolds. He died young, poor gentleman; he perished at sea, going to America."

"He was the young buck who brought the majolica out of Italy," I supplemented.

"Indeed, sir, I believe he did," said the housekeeper without wonder.

"He's the image of you, my dear Searle," I further observed.

"He's remarkably like the gentleman, saving his presence," said the housekeeper.

My friend stood staring. "Clement Searle—at sea—going to America—?" he broke out. Then with some sharpness to our old woman: "Why the devil did he go to America?"

"Why indeed, sir? You may well ask. I believe he had kinsfolk there. It was for them to come to him."

Searle broke into a laugh. "It was for them to come to him! Well, well," he said, fixing his eyes on our guide, "they've come to him at last!"

She blushed like a wrinkled rose-leaf. "Indeed, sir, I verily believe you're one of US!"

"My name's the name of that beautiful youth," Searle went on. "Dear kinsman I'm happy to meet you! And what do you think of this?" he pursued as he grasped me by the arm. "I have an idea. He perished at sea. His spirit came ashore and wandered about in misery till it got another incarnation—in this poor trunk!" And he tapped his hollow chest. "Here it has rattled about these forty years, beating its wings against its rickety cage, begging to be taken home again. And I never knew what was the matter with me! Now at last the bruised spirit can escape!"

Our old lady gaped at a breadth of appreciation—if not at the disclosure of a connexion—beyond her. The scene was really embarrassing, and my confusion increased as we became aware of another presence. A lady had appeared in the doorway and the housekeeper dropped just audibly: "Miss Searle!" My first impression of Miss Searle was that she was neither young nor beautiful. She stood without confidence on the threshold, pale, trying to smile and twirling my card in her fingers. I immediately bowed. Searle stared at her as if one of the pictures had stepped out of its frame.

"If I'm not mistaken one of you gentlemen is Mr. Clement Searle," the lady adventured.

"My friend's Mr. Clement Searle," I took upon myself to reply. "Allow me to add that I alone am responsible for your having received his name."

"I should have been sorry not to—not to see him," said Miss Searle, beginning to blush. "Your being from America has led me—perhaps to intrude!"

"The intrusion, madam, has been on our part. And with just that excuse—that we come from so far away."

Miss Searle, while I spoke, had fixed her eyes on my friend as he stood silent beneath Sir Joshua's portrait. The housekeeper, agitated and mystified, fairly let herself go. "Heaven preserve us, Miss! It's your great-uncle's picture come to life."

"I'm not mistaken then," said Miss Searle—"we must be distantly related." She had the air of the shyest of women, for whom it was almost anguish to make an advance without help. Searle eyed her with gentle wonder from head to foot, and I could easily read his thoughts. This then was his maiden-cousin, prospective mistress of these hereditary treasures. She was of some thirty-five years of age, taller than was then common and perhaps stouter than is now enjoined. She had small kind grey eyes, a considerable quantity of very light-brown hair and a smiling well-formed mouth. She was dressed in a lustreless black satin gown with a short train. Disposed about her neck was a blue handkerchief, and over this handkerchief, in many convolutions, a string of amber beads. Her appearance was singular; she was large yet somehow vague, mature yet undeveloped. Her manner of addressing us spoke of all sorts of deep diffidences. Searle, I think, had prefigured to himself some proud cold beauty of five-and-twenty; he was relieved at finding the lady timid and not obtrusively fair. He at once had an excellent tone.

"We're distant cousins, I believe. I'm happy to claim a relationship which you're so good as to remember. I hadn't counted on your knowing anything about me."

"Perhaps I've done wrong." And Miss Searle blushed and smiled anew. "But I've always known of there being people of our blood in America, and have often wondered and asked about them—without ever learning much. To-day, when this card was brought me and I understood a Clement Searle to be under our roof as a stranger, I felt I ought to do something. But, you know, I hardly knew what. My brother's in London. I've done what I think he would have done. Welcome as a cousin." And with a resolution that ceased to be awkward she put out her hand.

"I'm welcome indeed if he would have done it half so graciously!" Again Searle, taking her hand, acquitted himself beautifully.

"You've seen what there is, I think," Miss Searle went on. "Perhaps now you'll have luncheon." We followed her into a small breakfast-room where a deep bay window opened on the mossy flags of a terrace. Here, for some moments, she remained dumb and abashed, as if resting from a measurable effort. Searle too had ceased to overflow, so that I had to relieve the silence. It was of course easy to descant on the beauties of park and mansion, and as I did so I observed our hostess. She had no arts, no impulses nor graces—scarce even any manners; she was queerly, almost frowsily dressed; yet she pleased me well. She had an antique sweetness, a homely fragrance of old traditions. To be so simple, among those complicated treasures, so pampered and yet so fresh, so modest and yet so placid, told of just the spacious leisure in which Searle and I had imagined human life to be steeped in such places as that. This figure was to the Sleeping Beauty in the Wood what a fact is to a fairy-tale, an interpretation to a myth. We, on our side, were to our hostess subjects of a curiosity not cunningly veiled.

"I should like so to go abroad!" she exclaimed suddenly, as if she meant us to take the speech for an expression of interest in ourselves.

"Have you never been?" one of us asked.

"Only once. Three years ago my brother took me to Switzerland. We thought it extremely beautiful. Except for that journey I've always lived here. I was born in this house. It's a dear old place indeed, and I know it well. Sometimes one wants a change." And on my asking her how she spent her time and what society she saw, "Of course it's very quiet," she went on, proceeding by short steps and simple statements, in the manner of a person called upon for the first time to analyse to that extent her situation. "We see very few people. I don't think there are many nice ones hereabouts. At least we don't know them. Our own family's very small. My brother cares for nothing but riding and books. He had a great sorrow ten years ago. He lost his wife and his only son, a dear little boy, who of course would have had everything. Do you know that that makes me the heir, as they've done something—I don't quite know what—to the entail? Poor old me! Since his loss my brother has preferred to be quite alone. I'm sorry he's away. But you must wait till he comes back. I expect him in a day or two." She talked more and more, as if our very strangeness led her on, about her circumstances, her solitude, her bad eyes, so that she couldn't read, her flowers, her ferns, her dogs, and the vicar, recently presented to the living by her brother and warranted quite safe, who had lately begun to light his altar candles; pausing every now and then to gasp in self-surprise, yet, in the quaintest way in the world, keeping up her story as if it were a slow rather awkward old-time dance, a difficult pas seul in which she would have been better with more practice, but of which she must complete the figure. Of all the old things I had seen in England this exhibited mind of Miss Searle's seemed to me the oldest, the most handed down and taken for granted; fenced and protected as it was by convention and precedent and usage, thoroughly acquainted with its subordinate place. I felt as if I were talking with the heroine of a last-century novel. As she talked she rested her dull eyes on her kinsman with wondering kindness. At last she put it to him: "Did you mean to go away without asking for us?"

"I had thought it over, Miss Searle, and had determined not to trouble you. You've shown me how unfriendly I should have been."

"But you knew of the place being ours, and of our relationship?"

"Just so. It was because of these things that I came down here—because of them almost that I came to England. I've always liked to think of them," said my companion.

"You merely wished to look then? We don't pretend to be much to look at."

He waited; her words were too strange. "You don't know what you are, Miss Searle."

"You like the old place then?"

Searle looked at her again in silence. "If I could only tell you!" he said at last.

"Do tell me. You must come and stay with us."

It moved him to an oddity of mirth. "Take care, take care—I should surprise you! I'm afraid I should bore you. I should never leave you."

"Oh you'd get homesick—for your real home!"

At this he was still more amused. "By the way, tell Miss Searle about our real home," he said to me. And he stepped, through the window, out upon the terrace, followed by two beautiful dogs, a setter and a young stag-hound who from the moment we came in had established the fondest relation with him. Miss Searle looked at him, while he went, as if she vaguely yearned over him; it began to be plain that she was interested in her exotic cousin. I suddenly recalled the last words I had heard spoken by my friend's adviser in London and which, in a very crude form, had reference to his making a match with this lady. If only Miss Searle could be induced to think of that, and if one had but the tact to put it in a light to her! Something assured me that her heart was virgin-soil, that the flower of romantic affection had never bloomed there. If I might just sow the seed! There seemed to shape itself within her the perfect image of one of the patient wives of old.

"He has lost his heart to England," I said. "He ought to have been born here."

"And yet he doesn't look in the least an Englishman," she still rather guardedly prosed.

"Oh it isn't his looks, poor fellow."

"Of course looks aren't everything. I never talked with a foreigner before; but he talks as I have fancied foreigners."

"Yes, he's foreign enough."

"Is he married?"

"His wife's dead and he's all alone in the world."

"Has he much property?"

"None to speak of."

"But he has means to travel."

I meditated. "He has not expected to travel far," I said at last. "You know, he's in very poor health."

"Poor gentleman! So I supposed."

"But there's more of him to go on with than he thinks. He came here because he wanted to see your place before he dies."

"Dear me—kind man!" And I imagined in the quiet eyes the hint of a possible tear. "And he was going away without my seeing him?"

"He's very modest, you see."

"He's very much the gentleman."

I couldn't but smile. "He's ALL—"

At this moment we heard on the terrace a loud harsh cry. "It's the great peacock!" said Miss Searle, stepping to the window and passing out while I followed her. Below us, leaning on the parapet, stood our appreciative friend with his arm round the neck of the setter. Before him on the grand walk strutted the familiar fowl of gardens—a splendid specimen—with ruffled neck and expanded tail. The other dog had apparently indulged in a momentary attempt to abash the gorgeous biped, but at Searle's summons had bounded back to the terrace and leaped upon the ledge, where he now stood licking his new friend's face. The scene had a beautiful old-time air: the peacock flaunting in the foreground like the genius of stately places; the broad terrace, which flattered an innate taste of mine for all deserted walks where people may have sat after heavy dinners to drink coffee in old Sevres and where the stiff brocade of women's dresses may have rustled over grass or gravel; and far around us, with one leafy circle melting into another, the timbered acres of the park. "The very beasts have made him welcome," I noted as we rejoined our companion.

"The peacock has done for you, Mr. Searle," said his cousin, "what he does only for very great people. A year ago there came here a great person—a grand old lady—to see my brother. I don't think that since then he has spread his tail as wide for any one else—not by a dozen feathers."

"It's not alone the peacock," said Searle. "Just now there came slipping across my path a little green lizard, the first I ever saw, the lizard of literature! And if you've a ghost, broad daylight though it be, I expect to see him here. Do you know the annals of your house, Miss Searle?"

"Oh dear, no! You must ask my brother for all those things."

"You ought to have a collection of legends and traditions. You ought to have loves and murders and mysteries by the roomful. I shall be ashamed of you if you haven't."

"Oh Mr. Searle! We've always been a very well-behaved family," she quite seriously pleaded. "Nothing out of the way has ever happened, I think."

"Nothing out of the way? Oh that won't do! We've managed better than that in America. Why I myself!"—and he looked at her ruefully enough, but enjoying too his idea that he might embody the social scandal or point to the darkest drama of the Searles. "Suppose I should turn out a better Searle than you—better than you nursed here in romance and extravagance? Come, don't disappoint me. You've some history among you all, you've some poetry, you've some accumulation of legend. I've been famished all my days for these things. Don't you understand? Ah you can't understand! Tell me," he rambled on, "something tremendous. When I think of what must have happened here; of the lovers who must have strolled on this terrace and wandered under the beeches, of all the figures and passions and purposes that must have haunted these walls! When I think of the births and deaths, the joys and sufferings, the young hopes and the old regrets, the rich experience of life—!" He faltered a moment with the increase of his agitation. His humour of dismay at a threat of the commonplace in the history he felt about him had turned to a deeper reaction. I began to fear however that he was really losing his head. He went on with a wilder play. "To see it all called up there before me, if the Devil alone could do it I'd make a bargain with the Devil! Ah Miss Searle," he cried, "I'm a most unhappy man!"

"Oh dear, oh dear!" she almost wailed while I turned half away.

"Look at that window, that dear little window!" I turned back to see him point to a small protruding oriel, above us, relieved against the purple brickwork, framed in chiselled stone and curtained with ivy.

"It's my little room," she said.

"Of course it's a woman's room. Think of all the dear faces—all of them so mild and yet so proud—that have looked out of that lattice, and of all the old-time women's lives whose principal view of the world has been this quiet park! Every one of them was a cousin of mine. And you, dear lady, you're one of them yet." With which he marched toward her and took her large white hand. She surrendered it, blushing to her eyes and pressing her other hand to her breast. "You're a woman of the past. You're nobly simple. It has been a romance to see you. It doesn't matter what I say to you. You didn't know me yesterday, you'll not know me to-morrow. Let me to-day do a mad sweet thing. Let me imagine in you the spirit of all the dead women who have trod the terrace-flags that lie here like sepulchral tablets in the pavement of a church. Let me say I delight in you!"—he raised her hand to his lips. She gently withdrew it and for a moment averted her face. Meeting her eyes the next instant I saw the tears had come. The Sleeping Beauty was awake.

There followed an embarrassed pause. An issue was suddenly presented by the appearance of the butler bearing a letter. "A telegram, Miss," he announced.

"Oh what shall I do?" cried Miss Searle. "I can't open a telegram. Cousin, help me."

Searle took the missive, opened it and read aloud: "I shall be home to dinner. Keep the American."

III

"KEEP the American!" Miss Searle, in compliance with the injunction conveyed in her brother's telegram (with something certainly of telegraphic curtness), lost no time in expressing the pleasure it would give her that our friend should remain. "Really you must," she said; and forthwith repaired to the house-keeper to give orders for the preparation of a room.

"But how in the world did he know of my being here?" my companion put to me.

I answered that he had probably heard from his solicitor of the other's visit. "Mr. Simmons and that gentleman must have had another interview since your arrival in England. Simmons, for reasons of his own, has made known to him your journey to this neighbourhood, and Mr. Searle, learning this, has immediately taken for granted that you've formally presented yourself to his sister. He's hospitably inclined and wishes her to do the proper thing by you. There may even," I went on, "be more in it than that. I've my little theory that he's the very phoenix of usurpers, that he has been very much struck with what the experts have had to say for you, and that he wishes to have the originality of making over to you your share—so limited after all—of the estate."

"I give it up!" my friend mused. "Come what come will!"

"You, of course," said Miss Searle, reappearing and turning to me, "are included in my brother's invitation. I've told them to see about a room for you. Your luggage shall immediately be sent for."

It was arranged that I in person should be driven over to our little inn and that I should return with our effects in time to meet Mr. Searle at dinner. On my arrival several hours later I was immediately conducted to my room. The servant pointed out to me that it communicated by a door and a private passage with that of my fellow visitor. I made my way along this passage—a low narrow corridor with a broad latticed casement through which there streamed upon a series of grotesquely sculptured oaken closets and cupboards the vivid animating glow of the western sun—knocked at his door and, getting no answer, opened it. In an armchair by the open window sat my friend asleep, his arms and legs relaxed and head dropped on his breast. It was a great relief to see him rest thus from his rhapsodies, and I watched him for some moments before waking him. There was a faint glow of colour in his cheek and a light expressive parting of his lips, something nearer to ease and peace than I had yet seen in him. It was almost happiness, it was almost health. I laid my hand on his arm and gently shook it. He opened his eyes, gazed at me a moment, vaguely recognised me, then closed them again. "Let me dream, let me dream!"

"What are you dreaming about?"

A moment passed before his answer came. "About a tall woman in a quaint black dress, with yellow hair and a sweet, sweet smile, and a soft low delicious voice! I'm in love with her."

"It's better to see her than to dream about her," I said. "Get up and dress; then we'll go down to dinner and meet her."

"Dinner—dinner—?" And he gradually opened his eyes again. "Yes, upon my word I shall dine!"

"Oh you're all right!" I declared for the twentieth time as he rose to his feet. "You'll live to bury Mr. Simmons." He told me he had spent the hours of my absence with Miss Searle—they had strolled together half over the place. "You must be very intimate," I smiled.

"She's intimate with ME. Goodness knows what rigmarole I've treated her to!" They had parted an hour ago; since when, he believed, her brother had arrived.

The slow-fading twilight was still in the great drawing-room when we came down. The housekeeper had told us this apartment was rarely used, there being others, smaller and more convenient, for the same needs. It seemed now, however, to be occupied in my comrade's honour. At the furthest end, rising to the roof like a royal tomb in a cathedral, was a great chimney-piece of chiselled white marble, yellowed by time, in which a light fire was crackling. Before the fire stood a small short man, with his hands behind him; near him was Miss Searle, so transformed by her dress that at first I scarcely knew her. There was in our entrance and reception something remarkably chilling and solemn. We moved in silence up the long room; Mr. Searle advanced slowly, a dozen steps, to meet us; his sister stood motionless. I was conscious of her masking her visage with a large white tinselled fan, and that her eyes, grave and enlarged, watched us intently over the top of it. The master of Lackley grasped in silence the proffered hand of his kinsman and eyed him from head to foot, suppressing, I noted, a start of surprise at his resemblance to Sir Joshua's portrait. "This is a happy day." And then turning to me with an odd little sharp stare: "My cousin's friend is my friend." Miss Searle lowered her fan.

The first thing that struck me in Mr. Searle's appearance was his very limited stature, which was less by half a head than that of his sister. The second was the preternatural redness of his hair and beard. They intermingled over his ears and surrounded his head like a huge lurid nimbus. His face was pale and attenuated, the face of a scholar, a dilettante, a comparer of points and texts, a man who lives in a library bending over books and prints and medals. At a distance it might have passed for smooth and rather blankly composed; but on a nearer view it revealed a number of wrinkles, sharply etched and scratched, of a singularly aged and refined effect. It was the complexion of a man of sixty. His nose was arched and delicate, identical almost with the nose of my friend. His eyes, large and deep-set, had a kind of auburn glow, the suggestion of a keen metal red-hot—or, more plainly, were full of temper and spirit. Imagine this physiognomy—grave and solemn, grotesquely solemn, in spite of the bushy brightness which made a sort of frame for it—set in motion by a queer, quick, defiant, perfunctory, preoccupied smile, and you will have an imperfect notion of the remarkable presence of our host; something better worth seeing and knowing, I perceived as I quite breathlessly took him in, than anything we had yet encountered. How thoroughly I had entered into sympathy with my poor picked-up friend, and how effectually I had associated my sensibilities with his own, I had not suspected till, within the short five minutes before the signal for dinner, I became aware, without his giving me the least hint, of his placing himself on the defensive. To neither of us was Mr. Searle sympathetic. I might have guessed from her attitude that his sister entered into our thoughts. A marked change had been wrought in her since the morning; during the hour, indeed—as I read in the light of the wondering glance he cast at her—that had elapsed since her parting with her cousin. She had not yet recovered from some great agitation. Her face was pale and she had clearly been crying. These notes of trouble gave her a new and quite perverse dignity, which was further enhanced by something complimentary and commemorative in her dress.

Whether it was taste or whether it was accident I know not; but the amiable creature, as she stood there half in the cool twilight, half in the arrested glow of the fire as it spent itself in the vastness of its marble cave, was a figure for a painter. She was habited in some faded splendour of sea-green crape and silk, a piece of millinery which, though it must have witnessed a number of dull dinners, preserved still a festive air. Over her white shoulders she wore an ancient web of the most precious and venerable lace and about her rounded throat a single series of large pearls. I went in with her to dinner, and Mr. Searle, following with my friend, took his arm, as the latter afterwards told me, and pretended jocosely to conduct him. As dinner proceeded the feeling grew within me that a drama had begun to be played in which the three persons before me were actors—each of a really arduous part. The character allotted to my friend, however, was certainly the least easy to represent with effect, though I overflowed with the desire that he should acquit himself to his honour. I seemed to see him urge his faded faculties to take their cue and perform. The poor fellow tried to do himself credit more seriously than ever in his old best days. With Miss Searle, credulous passive and pitying, he had finally flung aside all vanity and propriety and shown the bottom of his fantastic heart. But with our host there might be no talking of nonsense nor taking of liberties; there and then, if ever, sat a consummate conservative, breathing the fumes of hereditary privilege and security. For an hour, accordingly, I saw my poor protege attempt, all in pain, to meet a new decorum. He set himself the task of appearing very American, in order that his appreciation of everything Mr. Searle represented might seem purely disinterested. What his kinsman had expected him to be I know not; but

I made Mr. Searle out as annoyed, in spite of his exaggerated urbanity, at finding him so harmless. Our host was not the man to show his hand, but I think his best card had been a certain implicit confidence that so provincial a parasite would hardly have good manners.

He led the conversation to the country we had left; rather as if a leash had been attached to the collar of some lumpish and half-domesticated animal the tendency of whose movements had to be recognised. He spoke of it indeed as of some fabled planet, alien to the British orbit, lately proclaimed to have the admixture of atmospheric gases required to support animal life, but not, save under cover of a liberal afterthought, to be admitted into one's regular conception of things. I, for my part, felt nothing but regret that the spheric smoothness of his universe should be disfigured by the extrusion even of such inconsiderable particles as ourselves.

"I knew in a general way of our having somehow ramified over there," Mr. Searle mentioned; "but had scarcely followed it more than you pretend to pick up the fruit your long-armed pear tree may drop, on the other side of your wall, in your neighbour's garden. There was a man I knew at Cambridge, a very odd fellow, a decent fellow too; he and I were rather cronies; I think he afterwards went to the Middle States. They'll be, I suppose, about the Mississippi? At all events, there was that great-uncle of mine whom Sir Joshua painted. He went to America, but he never got there. He was lost at sea. You look enough like him to make one fancy he DID get there and that you've kept him alive by one of those beastly processes—I think you have 'em over there: what do you call it, 'putting up' things? If you're he you've not done a wise thing to show yourself here. He left a bad name behind him. There's a ghost who comes sobbing about the house every now and then, the ghost of one to whom he did a wrong."

"Oh mercy ON us!" cried Miss Searle in simple horror.

"Of course YOU know nothing of such things," he rather dryly allowed. "You're too sound a sleeper to hear the sobbing of ghosts."

"I'm sure I should like immensely to hear the sobbing of a ghost," said my friend, the light of his previous eagerness playing up into his eyes. "Why does it sob? I feel as if that were what we've come above all to learn."

Mr. Searle eyed his audience a moment gaugingly; he held the balance as to measure his resources. He wished to do justice to his theme. With the long finger-nails of his left hand nervously playing against the tinkling crystal of his wineglass and his conscious eyes betraying that, small and strange as he sat there, he knew himself, to his pleasure and advantage, remarkably impressive, he dropped into our untutored minds the sombre legend of his house. "Mr. Clement Searle, from all I gather, was a young man of great talents but a weak disposition. His mother was left a widow early in life, with two sons, of whom he was the elder and the more promising. She educated him with the greatest affection and care. Of course when he came to manhood she wished him to marry well. His means were quite sufficient to enable him to overlook the want of money in his wife; and Mrs. Searle selected a young lady who possessed, as she conceived, every good gift save a fortune—a fine proud handsome girl, the daughter of an old friend, an old lover I suspect, of her own. Clement, however, as it appeared, had either chosen otherwise or was as yet unprepared to choose. The young lady opened upon him in vain the battery of her attractions; in vain his mother urged her cause. Clement remained cold, insensible, inflexible. Mrs. Searle had a character which appears to have gone out of fashion in my family nowadays; she was a great manager, a maitresse-femme. A proud passionate imperious woman, she had had immense cares and ever so many law-suits; they had sharpened her temper and her will. She suspected that her son's affections had another object, and this object she began to hate. Irritated by his stubborn defiance of her wishes she persisted in her purpose. The more she watched him the more she was convinced he loved in secret. If he loved in secret of course he loved beneath him. He went about the place all sombre and sullen and brooding. At last, with the rashness of an angry woman, she threatened to bring the young lady of her choice—who, by the way, seems to have been no shrinking blossom— to stay in the house. A stormy scene was the result. He threatened that if she did so he would leave the country and sail for America. She probably disbelieved him; she knew him to be weak, but she overrated his weakness. At all events the rejected one arrived and Clement Searle departed. On a dark December day he took ship at Southampton. The two women, desperate with rage and sorrow, sat alone in this big house, mingling their tears and imprecations. A fortnight later, on Christmas Eve, in the midst of a great snowstorm long famous in the country, something happened that quickened their bitterness. A young woman, battered and chilled by the storm, gained entrance to the house and, making her way into the presence of the mistress and her guest, poured out her tale. She was a poor curate's daughter out of some little hole in Gloucestershire. Clement Searle had loved her—loved her all too well! She had been turned out in wrath from her father's house; his mother at least might pity her—if not for herself then for the child she was soon to bring forth. Hut the poor girl had been a second time too trustful. The women, in scorn, in horror, with blows possibly, drove her forth again into the storm. In the storm she wandered and in the deep snow she died. Her lover, as you know, perished in that hard winter weather at sea; the news came to his mother late, but soon enough. We're haunted by the curate's daughter!"

Mr. Searle retailed this anecdote with infinite taste and point, the happiest art; when he ceased there was a pause of some moments. "Ah well we may be!" Miss Searle then mournfully murmured.

Searle blazed up into enthusiasm. "Of course, you know"—with which he began to blush violently—"I should be sorry to claim any identity with the poor devil my faithless namesake. But I should be immensely gratified if the young lady's spirit, deceived by my resemblance, were to mistake me for her cruel lover. She's welcome to the comfort of it. What one can do in the case I shall be glad to do. But can a ghost haunt a ghost? I AM a ghost!"

Mr. Searle stared a moment and then had a subtle sneer. "I could almost believe you are!"

"Oh brother—and cousin!" cried Miss Searle with the gentlest yet most appealing dignity. "How can you talk so horribly?" The horrible talk, however, evidently possessed a potent magic for my friend; and his imagination, checked a while by the influence of his kinsman, began again to lead him a dance. From this moment he ceased to steer his frail bark, to care what he said or how he said it, so long as he expressed his passionate appreciation of the scene around him. As he kept up this strain I ceased even secretly to wish he wouldn't. I have wondered since that I shouldn't have been annoyed by the way he reverted constantly to himself. But a great frankness, for the time, makes its own law and a great passion its own channel. There was moreover an irresponsible indescribable effect of beauty in everything his lips uttered. Free alike from adulation and from envy, the essence of his discourse was a divine apprehension, a romantic vision free as the flight of Ariel, of the poetry of his companions' situation and their contrasted general irresponsiveness.

"How does the look of age come?" he suddenly broke out at dessert. "Does it come of itself, unobserved, unrecorded, unmeasured? Or do you woo it and set baits and traps for it, and watch it like the dawning brownness of a meerschaum pipe, and make it fast, when it appears, just where it peeps out, and light a votive taper beneath it and give thanks to it daily? Or do you forbid it and fight it and resist it, and yet feel it settling and deepening about you as irresistible as fate?"

"What the deuce is the man talking about?" said the smile of our host.

"I found a little grey hair this morning," Miss Searle incoherently prosed.

"Well then I hope you paid it every respect!" cried her visitor.

"I looked at it for a long time in my hand-glass," she answered with more presence of mind.

"Miss Searle can for many years to come afford to be amused at grey hairs," I interposed in the hope of some greater ease. It had its effect. "Ten years from last Thursday I shall be forty-four," she almost comfortably smiled.

"Well, that's just what I am," said Searle. "If I had only come here ten years ago! I should have had more time to enjoy the feast, but I should have had less appetite. I needed first to get famished."

"Oh why did you wait for that?" his entertainer asked. "To think of these ten years that we might have been enjoying you!" At the vision of which waste and loss Mr. Searle had a fine shrill laugh.

"Well," my friend explained, "I always had a notion—a stupid vulgar notion if there ever was one—that to come abroad properly one had to have a pot of money. My pot was too nearly empty. At last I came with my empty pot!"

Mr. Searle had a wait for delicacy, but he proceeded. "You're reduced, you're—a—straitened?"

Our companion's very breath blew away the veil. "Reduced to nothing. Straitened to the clothes on my back!"

"You don't say so!" said Mr. Searle with a large vague gasp. "Well—well—well!" he added in a voice which might have meant everything or nothing; and then, in his whimsical way, went on to finish a glass of wine. His searching eye, as he drank, met mine, and for a moment we each rather deeply sounded the other, to the effect no doubt of a slight embarrassment. "And you," he said by way of carrying this off—"how about YOUR wardrobe?"

"Oh his!" cried my friend; "his wardrobe's immense. He could dress up a regiment!" He had drunk more champagne—I admit that the champagne was good—than was from any point of view to have been desired. He was rapidly drifting beyond any tacit dissuasion of mine. He was feverish and rash, and all attempt to direct would now simply irritate him. As we rose from the table he caught my troubled look. Passing his arm for a moment into mine, "This is the great night!" he strangely and softly said; "the night and the crisis that will settle me."

Mr. Searle had caused the whole lower portion of the house to be thrown open and a multitude of lights to be placed in convenient and effective positions. Such a marshalled wealth of ancient candlesticks and flambeaux I had never beheld. Niched against the dusky wainscots, casting great luminous circles upon the pendent stiffness of sombre tapestries, enhancing and completing with admirable effect the variety and mystery of the great ancient house, they seemed to people the wide rooms, as our little group passed slowly from one to another, with a dim expectant presence. We had thus, in spite of everything, a wonderful hour of it. Mr. Searle at once assumed the part of cicerone, and—I had not hitherto done him justice—Mr. Searle became almost agreeable. While I lingered behind with his sister he walked in advance with his kinsman. It was as if he had said: "Well, if you want the old place you shall have it—so far as the impression goes!" He spared us no thrill—I had almost said no pang—of that experience. Carrying a tall silver candlestick in his left hand, he raised it and lowered it and cast the light hither and thither, upon pictures and hangings and carvings and cornices. He knew his house to perfection. He touched upon a hundred traditions and memories, he threw off a cloud of rich reference to its earlier occupants. He threw off again, in his easy elegant way, a dozen—happily lighter—anecdotes. His relative attended with a brooding deference. Miss Searle and I meanwhile were not wholly silent.

"I suppose that by this time you and your cousin are almost old friends," I remarked.

She trifled a moment with her fan and then raised her kind small eyes. "Old friends—yet at the same time strangely new! My cousin, my cousin"— and her voice lingered on the word—"it seems so strange to call him my cousin after thinking these many years that I've no one in the world but my brother. But he's really so very odd!"

"It's not so much he as—well, as his situation, that deserves that name," I tried to reason.

"I'm so sorry for his situation. I wish I could help it in some way. He interests me so much." She gave a sweet-sounding sigh. "I wish I could have known him sooner—and better. He tells me he's but the shadow of what he used to be."

I wondered if he had been consciously practising on the sensibilities of this gentle creature. If he had I believed he had gained his point. But his position had in fact become to my sense so precarious that I hardly ventured to be glad. "His better self just now seems again to be taking shape," I said. "It will have been a good deed on your part if you help to restore him to all he ought to be."

She met my idea blankly. "Dear me, what can I do?"

"Be a friend to him. Let him like you, let him love you. I dare say you see in him now much to pity and to wonder at. But let him simply enjoy a while the grateful sense of your nearness and dearness. He'll be a better and stronger man for it, and then you can love him, you can esteem him, without restriction."

She fairly frowned for helplessness. "It's a hard part for poor stupid me to play!"

Her almost infantine innocence left me no choice but to be absolutely frank. "Did you ever play any part at all?"

She blushed as if I had been reproaching her with her insignificance. "Never! I think I've hardly lived."

"You've begun to live now perhaps. You've begun to care for something else than your old-fashioned habits. Pardon me if I seem rather meddlesome; you know we Americans are very rough and ready. It's a great moment. I wish you joy!"

"I could almost believe you're laughing at me. I feel more trouble than joy."

"Why do you feel trouble?"

She paused with her eyes fixed on our companions. "My cousin's arrival's a great disturbance," she said at last.

"You mean you did wrong in coming to meet him? In that case the fault's mine. He had no intention of giving you the opportunity."

"I certainly took too much on myself. But I can't find it in my heart to regret it. I never shall regret it! I did the only thing I COULD, heaven forgive me!"

"Heaven bless you, Miss Searle! Is any harm to come of it? I did the evil; let me bear the brunt!"

She shook her head gravely. "You don't know my brother!"

"The sooner I master the subject the better then," I said. I couldn't help relieving myself—at least by the tone of my voice—of the antipathy with which, decidedly, this gentleman had inspired me. "Not perhaps that we should get on so well together!" After which, as she turned away, "Are you VERY much afraid of him?" I added.

She gave me a shuddering sidelong glance. "He's looking at me!"

He was placed with his back to us, holding a large Venetian hand-mirror, framed in chiselled silver, which he had taken from a shelf of antiquities, just at such an angle that he caught the reflexion of his sister's person. It was evident that I too was under his attention, and was resolved I wouldn't be suspected for nothing. "Miss Searle," I said with urgency, "promise me something."

She turned upon me with a start and a look that seemed to beg me to spare her. "Oh don't ask me—please don't!" It was as if she were standing on the edge of a place where the ground had suddenly fallen away, and had been called upon to make a leap. I felt retreat was impossible, however, and that it was the greater kindness to assist her to jump.

"Promise me," I repeated.

Still with her eyes she protested. "Oh what a dreadful day!" she cried at last.

"Promise me to let him speak to you alone if he should ask you—any wish you may suspect on your brother's part notwithstanding." She coloured deeply. "You mean he has something so particular to say?"

"Something so particular!"

"Poor cousin!"

"Well, poor cousin! But promise me."

"I promise," she said, and moved away across the long room and out of the door.

"You're in time to hear the most delightful story," Searle began to me as I rejoined him and his host. They were standing before an old sombre portrait of a lady in the dress of Queen Anne's time, whose ill-painted flesh-tints showed livid, in the candle-light, against her dark drapery and background. "This is Mrs. Margaret Searle—a sort of Beatrix Esmond—qui se passait ses fantaisies. She married a paltry Frenchman, a penniless fiddler, in the teeth of her whole family. Pretty Mrs. Margaret, you must have been a woman of courage! Upon my word, she looks like Miss Searle! But pray go on. What came of it all?"

Our companion watched him with an air of distaste for his boisterous homage and of pity for his crude imagination. But he took up the tale with an effective dryness: "I found a year ago, in a box of very old papers, a letter from the lady in question to a certain Cynthia Searle, her elder sister. It was dated from Paris and dreadfully ill-spelled. It contained a most passionate appeal for pecuniary assistance. She had just had a baby, she was starving and dreadfully neglected by her husband—she cursed the day she had left England. It was a most dismal production. I never heard she found means to return."

"So much for marrying a Frenchman!" I said sententiously.

Our host had one of his waits. "This is the only lady of the family who ever was taken in by an adventurer."

"Does Miss Searle know her history?" asked my friend with a stare at the rounded whiteness of the heroine's cheek.

"Miss Searle knows nothing!" said our host with expression.

"She shall know at least the tale of Mrs. Margaret," their guest returned; and he walked rapidly away in search of her.

Mr. Searle and I pursued our march through the lighted rooms. "You've found a cousin with a vengeance," I doubtless awkwardly enough laughed.

"Ah a vengeance?" my entertainer stiffly repeated.

"I mean that he takes as keen an interest in your annals and possessions as yourself."

"Oh exactly so! He tells me he's a bad invalid," he added in a moment. "I should never have supposed it."

"Within the past few hours he's a changed man. Your beautiful house, your extreme kindness, have refreshed him immensely." Mr. Searle uttered the vague ejaculation with which self-conscious Britons so often betray the concussion of any especial courtesy of speech. But he followed this by a sudden odd glare and the sharp declaration: "I'm an honest man!" I was quite prepared to assent; but he went on with a fury of frankness, as if it were the first time in his life he had opened himself to any one, as if the process were highly disagreeable and he were hurrying through it as a task. "An honest man, mind you! I know nothing about Mr. Clement Searle! I never expected to see him. He has been to me a—a—!" And here he paused to select a word which should vividly enough express what, for good or for ill, his kinsman represented. "He has been to me an Amazement! I've no doubt he's a most amiable man. You'll not deny, however, that he's a very extraordinary sort of person. I'm sorry he's ill. I'm sorry he's poor. He's my fiftieth cousin. Well and good. I'm an honest man. He shall not have it to say that he wasn't received at my house."

"He too, thank heaven, is an honest man!" I smiled.

"Why the devil then," cried Mr. Searle, turning almost fiercely on me, "has he put forward this underhand claim to my property?"

The question, quite ringing out, flashed backward a gleam of light upon the demeanour of our host and the suppressed agitation of his sister. In an instant the jealous gentleman revealed itself. For a moment I was so surprised and scandalised at the directness of his attack that I lacked words to reply. As soon as he had spoken indeed Mr. Searle appeared to feel he had been wanting in form. "Pardon me," he began afresh, "if I speak of this matter with heat. But I've been more disgusted than I can say to hear, as I heard this morning from my solicitor, of the extraordinary proceedings of Mr. Clement Searle. Gracious goodness, sir, for what does the man take me? He pretends to the Lord knows what fantastic admiration for my place. Let him then show his respect for it by not taking too many liberties! Let him, with his high-flown parade of loyalty, imagine a tithe of what *I* feel! I love my estate; it's my passion, my conscience, my life! Am I to divide it up at this time of day with a beggarly foreigner—a man without means, without appearance, without proof, a pretender, an adventurer, a chattering mountebank? I thought America boasted having lands for all men! Upon my soul, sir, I've never been so shocked in my life."

I paused for some moments before speaking, to allow his passion fully to expend itself and to flicker up again if it chose; for so far as I was concerned in the whole awkward matter I but wanted to deal with him discreetly. "Your apprehensions, sir," I said at last, "your not unnatural surprise, perhaps, at the candour of our interest, have acted too much on your nerves. You're attacking a man of straw, a creature of unworthy illusion; though I'm sadly afraid you've wounded a man of spirit and conscience. Either my friend has no valid claim on your estate, in which case your agitation is superfluous; or he HAS a valid claim—"

Mr. Searle seized my arm and glared at me; his pale face paler still with the horror of my suggestion, his great eyes of alarm glowing and his strange red hair erect and quivering. "A valid claim!" he shouted. "Let him try it—let him bring it into court!"

We had emerged into the great hall and stood facing the main doorway. The door was open into the portico, through the stone archway of which I saw the garden glitter in the blue light of a full moon. As the master of the house uttered the words I have just repeated my companion came slowly up into the porch from without, bareheaded, bright in the outer moonlight, dark in the shadow of the archway, and bright again in the lamplight at the entrance of the hall. As he crossed the threshold the butler made an appearance at the head of the staircase on our left, faltering visibly a moment at sight of Mr. Searle; after which, noting my friend, he gravely descended. He bore in his hand a small silver tray. On the tray, gleaming in the light of the suspended lamp, lay a folded note. Clement Searle came forward, staring a little and startled, I think, by some quick nervous prevision of a catastrophe. The butler applied the match to the train. He advanced to my fellow visitor, all solemnly, with the offer of his missive. Mr. Searle made a movement as if to spring forward, but controlled himself. "Tottenham!" he called in a strident voice.

"Yes, sir!" said Tottenham, halting.

"Stand where you are. For whom is that note?"

"For Mr. Clement Searle," said the butler, staring straight before him and dissociating himself from everything.

"Who gave it to you?"

"Mrs. Horridge, sir." This personage, I afterwards learned, was our friend the housekeeper.

"Who gave it Mrs. Horridge?"

There was on Tottenham's part just an infinitesimal pause before replying.

"My dear sir," broke in Searle, his equilibrium, his ancient ease, completely restored by the crisis, "isn't that rather my business?"

"What happens in my house is my business, and detestable things seem to be happening." Our host, it was clear, now so furiously detested them that I was afraid he would snatch the bone of contention without more ceremony. "Bring me that thing!" he cried; on which Tottenham stiffly moved to obey.

"Really this is too much!" broke out my companion, affronted and helpless.

So indeed it struck me, and before Mr. Searle had time to take the note I possessed myself of it. "If you've no consideration for your sister let a stranger at least act for her." And I tore the disputed object into a dozen pieces.

"In the name of decency, what does this horrid business mean?" my companion quavered.

Mr. Searle was about to open fire on him, but at that moment our hostess appeared on the staircase, summoned evidently by our high-pitched contentious voices. She had exchanged her dinner-dress for a dark wrapper, removed her ornaments and begun to disarrange her hair, a thick tress of which escaped from the comb. She hurried down with a pale questioning face. Feeling distinctly that, for ourselves, immediate departure was in the air, and divining Mr. Tottenham to be a person of a few deep-seated instincts and of much latent energy, I seized the opportunity to request him, sotto voce, to send a carriage to the door without delay. "And put up our things," I added.

Our host rushed at his sister and grabbed the white wrist that escaped from the loose sleeve of her dress. "What was in that note?" he quite hissed at her.

Miss Searle looked first at its scattered fragments and then at her cousin. "Did you read it?"

"No, but I thank you for it!" said Searle.

Her eyes, for an instant, communicated with his own as I think they had never, never communicated with any other source of meaning; then she transferred them to her brother's face, where the sense went out of them, only to leave a dull sad patience. But there was something even in this flat humility that seemed to him to mock him, so that he flushed crimson with rage and spite and flung her away. "You always were an idiot! Go to bed."

In poor Searle's face as well the gathered serenity had been by this time all blighted and distorted and the reflected brightness of his happy day turned to blank confusion. "Have I been dealing these three hours with a madman?" he woefully cried.

"A madman, yes, if you will! A man mad with the love of his home and the sense of its stability. I've held my tongue till now, but you've been too much for me. Who the devil are you, and what and why and whence?" the terrible little man continued. "From what paradise of fools do you come that you fancy I shall make over to you, for the asking, a part of my property and my life? I'm forsooth, you ridiculous person, to go shares with you? Prove your preposterous claim! There isn't THAT in it!" And he kicked one of the bits of paper on the floor.

Searle received this broadside gaping. Then turning away he went and seated himself on a bench against the wall and rubbed his forehead amazedly. I looked at my watch and listened for the wheels of our carriage.

But his kinsman was too launched to pull himself up. "Wasn't it enough that you should have plotted against my rights? Need you have come into my very house to intrigue with my sister?"

My friend put his two hands to his face. "Oh, oh, oh!" he groaned while Miss Searle crossed rapidly and dropped on her knees at his side.

"Go to bed, you fool!" shrieked her brother.

"Dear cousin," she said, "it's cruel you're to have so to think of us!"

"Oh I shall think of YOU as you'd like!" He laid a hand on her head.

"I believe you've done nothing wrong," she brought bravely out.

"I've done what I could," Mr. Searle went on—"but it's arrant folly to pretend to friendship when this abomination lies between us. You were welcome to my meat and my wine, but I wonder you could swallow them. The sight spoiled MY appetite!" cried the master of Lackley with a laugh. "Proceed with your trumpery case! My people in London are instructed and prepared."

"I shouldn't wonder if your case had improved a good deal since you gave it up," I was moved to observe to Searle.

"Oho! you don't feign ignorance then?" and our insane entertainer shook his shining head at me. "It's very kind of you to give it up! Perhaps you'll also give up my sister!"

Searle sat staring in distress at his adversary. "Ah miserable man—I thought we had become such beautiful friends."

"Boh, you hypocrite!" screamed our host.

Searle seemed not to hear him. "Am I seriously expected," he slowly and painfully pursued, "to defend myself against the accusation of any real indelicacy—to prove I've done nothing underhand or impudent? Think what you please!" And he rose, with an effort, to his feet. "I know what YOU think!" he added to Miss Searle.

The wheels of the carriage resounded on the gravel, and at the same moment a footman descended with our two portmanteaux. Mr. Tottenham followed him with our hats and coats.

"Good God," our host broke out again, "you're not going away?"—an ejaculation that, after all that had happened, had the grandest comicality. "Bless my soul," he then remarked as artlessly, "of course you're going!"

"It's perhaps well," said Miss Searle with a great effort, inexpressibly touching in one for whom great efforts were visibly new and strange, "that I should tell you what my poor little note contained."

"That matter of your note, madam," her brother interrupted, "you and I will settle together!"

"Let me imagine all sorts of kind things!" Searle beautifully pleaded.

"Ah too much has been imagined!" she answered simply. "It was only a word of warning. It was to tell you to go. I knew something painful was coming."

He took his hat. "The pains and the pleasures of this day," he said to his kinsman, "I shall equally never forget. Knowing you," and he offered his hand to Miss Searle, "has been the pleasure of pleasures. I hoped something more might have come of it."

"A monstrous deal too much has come of it!" Mr. Searle irrepressibly declared.

His departing guest looked at him mildly, almost benignantly, from head to foot, and then with closed eyes and some collapse of strength, "I'm afraid so, I can't stand more," he went on. I gave him my arm and we crossed the threshold. As we passed out I heard Miss Searle break into loud weeping.

"We shall hear from each other yet, I take it!" her brother pursued, harassing our retreat.

My friend stopped, turning round on him fiercely. "You very impossible man!" he cried in his face.

"Do you mean to say you'll not prosecute?" Mr. Searle kept it up. "I shall force you to prosecute! I shall drag you into court, and you shall be beaten—beaten—beaten!" Which grim reiteration followed us on our course.

We drove of course to the little wayside inn from which we had departed in the morning so unencumbered, in all broad England, either with enemies or friends. My companion, as the carriage rolled along, seemed overwhelmed and exhausted. "What a beautiful horrible dream!" he confusedly wailed. "What a strange awakening! What a long long day! What a hideous scene! Poor me! Poor woman!" When we had resumed possession of our two little neighbouring rooms I asked him whether Miss Searle's note had been the result of anything that had passed between them on his going to rejoin her. "I found her on the terrace," he said, "walking restlessly up and down in the moonlight. I was greatly excited—I hardly know what I said. I asked her, I think, if she knew the story of Margaret Searle. She seemed frightened and troubled, and she used just the words her brother had used—'I know nothing.' For the moment, somehow, I felt as a man drunk. I stood before her and told her, with great emphasis, how poor Margaret had married a beggarly foreigner—all in obedience to her heart and in defiance to her family. As I talked the sheeted moonlight seemed to close about us, so that we stood there in a dream, in a world quite detached. She grew younger, prettier, more attractive—I found myself talking all kinds of nonsense. Before I knew it I had gone very far. I was taking her hand and calling her 'Margaret, dear Margaret!' She had said it was impossible, that she could do nothing, that she was a fool, a child, a slave. Then with a sudden sense—it was odd how it came over me there—of the reality of my connexion with the place, I spoke of my claim against the estate. 'It exists,' I declared, 'but I've given it up. Be generous! Pay me for my sacrifice.' For an instant her face was radiant. 'If I marry you,' she asked, 'will it make everything right?' Of that I at once assured her—in our marriage the whole difficulty would melt away like a rain-drop in the great sea. 'Our marriage!' she repeated in wonder; and the deep ring of her voice seemed to wake us up and show us our folly. 'I love you, but I shall never see you again,' she cried; and she hurried away with her face in her hands. I walked up and down the terrace for some moments, and then came in and met you. That's the only witchcraft I've used!"

The poor man was at once so roused and so shaken by the day's events that I believed he would get little sleep. Conscious on my own part that I shouldn't close my eyes, I but partly undressed, stirred my fire and sat down to do some writing. I heard the great clock in the little parlour below strike twelve, one, half-past one. Just as the vibration of this last stroke was dying on the air the door of communication with Searle's room was flung open and my companion stood on the threshold, pale as a corpse, in his nightshirt, shining like a phantom against the darkness behind him. "Look well at me!" he intensely gasped; "touch me, embrace me, revere me! You see a man who has seen a ghost!"

"Gracious goodness, what do you mean?"

"Write it down!" he went on. "There, take your pen. Put it into dreadful words. How do I look? Am I human? Am I pale? Am I red? Am I speaking English? A ghost, sir! Do you understand?"

I confess there came upon me by contact a kind of supernatural shock. I shall always feel by the whole communication of it that I too have seen a ghost. My first movement—I can smile at it now—was to spring to the door, close it quickly and turn the key upon the gaping blackness from which Searle had emerged. I seized his two hands; they were wet with perspiration. I pushed my chair to the fire and forced him to sit down in it; then I got on my knees and held his hands as firmly as possible. They trembled and quivered; his eyes were fixed save that the pupil dilated and contracted with extraordinary force. I asked no questions, but waited there, very curious for what he would say. At last he spoke. "I'm not frightened, but I'm—oh excited! This is life! This is living! My nerves—my heart—my brain! They're throbbing—don't you feel it? Do you tingle? Are you hot? Are you cold? Hold me tight—tight—tight! I shall tremble away into waves—into surges—and know all the secrets of things and all the reasons and all the mysteries!" He paused a moment and then went on: "A woman—as clear as that candle: no, far clearer! In a blue dress, with a black mantle on her head and a little black muff. Young and wonderfully pretty, pale and ill; with the sadness of all the women who ever loved and suffered pleading and accusing in her wet-looking eyes. God knows I never did any such thing! But she took me for my elder, for the other Clement. She came to me here as she would have come to me there. She wrung her hands and she spoke to me 'marry me!' she moaned; 'marry me and put an end to my shame!' I sat up in bed, just as I sit here, looked at her, heard her—heard her voice melt away, watched her figure fade away. Bless us and save us! Here I be!"

I made no attempt either to explain or to criticise this extraordinary passage. It's enough that I yielded for the hour to the strange force of my friend's emotion. On the whole I think my own vision was the more interesting of the two. He beheld but the transient irresponsible spectre—I beheld the human subject hot from the spectral presence. Yet I soon recovered my judgement sufficiently to be moved again to try to guard him against the results of excitement and exposure. It was easily agreed that he was not for the night to return to his room, and I made him fairly comfortable in his place by my fire. Wishing above all to preserve him from a chill I removed my bedding and wrapped him in the blankets and counterpane. I had no nerves either for writing or for sleep; so I put out my lights, renewed the fuel and sat down on the opposite side of the hearth. I found it a great and high solemnity just to watch my companion. Silent, swathed and muffled to his chin, he sat rigid and erect with the dignity of his adventure. For the most part his eyes were closed; though from time to time he would open them with a steady expansion and stare, never blinking, into the flame, as if he again beheld without terror the image of the little woman with the muff. His cadaverous emaciated face, his tragic wrinkles intensified by the upward glow from the hearth, his distorted moustache, his extraordinary gravity and a certain fantastical air as the red light flickered over him, all re-enforced his fine likeness to the vision-haunted knight of La Mancha when laid up after some grand exploit. The night passed wholly without speech. Toward its close I slept for half an hour. When I awoke the awakened birds had begun to twitter and Searle, unperturbed, sat staring at me. We exchanged a long look, and I felt with a pang that his glittering eyes had tasted their last of natural sleep. "How is it? Are you comfortable?" I nevertheless asked.

He fixed me for a long time without replying and then spoke with a weak extravagance and with such pauses between his words as might have represented the slow prompting of an inner voice. "You asked me when you first knew me what I was. 'Nothing,' I said, 'nothing of any consequence.' Nothing I've always supposed myself to be. But I've wronged myself—I'm a great exception. I'm a haunted man!"

If sleep had passed out of his eyes I felt with even a deeper pang that sanity had abandoned his spirit. From this moment I was prepared for the worst. There were in my friend, however, such confirmed habits of mildness that I found myself not in the least fearing he would prove unmanageable. As morning began fully to dawn upon us I brought our curious vigil to a close. Searle was so enfeebled that I gave him my hands to help him out of his chair, and he retained them for some moments after rising to his feet, unable as he seemed to keep his balance. "Well," he said, "I've been once favoured, but don't think I shall be favoured again. I shall soon be myself as fit to 'appear' as any of them. I shall haunt the master of Lackley! It can only mean one thing—that they're getting ready for me on the other side of the grave."

When I touched the question of breakfast he replied that he had his breakfast in his pocket; and he drew from his travelling-bag a phial of morphine. He took a strong dose and went to bed. At noon I found him on foot again, dressed, shaved, much refreshed. "Poor fellow," he said, "you've got more than you bargained for—not only a man with a grievance but a man with a ghost. Well, it won't be for long!" It had of course promptly become a question whither we should now direct our steps. "As I've so little time," he argued for this, "I should like to see the best, the best alone." I answered that either for time or eternity I had always supposed Oxford to represent the English maximum, and for Oxford in the course of an hour we accordingly departed.

IV

Of that extraordinary place I shall not attempt to speak with any order or indeed with any coherence. It must ever remain one of the supreme gratifications of travel for any American aware of the ancient pieties of race. The impression it produces, the emotions it kindles in the mind of such a visitor, are too rich and various to be expressed in the halting rhythm of prose. Passing through the small oblique streets in which the long grey battered public face of the colleges seems to watch jealously for sounds that may break upon the stillness of study, you feel it the most dignified and most educated of cities. Over and through it all the great corporate fact of the University slowly throbs after the fashion of some steady bass in a concerted piece or that of the mediaeval mystical presence of the Empire in the old States of Germany. The plain perpendicular of the so mildly conventual fronts, masking blest seraglios of culture and leisure, irritates the imagination scarce less than the harem-walls of Eastern towns. Within their arching portals, however, you discover more sacred and sunless courts, and the dark verdure soothing and cooling to bookish eyes. The grey-green quadrangles stand for ever open with a trustful hospitality. The seat of the humanities is stronger in her own good manners than in a marshalled host of wardens and beadles. Directly after our arrival my friend and I wandered forth in the luminous early dusk. We reached the bridge that under-spans the walls of Magdalen and saw the eight-spired tower, delicately fluted and embossed, rise in temperate beauty—the perfect prose of Gothic—wooing the eyes to the sky that was slowly drained of day. We entered the low monkish doorway and stood in the dim little court that nestles beneath the tower, where the swallows niche more lovingly in the tangled ivy than elsewhere in Oxford, and passed into the quiet cloister and studied the small sculptured monsters on the entablature of the arcade. I rejoiced in every one of my unhappy friend's responsive vibrations, even while feeling that they might as direfully multiply as those that had preceded them. I may say that from this time forward I found it difficult to distinguish in his company between the riot of fancy and the labour of thought, or to fix the balance between what he saw and what he imagined. He had already begun playfully to exchange his identity for that of the earlier Clement Searle, and he now delivered himself almost wholly in the character of his old-time kinsman.

"THIS was my college, you know," he would almost anywhere break out, applying the words wherever we stood—"the sweetest and noblest in the whole place. How often have I strolled in this cloister with my intimates of the other world! They are all dead and buried, but many a young fellow as we meet him, dark or fair, tall or short, reminds me of the past age and the early attachment. Even as we stand here, they say, the whole thing feels about its massive base the murmurs of the tide of time; some of the foundation-stones are loosened, some of the breaches will have to be repaired. Mine was the old unregenerate Oxford, the home of rank abuses, of distinctions and privileges the most delicious and invidious. What cared I, who was a perfect gentleman and with my pockets full of money? I had an allowance of a thousand a year."

It was at once plain to me that he had lost the little that remained of his direct grasp on life and was unequal to any effort of seeing things in their order. He read my apprehension in my eyes and took pains to assure me I was right. "I'm going straight down hill. Thank heaven it's an easy slope, coated with English turf and with an English churchyard at the foot." The hysterical emotion produced by our late dire misadventure had given place to an unruffled calm in which the scene about us was reflected as in an old-fashioned mirror. We took an afternoon walk through Christ-Church meadow and at the river-bank procured a boat which I pulled down the stream to Iffley and to the slanting woods of Nuneham—the sweetest flattest reediest stream-side landscape that could be desired. Here of course we encountered the scattered phalanx of the young, the happy generation, clad in white flannel and blue, muscular fair-haired magnificent fresh, whether floated down the current by idle punts and lounging in friendly couples when not in a singleness that nursed ambitions, or straining together in rhythmic crews and hoarsely exhorted from the near bank. When to the exhibition of so much of the clearest joy of wind and limb we added the great sense of perfumed protection shed by all the enclosed lawns and groves and bowers, we felt that to be young in such scholastic shades must be a double, an infinite blessing. As my companion found himself less and less able to walk we repaired in turn to a series of gardens and spent long hours sitting in their greenest places. They struck us as the fairest things in England and the ripest and sweetest fruit of the English system. Locked in their antique verdure, guarded, as in the case of New College, by gentle battlements of silver-grey, outshouldering the matted leafage of undisseverable plants, filled with nightingales and memories, a sort of chorus of tradition; with vaguely-generous youths sprawling bookishly on the turf as if to spare it the injury of their boot-heels, and with the great conservative college countenance appealing gravely from the restless outer world, they seem places to lie down on the grass in for ever, in the happy faith that life is all a green old English garden and time an endless summer afternoon. This charmed seclusion was especially grateful to my friend, and his sense of it reached its climax, I remember, on one of the last of such occasions and while we sat in fascinated flanerie over against the sturdy back of Saint John's. The wide discreetly-windowed wall here perhaps broods upon the lawn with a more effective air of property than elsewhere. Searle dropped into fitful talk and spun his humour into golden figures. Any passing undergraduate was a peg to hang a fable, every feature of the place a pretext for more embroidery.

"Isn't it all a delightful lie?" he wanted to know. "Mightn't one fancy this the very central point of the world's heart, where all the echoes of the general life arrive but to falter and die? Doesn't one feel the air just thick with arrested voices? It's well there should be such places, shaped in the interest of factitious needs, invented to minister to the book-begotten longing for a medium in which one may dream unwaked and believe unconfuted; to foster the sweet illusion that all's well in a world where so much is so damnable, all right and rounded, smooth and fair, in this sphere of the rough and ragged, the pitiful unachieved especially, and the dreadful uncommenced. The world's made—work's over. Now for leisure! England's safe—now for Theocritus and Horace, for lawn and sky! What a sense it all gives one of the composite life of the country and of the essential furniture of its luckier minds! Thank heaven they had the wit to send me here in the other time. I'm not much visibly the braver perhaps, but think how I'm the happier! The misty spires and towers, seen far off on the level, have been all these years one of the constant things of memory. Seriously, what do the spires and towers do for these people? Are they wiser, gentler, finer, cleverer? My diminished dignity reverts in any case at moments to the naked background of our own education, the deadly dry air in which we gasp for impressions and comparisons. I assent to it all with a sort of desperate calmness; I accept it with a dogged pride. We're nursed at the opposite pole. Naked come we into a naked world. There's a certain grandeur in the lack of decorations, a certain heroic strain in that young imagination of ours which finds nothing made to its hands, which has to invent its own traditions and raise high into our morning-air, with a ringing hammer and nails, the castles in which we dwell. Noblesse oblige—Oxford must damnably do so. What a horrible thing not to rise to such examples! If you pay the pious debt to the last farthing of interest you may go through life with her blessing; but if you let it stand unhonoured you're a worse barbarian than we! But for the better or worse, in a myriad private hearts, think how she must be loved! How the youthful sentiment of mankind seems visibly to brood upon her! Think of the young lives now taking colour in her cloisters and halls. Think of the centuries' tale of dead lads—dead alike with the end of the young days to which these haunts were a present world, and the close of the larger lives which the general mother-scene has dropped into less bottomless traps. What are those two young fellows kicking their heels over on the grass there? One of them has the Saturday Review; the other—upon my soul—the other has Artemus Ward! Where do they live, how do they live, to what end do they live? Miserable boys! How can they read Artemus Ward under those windows of Elizabeth? What do you think loveliest in all Oxford? The poetry of certain windows. Do you see that one yonder, the second of those lesser bays, with the broken cornice and the lattice? That used to be the window of my bosom friend a hundred years ago. Remind me to tell you the story of that broken cornice. Don't pretend it's not a common thing to have one's bosom friend at another college. Pray was I committed to common things? He was a charming fellow. By the way, he was a good deal like you. Of course his cocked hat, his long hair in a black ribbon, his cinnamon velvet suit and his flowered waistcoat made a difference. We gentlemen used to wear swords."

There was really the touch of grace in my poor friend's divagations—the disheartened dandy had so positively turned rhapsodist and seer. I was particularly struck with his having laid aside the diffidence and self-consciousness of the first days of our acquaintance. He had become by this time a disembodied observer and critic; the shell of sense, growing daily thinner and more transparent, transmitted the tremor of his quickened spirit. He seemed to pick up acquaintances, in the course of our contemplations, merely by putting out his hand. If I left him for ten minutes I was sure to find him on my return in earnest conversation with some affable wandering scholar. Several young men with whom he had thus established relations invited him to their rooms and entertained him, as I gathered, with rather rash hospitality. For myself, I chose not to be present at these symposia; I shrank partly from being held in any degree responsible for his extravagance, partly from the pang of seeing him yield to champagne and an admiring circle. He reported such adventures with less keen a complacency than I had supposed he might use, but a certain method in his madness, a certain dignity in his desire to fraternise, appeared to save him from mischance. If they didn't think him a harmless lunatic they certainly thought him a celebrity of the Occident. Two things, however, grew evident—that he drank deeper than was good for him and that the flagrant freshness of his young patrons rather interfered with his predetermined sense of the element of finer romance. At the same time it completed his knowledge of the place. Making the acquaintance of several tutors and fellows, he dined in hall in half a dozen colleges, alluding afterwards to these banquets with religious unction. One evening after a participation indiscreetly prolonged he came back to the hotel in a cab, accompanied by a friendly undergraduate and a physician and looking deadly pale. He had swooned away on leaving table and remained so rigidly unconscious as much to agitate his banqueters. The following twenty-four hours he of course spent in bed, but on the third day declared himself strong enough to begin afresh. On his reaching the street his strength once more forsook him, so that I insisted on his returning to his room. He besought me with tears in his eyes not to shut him up. "It's my last chance—I want to go back for an hour to that garden of Saint John's. Let me eat and drink—to-morrow I die." It seemed to me possible that with a Bath-chair the expedition might be accomplished.

The hotel, it appeared, possessed such a convenience, which was immediately produced. It became necessary hereupon that we should have a person to propel the chair. As there was no one on the spot at liberty I was about to perform the office; but just as my patient had got seated and wrapped—he now had a perpetual chill—an elderly man emerged from a lurking-place near the door and, with a formal salute, offered to wait upon the gentleman. We assented, and he proceeded solemnly to trundle the chair before him. I recognised him as a vague personage whom I had observed to lounge shyly about the doors of the hotels, at intervals during our stay, with a depressed air of wanting employment and a poor semblance of finding it. He had once indeed in a half-hearted way proposed himself as an amateur cicerone for a tour through the colleges; and I now, as I looked at him, remembered with a pang that I had too curtly declined his ministrations. Since then his shyness, apparently, had grown less or his misery greater, for it was with a strange grim avidity that he now attached himself to our service. He was a pitiful image of shabby gentility and the dinginess of "reduced circumstances." He would have been, I suppose, some fifty years of age; but his pale haggard unwholesome visage, his plaintive drooping carriage and the irremediable disarray of his apparel seemed to add to the burden of his days and tribulations. His eyes were weak and bloodshot, his bold nose was sadly compromised, and his reddish beard, largely streaked with grey, bristled under a month's neglect of the razor. In all this rusty forlornness lurked a visible assurance of our friend's having known better days. Obviously he was the victim of some fatal depreciation in the market value of pure gentility. There had been something terribly affecting in the way he substituted for the attempt to touch the greasy rim of his antiquated hat some such bow as one man of the world might make another. Exchanging a few words with him as we went I was struck with the decorum of his accent. His fine whole voice should have been congruously cracked.

"Take me by some long roundabout way," said Searle, "so that I may see as many college-walls as possible."

"You know," I asked of our attendant, "all these wonderful ins and outs?"

"I ought to, sir," he said, after a moment, with pregnant gravity. And as we were passing one of the colleges, "That used to be my place," he added.

At these words Searle desired him to stop and come round within sight. "You say that's YOUR college?"

"The place might deny me, sir; but heaven forbid I should seem to take it ill of her. If you'll allow me to wheel you into the quad I'll show you my windows of thirty years ago."

Searle sat staring, his huge pale eyes, which now left nothing else worth mentioning in his wasted face, filled with wonder and pity. "If you'll be so kind," he said with great deference. But just as this perverted product of a liberal education was about to propel him across the threshold of the court he turned about, disengaged the mercenary hands, with one of his own, from the back of the chair, drew their owner alongside and turned to me. "While we're here, my dear fellow," he said, "be so good as to perform this service. You understand?" I gave our companion a glance of intelligence and we resumed our way. The latter showed us his window of the better time, where a rosy youth in a scarlet smoking-fez now puffed a cigarette at the open casement. Thence we proceeded into the small garden, the smallest, I believe, and certainly the sweetest, of all the planted places of Oxford. I pushed the chair along to a bench on the lawn, turned it round, toward the front of the college and sat down by it on the grass. Our attendant shifted mournfully from one foot to the other, his patron eyeing him open-mouthed. At length Searle broke out: "God bless my soul, sir, you don't suppose I expect you to stand! There's an empty bench."

"Thank you," said our friend, who bent his joints to sit.

"You English are really fabulous! I don't know whether I most admire or most abominate you! Now tell me: who are you? what are you? what brought you to this?"

The poor fellow blushed up to his eyes, took off his hat and wiped his forehead with an indescribable fabric drawn from his pocket. "My name's Rawson, sir. Beyond that it's a long story."

"I ask out of sympathy," said Searle. "I've a fellow-feeling. If you're a poor devil I'm a poor devil as well."

"I'm the poorer devil of the two," said the stranger with an assurance for once presumptuous.

"Possibly. I suppose an English poor devil's the poorest of all poor devils. And then you've fallen from a height. From a gentleman commoner—is that what they called you?—to a propeller of Bath-chairs. Good heavens, man, the fall's enough to kill you!"

"I didn't take it all at once, sir. I dropped a bit one time and a bit another."

"That's me, that's me!" cried Searle with all his seriousness.

"And now," said our friend, "I believe I can't drop any further."

"My dear fellow"—and Searle clasped his hand and shook it—"I too am at the very bottom of the hole."

Mr. Rawson lifted his eyebrows. "Well, sir, there's a difference between sitting in such a pleasant convenience and just trudging behind it!"

"Yes—there's a shade. But I'm at my last gasp, Mr. Rawson."

"I'm at my last penny, sir."

"Literally, Mr. Rawson?"

Mr. Rawson shook his head with large loose bitterness. "I've almost come to the point of drinking my beer and buttoning my coat figuratively; but I don't talk in figures."

Fearing the conversation might appear to achieve something like gaiety at the expense of Mr. Rawson's troubles, I took the liberty of asking him, with all consideration, how he made a living.

"I don't make a living," he answered with tearful eyes; "I can't make a living. I've a wife and three children—and all starving, sir. You wouldn't believe what I've come to. I sent my wife to her mother's, who can ill afford to keep her, and came to Oxford a week ago, thinking I might pick up a few half-crowns by showing people about the colleges. But it's no use. I haven't the assurance. I don't look decent. They want a nice little old man with black gloves and a clean shirt and a silver-headed stick. What do I look as if I knew about Oxford, sir?"

"Mercy on us," cried Searle, "why didn't you speak to us before?"

"I wanted to; half a dozen times I've been on the point of it. I knew you were Americans."

"And Americans are rich!" cried Searle, laughing. "My dear Mr. Rawson, American as I am I'm living on charity."

"And I'm exactly not, sir! There it is. I'm dying for the lack of that same. You say you're a pauper, but it takes an American pauper to go bowling about in a Bath-chair. America's an easy country."

"Ah me!" groaned Searle. "Have I come to the most delicious corner of the ancient world to hear the praise of Yankeeland?"

"Delicious corners are very well, and so is the ancient world," said Mr. Rawson; "but one may sit here hungry and shabby, so long as one isn't too shabby, as well as elsewhere. You'll not persuade me that it's not an easier thing to keep afloat yonder than here. I wish *I* were in Yankeeland, that's all!" he added with feeble force. Then brooding for a moment on his wrongs: "Have you a bloated brother? or you, sir? It matters little to you. But it has mattered to me with a vengeance! Shabby as I sit here I can boast that advantage—as he his five thousand a year. Being but a twelvemonth my elder he swaggers while I go thus. There's old England for you! A very pretty place for HIM!"

"Poor old England!" said Searle softly.

"Has your brother never helped you?" I asked.

"A five-pound note now and then! Oh I don't say there haven't been times when I haven't inspired an irresistible sympathy. I've not been what I should. I married dreadfully out of the way. But the devil of it is that he started fair and I started foul; with the tastes, the desires, the needs, the sensibilities of a gentleman—and not another blessed 'tip.' I can't afford to live in England."

"THIS poor gentleman fancied a couple of months ago that he couldn't afford to live in America," I fondly explained.

"I'd 'swap'—do you call it?—chances with him!" And Mr. Rawson looked quaintly rueful over his freedom of speech.

Searle sat supported there with his eyes closed and his face twitching for violent emotion, and then of a sudden had a glare of gravity. "My friend, you're a dead failure! Be judged! Don't talk about 'swapping.' Don't talk about chances. Don't talk about fair starts and false starts. I'm at that point myself that I've a right to speak. It lies neither in one's chance nor one's start to make one a success; nor in anything one's brother—however bloated—can do or can undo. It lies in one's character. You and I, sir, have HAD no character—that's very plain. We've been weak, sir; as weak as water. Here we are for it—sitting staring in each other's faces and reading our weakness in each other's eyes. We're of no importance whatever, Mr. Rawson!"

Mr. Rawson received this sally with a countenance in which abject submission to the particular affirmed truth struggled with the comparative propriety of his general rebellion against fate. In the course of a minute a due self-respect yielded to the warm comfortable sense of his being relieved of the cares of an attitude. "Go on, sir, go on," he said. "It's wholesome doctrine." And he wiped his eyes with what seemed his sole remnant of linen.

"Dear, dear," sighed Searle, "I've made you cry! Well, we speak as from man to man. I should be glad to think you had felt for a moment the side-light of that great undarkening of the spirit which precedes—which precedes the grand illumination of death."

Mr. Rawson sat silent a little, his eyes fixed on the ground and his well-cut nose but the more deeply dyed by his agitation. Then at last looking up: "You're a very good-natured man, sir, and you'll never persuade me you don't come of a kindly race. Say what you please about a chance; when a man's fifty—degraded, penniless, a husband and father—a chance to get on his legs again is not to be despised. Something tells me that my luck may be in your country—which has brought luck to so many. I can come on the parish here of course, but I don't want to come on the parish. Hang it, sir, I want to hold up my head. I see thirty years of life before me yet. If only by God's help I could have a real change of air! It's a fixed idea of mine. I've had it for the last ten years. It's not that I'm a low radical. Oh I've no vulgar opinions. Old England's good enough for me, but I'm not good enough for old England. I'm a shabby man that wants to get out of a room full of staring gentlefolk. I'm for ever put to the blush. It's a perfect agony of spirit; everything reminds me of my younger and better self. The thing for me would be a cooling cleansing plunge into the unknowing and the unknown! I lie awake thinking of it."

Searle closed his eyes, shivering with a long-drawn tremor which I hardly knew whether to take for an expression of physical or of mental pain. In a moment I saw it was neither. "Oh my country, my country, my country!" he murmured in a broken voice; and then sat for some time abstracted and lost. I signalled our companion that it was time we should bring our small session to a close, and he, without hesitating, possessed himself of the handle of the Bath-chair and pushed it before him. We had got halfway home before Searle spoke or moved. Suddenly in the High Street, as we passed a chop-house from whose open doors we caught a waft of old-fashioned cookery and other restorative elements, he motioned us to halt. "This is my last five pounds"—and he drew a note from his pocket-book. "Do me the favour, Mr. Rawson, to accept it. Go in there and order the best dinner they can give you. Call for a bottle of Burgundy and drink it to my eternal rest!"

Mr. Rawson stiffened himself up and received the gift with fingers momentarily irresponsive. But Mr. Rawson had the nerves of a gentleman. I measured the spasm with which his poor dispossessed hand closed upon the crisp paper, I observed his empurpled nostril convulsive under the other solicitation. He crushed the crackling note in his palm with a passionate pressure and jerked a spasmodic bow. "I shall not do you the wrong, sir, of anything but the best!" The next moment the door swung behind him.

Searle sank again into his apathy, and on reaching the hotel I helped him to get to bed. For the rest of the day he lay without motion or sound and beyond reach of any appeal. The doctor, whom I had constantly in attendance, was sure his end was near. He expressed great surprise that he should have lasted so long; he must have been living for a month on the very dregs of his strength. Toward evening, as I sat by his bedside in the deepening dusk, he roused himself with a purpose I had vaguely felt gathering beneath his stupor.

"My cousin, my cousin," he said confusedly. "Is she here?" It was the first time he had spoken of Miss Searle since our retreat from her brother's house, and he continued to ramble. "I was to have married her. What a dream! That day was like a string of verses—rhymed hours. But the last verse is bad measure. What's the rhyme to 'love'? ABOVE! Was she a simple woman, a kind sweet woman? Or have I only dreamed it? She had the healing gift; her touch would have cured my madness. I want you to do something. Write three lines, three words: 'Good-bye; remember me; be happy.'" And then after a long pause: "It's strange a person in my state should have a wish. Why should one eat one's breakfast the day one's hanged? What a creature is man! What a farce is life! Here I lie, worn down to a mere throbbing fever-point; I breathe and nothing more, and yet I DESIRE! My desire lives. If I could see her! Help me out with it and let me die."

Half an hour later, at a venture, I dispatched by post a note to Miss Searle: "Your cousin is rapidly sinking. He asks to see you." I was conscious of a certain want of consideration in this act, since it would bring her great trouble and yet no power to face the trouble; but out of her distress I fondly hoped a sufficient force might be born. On the following day my friend's exhaustion had become so great that I began to fear his intelligence altogether broken up. But toward evening he briefly rallied, to maunder about many things, confounding in a sinister jumble the memories of the past weeks and those of bygone years. "By the way," he said suddenly, "I've made no will. I haven't much to bequeath. Yet I have something." He had been playing listlessly with a large signet-ring on his left hand, which he now tried to draw off. "I leave you this"—working it round and round vainly—"if you can get it off. What enormous knuckles! There must be such knuckles in the mummies of the Pharaohs. Well, when I'm gone—! No, I leave you something more precious than gold—the sense of a great kindness. But I've a little gold left. Bring me those trinkets." I placed on the bed before him several articles of jewellery, relics of early foppery: his watch and chain, of great value, a locket and seal, some odds and ends of goldsmith's work. He trifled with them feebly for some moments, murmuring various names and dates associated with them. At last, looking up with clearer interest, "What has become," he asked, "of Mr. Rawson?"

"You want to see him?"

"How much are these things worth?" he went on without heeding me. "How much would they bring?" And he weighed them in his weak hands. "They're pretty heavy. Some hundred or so? Oh I'm richer than I thought! Rawson—Rawson—you want to get out of this awful England?"

I stepped to the door and requested the servant whom I kept in constant attendance in our adjacent sitting-room to send and ascertain if Mr. Rawson were on the premises. He returned in a few moments, introducing our dismal friend. Mr. Rawson was pale even to his nose and derived from his unaffectedly concerned state an air of some distinction. I led him up to the bed. In Searle's eyes, as they fell on him, there shone for a moment the light of a human message.

"Lord have mercy!" gasped Mr. Rawson.

"My friend," said Searle, "there's to be one American the less—so let there be at the same time one the more. At the worst you'll be as good a one as I. Foolish me! Take these battered relics; you can sell them; let them help you on your way. They're gifts and mementoes, but this is a better use. Heaven speed you! May America be kind to you. Be kind, at the last, to your own country!"

"Really this is too much; I can't," the poor man protested, almost scared and with tears in his eyes. "Do come round and get well and I'll stop here. I'll stay with you and wait on you."

"No, I'm booked for my journey, you for yours. I hope you don't mind the voyage."

Mr. Rawson exhaled a groan of helpless gratitude, appealing piteously from so strange a windfall. "It's like the angel of the Lord who bids people in the Bible to rise and flee!"

Searle had sunk back upon his pillow, quite used up; I led Mr. Rawson back into the sitting-room, where in three words I proposed to him a rough valuation of our friend's trinkets. He assented with perfect good-breeding; they passed into my possession and a second bank-note into his.

From the collapse into which this wondrous exercise of his imagination had plunged him my charge then gave few signs of being likely to emerge. He breathed, as he had said, and nothing more. The twilight deepened; I lighted the night-lamp. The doctor sat silent and official at the foot of the bed; I resumed my constant place near the head. Suddenly our patient opened his eyes wide. "She'll not come," he murmured. "Amen! she's an English sister." Five minutes passed; he started forward. "She's come, she's here!" he confidently quavered. His words conveyed to my mind so absolute an assurance that I lightly rose and passed into the sitting-room. At the same moment, through the opposite door, the servant introduced a lady. A lady, I say; for an instant she was simply such—tall pale dressed in deep mourning. The next instant I had uttered her name—"Miss Searle!" She looked ten years older.

She met me with both hands extended and an immense question in her face. "He has just announced you," I said. And then with a fuller consciousness of the change in her dress and countenance: "What has happened?"

"Oh death, death!" she wailed. "You and I are left."

There came to me with her words a sickening shock, the sense of poetic justice somehow cheated, defeated. "Your brother?" I panted.

She laid her hand on my arm and I felt its pressure deepen as she spoke. "He was thrown from his horse in the park. He died on the spot. Six days have passed. Six months!"

She accepted my support and a moment later we had entered the room and approached the bedside, from which the doctor withdrew. Searle opened his eyes and looked at her from head to foot. Suddenly he seemed to make out her mourning. "Already!" he cried audibly and with a smile, as I felt, of pleasure.

She dropped on her knees and took his hand. "Not for you, cousin," she whispered. "For my poor brother."

He started, in all his deathly longitude, as with a galvanic shock. "Dead! HE dead! Life itself!" And then after a moment and with a slight rising inflexion: "You're free?"

"Free, cousin. Too sadly free. And now—NOW—with what use for freedom?"

He looked steadily into her eyes, dark in the heavy shadow of her musty mourning-veil. "For me wear colours!"

In a moment more death had come, the doctor had silently attested it, and she had burst into sobs.

We buried him in the little churchyard in which he had expressed the wish to lie; beneath one of the blackest and widest of English yews and the little tower than which none in all England has a softer and hoarier grey. A year has passed; Miss Searle, I believe, has begun to wear colours.

A SMALL BOY AND OTHERS

I

In the attempt to place together some particulars of the early life of William James and present him in his setting, his immediate native and domestic air, so that any future gathered memorials of him might become the more intelligible and interesting, I found one of the consequences of my interrogation of the past assert itself a good deal at the expense of some of the others. For it was to memory in the first place that my main appeal for particulars had to be made; I had been too near a witness of my brother's beginnings of life, and too close a participant, by affection, admiration and sympathy, in whatever touched and moved him, not to feel myself in possession even of a greater quantity of significant truth, a larger handful of the fine substance of history, than I could hope to express or apply. To recover anything like the full treasure of scattered, wasted circumstance was at the same time to live over the spent experience itself, so deep and rich and rare, with whatever sadder and sorer intensities, even with whatever poorer and thinner passages, after the manner of every one's experience; and the effect of this in turn was to find discrimination among the parts of my subject again and again difficult—so inseparably and beautifully they seemed to hang together and the comprehensive case to decline mutilation or refuse to be treated otherwise than handsomely. This meant that aspects began to multiply and images to swarm, so far at least as they showed, to appreciation, as true terms and happy values; and that I might positively and exceedingly rejoice in my relation to most of them, using it for all that, as the phrase is, it should be worth. To knock at the door of the past was in a word to see it open to me quite wide—to see the world within begin to "compose" with a grace of its own round the primary figure, see it people itself vividly and insistently. Such then is the circle of my commemoration and so much these free and copious notes a labour of love and loyalty. We were, to my sense, the blest group of us, such a company of characters and such a picture of differences, and withal so fused and united and interlocked, that each of us, to that fond fancy, pleads for preservation, and that in respect to what I speak of myself as possessing I think I shall be ashamed, as of a cold impiety, to find any element altogether negligible. To which I may add perhaps that I struggle under the drawback, innate and inbred, of seeing the whole content of memory and affection in each enacted and recovered moment, as who should say, in the vivid image and the very scene; the light of the only terms in which life has treated me to experience. And I cherish the moment and evoke the image and repaint the scene; though meanwhile indeed scarce able to convey how prevailingly and almost exclusively, during years and years, the field was animated and the adventure conditioned for me by my brother's nearness and that play of genius in him of which I had never had a doubt from the first.

The "first" then—since I retrace our steps to the start, for the pleasure, strangely mixed though it be, of feeling our small feet plant themselves afresh and artlessly stumble forward again—the first began long ago, far off, and yet glimmers at me there as out of a thin golden haze, with all the charm, for imagination and memory, of pressing pursuit rewarded, of distinctness in the dimness, of the flush of life in the grey, of the wonder of consciousness in everything; everything having naturally been all the while but the abject little matter of course. Partly doubtless as the effect of a life, now getting to be a tolerably long one, spent in the older world, I see the world of our childhood as very young indeed, young with its own juvenility as well as with ours; as if it wore the few and light garments and had gathered in but the scant properties and breakable toys of the tenderest age, or were at the most a very unformed young person, even a boisterous hobbledehoy. It exhaled at any rate a simple freshness, and I catch its pure breath, at our infantile Albany, as the very air of long summer afternoons—occasions tasting of ample leisure, still bookless, yet beginning to be bedless, or cribless; tasting of accessible garden peaches in a liberal backward territory that was still almost part of a country town; tasting of many-sized uncles, aunts, cousins, of strange legendary domestics, inveterately but archaically Irish, and whose familiar remarks and "criticism of life" were handed down, as well as of dim family ramifications and local allusions—mystifications always—that flowered into anecdote as into small hard plums; tasting above all of a big much-shaded savoury house in which a softly-sighing widowed grandmother, Catherine Barber by birth, whose attitude was a resigned consciousness of complications and accretions, dispensed an hospitality seemingly as joyless as it was certainly boundless.

What she *liked*, dear gentle lady of many cares and anxieties, was the "fiction of the day," the novels, at that time promptly pirated, of Mrs. Trollope and Mrs. Gore, of Mrs. Marsh, Mrs. Hubback and the Misses Kavanagh and Aguilar, whose very names are forgotten now, but which used to drive her away to quiet corners whence her figure comes back to me bent forward on a table with the book held out at a distance and a tall single candle placed, apparently not at all to her discomfort, in that age of sparer and braver habits, straight between the page and her eyes. There is a very animated allusion to one or two of her aspects in the fragment of a "spiritual autobiography," the reminiscences of a so-called Stephen Dewhurst printed by W. J. (1885) in The Literary Remains of Henry James; a reference which has the interest of being very nearly as characteristic of my father himself (which his references in almost any connection were wont to be) as of the person or the occasion evoked. I had reached my sixteenth year when she died, and as my only remembered grandparent she touches the chord of attachment to a particular vibration. She represented for us in our generation the only English blood—that of both her own parents—flowing in our veins; I confess that out of that association, for reasons and reasons, I feel her image most beneficently bend. We were, as to three parts, of two other stocks; and I recall how from far back I reflected—for I see I must have been always reflecting—that, mixed as such a mixture, our Scotch with our Irish, might be, it had had still a grace to borrow from the third infusion or dimension. If I could freely have chosen moreover it was precisely from my father's mother that, fond votary of the finest faith in the vivifying and characterising force of mothers, I should have wished to borrow it; even while conscious that Catherine Barber's own people had drawn breath in American air for at least two generations before her. Our father's father, William James, an Irishman and a Protestant born (of county Cavan) had come to America, a very young man and then sole of his family, shortly after the Revolutionary War; my father, the second son of the third of the marriages to which the country of his adoption was liberally to help him, had been born in Albany in 1811. Our maternal greatgrandfather on the father's side, Hugh Walsh, had reached our shores from a like Irish home, Killyleagh, county Down, somewhat earlier, in 1764, he being then nineteen; he had settled at Newburgh-on-the-Hudson, half way to Albany, where some of his descendants till lately lingered. Our maternal greatgrandfather on the mother's side—that is our mother's mother's father, Alexander Robertson of Polmont near Edinburgh—had likewise crossed the sea in the mid-century and prospered in New York very much as Hugh Walsh was prospering and William James was still more markedly to prosper, further up the Hudson; as unanimous and fortunate beholders of the course of which admirable stream I like to think of them. I find Alexander Robertson inscribed in a wee New York directory of the close of the century as Merchant; and our childhood in that city was passed, as to some of its aspects, in a sense of the afterglow, reduced and circumscribed, it is true, but by no means wholly inanimate, of his shining solidity.

The sweet taste of Albany probably lurked most in its being our admired antithesis to New York; it was holiday, whereas New York was home; at least that presently came to be the relation, for to my very very first fleeting vision, I apprehend, Albany itself must have been the scene exhibited. Our parents had gone there for a year or two to be near our grandmother on their return from their first (that is our mother's first) visit to Europe, which had quite immediately followed my birth, which appears to have lasted some year and a half, and of which I shall have another word to say. The Albany experiment would have been then their first founded housekeeping, since I make them out to have betaken themselves for the winter following their marriage to the ancient Astor House—not indeed at that time ancient, but the great and appointed modern hotel of New York, the only one of such pretensions, and which somehow continued to project its massive image, that of a great square block of granite with vast dark warm interiors, across some of the later and more sensitive stages of my infancy. Clearly—or I should perhaps rather say dimly—recourse to that hospitality was again occasionally had by our parents; who had originally had it to such a happy end that on January 9th, 1842, my elder brother had come into the world there. It remained a tradition with him that our father's friend from an early time, R. W. Emerson, then happening to be in New York and under that convenient roof, was proudly and pressingly "taken upstairs" to admire and give his blessing to the lately-born babe who was to become the second American William James. The blessing was to be renewed, I may mention, in the sense that among the impressions of the next early years I easily distinguish that of the great and urbane Emerson's occasional presence in Fourteenth Street, a centre of many images, where the parental tent was before long to pitch itself and rest awhile. I am interested for the moment, however, in identifying the scene of our very first perceptions—of my very own at least, which I can here best speak for.

One of these, and probably the promptest in order, was that of my brother's occupying a place in the world to which I couldn't at all aspire—to any approach to which in truth I seem to myself ever conscious of having signally forfeited a title. It glimmers back to me that I quite definitely and resignedly thought of him as in the most exemplary manner already beforehand with me, already seated at his task when the attempt to drag me crying and kicking to the first hour of my education failed on the threshold of the Dutch House in Albany after the fashion I have glanced at in a collection of other pages than these (just as I remember to have once borrowed a hint from our grandmother's "interior" in a work of imagination). That failure of my powers or that indifference to them, my retreat shrieking from the Dutch House, was to leave him once for all already there an embodied demonstration of the possible—already wherever it might be that there was a question of my arriving, when arriving at all, belatedly and ruefully; as if he had gained such an advance of me in his sixteen months' experience of the world before mine began that I never for all the time of childhood and youth in the least caught up with him or overtook him. He was always round the corner and out of sight, coming back into view but at his hours of extremest ease. We were never in the same schoolroom, in the same game, scarce even in step together or in the same phase at the same time; when our phases overlapped, that is, it was only for a moment—he was clean out before I had got well in. How far he had really at any moment dashed forward it is not for me now to attempt to say; what comes to me is that I at least hung inveterately and woefully back, and that this relation alike to our interests and to each other seemed proper and preappointed. I lose myself in wonder at the loose ways, the strange process of waste, through which nature and fortune may deal on occasion with those whose faculty for application is all and only in their imagination and their sensibility. There may be during those bewildered and brooding years so little for them to "show" that I liken the individual dunce—as he so often must appear—to some commercial traveller who has lost the key to his packed case of samples and can but pass for a fool while other exhibitions go forward.

I achieve withal a dim remembrance of my final submission, though it is the faintest ghost of an impression and consists but of the bright blur of a dame's schoolroom, a mere medium for small piping shuffling sound and suffered heat, as well as for the wistfulness produced by "glimmering squares" that were fitfully screened, though not to any revival of cheer, by a huge swaying, yet dominant object. This dominant object, the shepherdess of the flock, was Miss Bayou or Bayhoo—I recover but the alien sound of her name, which memory caresses only because she may have been of like race with her temple of learning, which faced my grandmother's house in North Pearl Street and really justified its exotic claim by its yellow archaic gable-end: I think of the same as of brick baked in the land of dykes and making a series of small steps from the base of the gable to the point. These images are subject, I confess, to a soft confusion—which is somehow consecrated, none the less, and out of which, with its shade of contributory truth, some sort of scene insists on glancing. The very flush of the uneven bricks of the pavement lives in it, the very smell of the street cobbles, the imputed grace of the arching umbrage—I see it all as from under trees; the form of Steuben Street, which crossed our view, as steep even to the very essence of adventure, with a summit, and still more with a nethermost and riskiest incline, very far away. There lives in it the aspect of the other house—the other and much smaller than my grandmother's, conveniently near it and within sight; which was pinkish-red picked out with white, whereas my grandmother's was greyish-brown and very grave, and which must have stood back a little from the street, as I seem even now to swing, or at least to perch, on a relaxed gate of approach that was conceived to work by an iron chain weighted with a big ball; all under a spreading tree again and with the high, oh so high white stone steps (mustn't they have been marble?) and fan-lighted door of the pinkish-red front behind me. I lose myself in ravishment before the marble and the pink. There were other houses too—one of them the occasion of the first "paid" visit that struggles with my twilight of social consciousness; a call with my father, conveying me presumably for fond exhibition (since if my powers were not exhibitional my appearance and my long fair curls, of which I distinctly remember the lachrymose sacrifice, suppositiously were), on one of our aunts, the youngest of his three sisters, lately married and who, predestined to an early death, hovers there for me, softly spectral, in long light "front" ringlets, the fashion of the time and the capital sign of all our paternal aunts seemingly; with the remembered enhancement of her living in Elk Street, the name itself vaguely portentous, as through beasts of the forest not yet wholly exorcised, and more or less under the high brow of that Capitol which, as aloft somewhere and beneath the thickest shades of all, loomed, familiar yet impressive, at the end of almost any Albany vista of reference. I have seen other capitols since, but the whole majesty of the matter must have been then distilled into my mind—even though the connection was indirect and the concrete image, that of the primitive structure, long since pretentiously and insecurely superseded—so that, later on, the impression was to find itself, as the phrase is, discounted. Had it not moreover been reinforced at the time, for that particular Capitoline hour, by the fact that our uncle, our aunt's husband, was a son of Mr. Martin Van Buren, and that *he* was the President? This at least led the imagination on—or leads in any case my present imagination of that one; ministering to what I have called the soft confusion.

The confusion clears, however, though the softness remains, when, ceasing to press too far backward, I meet the ampler light of conscious and educated little returns to the place; for the education of New York, enjoyed up to my twelfth year, failed to blight its romantic appeal. The images I really distinguish flush through the maturer medium, but with the sense of them only the more wondrous. The other house, the house of my parents' limited early sojourn, becomes that of those of our cousins, numerous at that time, who pre-eminently figured for us; the various brood presided over by my father's second sister, Catherine James, who had married at a very early age Captain Robert Temple, U.S.A. Both these parents were to die young, and their children, six in number, the two eldest boys, were very markedly to people our preliminary scene; this being true in particular of three of them, the sharply differing brothers and the second sister, Mary Temple, radiant and rare, extinguished in her first youth, but after having made an impression on many persons, and on ourselves not least, which was to become in the harmonious circle, for all time, matter of sacred legend and reference, of associated piety. Those and others with them were the numerous dawnings on which in many cases the deepening and final darknesses were so soon to follow: our father's family was to offer such a chronicle of early deaths, arrested careers, broken promises, orphaned children. It sounds cold-blooded, but part of the charm of our grandmother's house for us—or I should perhaps but speak for myself—was in its being so much and so sociably a nurseried and playroomed orphanage. The children of her lost daughters and daughters-in-law overflowed there, mainly as girls; on whom the surviving sons-in-law and sons occasionally and most trustingly looked in. Parentally bereft cousins were somehow more thrilling than parentally provided ones; and most thrilling when, in the odd fashion of that time, they were sent to school in New York as a preliminary to their being sent to school in Europe. They spent scraps of holidays with us in Fourteenth Street, and I think my first childish conception of the enviable lot, formed amid these associations, was to be so little fathered or mothered, so little sunk in the short range, that the romance of life seemed to lie in some constant improvisation, by vague overhovering authorities, of new situations and horizons. We were intensely domesticated, yet for the very reason perhaps that we felt our young bonds easy; and they were so easy compared to other small plights of which we had stray glimpses that my first assured conception of true richness was that we should be sent separately off among cold or even cruel aliens in order to be there thrillingly homesick. Homesickness was a luxury I remember craving from the tenderest age—a luxury of which I was unnaturally, or at least prosaically, deprived. Our motherless cousin Augustus Barker came up from Albany to the Institution Charlier—unless it was, as I suspect, a still earlier specimen, with a name that fades from me, of that type of French establishment for boys which then and for years after so incongruously flourished in New York; and though he professed a complete satisfaction with pleasures tasted in our innocent society I felt that he was engaged in a brave and strenuous adventure while we but hugged the comparatively safe shore.

II

We were day-boys, William and I, at dispensaries of learning the number and succession of which to-day excite my wonder; we couldn't have changed oftener, it strikes me as I look back, if our presence had been inveterately objected to, and yet I enjoy an inward certainty that, my brother being vividly bright and I quite blankly innocuous, this reproach was never brought home to our house. It was an humiliation to me at first, small boys though we were, that our instructors kept being instructresses and thereby a grave reflection both on our attainments and our spirit. A bevy of these educative ladies passes before me, I still possess their names; as for instance that of Mrs. Daly and that of Miss Rogers (previously of the "Chelsea Female Institute," though at the moment of Sixth Avenue this latter), whose benches indeed my brother didn't haunt, but who handled us literally with gloves—I still see the elegant objects as Miss Rogers beat time with a long black ferule to some species of droning chant or chorus in which we spent most of our hours; just as I see her very tall and straight and spare, in a light blue dress, her firm face framed in long black glossy ringlets and the stamp of the Chelsea Female Institute all over her. Mrs. Daly, clearly the immediate successor to the nebulous Miss Bayou, remains quite substantial—perhaps because the sphere of her small influence has succeeded in not passing away, up to this present writing; so that in certain notes on New York published a few years since I was moved to refer to it with emotion as one of the small red houses on the south side of Waverley Place that really carry the imagination back to a vanished social order. They carry mine to a stout red-faced lady with grey hair and a large apron, the latter convenience somehow suggesting, as she stood about with a resolute air, that she viewed her little pupils as so many small slices cut from the loaf of life and on which she was to dab the butter of arithmetic and spelling, accompanied by way of jam with a light application of the practice of prize-giving. I recall an occasion indeed, I must in justice mention, when the jam really was thick—my only memory of a schoolfeast, strange to say, throughout our young annals: something uncanny in the air of the schoolroom at the unwonted evening or late afternoon hour, and tables that seemed to me prodigiously long and on which the edibles were chunky and sticky. The stout red-faced lady must have been Irish, as the name she bore imported—or do I think so but from the indescribably Irish look of her revisited house? It refers itself at any rate to a New York age in which a little more or a little less of the colour was scarce notable in the general flush.

Of pure unimported strain, however, were Miss Sedgwick and Mrs. Wright (Lavinia D.), the next figures in the procession—the procession that was to wind up indeed with two foreign recruits, small brown snappy Mademoiselle Delavigne, who plied us with the French tongue at home and who had been introduced to us as the niece—or could it have been the grandniece?—of the celebrated Casimir, and a large Russian lady in an extraordinarily short cape (I like to recall the fashion of short capes) of the same stuff as her dress, and Merovingian sidebraids that seemed to require the royal crown of Frédégonde or Brunéhaut to complete their effect. This final and aggravational representative of the compromising sex looms to my mind's eye, I should add, but as the creature of an hour, in spite of her having been domiciled with us; whereas I think of Mademoiselle Delavigne as flitting in and out on quick, fine, more or less cloth-shod feet of exemplary neatness, the flat-soled feet of Louis Philippe and of the female figures in those volumes of Gavarni then actual, then contemporaneous, which were kept in a piece of furniture that stood between the front-parlour windows in Fourteenth Street, together with a set of Béranger enriched by steel engravings to the strange imagery of which I so wonderingly responded that all other art of illustration, ever since, has been for me comparatively weak and cold. These volumes and the tall entrancing folios of Nash's lithographed Mansions of England in the Olden Time formed a store lending itself particularly to distribution on the drawingroom carpet, with concomitant pressure to the same surface of the small student's stomach and relieving agitation of his backward heels. I make out that it had decidedly been given to Mlle. Delavigne to represent to my first perception personal France; she was, besides not being at all pink or shy, oval and fluent and mistress somehow of the step—the step of levity that involved a whisk of her short skirts; there she was, to the life, on the page of Gavarni, attesting its reality, and there again did that page in return (I speak not of course of the unplumbed depths of the appended text) attest her own felicity. I was later on to feel—that is I was to learn—how many impressions and appearances, how large a sense of things, her type and tone prefigured. The evanescence of the large Russian lady, whom I think of as rather rank, I can't express it otherwise, may have been owing to some question of the purity of her accent in French; it was one of her attributes and her grounds of appeal to us that she had come straight from Siberia, and it is distinct to me that the purity was challenged by a friend of the house, and without— pathetically enough!—provoking the only answer, the plea that the missing Atticism would have been wasted on young barbarians. The Siberian note, on our inmate's part, may perhaps have been the least of her incongruities; she was above all too big for a little job, towered over us doubtless too heroically; and her proportions hover but to lose themselves—with the successors to her function awaiting us a little longer.

Meanwhile, to revert an instant, if the depressed consciousness of our still more or less quailing, educationally, beneath the female eye—and there was as well the deeper depth, there was the degrading fact, that with us literally consorted and contended Girls, that we sat and strove, even though we drew the line at playing with them and at knowing them, when not of the swarming cousinship, at home—if that felt awkwardness didn't exactly coincide with the ironic effect of "Gussy's" appearances, his emergence from rich mystery and his return to it, our state was but comparatively the braver: he always had so much more to tell us than we could possibly have to tell him. On reflection I see that the most completely rueful period couldn't after all greatly have prolonged itself; since the female eye last bent on us would have been that of Lavinia D. Wright, to our connection with whom a small odd reminiscence attaches a date. A little schoolmate displayed to me with pride, while the connection lasted, a beautiful coloured, a positively iridescent and gilded card representing the first of all the "great exhibitions" of our age, the London Crystal Palace of 1851—his father having lately gone out to it and sent him the dazzling memento. In 1851 I was eight years old and my brother scarce more than nine; in addition to which it is distinct to me in the first place that we were never faithful long, or for more than one winter, to the same studious scene, and in the second that among our instructors Mrs.

Lavinia had no successor of her own sex unless I count Mrs. Vredenburg, of New Brighton, where we spent the summer of 1854, when I had reached the age of eleven and found myself bewildered by recognition of the part that "attendance at school" was so meanly to play in the hitherto unclouded long vacation. This was true at least for myself and my next younger brother, Wilky, who, under the presumption now dawning of his "community of pursuits" with my own, was from that moment, off and on, for a few years, my extremely easy yokefellow and playfellow. On William, charged with learning—I thought of him inveterately from our younger time as charged with learning—no such trick was played; he rested or roamed, that summer, on his accumulations; a fact which, as I was sure I saw these more and more richly accumulate, didn't in the least make me wonder. It comes back to me in truth that I had been prepared for anything by his having said to me toward the end of our time at Lavinia D's and with characteristic authority—his enjoyment of it coming from my character, I mean, quite as much as from his own—that that lady was a very able woman, as shown by the Experiments upstairs. He was upstairs of course, and I was down, and I scarce even knew what Experiments were, beyond their indeed requiring capability. The region of their performance was William's natural sphere, though I recall that I had a sense of peeping into it to a thrilled effect on seeing our instructress illustrate the proper way to extinguish a candle. She firmly pressed the flame between her thumb and her two forefingers, and, on my remarking that I didn't see how she could do it, promptly replied that I of course couldn't do it myself (as *he* could) because I should be afraid.

That reflection on my courage awakes another echo of the same scant season—since the test involved must have been that of our taking our way home through Fourth Avenue from some point up town, and Mrs. Wright's situation in East Twenty-first Street was such a point. The Hudson River Railroad was then in course of construction, or was being made to traverse the upper reaches of the city, through that part of which raged, to my young sense, a riot of explosion and a great shouting and waving of red flags when the gunpowder introduced into the rocky soil was about to take effect. It was our theory that our passage there, in the early afternoon, was beset with danger, and our impression that we saw fragments of rock hurtle through the air and smite to the earth another and yet another of the persons engaged or exposed. The point of honour, among several of us, was of course nobly to defy the danger, and I feel again the emotion with which I both hoped and feared that the red flags, lurid signals descried from afar, would enable or compel us to renew the feat. That I didn't for myself inveterately renew it I seem to infer from the memory of other perambulations of the period—as to which I am divided between their still present freshness and my sense of perhaps making too much of these tiny particles of history. My stronger rule, however, I confess, and the one by which I must here consistently be guided, is that, from the moment it is a question of projecting a picture, no particle that counts for memory or is appreciable to the spirit *can* be too tiny, and that experience, in the name of which one speaks, is all compact of them and shining with them. There was at any rate another way home, with other appeals, which consisted of getting straight along westward to Broadway, a sphere of a different order of fascination and bristling, as I seem to recall, with more vivid aspects, greater curiosities and wonderments. *The* curiosity was of course the country-place, as I supposed it to be, on the northeast corner of Eighteenth Street, if I am not mistaken; a big brown house in "grounds" peopled with animal life, which, little as its site may appear to know it to-day, lingered on into considerably later years. I have but to close my eyes in order to open them inwardly again, while I lean against the tall brown iron rails and peer through, to a romantic view of browsing and pecking and parading creatures, not numerous, but all of distinguished appearance: two or three elegant little cows of refined form and colour, two or three nibbling fawns and a larger company, above all, of peacocks and guineafowl, with, doubtless—though as to this I am vague—some of the commoner ornaments of the barnyard. I recognise that the scene as I evoke it fails of grandeur; but it none the less had for me the note of greatness—all of which but shows of course what a very town-bred small person I was, and was to remain.

I see myself moreover as somehow always alone in these and like New York *flâneries* and contemplations, and feel how the sense of my being so, being at any rate master of my short steps, such as they were, through all the beguiling streets, was probably the very savour of each of my chance feasts. Which stirs in me at the same time some wonder at the liberty of range and opportunity of adventure allowed to my tender age; though the puzzle may very well drop, after all, as I ruefully reflect that I couldn't have been judged at home reckless or adventurous. What I look back to as my infant license can only have had for its ground some timely conviction on the part of my elders that the only form of riot or revel ever known to me would be that of the visiting mind. Wasn't I myself for that matter even at that time all acutely and yet resignedly, even quite fatalistically, aware of what to think of this? I at any rate watch the small boy dawdle and gape again. I smell the cold dusty paint and iron as the rails of the Eighteenth Street corner rub his contemplative nose, and, feeling him foredoomed, withhold from him no grain of my sympathy. He is a convenient little image or warning of all that was to be for him, and he might well have been even happier than he was. For there was the very pattern and measure of all he was to demand: just to *be* somewhere—almost anywhere would do—and somehow receive an impression or an accession, feel a relation or a vibration. He was to go without many things, ever so many—as all persons do in whom contemplation takes so much the place of action; but everywhere, in the years that came soon after, and that in fact continued long, in the streets of great towns, in New York still for some time, and then for a while in London, in Paris, in Geneva, wherever it might be, he was to enjoy more than anything the so far from showy practice of wondering and dawdling and gaping: he was really, I think, much to profit by it. What it at all appreciably gave him—that is gave him in producible form—would be difficult to state; but it seems to him, as he even now thus indulges himself, an education like another: feeling, as he has come to do more and more, that no education avails for the intelligence that doesn't stir in it some subjective passion, and that on the other hand almost anything that does so act is largely educative, however small a figure the process might make in a scheme of training. Strange indeed, furthermore, are some of the things that *have* stirred a subjective passion—stirred it, I mean, in young persons predisposed to a more or less fine inspired application.

III

But I positively dawdle and gape here—I catch myself in the act; so that I take up the thread of fond reflection that guides me through that mystification of the summer school, which I referred to a little way back, at the time when the Summer School as known in America to-day was so deep in the bosom of the future. The seat of acquisition I speak of must have been contiguous to the house we occupied—I recall it as most intimately and objectionably near—and carried on in the interest of those parents from New York who, in villeggiatura under the queer conditions of those days, with the many modern mitigations of the gregarious lot still unrevealed and the many refinements on the individual one still undeveloped, welcomed almost any influence that might help at all to form their children to civility. Yet I remember that particular influence as more noisy and drowsy and dusty than anything else—as to which it must have partaken strongly of the general nature of New Brighton; a neighbourhood that no apt agency whatever had up to that time concerned itself to fashion, and that was indeed to remain shabbily shapeless for years; since I recall almost as dire an impression of it received in the summer of 1875. I seem more or less to have begun life, for that matter, with impressions of New Brighton; there comes back to me another, considerably more infantile than that of 1854, so infantile indeed that I wonder at its having stuck—that of a place called the Pavilion, which must have been an hotel sheltering us for July and August, and the form of which to childish retrospect, unprejudiced by later experience, was that of a great Greek temple shining over blue waters in the splendour of a white colonnade and a great yellow pediment. The elegant image remained, though imprinted in a child so small as to be easily portable by a stout nurse, I remember, and not less easily duckable; I gasp again, and was long to gasp, with the sense of salt immersion received at her strong hands. Wonderful altogether in fact, I find as I write, the quantity, the intensity of picture recoverable from even the blankest and tenderest state of the little canvas.

I connect somehow with the Pavilion period a visit paid with my father—who decidedly must have liked to take me about, I feel so rich in that general reminiscence—to a family whom we reached in what struck me as a quite lovely embowered place, on a very hot day, and among whom luxuries and eccentricities flourished together. They were numerous, the members of this family, they were beautiful, they partook of their meals, or were at the moment partaking of one, out of doors, and the then pre-eminent figure in the group was a very big Newfoundland dog on whose back I was put to ride. That must have been my first vision of the liberal life—though I further ask myself what my age could possibly have been when my weight was so fantastically far from hinting at later developments. But the romance of the hour was particularly in what I have called the eccentric note, the fact that the children, my entertainers, riveted my gaze to stockingless and shoeless legs and feet, conveying somehow at the same time that they were not poor and destitute but rich and provided—just as I took their garden-feast for a sign of overflowing food—and that their state as of children of nature was a refinement of freedom and grace. They were to become great and beautiful, the household of that glimmering vision, they were to figure historically, heroically, and serve great public ends; but always, to my remembering eyes and fond fancy, they were to move through life as with the bare white feet of that original preferred fairness and wildness. This is rank embroidery, but the old surface itself insists on spreading—it waits at least with an air of its own. The rest is silence; I can—extraordinary encumbrance even for the most doating of parents on a morning call—but have returned with my father to "our hotel"; since I feel that I must not only to this but to a still further extent face the historic truth that we were for considerable periods, during our earliest time, nothing less than hotel children. Between the far-off and the later phases at New Brighton stretched a series of summers that had seen us all regularly installed for a couple of months at an establishment passing in the view of that simpler age for a vast caravansery—the Hamilton House, on the south Long Island shore, so called from its nearness to the Fort of that name, which had Fort Lafayette, the Bastille of the Civil War, out in the channel before it and which probably cast a stronger spell upon the spirit of our childhood, William's and mine at least, than any scene presented to us up to our reaching our teens.

I find that I draw from the singularly unobliterated memory of the particulars of all that experience the power quite to glory in our shame; of so entrancing an interest did I feel it at the time to *be* an hotel child, and so little would I have exchanged my lot with that of any small person more privately bred. We were private enough in all conscience, I think I must have felt, the rest of the year; and at what age mustn't I quite have succumbed to the charm of the world seen in a larger way? For there, incomparably, was the chance to dawdle and gape; there were human appearances in endless variety and on the exhibition-stage of a piazza that my gape measured almost as by miles; it was even as if I had become positively conscious that the social scene so peopled would pretty well always say more to me than anything else. What it did say I of course but scantly understood; but I none the less knew it spoke, and I listened to its voice, I seem to recall, very much as "young Edwin," in Dr. Beattie's poem, listened to the roar of tempests and torrents from the nobler eminence of beetling crags and in exposure to still deeper abysses. I cling for the moment, however, to the small story of our Vredenburg summer, as we were for long afterwards invidiously to brand it; the more that it so plays its part in illustration, under the light of a later and happier age, of the growth, when not rather of the arrest, of manners and customs roundabout our birthplace. I think we had never been so much as during these particular months disinherited of the general and public amenities that reinforce for the young private precept and example—disinherited in favour of dust and glare and mosquitoes and pigs and shanties and rumshops, of no walks and scarce more drives, of a repeated no less than of a strong emphasis on the more sordid sides of the Irish aspect in things. There was a castellated residence on the hill above us—very high I remember supposing the hill and very stately the structure; it had towers and views and pretensions and belonged to a Colonel, whom we thought very handsome and very costumed, (as if befrogged and high-booted, which he couldn't have been at all, only *ought* to have been, would even certainly have been at a higher pitch of social effect,) and whose son and heir, also very handsome and known familiarly and endearingly as Chick, had a velvet coat and a pony and I think spurs, all luxuries we were without, and was cousin to boys, the De Coppets, whom we had come to know at our school of the previous winter and who somehow—

doubtless partly as guests of the opulent Chick—hovered again about the field of idleness.

The De Coppets, particularly in the person of the first-born Louis, had been a value to us, or at any rate to me—for though I was, in common with my elders then, unacquainted with the application of that word as I use it here, what was my incipient sense of persons and things, what were my first stirred observant and imaginative reactions, discriminations and categories, but a vague groping for it? The De Coppets (again as more especially and most impressively interpreted by the subtle Louis) enjoyed the pre-eminence of being European; they had dropped during the scholastic term of 1853-4 straight from the lake of Geneva into the very bosom of Mr. Richard Pulling Jenks's select resort for young gentlemen, then situated in Broadway below Fourth Street; and had lately been present at an historic pageant—whether or no celebrating the annals of the town of Coppet I know not—in which representatives of their family had figured in armour and on horseback as the Barons (to our comprehension) de Coup or Cou. Their father was thus of the Canton de Vaud—only their mother had been native among ourselves and sister to the Colonel of the castellations. But what was the most vivid mark of the brothers, and vividest on the part of the supersubtle Louis, was his French treatment of certain of our native local names, Ohio and Iowa for instance, which he rendered, as to their separate vowels, with a daintiness and a delicacy invidious and imperturbable, so that he might have been Chateaubriand declaiming Les Natchez at Madame Récamier's—O-ee-oh and Ee-o-wah; a proceeding in him, a violence offered to his serried circle of little staring and glaring New Yorkers supplied with the usual allowance of fists and boot-toes, which, as it was clearly conscious, I recollect thinking unsurpassed for cool calm courage. Those *were* the right names—which we owed wholly to the French explorers and Jesuit Fathers; so much the worse for us if we vulgarly didn't know it. I lose myself in admiration of the consistency, the superiority, the sublimity, of the not at all game-playing, yet in his own way so singularly sporting, Louis. He was naturally and incorruptibly French—as, so oddly, I have known other persons of both sexes to be whose English was naturally and incorruptibly American; the appearance being thus that the possession of indigenous English alone forms the adequate barrier and the assured racial ground. (Oh the queer reversions observed on the part of Latinized compatriots in the course of a long life—the remarkable drops from the quite current French or Italian to the comparatively improvised native idiom, with the resulting effect of the foreign tongue used as a domestic and the domestic, that is the original American, used as a foreign tongue, or without inherited confidence!)

Louis De Coppet, though theoretically American and domiciled, was *naturally* French, and so pressed further home to me that "sense of Europe" to which I feel that my very earliest consciousness waked—a perversity that will doubtless appear to ask for all the justification I can supply and some of which I shall presently attempt to give. He opened vistas, and I count ever as precious anyone, everyone, who betimes does that for the small straining vision; performing this office never so much, doubtless, as when, during that summer, he invited me to collaborate with him in the production of a romance which *il se fit fort* to get printed, to get published, when success, or in other words completion, should crown our effort. Our effort, alas, failed of the crown, in spite of sundry solemn and mysterious meetings—so much devoted, I seem to remember, to the publishing question that others more fundamental dreadfully languished; leaving me convinced, however, that my friend would have got our fiction published if he could only have got it written. I think of my participation in this vain dream as of the very first gage of visiting approval offered to the exercise of a gift—though quite unable to conceive my companion's ground for suspecting a gift of which I must at that time quite have failed to exhibit a single in the least "phenomenal" symptom. It had none the less by his overtures been handsomely *imputed* to me; that was in a manner a beginning—a small start, yet not wholly unattended with bravery. Louis De Coppet, I must add, brought to light later on, so far as I know, no compositions of his own; we met him long after in Switzerland and eventually heard of his having married a young Russian lady and settled at Nice. If I drop on his memory this apology for a bay-leaf it is from the fact of his having given the earliest, or at least the most personal, tap to that pointed prefigurement of the manners of "Europe," which, inserted wedge-like, if not to say peg-like, into my young allegiance, was to split the tender organ into such unequal halves. His the toy hammer that drove in the very point of the golden nail.

It was as if there had been a mild magic in that breath, however scant, of another world; but when I ask myself what element of the pleasing or the agreeable may have glimmered through the then general, the outer and enveloping conditions, I recover many more of the connections in which forms and civilities lapsed beyond repair than of those in which they struggled at all successfully. It is for some record of the question of taste, of the consciousness of an æsthetic appeal, as reflected in forms and aspects, that I shall like best to testify; as the promise and the development of these things on our earlier American scene are the more interesting to trace for their doubtless demanding a degree of the finer attention. The plain and happy profusions and advances and successes, as one looks back, reflect themselves at every turn; the quick beats of material increase and multiplication, with plenty of people to tell of them and throw up their caps for them; but the edifying matters to recapture would be the adventures of the "higher criticism" so far as there was any—and so far too as it might bear on the real quality and virtue of things; the state of manners, the terms of intercourse, the care for excellence, the sense of appearances, the intellectual reaction generally. However, any breasting of those deep waters must be but in the form for me of an occasional dip. It meanwhile fairly overtakes and arrests me here as a contributive truth that our general medium of life in the situation I speak of was such as to make a large defensive verandah, which seems to have very stoutly and completely surrounded us, play more or less the part of a raft of rescue in too high a tide—too high a tide there beneath us, as I recover it, of the ugly and the graceless. My particular perspective may magnify a little wildly—when it doesn't even more weirdly diminish; but I read into the great hooded and guarded resource in question an evidential force: as if it must really have played for us, so far as its narrowness and its exposure permitted, the part of a buffer-state against the wilderness immediately near, that of the empty, the unlovely and the mean. Interposing a little ease, didn't it interpose almost all the ease we knew?—so that when amiable friends, arriving from New York by the boat, came to see us, there was no rural view for them but that of our great shame, a view of the pigs and the shanties and the loose planks and scattered refuse and rude public ways; never even a field-path for a gentle walk or a garden nook in afternoon shade. I recall my prompt distaste, a strange precocity of criticism, for so much aridity—since of what lost Arcadia, at that age, had I really had the least glimpse?

Our scant margin must have affected me more nobly, I should in justice add, when old Mrs. L. passed or hovered, for she sometimes caustically joined the circle and sometimes, during the highest temperatures, which were very high that summer, but flitted across it in a single flowing garment, as we amazedly conceived; one of the signs of that grand impertinence, I supposed, which belonged to "dowagers"—dowagers who were recognised characters and free speakers, doing and saying what they liked. This ancient lady was lodged in some outlying tract of the many-roomed house, which in more than one quarter stretched away into mystery; but the piazza, to which she had access, was unbroken, and whenever she strayed from her own territory she swam afresh into ours. I definitely remember that, having heard and perhaps read of dowagers, who, as I was aware, had scarce been provided for in our social scheme, I said to myself at first sight of our emphatic neighbour, a person clearly used to exceptional deference, "This must be a perfect specimen;" which was somehow very wonderful. The absolute first sight, however, had preceded the New Brighton summer, and it makes me lose myself in a queer dim vision, all the obscurities attendant on my having been present, as a very small boy indeed, at an evening entertainment where Mrs. L. figured in an attire that is still vivid to me: a blue satin gown, a long black lace shawl and a head-dress consisting in equally striking parts of a brown wig, a plume of some sort waving over it and a band or fillet, whether of some precious metal or not I forget, keeping it in place by the aid of a precious stone which adorned the centre of her brow. Such was my first view of the *féronnière* of our grandmothers, when not of our greatgrandmothers. I see its wearer at this day bend that burdened brow upon me in a manner sufficiently awful, while her knuckly white gloves toyed with a large fan and a vinaigrette attached to her thumb by a chain; and as she was known to us afterwards for a friend of my Albany grandmother's it may have been as a tribute to this tie that she allowed me momentarily to engage her attention. *Then* it predominantly must have been that I knew her for a dowager—though this was a light in which I had never considered my grandmother herself; but what I have quite lost the clue to is the question of my extraordinary footing in such an assembly, the occasion of a dance of my elders, youthful elders but young married people, into which, really, my mother, as a participant, must have introduced me.

IV

It took place in the house of our cousins Robert and Kitty Emmet the elder—for we were to have two cousin Kittys of that ilk and yet another consanguineous Robert at least; the latter name being naturally, among them all, of a pious, indeed of a glorious, tradition, and three of my father's nieces marrying three Emmet brothers, the first of these the Robert aforesaid. Catherine James, daughter of my uncle Augustus, his then quite recent and, as I remember her, animated and attractive bride, whose fair hair framed her pointed smile in full and far-drooping "front" curls, I easily evoke as my first apprehended image of the free and happy young woman of fashion, a sign of the wondrous fact that ladies might live for pleasure, pleasure always, pleasure alone. She was distinguished for nothing whatever so much as for an insatiable love of the dance; that passion in which I think of the "good," the best, New York society of the time as having capered and champagned itself away. Her younger sister Gertrude, afterwards married to James—or more inveterately Jim—Pendleton, of Virginia, followed close upon her heels, literally speaking, and though emulating her in other respects too, was to last, through many troubles, much longer (looking extraordinarily the while like the younger portraits of Queen Victoria) and to have much hospitality, showing it, and showing everything, in a singularly natural way, for a considerable collection of young hobbledehoy kinsmen. But I am solicited a moment longer by the queer little issues involved—as if a social light would somehow stream from them—in my having been taken, a mere mite of observation, to Kitty Emmet's "grown-up" assembly. Was it that my mother really felt that to the scrap that I was other scraps would perhaps strangely adhere, to the extent thus of something to distinguish me by, nothing else probably having as yet declared itself—such a scrap for instance as the fine germ of this actual ferment of memory and play of fancy, a retroactive vision almost intense of the faded hour and a fond surrender to the questions with which it bristles? All the female relatives on my father's side who reappear to me in these evocations strike me as having been intensely and admirably, but at the same time almost indescribably, *natural*; which fact connects itself for the brooding painter and fond analyst with fifty other matters and impressions, his vision of a whole social order—if the American scene might indeed have been said at that time to be positively ordered. Wasn't the fact that the dancing passion was so out of proportion to any social resource just one of the signs of the natural?—and for that matter in both sexes alike of the artless kindred. It was shining to us that Jim Pendleton had a yacht—though I was not smuggled aboard it; there the line was drawn—but the deck must have been more used for the "German" than for other manœuvres, often doubtless under the lead of our cousin Robert, the eldest of the many light irresponsibles to whom my father was uncle: distinct to me still being the image of that phenomenally lean and nimble choreographic hero, "Bob" James to us always, who, almost ghost-fashion, led the cotillion on from generation to generation, his skull-like smile, with its accent from the stiff points of his long moustache and the brightly hollow orbits of his eyes, helping to make of him an immemorial elegant skeleton.

It is at all events to the sound of fiddles and the popping of corks that I see even young brides, as well as young grooms, originally so formed to please and to prosper as our hosts of the restless little occasion I have glanced at, vanish untimely, become mysterious and legendary, with such unfathomed silences and significant headshakes replacing the earlier concert; so that I feel how one's impression of so much foredoomed youthful levity received constant and quite thrilling increase. It was of course an impression then obscurely gathered, but into which one was later on to read strange pages—to some of which I may find myself moved to revert. Mere mite of observation though I have dubbed myself, I won't pretend to have deciphered any of them amid the bacchanal sounds that, on the evening so suggestively spent, floated out into the region of Washington Place. It is round that general centre that my richest memories of the "gay" little life in general cluster—as if it had been, for the circle in which I seem justified in pretending to have "moved," of the finer essence of "town"; covering as it did the stretch of Broadway down to Canal Street, with, closer at hand, the New York Hotel, which figured somehow inordinately in our family annals (the two newer ones, the glory of their brief and discredited, their flouted and demolished age, the brown

Metropolitan and the white St. Nicholas, were much further down) and rising northward to the Ultima Thule of Twenty-third Street, only second then in the supposedly ample scheme of the regular ninth "wide" street. I can't indeed have moved much on that night of revelations and yet of enigmas over which I still hang fascinated; I must have kept intensely still in my corner, all wondering and all fearing—fearing notice most; and in a definite way I but remember the formidable interest of my so convincing dowager (to hark back for a second to *her*) and the fact that a great smooth white cloth was spread across the denuded room, converted thus into a field of frolic the prospect of which much excited my curiosity. I but recover the preparations, however, without recovering the performance; Mrs. L. and I must have been the only persons not shaking a foot, and premature unconsciousness clearly in my case supervened. Out of it peeps again the riddle, the so quaint *trait de mœurs*, of my infant participation. But I set that down as representative and interesting, and have done with it.

The manners of the time had obviously a *bonhomie* of their own— certainly so on our particularly indulgent and humane little field; as to which general proposition the later applications and transformations of the bonhomie would be interesting to trace. It has lingered and fermented and earned other names, but I seem on the track of its prime evidence with that note of the sovereign ease of all the young persons with whom we grew up. In the after-time, as our view took in, with new climes and new scenes, other examples of the class, these were always to affect us as more formed and finished, more tutored and governessed, warned and armed at more points for, and doubtless often against, the social relation; so that this prepared state on their part, and which at first appeared but a preparation for shyness or silence or whatever other ideal of the unconversable, came to be for us the normal, since it was the relative and not the positive, still less the superlative, state. No charming creatures of the growing girl sort were ever to be natural in the degree of these nearer and remoter ornaments of our family circle in youth; when after intervals and absences the impression was renewed we saw how right we had been about it, and I feel as if we had watched it for years under the apprehension and the vision of some inevitable change, wondering with an affectionate interest what effect the general improvement in manners might, perhaps all unfortunately, have upon it. I make out as I look back that it was really to succumb at no point to this complication, that it was to keep its really quite inimitable freshness to the end, or, in other words, when it had been the first free growth of the old conditions, was to pass away but with the passing of those themselves for whom it had been the sole possible expression. For it was as of an altogether special shade and sort that the New York young naturalness of our prime was touchingly to linger with us—so that to myself, at present, with only the gentle ghosts of the so numerous exemplars of it before me, it becomes the very stuff of the soft cerements in which their general mild mortality is laid away. We used to have in the after-time, amid fresh recognitions and reminders, the kindest "old New York" identifications for it. The special shade of its identity was thus that it was not conscious— really not conscious of anything in the world; or was conscious of so few possibilities at least, and these so immediate and so a matter of course, that it came almost to the same thing. That was the testimony that the slight subjects in question strike me as having borne to their surrounding medium—the fact that their unconsciousness could be so preserved. They played about in it so happily and serenely and sociably, as unembarrassed and loquacious as they were unadmonished and uninformed—only aware at the most that a good many people within their horizon were "dissipated"; as in point of fact, alas, a good many *were*. What it was to be dissipated—that, however, was but in the most limited degree a feature of their vision; they would have held, under pressure, that it consisted more than anything else in getting tipsy.

Infinitely queer and quaint, almost incongruously droll, the sense somehow begotten in ourselves, as very young persons, of our being surrounded by a slightly remote, yet dimly rich, outer and quite kindred circle of the tipsy. I remember how, once, as a very small boy, after meeting in the hall a most amiable and irreproachable gentleman, all but closely consanguineous, who had come to call on my mother, I anticipated his further entrance by slipping in to report to that parent that I thought *he* must be tipsy. And I was to recall perfectly afterwards the impression I so made on her—in which the general proposition that the gentlemen of a certain group or connection might on occasion be best described by the term I had used sought to destroy the particular presumption that our visitor wouldn't, by his ordinary measure, show himself for one of those. He didn't, to all appearance, for I was afterwards disappointed at the lapse of lurid evidence: that memory remained with me, as well as a considerable subsequent wonder at my having leaped to so baseless a view. The truth was indeed that we had too, in the most innocent way in the world, our sense of "dissipation" as an abounding element in family histories; a sense fed quite directly by our fondness for making our father—I can at any rate testify for the urgency of my own appeal to him—tell us stories of the world of his youth. He regaled us with no scandals, yet it somehow rarely failed to come out that each contemporary on his younger scene, each hero of each thrilling adventure, had, in spite of brilliant promise and romantic charm, ended badly, as badly as possible. This became our gaping generalisation—it gaped even under the moral that the anecdote was always, and so familiarly, humanly and vividly, designed to convey: everyone in the little old Albany of the Dutch houses and the steep streets and the recurrent family names—Townsends, Clintons, Van Rensselaers, Pruyns: I pick them up again at hazard, and all uninvidiously, out of reverberations long since still—everyone without exception had at last taken a turn as far as possible from edifying. And what they had most in common, the hovering presences, the fitful apparitions that, speaking for myself, so engaged my imagination, was just the fine old Albany drama—in the light of which a ring of mystery as to their lives (mainly carried on at the New York Hotel aforesaid) surrounded them, and their charm, inveterate, as I believed, shone out as through vaguely-apprehended storm-clouds. Their charm was in various marks of which I shall have more to say—for as I breathe all this hushed air again even the more broken things give out touching human values and faint sweet scents of character, flushes of old beauty and good-will.

The grim little generalisation remained, none the less, and I may speak of it—since I speak of everything—as still standing: the striking evidence that scarce aught but disaster *could*, in that so unformed and unseasoned society, overtake young men who were in the least exposed. Not to have been immediately launched in business of a rigorous sort was to *be* exposed—in the absence I mean of some fairly abnormal predisposition to virtue; since it was a world so simply constituted that whatever wasn't business, or exactly an office or a "store," places in which people sat close and made money, was just simply pleasure, sought, and sought only, in places in which people got tipsy. There was clearly no mean, least of all the golden one, for it was just the ready, even when the moderate, possession of gold that determined, that hurried on, disaster. There were whole sets and groups, there were "sympathetic," though too susceptible, races, that seemed scarce to recognise or to find possible any practical application of moneyed, that is of transmitted, ease, however limited, but to go more or less rapidly to the bad with it—which meant even then going as often as possible to Paris. The bright and empty air was as void of "careers" for a choice as of cathedral towers for a sketcher, and I passed my younger time, till within a year or two of the Civil War, with an absolute vagueness of impression as to how the political life of the country was carried on. The field was strictly covered, to my young eyes, I make out, by three classes, the busy, the tipsy, and Daniel Webster. This last great man must have represented for us a class in himself; as if to be "political" was just to *be* Daniel Webster in his proper person and with room left over for nobody else. That he should have filled the sky of public life from pole to pole, even to a childish consciousness not formed in New England and for which that strenuous section was but a name in the geography-book, is probably indeed a sign of how large, in the general air, he comparatively loomed. The public scene was otherwise a blank to our young vision, I discern, till, later on, in Paris, I saw—for at that unimproved period we of the unfledged didn't suppose ourselves to "meet"—Charles Sumner; with whose name indeed there further connects itself the image of a thrilled hour in the same city some months before: the gathering of a group of indignant persons on the terrace of a small old-world *hôtel* or pavilion looking out on the Avenue des Champs Elysées, slightly above the Rond-Point and just opposite the antediluvian Jardin d'Hiver (who remembers the Jardin d'Hiver, who remembers the ancient lodges of the *octroi*, the pair of them facing each other at the Barrière de l'Étoile?) and among them a passionate lady in tears over the news, fresh that morning, of the assault on Sumner by the South Carolina ruffian of the House. The wounded Senator, injured in health, had come to Europe later on to recuperate, and he offered me my first view, to the best of my belief, not only of a "statesman," but of any person whomsoever concerned in political life. I distinguish in the earlier twilight of Fourteenth Street my father's return to us one November day—we knew he had been out to vote—with the news that General Winfield Scott, his and the then "Whig" candidate, had been defeated for the Presidency; just as I rescue from the same limbo my afterwards proud little impression of having "met" that high-piled hero of the Mexican War, whom the Civil War was so soon and with so little ceremony to extinguish, literally met him, at my father's side, in Fifth Avenue, where he had just emerged from a cross-street. I remain vague as to what had then happened and scarce suppose I was, at the age probably of eight or nine, "presented"; but we must have been for some moments face to face while from under the vast amplitude of a dark blue military cloak with a big velvet collar and loosened silver clasp, which spread about him like a symbol of the tented field, he greeted my parent—so clear is my sense of the time it took me to gape *all* the way up to where he towered aloft.

V

The not very glorious smoke of the Mexican War, I note for another touch, had been in the air when I was a still smaller boy, and I have an association with it that hovers between the definite and the dim, a vision of our uncle (Captain as he then was) Robert Temple, U.S.A., in regimentals, either on his way to the scene of action or on the return from it. I see him as a person half asleep sees some large object across the room and against the window-light—even if to the effect of my now asking myself why, so far from the scene of action, he was in panoply of war. I seem to see him cock-hatted and feathered too—an odd vision of dancing superior plumes which doesn't fit if he was only a captain. However, I cultivate the wavering shade merely for its value as my earliest glimpse of any circumstance of the public order— unless indeed another, the reminiscence to which I owe to-day my sharpest sense of personal antiquity, had already given me the historic thrill. The scene of this latter stir of consciousness is, for memory, an apartment in one of the three Fifth Avenue houses that were not long afterward swallowed up in the present Brevoort Hotel, and consists of the admired appearance of my uncles "Gus" and John James to announce to my father that the Revolution had triumphed in Paris and Louis Philippe had fled to England. These last words, the flight of the king, linger on my ear at this hour even as they fell there; we had somehow waked early to a perception of Paris, and a vibration of my very most infantine sensibility under its sky had by the same stroke got itself preserved for subsequent wondering reference. I had been there for a short time in the second year of my life, and I was to communicate to my parents later on that as a baby in long clothes, seated opposite to them in a carriage and on the lap of another person, I had been impressed with the view, framed by the clear window of the vehicle as we passed, of a great stately square surrounded with high-roofed houses and having in its centre a tall and glorious column. I had naturally caused them to marvel, but I had also, under cross-questioning, forced them to compare notes, as it were, and reconstitute the miracle. They knew what my observation of monumental squares had been—and alas hadn't; neither New York nor Albany could have offered me the splendid perspective, and, for that matter, neither could London, which moreover I had known at a younger age still. Conveyed along the Rue St.-Honoré while I waggled my small feet, as I definitely remember doing, under my flowing robe, I had crossed the Rue de Castiglione and taken in, for all my time, the admirable aspect of the Place and the Colonne Vendôme. I don't now pretend to measure the extent to which my interest in the events of 1848—I was five years old—was quickened by that *souvenir*, a tradition further reinforced, I should add, by the fact that some relative or other, some member of our circle, was always either "there" ("there" being of course generally Europe, but particularly and pointedly Paris) or going there or coming back from there: I at any rate revert to the sound of the rich words on my uncles' lips as to my positive initiation into History. It was as if I had been ready for them and could catch on; I had heard of kings presumably, and also of fleeing: but that kings had sometimes to flee was a new and striking image, to which the apparent consternation of my elders added dramatic force. So much, in any case, for what I may claim—perhaps too idly—on behalf of my backward reach.

It has carried me far from my rather evident proposition that if we saw the "natural" so happily embodied about us—and in female maturity, or comparative maturity, scarce less than in female adolescence—this was because the artificial, or in other words the complicated, was so little there to threaten it. The complicated, as we were later on to define it, was but another name for those more massed and violent assaults upon the social sense that we were to recognise subsequently by their effects—observing thus that a sense more subtly social had so been created, and that it quite differed from that often almost complete inward blankness, in respect to any circumjacent, any constituted, order to the exhibition of which our earlier air and our family scene had inimitably treated us. We came more or less to see that our young contemporaries of another world, the trained and admonished, the disciplined and governessed, or in a word the formed, relatively speaking, had been made aware of many things of which those at home hadn't been; yet we were also to note—so far as we may be conceived as so precociously "noting," though we were certainly incorrigible observers—that, the awareness in question remaining at the best imperfect, our little friends as distinguished from our companions of the cousinship, greater and less, advanced and presumed but to flounder and recede, elated at once and abashed and on the whole but *feebly* sophisticated. The cousinship, on the other hand, all unalarmed and unsuspecting and unembarrassed, lived by pure serenity, sociability and loquacity; the oddest fact about its members being withal that it didn't make them bores, I seem to feel as I look back, or at least not worse bores than sundry specimens of the other growth. There can surely never have been anything like their good faith and, generally speaking, their amiability. I should have but to let myself go a little to wish to cite examples—save that in doing so I should lose sight of my point; which is to recall again that whether we were all amiable or not (and, frankly, I claim it in a high degree for most of us) the scene on which we so freely bloomed does strike me, when I reckon up, as extraordinarily unfurnished. How came it then that for the most part so simple we yet weren't more inane? This was doubtless by reason of the quantity of our inward life—ours of our father's house in especial I mean—which made an excellent, in some cases almost an incomparable, *fond* for a thicker civility to mix with when growing experience should begin to take that in. It was also quaint, among us, I may be reminded, to have *begun* with the inward life; but we began, after the manner of all men, as we could, and I hold that if it comes to that we might have begun much worse.

I was in my seventeenth year when the raid and the capture of John Brown, of Harper's Ferry fame, enjoyed its sharp reverberation among us, though we were then on the other side of the world; and I count this as the very first reminder that reached me of our living, on our side, in a political order: I had perfectly taken in from the pages of "Punch," which contributed in the highest degree to our education, that the peoples on the other side so lived. As there was no American "Punch," and to this time has been none, to give small boys the sense and the imagination of living with their public administrators, Daniel Webster and Charles Sumner had never become, for my fancy, members of a class, a class which numbered in England, by John Leech's showing, so many other members still than Lords Brougham, Palmerston and John Russell. The war of Secession, soon arriving, was to cause the field to bristle with features and the sense of the State, in our generation, infinitely to quicken; but that alarm came upon the country like a thief at night, and we might all have been living in a land in which there seemed at least nothing save a comparatively small amount of quite private property to steal. Even private property in other than the most modest amounts scarce figured for our particular selves; which doubtless came partly from the fact that amid all the Albany issue there was ease, with the habit of ease, thanks to our grandfather's fine old ability—he had decently provided for so large a generation; but our consciousness was positively disfurnished, as that of young Americans went, of the actualities of "business" in a world of business. As to that we all formed together quite a monstrous exception; business in a world of business was the thing we most agreed (differ as we might on minor issues) in knowing nothing about. We touched it and it touched us neither directly nor otherwise, and I think our fond detachment, not to say our helpless ignorance and on occasion (since I can speak for one fine instance) our settled density of understanding, made us an unexampled and probably, for the ironic "smart" gods of the American heaven, a lamentable case. Of course even the office and the "store" leave much of the provision for an approximately complete scheme of manners to be accounted for; still there must have been vast numbers of people about us for whom, under the usages, the assault on the imagination from without was much stronger and the filling-in of the general picture much richer. It was exactly by the lack of that filling-in that we—we more especially who lived at near view of my father's admirable example—had been thrown so upon the inward life. No one could ever have taken to it, even in the face of discouragement, more kindly and naturally than he; but the situation had at least that charm that, in default of so many kinds of the outward, people had their choice of as many kinds of the inward as they would, and might practise those kinds with whatever consistency, intensity and brilliancy. Of our father's perfect gift for practising *his* kind I shall have more to say; but I meanwhile glance yet again at those felicities of destitution which kept us, collectively, so genially interested in almost nothing but each other and which come over me now as one of the famous blessings in disguise.

There were "artists" in the prospect—didn't Mr. Tom Hicks and Mr. Paul Duggan and Mr. C. P. Cranch and Mr. Felix Darley, this last worthy of a wider reputation, capable perhaps even of a finer development, than he attained, more or less haunt our friendly fireside, and give us also the sense of others, landscapist Cropseys and Coles and Kensetts, and bust-producing Iveses and Powerses and Moziers, hovering in an outer circle? There were authors not less, some of them vague and female and in this case, as a rule, glossily ringletted and monumentally breastpinned, but mostly frequent and familiar, after the manner of George Curtis and Parke Godwin and George Ripley and Charles Dana and N. P. Willis and, for brighter lights or those that in our then comparative obscurity almost deceived the morn, Mr. Bryant, Washington Irving and E. A. Poe—the last-named of whom I cite not so much because he was personally present (the extremity of personal absence had just overtaken him) as by reason of that predominant lustre in him which our small opening minds themselves already recognised and which makes me wonder to-day at the legend of the native neglect of him. Was he not even at that time on all lips, had not my brother, promptly master of the subject, beckoned on my lagging mind with a recital of The Gold-Bug and The Pit and the Pendulum?—both of which, however, I was soon enough to read for myself, adding to them The Murders in the Rue Morgue. Were we not also forever mounting on little platforms at our infant schools to "speak" The Raven and Lenore and the verses in which we phrased the heroine as Annabellee?—falling thus into the trap the poet had so recklessly laid for us, as he had laid one for our interminable droning, not less, in the other pieces I have named. So far from misprizing our ill-starred magician we acclaimed him surely at every turn; he lay upon our tables and resounded in our mouths, while we communed to satiety, even for boyish appetites, over the thrill of his choicest pages. Don't I just recognise the ghost of a dim memory of a children's Christmas party at the house of Fourteenth Street neighbours— they come back to me as "the Beans": who and what and whence and whither the kindly Beans?—where I admired over the chimney piece the full-length portrait of a lady seated on the ground in a Turkish dress, with hair flowing loose from a cap which was not as the caps of ladies known to me, and I think with a tambourine, who was somehow identified to my enquiring mind as the wife of the painter of the piece, Mr. Osgood, and the so ministering friend of the unhappy Mr. Poe. There she throned in honour, like Queen Constance on the "huge firm earth"—all for *that* and her tambourine; and surely we could none of us have done more for the connection.

Washington Irving I "met," with infant promptitude, very much as I had met General Scott; only this time it was on a steamboat that I apprehended the great man; my father, under whose ever-patient protection I then was—during the summer afternoon's sail from New York to Fort Hamilton—having named him to me, for this long preservation, before they greeted and talked, and having a fact of still more moment to mention, with the greatest concern, afterwards: Mr. Irving had given him the news of the shipwreck of Margaret Fuller in those very waters (Fire Island at least was but just without our big Bay) during the great August storm that had within the day or two passed over us. The unfortunate lady was essentially of the Boston connection; but she must have been, and probably through Emerson, a friend of my parents—mustn't she have held "conversations," in the finest exotic Bostonese, in New York, Emerson himself lecturing there to admiration?—since the more I squeeze the sponge of memory the more its stored secretions flow, to remind me here again that, being with those elders late one evening at an exhibition of pictures, possibly that of the National Academy, then confined to scant quarters, I was shown a small full-length portrait of Miss Fuller, seated as now appears to me and wrapped in a long white shawl, the failure of which to do justice to its original my companions denounced with some emphasis. Was this work from the hand of Mr. Tom Hicks aforesaid, or was that artist concerned only with the life-sized, the enormous (as I took it to be) the full-length, the violently protruded accessories in which come back to me with my infant sense of the wonder and the beauty of them, as expressed above all in the image of a very long and lovely lady, the new bride of the artist, standing at a window before a row of plants or bulbs in tall coloured glasses. The light of the window playing over the figure and the "treatment" of its glass and of the flower-pots and the other furniture, passed, by my impression, for the sign of the master hand; and *was* it all brave and charming, or was it only very hard and stiff, quite ugly and helpless? I put these questions as to a vanished world and by way of pressing back into it only the more clingingly and tenderly—wholly regardless in other words of whether the answers to them at all matter. They matter doubtless but for fond evocation, and if one tries to evoke one must neglect none of the arts, one must do it with all the forms. Why I *should* so like to do it is another matter—and what "outside interest" I may suppose myself to create perhaps still another: I fatuously proceed at any rate, I make so far as I can the small warm dusky homogeneous New York world of the mid-century close about us.

VI

I see a small and compact and ingenuous society, screened in somehow conveniently from north and west, but open wide to the east and comparatively to the south and, though perpetually moving up Broadway, none the less constantly and delightfully walking down it. Broadway was the feature and the artery, the joy and the adventure of one's childhood, and it stretched, and prodigiously, from Union Square to Barnum's great American Museum by the City Hall—or only went further on the Saturday mornings (absurdly and deplorably frequent alas) when we were swept off by a loving aunt, our mother's only sister, then much domesticated with us and to whom the ruthless care had assigned itself from the first, to Wall Street and the torture chamber of Dr. Parkhurst, our tremendously respectable dentist, who was so old and so empurpled and so polite, in his stock and dress-coat and dark and glossy wig, that he had been our mother's and our aunt's haunting fear in *their* youth as well, since, in their quiet Warren Street, not far off, they were, dreadful to think, comparatively under his thumb. He extremely resembles, to my mind's eye, certain figures in Phiz's illustrations to Dickens, and it was clear to us through our long ordeal that our elders must, by some mistaken law of compensation, some refinement of the vindictive, be making us "pay" for what they in like helplessness had suffered from him: as if *we* had done them any harm! Our analysis was muddled, yet in a manner relieving, and for us too there were compensations, which we grudged indeed to allow, but which I could easily, even if shyly, have named. One of these was Godey's Lady's Book, a sallow pile of which (it shows to me for sallow in the warmer and less stony light of the Wall Street of those days and through the smell of ancient anodynes) lay on Joey Bagstock's table for our beguilement while we waited: I was to encounter in Phiz's Dombey and Son that design for our tormentor's type. There is no doubt whatever that I succumbed to the spell of Godey, who, unlike the present essences, was an anodyne before the fact as well as after; since I remember poring, in his pages, over tales of fashionable life in Philadelphia while awaiting my turn in the chair, not less than doing so when my turn was over and to the music of my brother's groans. This must have been at the hours when we were left discreetly to our own fortitude, through our aunt's availing herself of the relative proximity to go and shop at Stewart's and then come back for us; the ladies' great shop, vast, marmorean, plate-glassy and notoriously fatal to the female nerve (we ourselves had wearily trailed through it, hanging on the skirts, very literally, of indecision) which bravely waylaid custom on the Broadway corner of Chambers Street. Wasn't part of the charm of life—since I assume that there *was* such a charm—in its being then (I allude to life itself) so much more down-towny, on the supposition at least that our young gravitation in that sense for most of the larger joys consorted with something of the general habit? The joy that had to be fished out, like Truth, from the very bottom of the well was attendance at Trinity Church, still in that age supereminent, pointedly absolute, the finest feature of the southward scene; to the privilege of which the elder Albany cousins were apt to be treated when they came on to stay with us; an indulgence making their enjoyment of our city as down-towny as possible too, for I seem otherwise to see them but as returning with the familiar Stewart headache from the prolonged strain of selection.

The great reward dispensed to us for our sessions in the house of pain—as to which it became our subsequent theory that we had been regularly dragged there on alternate Saturdays—was our being carried on the return to the house of delight, or to one of them, for there were specifically two, where we partook of ice-cream, deemed sovereign for sore mouths, deemed sovereign in fact, all through our infancy, for everything. Two great establishments for the service of it graced the prospect, one Thompson's and the other Taylor's, the former, I perfectly recall, grave and immemorial, the latter upstart but dazzling, and having together the effect that whichever we went to we wondered if we hadn't better have gone to the other—with that capacity of childhood for making the most of its adventures after a fashion that may look so like making the least. It is in our father's company indeed that, as I press the responsive spring, I see the bedizened saucers heaped up for our fond consumption (they bore the Taylor-title painted in blue and gilded, with the Christian name, as parentally pointed out to us, perverted to "Jhon" for John, whereas the Thompson-name scorned such vulgar and

above all such misspelt appeals;) whence I infer that still other occasions for
that experience waited on us—as almost any would serve, and a paternal
presence so associated with them was not in the least conceivable in the Wall
Street *repaire*. That presence is in fact not associated for me, to any effect of
distinctness, with the least of our suffered shocks or penalties—though partly
doubtless because our acquaintance with such was of the most limited; a
conclusion I form even while judging it to have been on the whole sufficient
for our virtue. This sounds perhaps as if we had borne ourselves as prodigies
or prigs—which was as far as possible from being the case; we were bred in
horror of *conscious* propriety, of what my father was fond of calling "flagrant"
morality; what I myself at any rate read back into our rare educational ease,
for the memory of some sides of which I was ever to be thankful, is, besides
the *general* humanisation of our apprehended world and our "social" tone, the
unmistakeable appearance that my father was again and again accompanied
in public by his small second son: so many young impressions come back to
me as gathered at his side and in his personal haunts. Not that he mustn't
have offered his firstborn at least equal opportunities; but I make out that he
seldom led us forth, such as we were, together, and my brother must have had
in *his* turn many a mild adventure of which the secret—I like to put it so—
perished with him. He was to remember, as I perceived later on, many things
that I didn't, impressions I sometimes wished, as with a retracing jealousy,
or at least envy, that I might also have fallen direct heir to; but he professed
amazement, and even occasionally impatience, at my reach of reminiscence—
liking as he did to brush away old moral scraps in favour of new rather than
to hoard and so complacently exhibit them. If in my way I collected the new
as well I yet cherished the old; the ragbag of memory hung on its nail in my
closet, though I learnt with time to control the habit of bringing it forth. And
I say that with a due sense of my doubtless now appearing to empty it into
these pages.

I keep picking out at hazard those passages of our earliest age that help
to reconstruct for me even by tiny touches the experience of our parents,
any shade of which seems somehow to signify. I cherish, to the extent of
here reproducing, an old daguerreotype all the circumstances of the taking
of which I intensely recall—though as I was lately turned twelve when I

figured for it the feat of memory is perhaps not remarkable. It documents for me in so welcome and so definite a manner my father's cultivation of my company. It documents at the same time the absurdest little legend of my small boyhood—the romantic tradition of the value of being taken up from wherever we were staying to the queer empty dusty smelly New York of midsummer: I apply that last term because we always arrived by boat and I have still in my nostril the sense of the *abords* of the hot town, the rank and rubbishy waterside quarters, where big loose cobbles, for the least of all the base items, lay wrenched from their sockets of pungent black mud and where the dependent streets managed by a law of their own to be all corners and the corners to be all groceries; groceries indeed largely of the "green" order, so far as greenness could persist in the torrid air, and that bristled, in glorious defiance of traffic, with the overflow of their wares and implements. Carts and barrows and boxes and baskets, sprawling or stacked, familiarly elbowed in its course the bumping hack (the comprehensive "carriage" of other days, the only vehicle of hire then known to us) while the situation was accepted by the loose citizen in the garb of a freeman save for the brass star on his breast—and the New York garb of the period was, as I remember it, an immense attestation of liberty. Why the throb of romance should have beat time for me to such visions I can scarce explain, or can explain only by the fact that the squalor was a squalor wonderfully mixed and seasoned, and that I should wrong the whole impression if I didn't figure it first and foremost as that of some vast succulent cornucopia. What did the stacked boxes and baskets of our youth represent but the boundless fruitage of that more bucolic age of the American world, and what was after all of so strong an assault as the rankness of such a harvest? Where is that fruitage now, where in particular are the peaches *d'antan?* where the mounds of Isabella grapes and Seckel pears in the sticky sweetness of which our childhood seems to have been steeped? It was surely, save perhaps for oranges, a more informally and familiarly fruit-eating time, and bushels of peaches in particular, peaches big and peaches small, peaches white and peaches yellow, played a part in life from which they have somehow been deposed; every garden, almost every bush and the very boys' pockets grew them; they were "cut up" and eaten with cream at every meal; domestically "brandied" they figured, the rest of the year, scarce less freely—if they were rather a "party dish" it was because they made the party whenever they appeared, and when ice-cream was added, or they were added *to* it, they formed the highest revel we knew. Above all the public heaps of them, the high-piled receptacles at every turn, touched the street as with a sort of southern plenty; the note of the rejected and scattered fragments, the memory of the slippery skins and rinds and kernels with which the old dislocated flags were bestrown, is itself endeared to me and contributes a further pictorial grace. We ate everything in those days by the bushel and the barrel, as from stores that were infinite; we handled watermelons as freely as cocoanuts, and the amount of stomach-ache involved was negligible in the general Eden-like consciousness.

The glow of this consciousness even in so small an organism was part of the charm of these retreats offered me cityward upon our base of provisions; a part of the rest of which, I disengage, was in my fond perception of that almost eccentrically home-loving habit in my father which furnished us with half the household humour of our childhood—besides furnishing *him* with any quantity of extravagant picture of his so prompt pangs of anguish in absence for celebration of his precipitate returns. It was traditional for us later on, and especially on the European scene, that for him to leave us in pursuit of some advantage or convenience, some improvement of our condition, some enlargement of our view, was for him breathlessly to reappear, after the shortest possible interval, with no account at all to give of the benefit aimed at, but instead of this a moving representation, a far richer recital, of his spiritual adventures at the horrid inhuman inns and amid the hard alien races which had stayed his advance. He reacted, he rebounded, in favour of his fireside, from whatever brief explorations or curiosities; these passionate spontaneities were the pulse of his life and quite some of the principal events of ours; and, as he was nothing if not expressive, whatever happened to him for inward intensity happened abundantly to us for pity and terror, as it were, as well as for an ease and a quality of amusement among ourselves that was really always to fail us among others. Comparatively late in life, after his death, I had occasion to visit, in lieu of my brother, then in Europe, an American city in which he had had, since his own father's death, interests that were of importance to us all. On my asking the agent in charge when the owner had last taken personal cognisance of his property that gentleman replied only half to my surprise that he had never in all his years of possession performed such an act. Then it was perhaps that I most took the measure of his fine faith in human confidence as an administrative function. He had to have a *relation*, somehow expressed—and as he was the vividest and happiest of letter-writers it rarely failed of coming; but once it was established it served him, in every case, much better than fussy challenges, which had always the drawback of involving lapses and inattentions in regard to solicitudes more pressing. He incurably took for granted—incurably because whenever he did so the process succeeded; with which association, however, I perhaps overdrench my complacent vision of our summer snatches at town. Through a grave accident in early life country walks on rough roads were, in spite of his great constitutional soundness, tedious and charmless to him; he liked on the other hand the peopled pavement, the thought of which made him restless when away. Hence the fidelities and sociabilities, however superficial, that he couldn't *not* reaffirm—if he could only reaffirm the others, the really intimate and still more communicable, soon enough afterwards.

It was these of the improvised and casual sort that I shared with him thus indelibly; for truly if we took the boat to town to do things I did them quite as much as he, and so that a little boy could scarce have done them more. My part may indeed but have been to surround his part with a thick imaginative aura; but that constituted for me an activity than which I could dream of none braver or wilder. We went to the office of The New York Tribune—my father's relations with that journal were actual and close; and that was a wonderful world indeed, with strange steepnesses and machineries and noises and hurrying bare-armed, bright-eyed men, and amid the agitation clever, easy, kindly, jocular, partly undressed gentlemen (it was always July or August) some of whom I knew at home, taking it all as if it were the most natural place in the world. It was big to me, big to me with the breath of great vague connections, and I supposed the gentlemen very old, though since aware that they must have been, for the connections, remarkably young; and the conversation of one of them, the one I saw oftenest up town, who attained to great local and to considerable national eminence afterwards, and who talked often and thrillingly about the theatres, I retain as many bright fragments of as if I had been another little Boswell. It was as if he had dropped into my mind the germ of certain interests that were long afterwards to flower—as for instance on his announcing the receipt from Paris of news of the appearance at the Théâtre Français of an actress, Madame Judith, who was formidably to compete with her coreligionary Rachel and to endanger that artist's laurels. Why should Madame Judith's name have stuck to me through all the years, since I was never to see her and she is as forgotten as Rachel is remembered? Why should that scrap of gossip have made a date for my consciousness, turning it to the Comédie with an intensity that was long afterwards to culminate? Why was it equally to abide for me that the same gentleman had on one of these occasions mentioned his having just come back from a wonderful city of the West, Chicago, which, though but a year or two old, with plank sidewalks when there were any, and holes and humps where there were none, and shanties where there were not big blocks, and everything where there had yesterday been nothing, had already developed a huge energy and curiosity, and also an appetite for lectures? I became aware of the Comédie, I became aware of Chicago; I also became aware that even the most alluring fiction was not always for little boys to read. It was mentioned at the Tribune office that one of its reporters, Mr. Solon Robinson, had put forth a novel rather oddly entitled "Hot Corn" and more or less having for its subject the career of a little girl who hawked that familiar American luxury in the streets. The volume, I think, was put into my father's hand, and I recall my prompt desire to make acquaintance with it no less than the remark, as promptly addressed to my companion, that the work, however engaging, was not one that should be left accessible to an innocent child. The pang occasioned by this warning has scarcely yet died out for me, nor my sense of my first wonder at the discrimination—so great became from that moment the mystery of the tabooed book, of whatever identity; the question, in my breast, of why, if it was to be so right for others, it was only to be wrong for me. I remember the soreness of the thought that it was I rather who was wrong for the book—which was somehow humiliating: in that amount of discredit one couldn't but be involved. Neither then nor afterwards was the secret of "Hot Corn" revealed to me, and the sense of privation was to be more prolonged, I fear, than the vogue of the tale, which even as a success of scandal couldn't have been great.

VII

Dimly queer and "pathetic" to me were to remain through much of the after time indeed most of those early indigenous vogues and literary flurries: so few of those that brushed by my childhood had been other than a tinkling that suddenly stopped. I am afraid I mean that what was touching was rather the fact that the tinkle *could* penetrate than the fact that it died away; the light of criticism might have beat so straight—if the sense of proportion and the fact of compassion hadn't waved it away—on the æsthetic phase during which the appeal was mainly *by* the tinkle. The Scarlet Letter and The Seven Gables had the deep tone as much as one would; but of the current efforts of the imagination they were alone in having it till Walt Whitman broke out in the later fifties—and I was to know nothing of that happy genius till long after. An absorbed perusal of The Lamplighter was what I was to achieve at the fleeting hour I continue to circle round; that romance was on every one's lips, and I recollect it as more or less thrust upon me in amends for the imposed sacrifice of a ranker actuality—that of the improper Mr. Robinson, I mean, as to whom there revives in me the main question of where his impropriety, in so general a platitude of the bourgeois, could possibly have dwelt. It was to be true indeed that Walt Whitman achieved an impropriety of the first magnitude; that success, however, but showed us the platitude returning in a genial rage upon itself and getting out of control by generic excess. There was no rage at any rate in The Lamplighter, over which I fondly hung and which would have been my first "grown-up" novel—it had been soothingly offered me for that—had I consented to take it as really and truly grown-up. I couldn't have said what it lacked for the character, I only had my secret reserves, and when one blest afternoon on the New Brighton boat I waded into The Initials I saw how right I had been. The Initials *was* grown-up and the difference thereby exquisite; it came over me with the very first page, assimilated in the fluttered little cabin to which I had retired with it—all in spite of the fact too that my attention was distracted by a pair of remarkable little girls who lurked there out of more public view as to hint that they weren't to be seen for nothing.

That must have been a rich hour, for I mix the marvel of the Boon Children, strange pale little flowers of the American theatre, with my conscious joy in bringing back to my mother, from our forage in New York, a gift of such happy promise as the history of the long-legged Mr. Hamilton and his two Bavarian beauties, the elder of whom, Hildegarde, was to figure for our small generation as the very type of the haughty as distinguished from the forward heroine (since I think our categories really came to no more than those). I couldn't have got very far with Hildegarde in moments so scant, but I memorably felt that romance was thick round me—everything, at such a crisis, seeming to make for it at once. The Boon Children, conveyed thus to New Brighton under care of a lady in whose aspect the strain of the resolute triumphed over the note of the battered, though the showy in it rather succumbed at the same time to the dowdy, were already "billed," as infant phenomena, for a performance that night at the Pavilion, where our attendance, it was a shock to feel, couldn't be promised; and in gazing without charge at the pair of weary and sleepy little mountebanks I found the histrionic character and the dramatic profession for the first time revealed to me. They filled me with fascination and yet with fear; they expressed a melancholy grace and a sort of peevish refinement, yet seemed awfully detached and indifferent, indifferent perhaps even to being pinched and slapped, for art's sake, at home; they honoured me with no notice whatever and regarded me doubtless as no better than one of the little louts peeping through the tent of the show. In return I judged their appearance dissipated though fascinating, and sought consolation for the memory of their scorn and the loss of their exhibition, as time went on, in noting that the bounds of their fame seemed somehow to have been stayed. I neither "met" them nor heard of them again. The little Batemans must have obscured their comparatively dim lustre, flourishing at the same period and with a larger command of the pictorial poster and the other primitive symbols in Broadway—such posters and such symbols as they were at that time!—the little Batemans who were to be reserved, in maturer form, for my much later and more grateful appreciation.

This weak reminiscence has obstructed, however, something more to the purpose, the retained impression of those choicest of our loiterings that took place, still far down-town, at the Bookstore, home of delights and haunt of fancy. It was at the Bookstore we had called on the day of The Initials and the Boon Children—and it was thence we were returning with our spoil, of which the charming novel must have been but a fragment. My impression composed itself of many pieces; a great and various practice of burying my nose in the half-open book for the strong smell of paper and printer's ink, known to us as the English smell, was needed to account for it. *That* was the exercise of the finest sense that hung about us, my brother and me—or of one at least but little less fine than the sense for the satisfaction of which we resorted to Thompson's and to Taylor's: it bore me company during all our returns from forages and left me persuaded that I had only to snuff up hard enough, fresh uncut volume in hand, to taste of the very substance of London. All our books in that age were English, at least all our down-town ones—I personally recall scarce any that were not; and I take the perception of that quality in them to have associated itself with more fond dreams and glimmering pictures than any other one principle of growth. It was all a result of the deeply *infected* state: I had been prematurely poisoned—as I shall presently explain. The Bookstore, fondest of my father's resorts, though I remember no more of its public identity than that it further enriched the brave depth of Broadway, was overwhelmingly and irresistibly English, as not less tonically English was our principal host there, with whom we had moreover, my father and I, thanks to his office, such personal and genial relations that I recall seeing him grace our board at home, in company with his wife, whose vocal strain and complexion and coiffure and flounces I found none the less informing, none the less "racial," for my not being then versed in the language of analysis.

The true inwardness of these rich meanings—those above all of the Bookstore itself—was that a tradition was thus fed, a presumption thus created, a vague vision thus filled in: all expression is clumsy for so mystic a process. What else can have happened but that, having taken over, under suggestion and with singular infant promptitude, a particular throbbing consciousness, I had become aware of the source at which it could best be refreshed? That consciousness, so communicated, was just simply of certain impressions, certain *sources* of impression again, proceeding from over the sea and situated beyond it—or even much rather of my parents' own impression of such, the fruit of a happy time spent in and about London with their two babies and reflected in that portion of their talk with each other to which I best attended. Had *all* their talk for its subject, in my infant ears, that happy time?—did it deal only with London and Piccadilly and the Green Park, where, over against their dwelling, their two babies mainly took the air under charge of Fanny of Albany, their American nurse, whose remark as to the degree to which the British Museum fell short for one who had had the privilege of that of Albany was handed down to us? Did it never forbear from Windsor and Richmond and Sudbrook and Ham Common, amid the rich complexity of which, crowding their discourse with echoes, they had spent their summer?—all a scattering of such pearls as it seemed that their second-born could most deftly and instinctively pick up. Our sole maternal aunt, already mentioned as a devoted and cherished presence during those and many later years, was in a position to share with them the treasure of these mild memories, which strike me as having for the most part, through some bright household habit, overflowed at the breakfast-table, where I regularly attended with W. J.; she had imbibed betimes in Europe the seeds of a long nostalgia, and I think of her as ever so patiently communicative on that score under pressure of my artless appeal. That I should have been so inquiring while still so destitute of primary data was doubtless rather an anomaly; and it was for that matter quite as if my infant divination proceeded by the light of nature: I divined that it would matter to me in the future that "English life" should be of this or that fashion. My father had subscribed for me to a small periodical of quarto form, covered in yellow and entitled The Charm, which shed on the question the softest lustre, but of which the appearances were sadly intermittent, or then struck me as being; inasmuch as many of our visits to the Bookstore were to ask for the new number—only to learn with painful frequency that the last consignment from London had arrived without it. I feel again the pang of that disappointment—as if through the want of what I needed most for going on; the English smell was exhaled by The Charm in a peculiar degree, and I see myself affected by the failure as by that of a vital tonic. It was not, at the same time, by a Charm the more or the less that my salvation was to be, as it were, worked out, or my imagination at any rate duly convinced; conviction was the result of the very air of home, so far as I most consciously inhaled it. This represented, no doubt, a failure to read into matters close at hand all the interest they were capable of yielding; but I had taken the twist, had sipped the poison, as I say, and was to feel it to that end the most salutary cup. I saw my parents homesick, as I conceived, for the ancient order and distressed and inconvenienced by many of the more immediate features of the modern, as the modern pressed upon us, and since their theory of our better living was from an early time that we should renew the quest of the ancient on the very first possibility I simply grew greater in the faith that somehow to manage that would constitute success in life. I never found myself deterred from this fond view, which was implied in every question I asked, every answer I got, and every plan I formed.

Those are great words for the daydream of infant ignorance, yet if success in life may perhaps be best defined as the performance in age of some intention arrested in youth I may frankly put in a claim to it. To press my nose against the sources of the English smell, so different for young bibliophiles from any American, was to adopt that sweetness as the sign of my "atmosphere"; roundabout might be the course to take, but one was in motion from the first and one never lost sight of the goal. The very names of places and things in the other world—the marked opposite in most ways of that in which New York and Albany, Fort Hamilton and New Brighton formed so fallacious a maximum—became to me values and secrets and shibboleths; they were probably often on my tongue and employed as ignorance determined, but I quite recall being ashamed to use them as much as I should have liked. It was New Brighton, I reconstruct (and indeed definitely remember) that "finished" us at last—that and our final sordid school, W. J.'s and mine, in New York: the ancient order *had* somehow to be invoked when such "advantages" as those were the best within our compass and our means. Not further to anticipate, at all events, that climax was for a while but vaguely in sight, and the illusion of felicity continued from season to season to shut us in. It is only of what I took for felicity, however few the years and however scant the scene, that I am pretending now to speak; though I shall have strained the last drop of romance from this vision of our towny summers with the quite sharp reminiscence of my first sitting for my daguerreotype. I repaired with my father on an August day to the great Broadway establishment of Mr. Brady, supreme in that then beautiful art, and it is my impression—the only point vague with me—that though we had come up by the Staten Island boat for the purpose we were to keep the affair secret till the charming consequence should break, at home, upon my mother. Strong is my conviction that our mystery, in the event, yielded almost at once to our elation, for no tradition had a brighter household life with us than that of our father's headlong impatience. He moved in a cloud, if not rather in a high radiance, of precipitation and divulgation, a chartered rebel against cold reserves. The good news in his hand refused under any persuasion to grow stale, the sense of communicable pleasure in his breast was positively explosive; so that we saw those "surprises" in which he had conspired with our mother for our benefit converted by him in every case, under our shamelessly encouraged guesses, into common conspiracies against her—against her knowing, that is, how thoroughly we were all compromised. He had a special and delightful sophistry at the service of his overflow, and never so fine a fancy as in defending it on "human" grounds. He was something very different withal from a parent of weak mercies; weakness was never so positive and plausible, nor could the attitude of sparing you be more handsomely or on occasion even more comically aggressive.

My small point is simply, however, that the secresy of our conjoined portrait was probably very soon, by his act, to begin a public and shining life and to enjoy it till we received the picture; as to which moreover still another remembrance steals on me, a proof of the fact that our adventure was improvised. Sharp again is my sense of not being so adequately dressed as I should have taken thought for had I foreseen my exposure; though the resources of my wardrobe as then constituted could surely have left me but few alternatives. The main resource of a small New York boy in this line at that time was the little sheath-like jacket, tight to the body, closed at the neck and adorned in front with a single row of brass buttons—a garment of scant grace assuredly and compromised to my consciousness, above all, by a strange ironic light from an unforgotten source. It was but a short time before those days that the great Mr. Thackeray had come to America to lecture on The English Humourists, and still present to me is the voice proceeding from my father's library, in which some glimpse of me hovering, at an opening of the door, in passage or on staircase, prompted him to the formidable words: "Come here, little boy, and show me your extraordinary jacket!" My sense of my jacket became from that hour a heavy one—further enriched as my vision is by my shyness of posture before the seated, the celebrated visitor, who struck me, in the sunny light of the animated room, as enormously big and who, though he laid on my shoulder the hand of benevolence, bent on my native costume the spectacles of wonder. I was to know later on why he had been so amused and why, after asking me if this were the common uniform of my age and class, he remarked that in England, were I to go there, I should be addressed as "Buttons." It had been revealed to me thus in a flash that we were somehow *queer*, and though never exactly crushed by it I became aware that I at least felt so as I stood with my head in Mr. Brady's vise. Beautiful most decidedly the lost art of the daguerreotype; I remember the "exposure" as on this occasion interminably long, yet with the result of a facial anguish far less harshly reproduced than my suffered snapshots of a later age. Too few, I may here interject, were to remain my gathered impressions of the great humourist, but one of them, indeed almost the only other, bears again on the play of his humour over our perversities of dress. It belongs to a later moment, an occasion on which I see him familiarly seated with us, in Paris, during the spring of 1857, at some repast at which the younger of us too, by that time, habitually flocked, in our affluence of five. Our youngest was beside him, a small sister, then not quite in her eighth year, and arrayed apparently after the fashion of the period and place; and the tradition lingered long of his having suddenly laid his hand on her little flounced person and exclaimed with ludicrous horror: "Crinoline?—I was suspecting it! So young and so depraved!"

A fainter image, that of one of the New York moments, just eludes me, pursue it as I will; I recover but the setting and the fact of his brief presence in it, with nothing that was said or done beyond my being left with my father to watch our distinguished friend's secretary, who was also a young artist, establish his easel and proceed to paint. The setting, as I recall it, was an odd, oblong, blank "private parlour" at the Clarendon Hotel, then the latest thing in hotels, but whose ancient corner of Fourth Avenue and—was it Eighteenth Street?—long ago ceased to know it; the gentle, very gentle, portraitist was Mr. Eyre Crowe and the obliging sitter my father, who sat in response to Mr. Thackeray's desire that his protégé should find employment. The protector after a little departed, blessing the business, which took the form of a small full-length of the model seated, his arm extended and the hand on the knob of his cane. The work, it may at this time of day be mentioned, fell below its general possibilities; but I note the scene through which I must duly have gaped and wondered (for I had as yet seen no one, least of all a casual acquaintance in an hotel parlour, "really paint" before,) as a happy example again of my parent's positive cultivation of my society, it would seem, and thought for my social education. And then there are other connections; I recall it as a Sunday morning, I recover the place itself as a featureless void—bleak and bare, with its developments all to come, the hotel parlour of other New York days—but vivid still to me is my conscious assistance for the first time at operations that were to mean much for many of my coming years. Those of quiet Mr. Crowe held me spellbound—I was to circle so wistfully, as from that beginning, round the practice of his art, which in spite of these earnest approaches and intentions never on its own part in the least acknowledged our acquaintance; scarcely much more than it was ever to respond, for that matter, to the overtures of the mild aspirant himself, known to my observation long afterwards, in the London years, as the most touchingly resigned of the children of disappointment. Not only by association was he a Thackerayan figure, but much as if the master's hand had stamped him with the outline and the value, with life and sweetness and patience—shown, as after the long futility, seated in a quiet wait, very long too, for the end. That was sad, one couldn't but feel; yet it was in the oddest way impossible to take him for a failure. He might have been one of fortune's, strictly; but what was that when he was one of Thackeray's own successes?— in the minor line, but with such a grace and such a truth, those of some dim second cousin to Colonel Newcome.

VIII

I feel that at such a rate I remember too much, and yet this mild apparitionism is only part of it. To look back at all is to meet the apparitional and to find in its ghostly face the silent stare of an appeal. When I fix it, the hovering shade, whether of person or place, it fixes me back and seems the less lost—not to my consciousness, for that is nothing, but to its own—by my stopping however idly for it. The day of the daguerreotype, the August afternoon, what was it if not one of the days when we went to Union Square for luncheon and for more ice-cream and more peaches and even more, even most, enjoyment of ease accompanied by stimulation of wonder? It may have been indeed that a visit to Mrs. Cannon rather on that occasion engaged us—memory selects a little confusedly from such a wealth of experience. For the wonder was the experience, and that was everywhere, even if I didn't so much find it as take it with me, to be sure of not falling short. Mrs. Cannon lurked near Fourth Street—*that* I abundantly grasp, not more definitely placing her than in what seemed to me a labyrinth of grave bye-streets westwardly "back of" Broadway, yet at no great distance from it, where she must have occupied a house at a corner, since we reached her not by steps that went up to a front door but by others that went slightly down and formed clearly an independent side access, a feature that affected me as rich and strange. What the steps went down to was a spacious room, light and friendly, so that it couldn't have been compromised by an "area," which offered the brave mystification, amid other mystifications, of being at once a parlour and a shop, a shop in particular for the relief of gentlemen in want of pockethandkerchiefs, neckties, collars, umbrellas and straw-covered bottles of the essence known in old New York as "Cullone"—with a very long and big O. Mrs. Cannon was always seated at some delicate white or other needlework, as if she herself made the collars and the neckties and hemmed the pockethandkerchiefs, though the air of this conflicts with the sense of importation from remoter centres of fashion breathed by some of the more thrilling of the remarks I heard exchanged, at the same time that it quickened the oddity of the place. For the oddity was in many things—above all perhaps in there being no counter, no rows of shelves and no vulgar till for Mrs. Cannon's commerce; the parlour clearly dissimulated the shop—and positively to that extent that I might uncannily have wondered what the shop dissimulated. It represented, honestly, I made out in the course of visits that seem to me to have been delightfully repeated, the more informal of the approaches to our friend's brave background or hinterland, the realm of her main industry, the array of the furnished apartments for gentlemen—gentlemen largely for whom she imported the Eau de Cologne and the neckties and who struck me as principally consisting of the ever remarkable Uncles, desirous at times, on their restless returns from Albany or wherever, of an intimacy of comfort that the New York Hotel couldn't yield. Fascinating thus the implications of Mrs. Cannon's establishment, where the talk took the turn, in particular, of Mr. John and Mr. Edward and Mr. Howard, and where Miss Maggie or Miss Susie, who were on the spot in other rocking chairs and with other poised needles, made their points as well as the rest of us. The interest of the place was that the uncles were somehow always under discussion—as to where they at the moment might be, or as to when they were expected, or above all as to how (the "how" was the great matter and the fine emphasis) they had last appeared and might be conceived as carrying themselves; and that their consumption of neckties and Eau de Cologne was somehow inordinate: I might have been judging it in my innocence as their only *consommation*. I refer to those sources, I say, the charm of the scene, the finer part of which must yet have been that it didn't, as it regularly lapsed, dispose of *all* mystifications. If I didn't understand, however, the beauty was that Mrs. Cannon understood (that was what she did most of all, even more than hem pockethandkerchiefs and collars) and my father understood, and each understood that the other did, Miss Maggie and Miss Susie being no whit behind. It was only I who didn't understand—save in so far as I understood *that*, which was a kind of pale joy; and meanwhile there would be more to come from uncles so attachingly, so almost portentously, discussable. The vision at any rate was to stick by me as through its old-world friendly grace, its light on the elder amenity; the prettier manners, the tender personal note in the good lady's importations and anxieties, that of the hand-made fabric and the discriminating service. Fit to figure as a value anywhere—by which I meant in the right corner of any social picture, I afterwards said to myself—that refined and composed significance of Mrs. Cannon's scene.

Union Square was a different matter, though with the element there also that I made out that I *didn't* make out (my sense of drama was in this case, I think, rather more frightened off than led on;) a drawback for which, however, I consoled myself by baked apples and custards, an inveterate feature of our Sunday luncheon there (those of weekdays being various and casual) and by a study of a great store, as it seemed to me, of steel-plated volumes, devoted mainly to the heroines of Romance, with one in particular, presenting those of Shakespeare, in which the plates were so artfully coloured and varnished, and complexion and dress thereby so endeared to memory, that it was for long afterwards a shock to me at the theatre not to see just those bright images, with their peculiar toggeries, come on. I was able but the other day, moreover, to renew almost on the very spot the continuity of contemplation; large lumpish presences, precarious creations of a day, seemed to have elbowed out of the Square all but one or two of the minor monuments, pleasant appreciable things, of the other time; yet close to University Place the old house of the picture-books and the custards and the domestic situation had, though disfigured and overscored, not quite received its death-stroke; I disengaged, by a mere identification of obscured window and profaned portico, a whole chapter of history; which fact should indeed be a warning to penetration, a practical plea here for the superficial—by its exhibition of the rate at which the relations of any gage of experience multiply and ramify from the moment the mind begins to handle it. I pursued a swarm of such relations, on the occasion I speak of, up and down West Fourteenth Street and over to Seventh Avenue, running most of them to earth with difficulty, but finding them at half a dozen points quite confess to a queer stale sameness. The gage of experience, as I say, had in these cases been strangely spared—the sameness had in two or three of them held out as with conscious craft. But these are impressions I shall presently find it impossible not to take up again at any cost.

I first "realised" Fourteenth Street at a very tender age, and I perfectly recall that flush of initiation, consisting as it did of an afternoon call with my father at a house there situated, one of an already fairly mature row on the south side and quite near Sixth Avenue. It was as "our" house, just acquired by us, that he thus invited my approval of it—heaping as that does once more the measure of my small adhesiveness. I thoroughly approved—quite as if I had foreseen that the place was to become to me for ever so long afterwards a sort of anchorage of the spirit, being at the hour as well a fascination for the eyes, since it was there I first fondly gaped at the process of "decorating." I saw charming men in little caps ingeniously formed of folded newspaper—where in the roaring city are those quaint badges of the handicrafts now?—mounted on platforms and casting plaster into moulds; I saw them in particular paste long strips of yellowish grained paper upon walls, and I vividly remember thinking the grain and the pattern (for there was a pattern from waist-high down, a complication of dragons and sphinxes and scrolls and other fine flourishes) a wonderful and sumptuous thing. I would give much, I protest, to recover its lost secret, to see what it really was—so interesting ever to retrace, and sometimes so difficult of belief, in a community of one's own knowing, is the general æsthetic adventure, are the dangers and delusions, the all but fatal accidents and mortal ailments, that Taste has smilingly survived and after which the fickle creature may still quite brazenly look one in the face. Our quarter must have bristled in those years with the very worst of the danger-signals—though indeed they figured but as coarse complacencies; the age of "brown stone" had just been ushered in, and that material, in deplorable, in monstrous form, over all the vacant spaces and eligible sites then numerous between the Fifth and Sixth Avenues, more and more affronted the day. We seemed to have come up from a world of quieter harmonies, the world of Washington Square and thereabouts, so decent in its dignity, so instinctively unpretentious. There were even there spots of shabbiness that I recall, such as the charmless void reaching westward from the two houses that formed the Fifth Avenue corner to our grandfather's, our New York grandfather's house, itself built by him, with the happiest judgment, not so long before, and at no distant time in truth to be solidly but much less pleasingly neighboured. The ancient name of the Parade-ground still hung about the

142

central space, and the ancient wooden palings, then so generally accounted proper for central spaces—the whole image infinitely recedes—affected even my innocent childhood as rustic and mean. Union Square, at the top of the Avenue—or what practically then counted for the top—was encased, more smartly, in iron rails and further adorned with a fountain and an aged amateur-looking constable, awful to my generation in virtue of his star and his switch. I associate less elegance with the Parade-ground, into which we turned for recreation from my neighbouring dame's-school and where the parades deployed on no scale to check our own evolutions; though indeed the switch of office abounded there, for what I best recover in the connection is a sense and smell of perpetual autumn, with the ground so muffled in the leaves and twigs of the now long defunct ailanthus-tree that most of our own motions were a kicking of them up—the semi-sweet rankness of the plant was all in the air—and small boys pranced about as cavaliers whacking their steeds. There were bigger boys, bolder still, to whom this vegetation, or something kindred that escapes me, yielded long black beanlike slips which they lighted and smoked, the smaller ones staring and impressed; I at any rate think of the small one I can best speak for as constantly wading through an Indian summer of these *disjecta*, fascinated by the leaf-kicking process, the joy of lonely trudges, over a course in which those parts and the slightly more northward pleasantly confound themselves. These were the homely joys of the nobler neighbourhood, elements that had their match, and more, hard by the Fourteenth Street home, in the poplars, the pigs, the poultry, and the "Irish houses," two or three in number, exclusive of a very fine Dutch one, seated then, this last, almost as among gardens and groves—a breadth of territory still apparent, on the spot, in that marginal ease, that spread of occupation, to the nearly complete absence of which New York aspects owe their general failure of "style."

But there were finer vibrations as well—for the safely-prowling infant, though none perhaps so fine as when he stood long and drank deep at those founts of romance that gushed from the huge placards of the theatre. These announcements, at a day when advertisement was contentedly but information, had very much the form of magnified playbills; they consisted of vast oblong sheets, yellow or white, pasted upon tall wooden screens or into hollow sockets, and acquainting the possible playgoer with every circumstance that might seriously interest him. These screens rested sociably against trees and lamp-posts as well as against walls and fences, to all of which they were, I suppose, familiarly attached; but the sweetest note of their confidence was that, in parallel lines and the good old way, characters facing performers, they gave the whole cast, which in the "palmy days" of the drama often involved many names. I catch myself again in the fact of endless stations in Fifth Avenue near the southwest corner of Ninth Street, as I think it must have been, since the dull long "run" didn't exist then for the young *badaud* and the poster there was constantly and bravely renewed. It engaged my attention, whenever I passed, as the canvas of a great master in a great gallery holds that of the pious tourist, and even though I can't at this day be sure of its special reference I was with precocious passion "at home" among the theatres—thanks to our parents' fond interest in them (as from this distance I see it flourish for the time) and to the liberal law and happy view under which the addiction was shared with us, they never caring much for things we couldn't care for and generally holding that what was good to them would be also good for their children. It had the effect certainly of preparing for these, so far as we should incline to cherish it, a strange little fund of theatrical reminiscence, a small hoard of memories maintaining itself in my own case for a lifetime and causing me to wonder to-day, before its abundance, on how many evenings of the month, or perhaps even of the week, we were torn from the pursuits of home.

IX

The truth is doubtless, however, much less in the wealth of my experience than in the tenacity of my impression, the fact that I have lost nothing of what I saw and that though I can't now quite divide the total into separate occasions the various items surprisingly swarm for me. I shall return to some of them, wishing at present only to make my point of when and how the seeds were sown that afterwards so thickly sprouted and flowered. I was greatly to love the drama, at its best, as a "form"; whatever variations of faith or curiosity I was to know in respect to the infirm and inadequate theatre. There was of course anciently no question for us of the drama at its best; and indeed while I lately by chance looked over a copious collection of theatrical portraits, beginning with the earliest age of lithography and photography as so applied, and documentary in the highest degree on the personalities, as we nowadays say, of the old American stage, stupefaction grew sharp in me and scepticism triumphed, so vulgar, so barbarous, seemed the array of types, so extraordinarily provincial the note of every figure, so less than scant the claim of such physiognomies and such reputations. Rather dismal, everywhere, I admit, the histrionic image with the artificial lights turned off—the fatigued and disconnected face reduced to its mere self and resembling some closed and darkened inn with the sign still swung but the place blighted for want of custom. That consideration weighs; but what a "gang," all the same, when thus left to their own devices, the performers, men and women alike, of that world of queer appreciations! I ought perhaps to bear on them lightly in view of what in especial comes back to me; the sense of the sacred thrill with which I began to watch the green curtain, the particular one that was to rise to The Comedy of Errors on the occasion that must have been, for what I recall of its almost unbearable intensity, the very first of my ever sitting at a play. I should have been indebted for the momentous evening in that case to Mr. William Burton, whose small theatre in Chambers Street, to the rear of Stewart's big shop and hard by the Park, as the Park was at that time understood, offered me then my prime initiation. Let me not complain of my having owed the adventure to a still greater William as well, nor think again without the right intensity, the scarce tolerable throb, of the way the torment of the curtain was mixed, half so dark a defiance and half so rich a promise. One's eyes bored into it in vain, and yet one knew it *would* rise at the named hour, the only question being if one could exist till then. The play had been read to us during the day; a celebrated English actor, whose name I inconsistently forget, had arrived to match Mr. Burton as the other of the Dromios; and the agreeable Mrs. Holman, who had to my relentless vision too retreating a chin, was so good as to represent Adriana. I regarded Mrs. Holman as a friend, though in no warmer light than that in which I regarded Miss Mary Taylor—save indeed that Mrs. Holman had the pull, on one's affections, of "coming out" to sing in white satin and quite irrelevantly between the acts; an advantage she shared with the younger and fairer and more dashing, the dancing, Miss Malvina, who footed it and tambourined it and shawled it, irruptively, in lonely state. When not admiring Mr. Burton in Shakespeare we admired him as Paul Pry, as Mr. Toodles and as Aminadab Sleek in The Serious Family, and we must have admired him very much—his huge fat person, his huge fat face and his vast slightly pendulous cheek, surmounted by a sort of elephantine wink, to which I impute a remarkable baseness, being still perfectly present to me.

We discriminated, none the less; we thought Mr. Blake a much finer comedian, much more of a gentleman and a scholar—"mellow" Mr. Blake, whom with the brave and emphatic Mrs. Blake (*how* they must have made their points!) I connect partly with the Burton scene and partly with that, of slightly subsequent creation, which, after flourishing awhile slightly further up Broadway under the charmlessly commercial name of Brougham's Lyceum (we had almost only Lyceums and Museums and Lecture Rooms and Academies of Music for playhouse and opera then,) entered upon a long career and a migratory life as Wallack's Theatre. I fail doubtless to keep *all* my associations clear, but what is important, or what I desire at least to make pass for such, is that when we most admired Mr. Blake we also again admired Miss Mary Taylor; and it was at Brougham's, not at Burton's, that we rendered *her* that tribute—reserved for her performance of the fond theatrical daughter in the English version of Le Père de la Débutante, where I see the charming panting dark-haired creature, in flowing white classically relieved by a gold tiara and a golden scarf, rush back from the supposed stage to the represented greenroom, followed by thunders of applause, and throw herself upon the neck of the broken-down old gentleman in a blue coat with brass buttons who must have been after all, on second thoughts, Mr. Placide. Greater flights or more delicate shades the art of pathetic comedy was at that time held not to achieve; only I straighten it out that Mr. and Mrs. Blake, not less than Miss Mary Taylor (who preponderantly haunts my vision, even to the disadvantage of Miss Kate Horn in Nan the Good-for-Nothing, until indeed she is displaced by the brilliant Laura Keene) did migrate to Brougham's, where we found them all themselves as Goldsmith's Hardcastle pair and other like matters. We rallied especially to Blake as Dogberry, on the occasion of my second Shakespearean night, for as such I seem to place it, when Laura Keene and Mr. Lester—the Lester Wallack that was to be—did Beatrice and Benedick. I yield to this further proof that we had our proportion of Shakespeare, though perhaps antedating that rapt vision of Much Ado, which may have been preceded by the dazzled apprehension of A Midsummer Night's Dream at the Broadway (there *was* a confessed Theatre;) this latter now present to me in every bright particular. It supplied us, we must have felt, our greatest conceivable adventure—I cannot otherwise account for its emerging so clear. Everything here is as of yesterday, the identity of the actors, the details of their dress, the charm imparted by the sisters Gougenheim, the elegant elder as the infatuated Helena and the other, the roguish "Joey" as the mischievous Puck. Hermia was Mrs. Nagle, in a short salmon-coloured peplum over a white petticoat, the whole bulgingly confined by a girdle of shining gilt and forming a contrast to the loose scarves of Helena, while Mr. Nagle, not devoid, I seem to remember, of a blue chin and the latency of a fine brogue, was either Lysander or Demetrius; Mr. Davidge (also, I surmise, with a brogue) was Bottom the weaver and Madame Ponisi Oberon—Madame Ponisi whose range must have been wide, since I see her also as the white-veiled heroine of The Cataract of the Ganges, where, preferring death to dishonour, she dashes up the more or less perpendicular waterfall on a fiery black steed and with an effect only a little blighted by the chance flutter of a drapery out of which peeps the leg of a trouser and a big male foot; and then again, though presumably at a somewhat later time or, in strictness, *after* childhood's fond hour, as this and that noble matron or tragedy queen. I descry her at any rate as representing all characters alike with a broad brown face framed in bands or crowns or other heavy headgear out of which cropped a row of very small tight black curls. The Cataract of the Ganges is all there as well, a tragedy of temples and idols and wicked rajahs and real water, with Davidge and Joey Gougenheim again for comic relief—though all in a coarser radiance, thanks to the absence of fairies and Amazons and moonlit mechanical effects, the charm above all, so seen, of the play within the play; and I rank it in that relation with Green Bushes, despite the celebrity in the latter of Madame Céleste, who came to us straight out of London and whose admired walk up the stage as Miami the huntress, a wonderful majestic and yet voluptuous stride enhanced by a short kilt, black velvet leggings and a gun haughtily borne on the shoulder, is vividly before me as I write. The piece in question was, I recall, from the pen of Mr. Bourcicault, as he then wrote his name—he was so early in the field and must have been from long before, inasmuch as he now appears to me to have supplied Mr. Brougham, of the Lyceum aforesaid, with his choicest productions.

I sit again at London Assurance, with Mrs. Wallack—"Fanny" Wallack, I think, not that I quite know who she was—as Lady Gay Spanker, flushed and vociferous, first in a riding-habit with a tail yards long and afterwards in yellow satin with scarce a tail at all; I am present also at Love in a Maze, in which the stage represented, with primitive art I fear, a supposedly intricate garden-labyrinth, and in which I admired for the first time Mrs. Russell, afterwards long before the public as Mrs. Hoey, even if opining that she wanted, especially for the low-necked ordeal, less osseous a structure. There are pieces of that general association, I admit, the clue to which slips from me; the drama of modern life and of French origin—though what was then not of French origin?—in which Miss Julia Bennett, fresh from triumphs at the Haymarket, made her first appearance, in a very becoming white bonnet, either as a brilliant adventuress or as the innocent victim of licentious design, I forget which, though with a sense somehow that the white bonnet, when of true elegance, was the note at that period of the adventuress; Miss Julia Bennett with whom at a later age one was to renew acquaintance as the artful and ample Mrs. Barrow, full of manner and presence and often Edwin Booth's Portia, Desdemona and Julie de Mortemer. I figure her as having in the dimmer phase succeeded to Miss Laura Keene at Wallack's on the secession thence of this original charmer of our parents, the flutter of whose prime advent is perfectly present to me, with the relish expressed for that "English" sweetness of her speech (I already wondered why it *shouldn't* be English) which was not as the speech mostly known to us. The Uncles, within my hearing, even imitated, for commendation, some of her choicer sounds, to which I strained my ear on seeing her afterwards as Mrs. Chillington in the refined comedietta of A Morning Call, where she made delightful game of Mr. Lester as Sir Edward Ardent, even to the point of causing him to crawl about on all fours and covered with her shawl after the fashion of a horse-blanket. That delightful impression was then unconscious of the blight to come—that of my apprehending, years after, that the brilliant comedietta was the tribute of our Anglo-Saxon taste to Alfred de Musset's elegant proverb of the Porte Ouverte ou Fermée, in which nothing could find itself less at home than the horseplay of the English version. Miss Laura Keene, with a native grace at the start, a fresh and delicate inspiration, I infer from the kind of pleasure she appears to have begun with giving, was to live to belie her promise and, becoming hard and raddled, forfeit (on the evidence) all claim to the higher distinction; a fact not surprising under the lurid light projected by such a sign of the atmosphere of ineptitude as an accepted and condoned perversion to vulgarity of Musset's perfect little work. How *could* quality of talent consort with so dire an absence of quality in the material offered it? where could such lapses lead but to dust and desolation and what happy instinct not be smothered in an air so dismally non-conducting? Is it a foolish fallacy that these matters may have been on occasion, at that time, worth speaking of? is it only presumable that everything was perfectly cheap and common and everyone perfectly bad and barbarous and that even the least corruptible of our typical spectators were too easily beguiled and too helplessly kind? The beauty of the main truth as to any remembered matter looked at in due detachment, or in other words through the haze of time, is that comprehension has then become one with criticism, compassion, as it may really be called, one with musing vision, and the whole company of the anciently restless, with their elations and mistakes, their sincerities and fallacies and vanities and triumphs, embalmed for us in the mild essence of their collective submission to fate. We needn't be strenuous about them unless we particularly want to, and are glad to remember in season all that this would imply of the strenuous about our own *origines*, our muddled initiations. If nothing is more certain for us than that many persons, within our recollection, couldn't help being rather generally unadmonished and unaware, so nothing is more in the note of peace than that such a perceived state, pushed to a point, makes our scales of judgment but ridiculously rattle. *Our* admonition, our superior awareness, is of many things—and, among these, of how infinitely, at the worst, they lived, the pale superseded, and how much it was by their virtue.

Which reflections, in the train of such memories as those just gathered, may perhaps seem over-strained—though they really to my own eyes cause the images to multiply. Still others of these break in upon me and refuse to be slighted; reconstituting as I practically am the history of my fostered imagination, for whatever it may be worth, I won't pretend to a disrespect for *any* contributive particle. I left myself just above staring at the Fifth Avenue poster, and I can't but linger there while the vision it evokes insists on swarming. It was the age of the arrangements of Dickens for the stage, vamped-up promptly on every scene and which must have been the roughest theatrical tinkers' work, but at two or three of which we certainly assisted. I associate them with Mr. Brougham's temple of the art, yet am at the same time beset with the Captain Cuttle of Dombey and Son in the form of the big Burton, who never, I earnestly conceive, graced that shrine, so that I wander a trifle confusedly. Isn't it he whom I remember as a monstrous Micawber, the coarse parody of a charming creation, with the entire baldness of a huge Easter egg and collar-points like the sails of Mediterranean feluccas? Dire of course for all temperance in these connections was the need to conform to the illustrations of Phiz, himself already an improvising parodist and happy only so long as not imitated, not literally reproduced. Strange enough the "æsthetic" of artists who could desire but literally to reproduce. I give the whole question up, however, I stray too in the dust, and with a positive sense of having, in the first place, but languished at home when my betters admired Miss Cushman—terribly out of the picture and the frame we should to-day pronounce her, I fear—as the Nancy of Oliver Twist: as far away this must have been as the lifetime of the prehistoric "Park," to which it was just within my knowledge that my elders went for opera, to come back on us sounding those rich old Italian names, Bosio and Badiali, Ronconi and Steffanone, I am not sure I have them quite right; signs, of a rueful sound to us, that the line as to our infant participation *was* somewhere drawn. It had not been drawn, I all the more like to remember, when, under proper protection, at Castle Garden, I listened to that rarest of infant phenomena, Adelina Patti, poised in an armchair that had been pushed to the footlights and announcing her incomparable gift. She was about of our own age, she was one of us, even though at the same time the most prodigious of fairies, of glittering fables. That principle of selection was indeed in abeyance while I sat with my mother either at Tripler Hall or at Niblo's—I am vague about the occasion, but the names, as for fine old confused reasons, plead alike to my pen—and paid a homage quite other than critical, I dare say, to the then slightly worn Henrietta Sontag, Countess Rossi, who struck us as supremely elegant in pink silk and white lace flounces and with whom there had been for certain members of our circle some contact or intercourse that I have wonderingly lost. I learned at that hour in any case what "acclamation" might mean, and have again before me the vast high-piled auditory thundering applause at the beautiful pink lady's clear bird-notes; a thrilling, a tremendous experience and my sole other memory of concert-going, at that age, save the impression of a strange huddled hour in some smaller public place, some very minor hall, under dim lamps and again in my mother's company, where we were so near the improvised platform that my nose was brushed by the petticoats of the distinguished amateur who sang "Casta Diva," a very fine fair woman with a great heaving of bosom and flirt of crinoline, and that the ringletted Italian gentleman in black velvet and a romantic voluminous cloak who represented, or rather who professionally and uncontrollably was, an Improvisatore, had for me the effect, as I crouched gaping, of quite bellowing down my throat. That occasion, I am clear, was a concert for a charity, with the volunteer performance and the social patroness, and it had squeezed in where it would—at the same time that I somehow connect the place, in Broadway, on the right going down and not much below Fourth Street (except that everything seems to me to have been just below Fourth Street when not just above,) with the scene of my great public exposure somewhat later, the wonderful exhibition of Signor Blitz, the peerless conjurer, who, on my attending his entertainment with W. J. and our frequent comrade of the early time "Hal" Coster, practised on my innocence to seduce me to the stage and there plunge me into the shame of my sad failure to account arithmetically for his bewilderingly subtracted or added or divided pockethandkerchiefs and playing-cards; a paralysis of wit as to which I once more, and with the same wan despair, feel my companions' shy telegraphy of relief, their snickerings and mouthings and raised numerical fingers, reach me from the benches.

The second definite matter in the Dickens connection is the Smike of Miss Weston—whose prænomen I frivolously forget (though I fear it was Lizzie,) but who was afterwards Mrs. E. L. Davenport and then, sequently to some public strife or chatter, Mrs. Charles Matthews—in a version of Nicholas Nickleby that gracelessly managed to be all tearful melodrama, long-lost foundlings, wicked Ralph Nicklebys and scowling Arthur Grides, with other baffled villains, and scarcely at all Crummleses and Kenwigses, much less Squeerses; though there must have been something of Dotheboys Hall for the proper tragedy of Smike and for the broad Yorkshire effect, a precious theatrical value, of John Brodie. The ineffaceability was the anguish, to my tender sense, of Nicholas's starved and tattered and fawning and whining protégé; in face of my sharp retention of which through all the years who shall deny the immense authority of the theatre, or that the stage is the mightiest of modern engines? Such at least was to be the force of the Dickens imprint, however applied, in the soft clay of our generation; it was to resist so serenely the wash of the waves of time. To be brought up thus against the author of it, or to speak at all of the dawn of one's early consciousness of it and of his presence and power, is to begin to tread ground at once sacred and boundless, the associations of which, looming large, warn us off even while they hold. He did too much for us surely ever to leave us free—free of judgment, free of reaction, even should we care to be, which heaven forbid: he laid his hand on us in a way to undermine as in no other case the power of detached appraisement. We react against other productions of the general kind without "liking" them the less, but we somehow liked Dickens the more for having forfeited half the claim to appreciation. That process belongs to the fact that criticism, roundabout him, is somehow futile and tasteless. His own taste is easily impugned, but he entered so early into the blood and bone of our intelligence that it always remained better than the taste of overhauling him. When I take him up to-day and find myself holding off, I simply stop: not holding off, that is, but holding on, and from the very fear to do so; which sounds, I recognise, like perusal, like renewal, of the scantest. I don't renew, I wouldn't renew for the world; wouldn't, that is, with one's treasure so hoarded in the dusty chamber of youth, let in the intellectual air. Happy the house of life in which such chambers still hold out, even with the draught of the intellect whistling through the passages. We were practically contemporary, contemporary with the issues, the fluttering monthly numbers—that was the point; it made for us a good fortune, constituted for us in itself romance, on which nothing, to the end, succeeds in laying its hands.

The whole question dwells for me in a single small reminiscence, though there are others still: that of my having been sent to bed one evening, in Fourteenth Street, as a very small boy, at an hour when, in the library and under the lamp, one of the elder cousins from Albany, the youngest of an orphaned brood of four, of my grandmother's most extravagant adoption, had begun to read aloud to my mother the new, which must have been the first, instalment of David Copperfield. I had feigned to withdraw, but had only retreated to cover close at hand, the friendly shade of some screen or drooping table-cloth, folded up behind which and glued to the carpet, I held my breath and listened. I listened long and drank deep while the wondrous picture grew, but the tense cord at last snapped under the strain of the Murdstones and I broke into the sobs of sympathy that disclosed my subterfuge. I was this time effectively banished, but the ply then taken was ineffaceable. I remember indeed just afterwards finding the sequel, in especial the vast extrusion of the Micawbers, beyond my actual capacity; which took a few years to grow adequate—years in which the general contagious consciousness, and our own household response not least, breathed heavily through Hard Times, Bleak House and Little Dorrit; the seeds of acquaintance with Chuzzlewit and Dombey and Son, these coming thickly on, I had found already sown. I was to feel that I had been born, born to a rich awareness, under the very meridian; there sprouted in those years no such other crop of ready references as the golden harvest of Copperfield. Yet if I was to wait to achieve the happier of these recognitions I had already pored over Oliver Twist—albeit now uncertain of the relation borne by that experience to the incident just recalled. When Oliver was new to me, at any rate, he was already old to my betters; whose view of his particular adventures and exposures must have been concerned, I think, moreover, in the fact of my public and lively wonder about them. It was an exhibition deprecated—to infant innocence I judge; unless indeed my remembrance of enjoying it only on the terms of fitful snatches in another, though a kindred, house is due mainly to the existence there of George Cruikshank's splendid form of the work, of which our own foreground was clear. It perhaps even seemed to me more Cruikshank's than Dickens's; it was a thing of such vividly terrible images, and all marked with that peculiarity of Cruikshank that the offered flowers or goodnesses, the scenes and figures intended to comfort and cheer, present themselves under his hand as but more subtly sinister, or more suggestively queer, than the frank badnesses and horrors. The nice people and the happy moments, in the plates, frightened me almost as much as the low and the awkward; which didn't however make the volumes a source of attraction the less toward that high and square old back-parlour just westward of Sixth Avenue (as we in the same street were related to it) that formed, romantically, half our alternative domestic field and offered to our small inquiring steps a larger range and privilege. If the Dickens of those years was, as I have just called him, the great actuality of the current imagination, so I at once meet him in force as a feature even of conditions in which he was but indirectly involved.

For the other house, the house we most haunted after our own, was that of our cousin Albert, still another of the blest orphans, though this time of our mother's kindred; and if it was my habit, as I have hinted, to attribute to orphans as orphans a circumstantial charm, a setting necessarily more delightful than our father'd and mother'd one, so there spread about this appointed comrade, the perfection of the type, inasmuch as he alone was neither brother'd nor sister'd, an air of possibilities that were none the less vivid for being quite indefinite. He was to embody in due course, poor young man, some of these possibilities—those that had originally been for me the vaguest of all; but to fix his situation from my present view is not so much to wonder that it spoke to me of a wild freedom as to see in it the elements of a rich and rounded picture. The frame was still there but a short time since, cracked and empty, broken and gaping, like those few others, of the general overgrown scene, that my late quest had puzzled out; and this has somehow helped me to read back into it the old figures and the old long story, told as with excellent art. We knew the figures well while they lasted and had with them the happiest relation, but without doing justice to their truth of outline, their felicity of character and force of expression and function, above all to the compositional harmony in which they moved. That lives again to my considering eyes, and I admire as never before the fine artistry of fate. Our cousin's guardian, the natural and the legal, was his aunt, his only one, who was the cousin of our mother and our own aunt, virtually *our* only one, so far as a felt and adopted closeness of kinship went; and the three, daughters of two sole and much-united sisters, had been so brought up together as to have quite all the signs and accents of the same strain and the same nest. The cousin Helen of our young prospect was thus all but the sister Helen of our mother's lifetime, as was to happen, and was scarcely less a stout brave presence and an emphasised character for the new generation than for the old; noted here as she is, in particular, for her fine old-time value of clearness and straightness. I see in her strong simplicity, that of an earlier, quieter world, a New York of better manners and better morals and homelier beliefs, the very elements of some portrait by a grave Dutch or other truth-seeking master; she looks out with some of the strong marks, the anxious honesty, the modest humour, the folded resting hands, the dark handsome serious attire, the important composed cap, almost the badge of a guild or an order, that hang together about the images of past worthies, of whichever sex, who have had, as one may say, the courage of their character, and qualify them for places in great collections. I note with appreciation that she was strenuously, actively good, and have the liveliest impression both that no one was ever better, and that her goodness somehow testifies for the whole tone of a society, a remarkable cluster of private decencies. Her value to my imagination is even most of all perhaps in her mere local consistency, her fine old New York ignorance and rigour. Her traditions, scant but stiff, had grown there, close to her—they were all she needed, and she lived by them candidly and stoutly. That there have been persons so little doubtful of duty helps to show us how societies grow. A proportionately small amount of absolute conviction about it will carry, we thus make out, a vast dead weight of mere comparative. She was as anxious over hers indeed as if it had ever been in question—which is a proof perhaps that being void of imagination, when you are quite entirely void, makes scarcely more for comfort than having too much, which only makes in a manner for a homeless freedom or even at the worst for a questioned veracity. With a big installed conscience there is virtue in a grain of the figurative faculty—it acts as oil to the stiff machine.

Yet this life of straight and narrow insistences seated so clearly in our view didn't take up all the room in the other house, the house of the pictured, the intermittent Oliver, though of the fewer books in general than ours, and of the finer proportions and less peopled spaces (there were but three persons to fill them) as well as of the more turbaned and powdered family portraits, one of these, the most antique, a "French pastel," which must have been charming, of a young collateral ancestor who had died on the European tour. A vast marginal range seemed to me on the contrary to surround the adolescent nephew, who was some three years, I judge, beyond me in age and had other horizons and prospects than ours. No question of "Europe," for him, but a patriotic preparation for acquaintance with the South and West, or what was then called the West—he was to "see his own country first," winking at us while he did so; though he was, in spite of differences, so nearly and naturally neighbour'd and brother'd with us that the extensions of his range and the charms of his position counted somehow as the limits and the humilities of ours. He went neither to our schools nor to our hotels, but hovered out of our view in some other educational air that I can't now point to, and had in a remote part of the State a vast wild property of his own, known as the Beaverkill, to which, so far from his aunt's and his uncle's taking him there, he affably took them, and to which also he vainly invited W. J. and me, pointing thereby to us, however, though indirectly enough perhaps, the finest childish case we were to know for the famous acceptance of the inevitable. It was apparently not to be thought of that instead of the inevitable we should accept the invitation; the place was in the wilderness, incalculably distant, reached by a whole day's rough drive from the railroad, through every danger of flood and field, with prowling bears thrown in and probable loss of limb, of which there were sad examples, from swinging scythes and axes; but we of course measured our privation just by those facts, and grew up, so far as we did then grow, to believe that pleasures beyond price had been cruelly denied us. I at any rate myself grew up sufficiently to wonder if poor Albert's type, as it developed to the anxious elder view from the first, mightn't rather have undermined countenance; his pleasant foolish face and odd shy air of being suspected or convicted on grounds less vague to himself than to us may well have appeared symptoms of the course, of the "rig," he was eventually to run. I could think of him but as the *fils de famille* ideally constituted; not that I could then use for him that designation, but that I felt he must belong to an important special class, which he in fact formed in his own person. Everything was right, truly, for these felicities—to speak of them only as dramatic or pictorial values; since if we were present all the while at more of a drama than we knew, so at least, to my vague divination, the scene and the figures were there, not excluding the chorus, and I must have had the instinct of their being as right as possible. I see the actors move again through the high, rather bedimmed rooms—it is always a matter of winter twilight, firelight, lamplight; each one appointed to his or her part and perfect for the picture, which gave a sense of fulness without ever being crowded.

That composition had to wait awhile, in the earliest time, to find its proper centre, having been from the free point of view I thus cultivate a little encumbered by the presence of the most aged of our relatives, the oldest person I remember to have familiarly known—if it can be called familiar to have stood off in fear of such strange proofs of accomplished time: our Great-aunt Wyckoff, our maternal grandmother's elder sister, I infer, and an image of living antiquity, as I figure her to-day, that I was never to see surpassed. I invest her in this vision with all the idol-quality that may accrue to the venerable—solidly seated or even throned, hooded and draped and tucked-in, with big protective protrusive ears to her chair which helped it to the effect of a shrine, and a large face in which the odd blackness of eyebrow and of a couple of other touches suggested the conventional marks of a painted image. She signified her wants as divinities do, for I recover from her presence neither sound nor stir, remembering of her only that, as described by her companions, the pious ministrants, she had "said" so and so when she hadn't spoken at all. Was she really, as she seemed, so tremendously old, so old that her daughter, our mother's cousin Helen and ours, would have had to come to her in middle life to account for it, or did antiquity at that time set in earlier and was surrender of appearance and dress, matching the intrinsic decay, only more complacent, more submissive and, as who should say, more abject? I have my choice of these suppositions, each in its way of so lively an interest that I scarce know which to prefer, though inclining perhaps a little to the idea of the backward reach. If Aunt Wyckoff was, as I first remember her, scarce more than seventy, say, the thought fills me with one sort of joy, the joy of our modern, our so generally greater and nobler effect of duration: who *wouldn't* more subtly strive for that effect and, intelligently so striving, reach it better, than such non-questioners of fate?—the moral of whose case is surely that if they gave up too soon and too softly we wiser witnesses can reverse the process and fight the whole ground. But I apologise to the heavy shade in question if she had really drained her conceivable cup, and for that matter rather like to suppose it, so rich and strange is the pleasure of finding the past—the Past above all—answered for to one's own touch, this being our only way to be sure of it. It was the Past that one touched in her, the American past of a preponderant unthinkable queerness; and great would seem the fortune of helping on the continuity at some other far end.

X

It was at all events the good lady's disappearance that more markedly cleared the decks—cleared them for that long, slow, sustained action with which I make out that nothing was afterwards to interfere. She had sat there under her stiff old father's portrait, with which her own, on the other side of the chimney, mildly balanced; but these presences acted from that time but with cautious reserves. A brave, finished, clear-eyed image of such properties as the last-named, in particular, our already-mentioned Alexander Robertson, a faint and diminished replica of whose picture (the really fine original, as I remember it, having been long since perverted from our view) I lately renewed acquaintance with in a pious institution of his founding, where, after more than one push northward and some easy accommodations, he lives on into a world that knows him not and of some of the high improvements of which he can little enough have dreamed. Of the world he had personally known there was a feature or two still extant; the legend of his acres and his local concerns, as well as of his solid presence among them, was considerably cherished by us, though for ourselves personally the relics of his worth were a lean feast to sit at. They were by some invidious turn of fate all to help to constitute the heritage of our young kinsman, the orphaned and administered *fils de famille*, whose father, Alexander Wyckoff, son of our great-aunt and one of the two brothers of cousin Helen, just discernibly flushes for me through the ominous haze that preceded the worst visitation of cholera New York was to know. Alexander, whom, early widowed and a victim of that visitation, I evoke as with something of a premature baldness, of a blackness of short whisker, of an expanse of light waistcoat and of a harmless pomp of manner, appeared to have quite predominantly "come in" for the values in question, which he promptly transmitted to his small motherless son and which were destined so greatly to increase. There are clues I have only lost, not making out in the least to-day why the sons of Aunt Wyckoff should have been so happily distinguished. Our great-uncle of the name isn't even a dim ghost to me—he had passed away beyond recall before I began to take notice; but I hold, rightly,

I feel, that it was not to his person these advantages were attached. They could have descended to our grandmother but in a minor degree—we should otherwise have been more closely aware of them. It comes to me that so far as we had at all been aware it had mostly gone off in smoke: I have still in my ears some rueful allusion to "lands," apparently in the general country of the Beaverkill, which had come to my mother and her sister as their share of their grandfather Robertson's amplitude, among the further-apportioned shares of their four brothers, only to be sacrificed later on at some scant appraisement. It is in the nature of "lands" at a distance and in regions imperfectly reclaimed to be spoken of always as immense, and I at any rate entertained the sense that we should have been great proprietors, in the far wilderness, if we had only taken more interest. Our interests were peculiarly urban—though not indeed that this had helped us much. Something of the mystery of the vanished acres hung for me about my maternal uncle, John Walsh, the only one who appeared to have been in respect to the dim possessions much on the spot, but I too crudely failed of my chance of learning from him what had become of them.

Not that they had seen *him*, poor gentleman, very much further, or that I had any strong sense of opportunity; I catch at but two or three projections of him, and only at one of his standing much at his ease: I see him before the fire in the Fourteenth Street library, sturdy, with straight black hair and as if the Beaverkill had rather stamped him, but clean-shaven, in a "stock" and a black frock-coat—I hear him perhaps still more than I see him deliver himself on the then great subject of Jenny Lind, whom he seemed to have emerged from the wilderness to listen to and as to whom I remember thinking it (strange small critic that I must have begun to be) a note of the wilderness in him that he spoke of her as "Miss Lind"; albeit I scarce know, and must even less have known then, what other form he could have used. The rest of my sense of him is tinged with the ancient pity—that of our so exercised response in those years to the general sad case of uncles, aunts and cousins obscurely afflicted (the uncles in particular) and untimely gathered. Sharp to me the memory of a call, one dusky wintry Sunday afternoon, in Clinton Place, at the house of my uncle Robertson Walsh, then the head of my mother's family, where the hapless younger brother lay dying; whom I was taken to the top of the house to see and of the sinister twilight grimness of whose lot, stretched there, amid odours of tobacco and of drugs, or of some especial strong drug, in one of the chambers of what I remember as a remote and unfriended arching attic, probably in fact the best place of prescribed quiet, I was to carry away a fast impression. All the uncles, of whichever kindred, were to come to seem sooner or later to be dying, more or less before our eyes, of melancholy matters; and yet their general story, so far as one could read it, appeared the story of life. I conceived at any rate that John Walsh, celibate, lonely and good-naturedly black-browed, had been sacrificed to the far-off Robertson acres, which on their side had been sacrificed to I never knew what. The point of my divagation, however, is that the Barmecide banquet of another tract of the same *provenance* was always spread for us opposite the other house, from which point it stretched, on the north side of the street, to Sixth Avenue; though here we were soon to see it diminished at the corner by a structure afterwards known to us as our prosiest New York school. This edifice, devoted to-day to other uses, but of the same ample insignificance, still left for exploitation at that time an uncovered town-territory the transmitted tale of which was that our greatgrandfather, living down near the Battery, had had his country villa or, more strictly speaking, his farm there, with free expanses roundabout. Shrunken though the tract a part of it remained—in particular a space that I remember, though with the last faintness, to have seen appeal to the public as a tea-garden or open-air café, a haunt of dance and song and of other forms of rather ineffective gaiety. The subsequent conversion of the site into the premises of the French Theatre I was to be able to note more distinctly; resorting there in the winter of 1874-5, though not without some wan detachment, to a series of more or less exotic performances, and admiring in especial the high and hard virtuosity of Madame Ristori, the unfailing instinct for the wrong emphasis of the then acclaimed Mrs. Rousby (I still hear the assured "Great woman, great woman!" of a knowing friend met as I went out,) and the stout fidelity to a losing game, as well as to a truth not quite measurable among us, of the late, the but lugubriously-comic, the blighted John Toole.

These are glimmering ghosts, though that drama of the scene hard by at which I have glanced gives me back its agents with a finer intensity. For the long action set in, as I have hinted, with the death of Aunt Wyckoff, and, if rather taking its time at first to develop, maintained to the end, which was in its full finality but a few years since, the finest consistency and unity; with cousin Helen, in rich prominence, for the heroine; with the pale adventurous Albert for the hero or young protagonist, a little indeed in the sense of a small New York Orestes ridden by Furies; with a pair of confidants in the form first of the heroine's highly respectable but quite negligible husband and, second, of her close friend and quasi-sister our own admirable Aunt; with Alexander's younger brother, above all, the odd, the eccentric, the attaching Henry, for the stake, as it were, of the game. So for the spectator did the figures distribute themselves; the three principal, on the large stage—it became a field of such spreading interests—well in front, and the accessory pair, all sympathy and zeal, prompt comment and rich resonance, hovering in the background, responsive to any call and on the spot at a sign: this most particularly true indeed of our anything but detached Aunt, much less a passive recipient than a vessel constantly brimming, and destined herself to become the outstanding agent, almost the *dea ex machina*, in the last act of the story. Her colleague of the earlier periods (though to that title she would scarce have granted his right) I designate rather as our earnest cousin's husband than as our kinsman even by courtesy; since he was "Mr." to his own wife, for whom the dread of liberties taken in general included even those that might have been allowed to herself: he had not in the least, like the others in his case, married into the cousinship with us, and this apparently rather by his defect than by ours. His christian name, if certainly not for use, was scarce even for ornament— which consorted with the felt limits roundabout him of aids to mention and with the fact that no man could on his journey through life well have been less eagerly designated or apostrophised. If there are persons as to whom the "Mr." never comes up at all, so there are those as to whom it never subsides; but some of them all keep it by the greatness and others, oddly enough, by the smallness of their importance. The subject of my present reference, as I think of him, nevertheless—by which I mean in spite of his place in the latter group—greatly helps my documentation; he must have been of so excellent and consistent a shade of nullity. To that value, if value it be, there almost always attaches some question of the degree and the position: with adjuncts, with a relation, the zero may figure as a numeral—and the neglected zero is mostly, for that matter, endowed with a consciousness and subject to irritation. For this dim little gentleman, so perfectly a gentleman, no appeal and no redress, from the beginning to the end of his career, were made or entertained or projected; no question of how to treat him, or of how *he* might see it or feel it, could ever possibly rise; he was blank from whatever view, remaining so under application of whatever acid or exposure to whatever heat; the one identity he could have was to be part of the consensus.

Such a case is rare—that of being no case at all, that of not having even the interest of the grievance of not being one: we as a rule catch glimpses in the down-trodden of such resentments—they have at least sometimes the importance of feeling the weight of our tread. The phenomenon was here quite other—that of a natural platitude that had never risen to the level of sensibility. When you have been wronged you can be righted, when you have suffered you can be soothed; if you have that amount of grasp of the "scene," however humble, the drama of your life to some extent enacts itself, with the logical consequence of your being proportionately its hero and *having* to be taken for such. Let me not dream of attempting to say for what cousin Helen took her spectral spouse, though I think it the most marked touch in her portrait that she kept us from ever knowing. She was a person about whom you knew everything else, but there she was genially inscrutable, and above all claimed no damages on the score of slights offered him. She knew nothing whatever of these, yet could herself be much wounded or hurt—which latter word she sounded in the wondrous old New York manner so irreducible to notation. She covered the whole case with a mantle which was yet much more probably that of her real simplicity than of a feigned unconsciousness; I doubt whether she *knew* that men could be amiable in a different manner from that which had to serve her for supposing her husband amiable; when the mould and the men cast in it were very different she failed, or at least she feared, to conclude to amiability—though *some* women (as different themselves as such stranger men!) might take it for that. Directly interrogated she might (such was the innocence of these long-extinct manners) have approved of male society in stronger doses or more vivid hues—save where consanguinity, or indeed relationship by marriage, to which she greatly deferred, had honestly imposed it. The singular thing for the drama to which I return was that there it was just consanguinity that had made the burden difficult and strange and of a nature to call on great decisions and patient plans, even though the most ominous possibilities were not involved. I reconstruct and reconstruct of course, but the elements had to my childish vision at least nothing at all portentous; if any light of the lurid played in for me just a little it was but under much later information. What my childish vision was really most possessed of, I think, was the figure of the spectral spouse, the dim little gentleman, as I have called him, pacing the whole length of the two big parlours, in prolonged repetition, much as if they had been the deck of one of those ships anciently haunted by him, as "supercargo" or whatever, in strange far seas—according to the only legend connected with him save that of his early presumption in having approached, such as he was, so fine a young woman, and his remarkable luck in having approached her successfully; a luck surprisingly renewed for him, since it was also part of the legend that he had previously married and lost a bride beyond his deserts.

XI

I am, strictly speaking, at this point, on a visit to Albert, who at times sociably condescended to my fewer years—I still appreciate the man-of-the-world ease of it; but my host seems for the minute to have left me, and I am attached but to the rich perspective in which "Uncle" (for Albert too he was only all namelessly Uncle) comes and goes; out of the comparative high brownness of the back room, commanding brave extensions, as I thought them, a covered piazza over which, in season, Isabella grapes accessibly clustered and beyond which stretched, further, a "yard" that was as an ample garden compared to ours at home; I keep in view his little rounded back, at the base of which his arms are interlocked behind him, and I know how his bald head, yet with the hair bristling up almost in short-horn fashion at the sides, is thrust inquiringly, not to say appealingly, forward; I assist at his emergence, where the fine old mahogany doors of separation are rolled back on what used to seem to me silver wheels, into the brighter yet colder half of the scene, and attend him while he at last looks out awhile into Fourteenth Street for news of whatever may be remarkably, objectionably or mercifully taking place there; and then I await his regular return, preparatory to a renewed advance, far from indifferent as I innocently am to his discoveries or his comments. It is cousin Helen however who preferentially takes them up, attaching to them the right importance, which is for the moment the very greatest that could possibly be attached to anything in the world; I for my part occupied with those marks of character in our pacing companion—his long, slightly equine countenance, his eyebrows ever elevated as in the curiosity of alarm, and the so limited play from side to side of his extremely protrusive head, as if somehow through tightness of the "wash" neckcloths that he habitually wore and that, wound and re-wound in their successive stages, made his neck very long without making it in the least thick and reached their climax in a proportionately very small knot tied with the neatest art. I scarce can have known at the time that this was as complete a little old-world figure as any that might then have been noted there, far or near; yet if I didn't somehow "subtly" feel it, why am

I now so convinced that I must have had familiarly before me a masterpiece of the great Daumier, say, or Henri Monnier, or any other then contemporary projector of Monsieur Prudhomme, the timorous Philistine in a world of dangers, with whom I was later on to make acquaintance? I put myself the question, of scant importance though it may seem; but there is a reflection perhaps more timely than any answer to it. I catch myself in the act of seeing poor anonymous "Dear," as cousin Helen confined herself, her life long, to calling him, in the light of an image arrested by the French genius, and this in truth opens up vistas. I scarce know what it *doesn't* suggest for the fact of sharpness, of intensity of type; which fact in turn leads my imagination almost any dance, making me ask myself quite most of all whether a person so marked by it mustn't really have been a highly finished figure.

That degree of finish was surely rare among us—rare at a time when the charm of so much of the cousinship and the uncleship, the kinship generally, had to be found in their so engagingly dispensing with any finish at all. They happened to be amiable, to be delightful; but—I think I have already put the question—what would have become of us all if they hadn't been? a question the shudder of which could never have been suggested by the presence I am considering. He too was gentle and bland, as it happened—and I indeed see it all as a world quite unfavourable to arrogance or insolence or any hard and high assumption; but the more I think of him (even at the risk of thinking too much) the more I make out in him a tone and a manner that deprecated crude ease. Plenty of this was already in the air, but if he hadn't so spoken of an order in which forms still counted it might scarce have occurred to one that there had ever been any. It comes over me therefore that he testified— and perhaps quite beautifully; I remember his voice and his speech, which were not those of *that* New York at all, and with the echo, faint as it is, arrives the wonder of where he could possibly have picked such things up. They were, as forms, adjusted and settled things; from what finer civilisation therefore had they come down to him? To brood on this the least little bit is verily, as I have said, to open up vistas—out of the depths of one of which fairly glimmers the queerest of questions. Mayn't we accordingly have been, the rest of us, all wrong, and the dim little gentleman the only one among us who was right? May not his truth to type have been a matter that, as mostly typeless ourselves, we neither perceived nor appreciated?—so that if, as is conceivable, he felt and measured the situation and simply chose to be bland and quiet and keep his sense to himself, he was a hero without the laurel as well as a martyr without the crown. The light of which possibility is, however, too fierce; I turn it off, I tear myself from the view—noting further but the one fact in his history that, by my glimpse of it, quite escapes ambiguity. The youthful Albert, I have mentioned, was to resist successfully through those years that solicitation of "Europe" our own response to which, both as a general and a particular solution, kept breaking out in choral wails; but the other house none the less nourished projects so earnest that they could invoke the dignity of comparative silence and patience. The other house didn't aspire to the tongues, but it aspired to the grand tour, of which ours was on many grounds incapable. Only after years and when endless things had happened— Albert having long before, in especial, quite taken up his stake and ostensibly dropped out of the game—did the great adventure get itself enacted, with the effect of one of the liveliest illustrations of the irony of fate. What had most of all flushed through the dream of it during years was the legend, at last quite antediluvian, of the dim little gentleman's early Wanderjahre, that experience of distant lands and seas which would find an application none the less lively for having had long to wait. It had had to wait in truth half a century, yet its confidence had apparently not been impaired when New York, on the happy day, began to recede from view. Europe had surprises, none the less, and who knows to what extent it may after half a century have had shocks? The coming true of the old dream produced at any rate a snap of the tense cord, and the ancient worthy my imagination has, in the tenderest of intentions, thus played with, disembarked in England only to indulge in the last of his startled stares, only to look about him in vague deprecation and give it all up. He just landed and died; but the grand tour was none the less proceeded with—cousin Helen herself, aided by resources personal, social and financial that left nothing to desire, triumphantly performed it, though as with a feeling of delicacy about it firmly overcome.

But it has taken me quite out of the other house, so that I patch up again, at a stroke, that early scene of her double guardianship at which my small wonder assisted. It even then glimmered on me, I think, that if

Albert was, all so romantically, in charge of his aunt—which was a perfectly nondescript relation—so his uncle Henry, her odd brother, was her more or less legal ward, not less, despite his being so very much Albert's senior. In these facts and in the character of each of the three persons involved resided the drama; which must more or less have begun, as I have hinted, when simple-minded Henry, at a date I seem to have seized, definitely emerged from rustication—the Beaverkill had but for a certain term protected, or promoted, his simplicity—and began, on his side, to pace the well-worn field between the Fourteenth Street windows and the piazza of the Isabella grapes. I see him there less vividly than his fellow-pedestrian only because he was afterwards to loom so much larger, whereas his companion, even while still present, was weakly to shrink and fade. At this late day only do I devise for that companion a possible history; the simple-minded Henry's annals on the other hand grew in interest as soon as they became interesting at all. This happened as soon as one took in the ground and some of the features of his tutelage. The basis of it all was that, harmless as he appeared, he was not to be trusted; I remember how portentous that truth soon looked, both in the light of his intense amiability and of sister Helen's absolute certitude. He wasn't to be trusted—it was the sole very definite fact about him except the fact that he had so kindly come down from the far-off Beaverkill to regale us with the perfect demonstration, dutifully, resignedly setting himself among us to point the whole moral himself. He appeared, from the moment we really took it in, to be doing, in the matter, no more than he ought; he exposed himself to our invidious gaze, on this ground, with a humility, a quiet courtesy and an instinctive dignity that come back to me as simply heroic. He had himself accepted, under strenuous suggestion, the dreadful view, and I see him to-day, in the light of the grand dénouement, deferred for long years, but fairly dazzling when it came, as fairly sublime in his decision not to put anyone in the wrong about him a day sooner than he could possibly help. The whole circle of us would in that event be so dreadfully "sold," as to our wisdom and justice, he proving only noble and exquisite. It didn't so immensely matter to him as that, the establishment of his true character didn't; so he went on as if for all the years—and they really piled themselves up: his passing for a dangerous idiot, or at least for a slave of his passions from the moment he was allowed the wherewithal in the least to indulge them, was a less evil for him than seeing us rudely corrected. It was in truth an extraordinary situation and would have offered a splendid subject, as we used to say, to the painter of character, the novelist or the dramatist, with the hand to treat it. After I had read David Copperfield an analogy glimmered—it struck me even in the early time: cousin Henry was more or less another Mr. Dick, just as cousin Helen was in her relation to him more or less another Miss Trotwood. There were disparities indeed: Mr. Dick was the harmless lunatic on that lady's premises, but she admired him and appealed to him; lunatics, in her generous view, might be oracles, and there is no evidence, if I correctly remember, that she kept him low. Our Mr. Dick was suffered to indulge his passions but on ten cents a day, while his fortune, under conscientious, under admirable care— cousin Helen being no less the wise and keen woman of business than the devoted sister—rolled up and became large; likewise Miss Trotwood's inmate hadn't at all the perplexed brooding brow, with the troubled fold in it, that represented poor Henry's only form of criticism of adverse fate. They had alike the large smooth open countenance of those for whom life has been simplified, and if Mr. Dick had had a fortune he would have remained all his days as modestly vague about the figure of it as our relative consented to remain. The latter's interests were agricultural, while his predecessor's, as we remember, were mainly historical; each at any rate had in a general way his Miss Trotwood, not to say his sister Helen.

The good Henry's Miss Trotwood lived and died without an instant's visitation of doubt as to the due exercise of her authority, as to what would happen if it faltered; her victim waiting in the handsomest manner till she had passed away to show us all—all who remained, after so long, to do him justice—that nothing but what was charming and touching could possibly happen. This was, in part at least, the dazzling dénouement I have spoken of: he became, as soon as fortunate dispositions could take effect, the care of our admirable Aunt, between whom and his sister and himself close cousinship, from far back, had practically amounted to sisterhood: by which time the other house had long been another house altogether, its ancient site relinquished, its contents planted afresh far northward, with new traditions invoked, though with that of its great friendliness to all of us, for our mother's sake, still confirmed. Here with brief brightness, clouded at the very last, the solution emerged; we became aware, not without embarrassment, that poor Henry at large and supplied with funds was exactly as harmless and blameless as poor Henry stinted and captive; as to which if anything had been wanting to our confusion or to his own dignity it would have been his supreme abstinence, his suppression of the least "Didn't I tell you?" He didn't even pretend to have told us, when he so abundantly might, and nothing could exceed the grace with which he appeared to have noticed nothing. He "handled" dollars as decently, and just as profusely, as he had handled dimes; the only light shade on the scene—except of course for its being so belated, which did make it pathetically dim—was the question of how nearly he at all measured his resources. Not his heart, but his imagination, in the long years, had been starved; and though he was now all discreetly and wisely encouraged to feel rich, it was rather sadly visible that, thanks to almost half a century of over-discipline, he failed quite to rise to his estate. He did feel rich, just as he felt generous; the misfortune was only in his weak sense for meanings. That, with the whole situation, made delicacy of the first importance; as indeed what was perhaps most striking in the entire connection was the part played by delicacy from the first. It had all been a drama of the delicate: the consummately scrupulous and successful administration of his resources for the benefit of his virtue, so that they could be handed over, in the event, without the leakage of a fraction, what was that but a triumph of delicacy? So delicacy conspired, delicacy surrounded him; the case having been from the early time that, could he only be regarded as sufficiently responsible, could the sources of his bounty be judged fairly open to light pressure (there was question of none but the lightest) that bounty might blessedly flow. This had been Miss Trotwood's own enlightened view, on behalf of one of the oddest and most appealing collections of wistful wondering single gentlewomen that a great calculating benevolence perhaps ever found arrayed before it—ornaments these all of the second and third cousinship and interested spectators of the almost inexpressible facts.

I should have liked completely to express them, in spite of the difficulty— if not indeed just by reason of that; the difficulty of their consisting so much more of "character" than of "incident" (heaven save the artless opposition!)

though this last element figured bravely enough too, thanks to some of the forms taken by our young Albert's wild wilfulness. He was so weak—after the most approved fashion of distressing young men of means—that his successive exhibitions of it had a fine high positive effect, such as would have served beautifully, act after act, for the descent of the curtain. The issue, however (differing in this from the common theatrical trick) depended less on who should die than on who should live; the younger of cousin Helen's pair of wards—putting them even only as vessels of her attempted earnestness—had violently broken away, but a remedy to this grief, for reasons too many to tell, dwelt in the possible duration, could it only not be arrested, of two other lives, one of these her own, the second the guileless Henry's. The single gentlewomen, to a remarkable number, whom she regarded and treated as nieces, though they were only daughters of cousins, were such objects of her tender solicitude that, she and Henry and Albert being alike childless, the delightful thing to think of was, on certain contingencies, the nieces' prospective wealth. There were contingencies of course—and they exactly produced the pity and terror. Her estate would go at her death to her nearest of kin, represented by her brother and nephew; it would be only of her savings—fortunately, with her kind eye on the gentlewomen, zealous and long continued—that she might dispose by will; and it was but a troubled comfort that, should he be living at the time of her death, the susceptible Henry would profit no less than the wanton Albert. Henry was at any cost to be kept in life that he *might* profit; the woeful question, the question of delicacy, for a woman devoutly conscientious, was how could anyone else, how, above all, could fifteen other persons, be made to profit by his profiting? She had been as earnest a steward of her brother's fortune as if directness of pressure on him, in a sense favourable to her interests—that is to her sympathies, which were her only interests—had been a matter of course with her; whereas in fact she would have held it a crime, given his simplicity, to attempt in the least to guide his hand. If he didn't outlive his nephew—and he was older, though, as would appear, so much more virtuous—his inherited property, she being dead, would accrue to that unedifying person. *There* was the pity; and as for the question of the disposition of Henry's savings without the initiative of Henry's intelligence, in that, alas, was the terror. Henry's savings—there had been no terror for her, naturally, in beautifully husbanding his resources *for* him—dangled, naturally, with no small vividness, before the wistful gentlewomen, to whom, if he had but *had* the initiative, he might have made the most princely presents. Such was the oddity, not to say the rather tragic drollery, of the situation: that Henry's idea of a present was ten cents' worth of popcorn, or some similar homely trifle; and that when one had created for him a world of these proportions there was no honest way of inspiring him to write cheques for hundreds; all congruous though these would be with the generosity of his nature as shown by the exuberance of his popcorn. The ideal solution would be his flashing to intelligence just long enough to apprehend the case and, of his own magnanimous movement, sign away everything; but that was a fairy-tale stroke, and the fairies here somehow stood off.

Thus between the wealth of her earnestness and the poverty of her courage—her dread, that is, of exposing herself to a legal process for undue influence—our good lady was not at peace; or, to be exact, was only at such peace as came to her by the free bestowal of her own accumulations during her lifetime and after her death. She predeceased her brother and had the pang of feeling that if half her residuum would be deplorably diverted the other half would be, by the same stroke, imperfectly applied; the artless Henry remained at once so well provided and so dimly inspired. Here was suspense indeed for a last "curtain" but one; and my fancy glows, all expertly, for the disclosure of the final scene, than which nothing could well have been happier, on all the premises, save for a single flaw: the installation in Forty-fourth Street of our admirable aunt, often, through the later years, domiciled there, but now settled to community of life with a touching charge and representing near him his extinguished, *their* extinguished, sister. The too few years that followed were the good man's Indian summer and a very wonderful time—so charmingly it shone forth, for all concerned, that he was a person fitted to adorn, as the phrase is, almost any position. Our admirable aunt, not less devoted and less disinterested than his former protectress, had yet much more imagination; she had enough, in a word, for perfect confidence, and under confidence what remained of poor Henry's life bloomed like a garden freshly watered. Sad alas the fact that so scant a patch was now left. It sufficed, however, and he rose, just in time, to every conception; it was, as I have already noted, as if he had all the while known, as if he had really been a conscious victim to the superstition of his blackness. His final companion recognised, as it were, his powers; and it may be imagined whether when he absolutely himself proposed to benefit the gentlewomen she passed him, or not, the blessed pen. He had taken a year or two to publish by his behaviour the perfection of his civility, and so, on that safe ground, made use of the pen. His competence was afterwards attacked, and it emerged triumphant, exactly as his perfect charity and humility and amenity, and his long inward loneliness, of half a century, did. He had bowed his head and sometimes softly scratched it during that immense period; he had occasionally, after roaming downstairs with the troubled fold in his brow and the difficult, the smothered statement on his lips (his vocabulary was scant and stiff, the vocabulary of pleading explanation, often found too complicated by the witty,) retired once more to his room sometimes indeed for hours, to think it all over again; but had never failed of sobriety or propriety or punctuality or regularity, never failed of one of the virtues his imputed indifference to which had been the ground of his discipline. It was very extraordinary, and of all the stories I know is I think the most beautiful—so far at least as *he* was concerned! The flaw I have mentioned, the one break in the final harmony, was the death of our admirable aunt too soon, shortly before his own and while, taken with illness at the same time, he lay there deprived of her attention. He had that of the gentlewomen, however, two or three of the wisest and tenderest being deputed by the others; and if his original estate reverted at law they presently none the less had occasion to bless his name.

XII

I turn round again to where I last left myself gaping at the old ricketty bill-board in Fifth Avenue; and am almost as sharply aware as ever of the main source of its spell, the fact that it most often blazed with the rich appeal of Mr. Barnum, whose "lecture-room," attached to the Great American Museum, overflowed into posters of all the theatrical bravery disavowed by its title. It was my rueful theory of those days—though tasteful I may call it too as well as rueful—that on all the holidays on which we weren't dragged to the dentist's we attended as a matter of course at Barnum's, that is when we were so happy as to be able to; which, to my own particular consciousness, wasn't every time the case. The case was too often, to my melancholy view, that W. J., quite regularly, on the non-dental Saturdays, repaired to this seat of joy with the easy Albert—*he* at home there and master of the scene to a degree at which, somehow, neither of us could at the best arrive; he quite moulded, truly, in those years of plasticity, as to the æsthetic bent and the determination of curiosity, I seem to make out, by the general Barnum association and revelation. It was not, I hasten to add, that I too didn't, to the extent of my minor chance, drink at the spring; for how else should I have come by the whole undimmed sense of the connection?—the weary waiting, in the dusty halls of humbug, amid bottled mermaids, "bearded ladies" and chill dioramas, for the lecture-room, the true centre of the seat of joy, to open: vivid in especial to me is my almost sick wondering of whether I mightn't be rapt away before it did open. The impression appears to have been mixed; the drinking deep and the holding out, holding out in particular against failure of food and of stage-fares, provision for transport to and fro, being questions equally intense: the appeal of the lecture-room, in its essence a heavy extra, so exhausted our resources that even the sustaining doughnut of the refreshment-counter would mock our desire and the long homeward crawl, the length of Broadway and further, seem to defy repetition. Those desperate days, none the less, affect me now as having flushed with the very complexion of romance; their aches and inanitions were part of the adventure;

the homeward straggle, interminable as it appeared, flowered at moments into rapt contemplations—that for instance of the painted portrait, large as life, of the celebrity of the hour, then "dancing" at the Broadway Theatre, Lola Montes, Countess of Lansfeldt, of a dazzling and unreal beauty and in a riding-habit lavishly open at the throat.

It was thus quite in order that I should pore longest, there at my fondest corner, over the Barnum announcements—my present inability to be superficial about which has given in fact the measure of my contemporary care. These announcements must have been in their way marvels of attractive composition, the placard bristling from top to toe with its analytic "synopsis of scenery and incidents"; the synoptical view cast its net of fine meshes and the very word savoured of incantation. It is odd at the same time that when I question memory as to the living hours themselves, those of the stuffed and dim little hall of audience, smelling of peppermint and orange-peel, where the curtain rose on our gasping but rewarded patience, two performances only stand out for me, though these in the highest relief. Love, or the Countess and the Serf, by J. Sheridan Knowles—I see that still as the blazonry of one of them, just as I see Miss Emily Mestayer, large, red in the face, coifed in a tangle of small, fine, damp-looking short curls and clad in a light-blue garment edged with swans-down, shout at the top of her lungs that a "pur-r-r-se of gold" would be the fair guerdon of the minion who should start on the spot to do her bidding at some desperate crisis that I forget. I forget Huon the serf, whom I yet recall immensely admiring for his nobleness; I forget everyone but Miss Mestayer, who gave form to my conception of the tragic actress at her highest. She had a hooked nose, a great play of nostril, a vast protuberance of bosom and always the "crop" of close moist ringlets; I say always, for I was to see her often again, during a much later phase, the mid-most years of that Boston Museum which aimed at so vastly higher a distinction than the exploded lecture-room had really done, though in an age that snickered even abnormally low it still lacked the courage to call itself a theatre. She must have been in comedy, which I believe she also usefully and fearlessly practised, rather unimaginable; but there was no one like her in the Boston time for cursing queens and eagle-beaked mothers; the Shakespeare of the Booths and other such would have been unproducible without her; she had a rusty, rasping, heaving and tossing "authority" of which the bitterness is still in my ears. I am revisited by an outer glimpse of her in that after age when she had come, comparatively speaking, into her own—the sight of her, accidentally incurred, one tremendously hot summer night, as she slowly moved from her lodgings or wherever, in the high Bowdoin Street region, down to the not distant theatre from which even the temperature had given her no reprieve; and well remember how, the queer light of my young impression playing up again in her path, she struck me as the very image of mere sore histrionic habit and use, a worn and weary, a battered even though almost sordidly smoothed, *thing* of the theatre, very much as an old infinitely-handled and greasy violoncello of the orchestra might have been. It was but an effect doubtless of the heat that she scarcely seemed clad at all; slippered, shuffling and, though somehow hatted and vaguely veiled or streamered, wrapt in a gauzy sketch of a dressing-gown, she pointed to my extravagant attention the moral of thankless personal service, of the reverse of the picture, of the cost of "amusing the public" in a case of amusing it, as who should say, every hour. And I had thrilled before her as the Countess in "Love"—such contrasted combinations! But she carried her head very high, as with the habit of crowns and trains and tirades—had in fact much the air of some deposed and reduced sovereign living on a scant allowance; so that, all invisibly and compassionately, I took off my hat to her.

To which I must add the other of my two Barnumite scenic memories, my having anciently admired her as the Eliza of Uncle Tom's Cabin, her swelling bust encased in a neat cotton gown and her flight across the ice-blocks of the Ohio, if I rightly remember the perilous stream, intrepidly and gracefully performed. We lived and moved at that time, with great intensity, in Mrs. Stowe's novel—which, recalling my prompt and charmed acquaintance with it, I should perhaps substitute for The Initials, earlier mentioned here, as my first experiment in grown-up fiction. There was, however, I think, for that triumphant work no classified condition; it was for no sort of reader as distinct from any other sort, save indeed for Northern as differing from Southern: it knew the large felicity of gathering in alike the small and the simple and the big and the wise, and had above all the extraordinary fortune of finding itself, for an immense number of people, much less a book than a state of vision, of feeling and of consciousness, in which they didn't sit and read and appraise and pass the time, but walked and talked and laughed and cried and, in a manner of which Mrs. Stowe was the irresistible cause, generally conducted themselves. Appreciation and judgment, the whole impression, were thus an effect for which there had been no process—any process so related having in other cases *had* to be at some point or other critical; nothing in the guise of a written book, therefore, a book printed, published, sold, bought and "noticed," probably ever reached its mark, the mark of exciting interest, without having at least groped for that goal *as* a book or by the exposure of some literary side. Letters, here, languished unconscious, and Uncle Tom, instead of making even one of the cheap short cuts through the medium in which books breathe, even as fishes in water, went gaily roundabout it altogether, as if a fish, a wonderful "leaping" fish, had simply flown through the air. This feat accomplished, the surprising creature could naturally fly anywhere, and one of the first things it did was thus to flutter down on every stage, literally without exception, in America and Europe. If the amount of life represented in such a work is measurable by the ease with which representation is taken up and carried further, carried even violently furthest, the fate of Mrs. Stowe's picture was conclusive: it simply sat down wherever it lighted and made itself, so to speak, at home; thither multitudes flocked afresh and there, in each case, it rose to its height again and went, with all its vivacity and good faith, through all its motions.

These latter were to leave me, however, with a fonder vision still than that of the comparatively jejune "lecture-room" version; for the first exhibition of them to spring to the front was the fine free rendering achieved at a playhouse till then ignored by fashion and culture, the National Theatre, deep down on the East side, whence echoes had come faintest to ears polite, but where a sincerity vivid though rude was now supposed to reward the curious. Our numerous attendance there under this spell was my first experience of the "theatre party" as we have enjoyed it in our time—each emotion and impression of which is as fresh to me as the most recent of the same family. Precious through all indeed perhaps is the sense, strange only to later sophistication, of my small encouraged state as a free playgoer—a state doubly wondrous while I thus evoke the full contingent from Union Square; where, for that matter, I think, the wild evening must have been planned. I am lost again in all the goodnature from which small boys, on wild evenings, could dangle so unchidden—since the state of unchiddenness is what comes back to me well-nigh clearest. How without that complacency of conscience could every felt impression so live again? It is true that for my present sense of the matter snubs and raps would still tingle, would count double; just wherefore it is exactly, however, that I mirror myself in these depths of propriety. The social scheme, as we knew it, was, in its careless charity, worthy of the golden age— though I can't sufficiently repeat that we knew it both at its easiest and its safest: the fruits dropped right upon the board to which we flocked together, the least of us and the greatest, with differences of appetite and of reach, doubtless, but not with differences of place and of proportionate share. My appetite and my reach in respect to the more full-bodied Uncle Tom might have brooked certainly any comparison; I must have partaken thoroughly of the feast to have left the various aftertastes so separate and so strong. It was a great thing to have a canon to judge by—it helped conscious criticism, which was to fit on wings (for use ever after) to the shoulders of appreciation. In the light of that advantage I could be *sure* my second Eliza was less dramatic than my first, and that my first "Cassy," that of the great and blood-curdling Mrs. Bellamy of the lecture-room, touched depths which made the lady at the National prosaic and placid (I could already be "down" on a placid Cassy;) just as on the other hand the rocking of the ice-floes of the Ohio, with the desperate Eliza, infant in arms, balancing for a leap from one to the other, had here less of the audible creak of carpentry, emulated a trifle more, to my perception, the real water of Mr. Crummles's pump. They can't, even at that, have emulated it much, and one almost envies (quite making up one's mind not to denounce) the simple faith of an age beguiled by arts so rude.

However, the point exactly was that we attended this spectacle just in order *not* to be beguiled, just in order to enjoy with ironic detachment and, at the very most, to be amused ourselves at our sensibility should it prove to have been trapped and caught. To have become thus aware of our collective attitude constituted for one small spectator at least a great initiation; he got his first glimpse of that possibility of a "free play of mind" over a subject which was to throw him with force at a later stage of culture, when subjects had considerably multiplied, into the critical arms of Matthew Arnold. So he is himself at least interested in seeing the matter—as a progress in which the first step was taken, before that crude scenic appeal, by his wondering, among his companions, where the absurd, the absurd for *them*, ended and the fun, the real fun, which was the gravity, the tragedy, the drollery, the beauty, the thing itself, briefly, might be legitimately and tastefully held to begin. Uncanny though the remark perhaps, I am not sure I wasn't thus more interested in the pulse of our party, under my tiny recording thumb, than in the beat of the drama and the shock of its opposed forces—vivid and touching as the contrast was then found for instance between the tragi-comical Topsy, the slave-girl clad in a pinafore of sackcloth and destined to become for Anglo-Saxon millions the type of the absolute in the artless, and her little mistress the blonde Eva, a figure rather in the Kenwigs tradition of pantalettes and pigtails, whom I recall as perching quite suicidally, with her elbows out and a preliminary shriek, on that bulwark of the Mississippi steamboat which was to facilitate her all but fatal immersion in the flood. Why should I have duly noted that no little game on her part could well less have resembled or simulated an accident, and yet have been no less moved by her reappearance, rescued from the river but perfectly dry, in the arms of faithful Tom, who had plunged in to save her, without either so much as wetting his shoes, than if I had been engaged with her in a reckless romp? I could count the white stitches in the loose patchwork, and yet could take it for a story rich and harmonious; I could know we had all intellectually condescended and that we had yet had the thrill of an æsthetic adventure; and this was a brave beginning for a consciousness that was to be nothing if not mixed and a curiosity that was to be nothing if not restless.

The principle of this prolonged arrest, which I insist on prolonging a little further, is doubtless in my instinct to grope for our earliest æsthetic seeds. Careless at once and generous the hands by which they were sown, but practically appointed none the less to cause that peculiarly flurried hare to run—flurried because over ground so little native to it—when so many others held back. Is it *that* air of romance that gilds for me then the Barnum background—taking it as a symbol; that makes me resist, to this effect of a passionate adverse loyalty, any impulse to translate into harsh terms any old sordidities and poverties? The Great American Museum, the down-town scenery and aspects at large, and even the up-town improvements on them, as then flourishing?—why, they must have been for the most part of the last meanness: the Barnum picture above all ignoble and awful, its blatant face or frame stuck about with innumerable flags that waved, poor vulgar-sized ensigns, over spurious relics and catchpenny monsters in effigy, to say nothing of the promise within of the still more monstrous and abnormal living—from the total impression of which things we plucked somehow the flower of the ideal. It grew, I must in justice proceed, much more sweetly and naturally at Niblo's, which represented in our scheme the ideal evening, while Barnum figured the ideal day; so that I ask myself, with that sense of our resorting there under the rich cover of night (which was the supreme charm,) how it comes that this larger memory hasn't swallowed up all others. For here, absolutely, *was* the flower at its finest and grown as nowhere else—grown in the great garden of the Ravel Family and offered again and again to our deep inhalation. I see the Ravels, French acrobats, dancers and pantomimists, as representing, for our culture, pure grace and charm and civility; so that one doubts whether any candid community was ever so much in debt to a race of entertainers or had so happy and prolonged, so personal and grateful a relation with them. They must have been, with their offshoots of Martinettis and others, of three or four generations, besides being of a rich theatrical stock generally, and we had our particular friends and favourites among them; we seemed to follow them through every phase of their career, to assist at their tottering steps along the tight-rope as very small children kept in equilibrium by very big balancing-poles (caretakers here walking under in case of falls;) to greet them as Madame Axel, of robust maturity and in a Spanish costume, bounding on the same tense cord more heavily but more assuredly; and finally to know the climax of the art with them in Raoul or the Night-Owl and Jocko or the Brazilian Ape—and all this in the course of our own brief infancy. My impression of them bristles so with memories that we seem to have rallied to their different productions with much the same regularity with which we formed fresh educational connections; and they were so much our property and our pride that they supported us handsomely through all fluttered entertainment of the occasional Albany cousins. I remember how when one of these visitors, wound up, in honour of New York, to the very fever of perception, broke out one evening while we waited for the curtain to rise, "Oh don't you hear the cries? They're *beating* them, I'm sure they are; can't it be stopped?" we resented the charge as a slur on our very honour; for what our romantic relative had heatedly imagined to reach us, in a hushed-up manner from behind, was the sounds attendant on the application of blows to some acrobatic infant who had "funked" his little job. Impossible such horrors in the world of pure poetry opened out to us at Niblo's, a temple of illusion, of tragedy and comedy and pathos that, though its *abords* of stony brown Metropolitan Hotel, on the "wrong side," must have been bleak and vulgar, flung its glamour forth into Broadway. What more pathetic for instance, so that we publicly wept, than the fate of wondrous Martinetti Jocko, who, after befriending a hapless French family wrecked on the coast of Brazil and bringing back to life a small boy rescued from the waves (I see even now, with every detail, this inanimate victim supine on the strand) met his death by some cruel bullet of which I have forgotten the determinant cause, only remembering the final agony as something we could scarce bear and a strain of our sensibility to which our parents repeatedly questioned the wisdom of exposing us.

These performers and these things were in all probability but of a middling skill and splendour—it was the pre-trapèze age, and we were caught by mild marvels, even if a friendly good faith in them, something sweet and sympathetic, was after all a value, whether of their own humanity, their own special quality, or only of our innocence, never to be renewed; but I light this taper to the initiators, so to call them, whom I remembered, when we had left them behind, as if they had given us a silver key to carry off and so to refit, after long years, to sweet names never thought of from then till now. Signor Léon Javelli, in whom the French and the Italian charm appear to have met, who was he, and what did he brilliantly do, and why of a sudden do I thus recall and admire him? I am afraid he but danced the tight-rope, the most domestic of our friends' resources, as it brought them out, by the far stretch of the rope, into the bosom of the house and against our very hearts, where they leapt and bounded and wavered and recovered closely face to face with us; but I dare say he bounded, brave Signor Léon, to the greatest height of all: let this vague agility, in any case, connect him with that revelation of the ballet, the sentimental-pastoral, of other years, which, in The Four Lovers for example, a pantomimic lesson as in words of one syllable, but all quick and gay and droll, would have affected us as classic, I am sure, had we then had at our disposal that term of appreciation. When we read in English story-books about the pantomimes in London, which somehow cropped up in them so often, those were the only things that didn't make us yearn; so much we felt we were masters of the type, and so almost sufficiently was that a stop-gap for London constantly deferred. We hadn't the transformation-scene, it was true, though what this really seemed to come to was clown and harlequin taking liberties with policemen—these last evidently a sharp note in a picturesqueness that we lacked, our own slouchy "officers" saying nothing to us of that sort; but we had at Niblo's harlequin and columbine, albeit of less pure a tradition, and we knew moreover all about clowns, for we went to circuses too, and so repeatedly that when I add them to our list of recreations, the good old orthodox circuses under tents set up in vacant lots, with which New York appears at that time to have bristled, time and place would seem to have shrunken for most other pursuits, and not least for that of serious learning. And the case is aggravated as I remember Franconi's, which we more or less haunted and which, aiming at the grander style and the monumental effect, blazed with fresh paint and rang with Roman chariot-races up there among the deserts of Twenty-ninth Street or wherever; considerably south, perhaps, but only a little east, of the vaster desolations that gave scope to the Crystal Palace, second of its name since, following—not *passibus æquis*, alas—the London structure of 1851, this enterprise forestalled by a year or two the Paris Palais de l'Industrie of 1855. Such as it was I feel again its majesty on those occasions on which I dragged— if I must here once more speak for myself only—after Albany cousins through its courts of edification: I remember being very tired and cold and hungry there, in a little light drab and very glossy or shiny "talma" breasted with rather troublesome buttonhole-embroideries; though concomitantly conscious that I was somehow in Europe, since everything about me had been "brought over," which ought to have been consoling, and seems in fact to have been so in some degree, inasmuch as both my own pain and the sense of the cousinly, the Albany, headaches quite fade in that recovered presence of big European

Art embodied in Thorwaldsen's enormous Christ and the Disciples, a shining marble company ranged in a semicircle of dark maroon walls. If this was Europe then Europe was beautiful indeed, and we rose to it on the wings of wonder; never were we afterwards to see great showy sculpture, in whatever profuse exhibition or of whatever period or school, without some renewal of that charmed Thorwaldsen hour, some taste again of the almost sugary or confectionery sweetness with which the great white images had affected us under their supper-table gaslight. The Crystal Palace was vast and various and dense, which was what Europe was going to be; it was a deep-down jungle of impressions that were somehow challenges, even as we might, helplessly defied, find foreign words and practices; over which formidably towered Kiss's mounted Amazon attacked by a leopard or whatever, a work judged at that day sublime and the glory of the place; so that I felt the journey back in the autumn dusk and the Sixth Avenue cars (established just in time) a relapse into soothing flatness, a return to the Fourteenth Street horizon from a far journey and a hundred looming questions that would still, tremendous thought, come up for all the personal answers of which one cultivated the seed.

XIII

Let me hurry, however, to catch again that thread I left dangling from my glance at our small vague spasms of school—my personal sense of them being as vague and small, I mean, in contrast with the fuller and stronger cup meted out all round to the Albany cousins, much more privileged, I felt, in every stroke of fortune; or at least much more interesting, though it might be wicked to call them more happy, through those numberless bereavements that had so enriched their existence. I mentioned above in particular the enviable consciousness of our little red-headed kinsman Gus Barker, who, as by a sharp prevision, snatched what gaiety he might from a life to be cut short, in a cavalry dash, by one of the Confederate bullets of 1863: he blew out at us, on New York Sundays, as I have said, sharp puffs of the atmosphere of the Institution Charlier—strong to us, that is, the atmosphere of whose institutions was weak; but it was above all during a gregarious visit paid him in a livelier field still that I knew myself merely mother'd and brother'd. It had been his fate to be but scantly the latter and never at all the former—our aunt Janet had not survived his birth; but on this day of our collective pilgrimage to Sing-Sing, where he was at a "military" school and clad in a fashion that represented to me the very panoply of war, he shone with a rare radiance of privation. Ingenuous and responsive, of a social disposition, a candour of gaiety, that matched his physical activity—the most beautifully made athletic little person, and in the highest degree appealing and engaging—he not only did us the honours of his dazzling academy (dazzling at least to me) but had all the air of showing us over the great State prison which even then flourished near at hand and to which he accompanied us; a party of a composition that comes back to me as wonderful, the New York and Albany cousinships appearing to have converged and met, for the happy occasion, with the generations and sexes melting together and moving in a loose harmonious band. The party must have been less numerous than by the romantic tradition or confused notation of my youth, and what I mainly remember of it beyond my sense of our being at once an attendant train to my aged and gentle and in general most unadventurous grandmother, and a chorus of curiosity and amusement roundabout the vivid Gussy, is our collective impression that State prisons were on the whole delightful places, vast, bright and breezy, with a gay, free circulation in corridors and on stairs, a pleasant prevalence of hot soup and fresh crusty rolls, in tins, of which visitors admiringly partook, and for the latter, in chance corners and on sunny landings, much interesting light brush of gentlemen remarkable but for gentlemanly crimes—that is defalcations and malversations to striking and impressive amounts.

I recall our coming on such a figure at the foot of a staircase and his having been announced to us by our conductor or friend in charge as likely to be there; and what a charm I found in his cool loose uniform of shining white (as I was afterwards to figure it,) as well as in his generally refined and distinguished appearance and in the fact that he was engaged, while exposed to our attention, in the commendable act of paring his nails with a smart penknife and that he didn't allow us to interrupt him. One of my companions, I forget which, had advised me that in these contacts with illustrious misfortune I was to be careful not to stare; and present to me at this moment is the wonder of whether he would think it staring to note that *he* quite stared, and also that his hands were fine and fair and one of them adorned with a signet ring. I was to have later in life a glimpse of two or three dismal penitentiaries, places affecting me as sordid, as dark and dreadful; but if the revelation of Sing-Sing had involved the idea of a timely warning to the young mind my small sensibility at least was not reached by the lesson. I envied the bold-eyed celebrity in the array of a planter at his ease—we might have been *his* slaves—quite as much as I envied Gussy; in connection with which I may remark here that though in that early time I seem to have been constantly eager to exchange my lot for that of somebody else, on the assumed certainty of gaining by the bargain, I fail to remember feeling jealous of such happier persons—in the measure open to children of spirit. I had rather a positive lack of the passion, and thereby, I suppose, a lack of spirit; since if jealousy bears, as I think, on what one sees one's companions able to do—as against one's own falling short—envy, as I knew it at least, was simply of what they *were*, or in other words of a certain sort of richer consciousness supposed, doubtless often too freely supposed, in them. They were so *other*—

that was what I felt; and to *be* other, other almost anyhow, seemed as good as the probable taste of the bright compound wistfully watched in the confectioner's window; unattainable, impossible, of course, but as to which just this impossibility and just that privation kept those active proceedings in which jealousy seeks relief quite out of the question. A platitude of acceptance of the poor actual, the absence of all vision of how in any degree to change it, combined with a complacency, an acuity of perception of alternatives, though a view of them as only through the confectioner's hard glass—that is what I recover as the nearest approach to an apology, in the soil of my nature, for the springing seed of emulation. I never dreamed of competing—a business having in it at the best, for my temper, if not for my total failure of temper, a displeasing ferocity. If competing was bad snatching was therefore still worse, and jealousy was a sort of spiritual snatching. With which, nevertheless, all the while, one might have been "like" So-and-So, who had such horizons. A helpless little love of horizons I certainly cherished, and could sometimes even care for my own. These always shrank, however, under almost any suggestion of a further range or finer shade in the purple rim offered to other eyes—and that is what I take for the restlessness of envy. It wasn't that I wished to change with everyone, with anyone at a venture, but that I saw "gifts" everywhere but as mine and that I scarce know whether to call the effect of this miserable or monstrous. It was the effect at least of self-abandonment—I mean to visions.

There must have been on that occasion of the Sing-Sing day—which it deeply interests me to piece together—some state of connection for some of us with the hospitalities of Rhinebeck, the place of abode of the eldest of the Albany uncles—that is of the three most in our view; for there were two others, the eldest of all a half-uncle only, who formed a class quite by himself, and the very youngest, who, with lively interests of his own, had still less attention for us than either of his three brothers. The house at Rhinebeck and all its accessories (which struck our young sense as innumerable,) in especial the great bluff of the Hudson on which it stood, yields me images scarcely dimmed, though as the effect but of snatches of acquaintance; there at all events the gently-groaning—ever so gently and dryly—Albany grandmother, with the Albany cousins as to whom I here discriminate, her two adopted daughters, maturest and mildest of the general tribe, must have paused for a stay; a feature of which would be perhaps her juncture with the New York contingent, somewhere sociably achieved, for the befriending of juvenile Gussy. It shimmers there, the whole circumstance, with I scarce know what large innocence of charity and ease; the Gussy-pretext, for reunion, all so thin yet so important an appeal, the simplicity of the interests and the doings, the assumptions and the concessions, each to-day so touching, almost so edifying. We were surely all gentle and generous together, floating in such a clean light social order, sweetly proof against ennui—unless it be a bad note, as is conceivable, never, *never* to feel bored—and thankful for the smallest æsthetic or romantic mercies. My vision loses itself withal in vaster connections— above all in my general sense of the then grand newness of the Hudson River Railroad; so far at least as its completion to Albany was concerned, a modern blessing that even the youngest of us were in a position to appraise. The time had been when the steamboat had to content us—and I feel how amply it must have done so as I recall the thrill of docking in dim early dawns, the whole hour of the Albany waterside, the night of huge strange paddling and pattering and shrieking and creaking once ended, and contrast with it all certain long sessions in the train at an age and in conditions when neither train nor traveller had suffered chastening; sessions of a high animation, as I recast them, but at the same time of mortal intensities of lassitude. The elements here indeed are much confused and mixed—I must have known that discipline of the hectic interest and the extravagant strain in relation to Rhinebeck only; an *étape*, doubtless, on the way to New York, for the Albany kinship, but the limit to our smaller patiences of any northward land-journey. And yet not the young fatigue, I repeat, but the state of easy wonder, is what most comes back: the stops too repeated, but perversely engaging; the heat and the glare too great, but the river, by the window, making reaches and glimpses, so that the great swing of picture and force of light and colour were themselves a constant adventure; the uncles, above all, too pre-eminent, too recurrent, to the creation of a positive soreness of sympathy, of curiosity, and yet constituting by their presence half the enlargement of the time. For the presence of uncles, incoherent Albany uncles, is somehow what most gives these hours their stamp for memory. I scarce know why, nor do I much, I confess, distinguish occasions—but I see what I see: the long, the rattling car of the old open native form and the old harsh native exposure; the sense of arrival forever postponed, qualified however also by that of having in my hands a volume of M. Arsène Houssaye, Philosophes et Comédiennes, remarkably submitted by one of my relatives to my judgment. I see them always, the relatives, in slow circulation; restless and nervous and casual their note, not less than strikingly genial, but with vaguenesses, lapses, eclipses, that deprived their society of a tactless weight. They cheered us on, in their way; born optimists, clearly, if not logically determined ones, they were always reassuring and sustaining, though with a bright brevity that must have taken immensities, I think, for granted. They wore their hats slightly toward the nose, they strolled, they hung about, they reported of progress and of the company, they dropped suggestions, new magazines, packets of the edible deprecated for the immature; they figured in fine to a small nephew as the principal men of their time and, so far as the two younger and more familiar were concerned, the most splendid as to aspect and apparel. It was none the less to the least shining, though not essentially the least comforting, of this social trio that, if I rightly remember, I owed my introduction to the *chronique galante* of the eighteenth century.

There tags itself at any rate to the impression a flutter as of some faint, some recaptured, grimace for another of his kindly offices (which I associate somehow with the deck of a steamboat:) his production for our vague benefit of a literary classic, the Confessions, as he called our attention to them, of the celebrated "Rosseau" I catch again the echo of the mirth excited, to my surprise, by this communication, and recover as well my responsive advance toward a work that seemed so to promise; but especially have I it before me that some play of light criticism mostly attended, on the part of any circle, this speaker's more ambitious remarks. For all that, and in spite of oddities of appearance and type, it was Augustus James who spread widest, in default of towering highest, to my wistful view of the larger life, and who covered definite and accessible ground. This ground, the house and precincts of Linwood, at Rhinebeck, harboured our tender years, I surmise, but at few and brief moments; but it hadn't taken many of these to make it the image of an hospitality liberal as I supposed great social situations were liberal; suppositions on this score having in childhood (or at least they had in mine) as little as possible to do with dry data. Didn't Linwood bristle with great views and other glories, with gardens and graperies and black ponies, to say nothing of gardeners and grooms who were notoriously and quotedly droll; to say nothing, in particular, of our aunt Elizabeth, who had been Miss Bay of Albany, who was the mother of the fair and free young waltzing-women in New York, and who floats back to me through the Rhinebeck picture, aquiline but easy, with an effect of handsome highbrowed, high-nosed looseness, of dressing-gowns or streaming shawls (the dowdy, the delightful shawl of the period;) and of claws of bright benevolent steel that kept nipping for our charmed advantage: roses and grapes and peaches and currant-clusters, together with turns of phrase and scraps of remark that fell as by quite a like flash of shears. These are mere scrapings of gold-dust, but my mind owes her a vibration that, however tiny, was to insist all these years on *marking*—on figuring in a whole complex of picture and drama, the clearest note of which was that of worry and woe: a crisis prolonged, in deep-roofed outer galleries, through hot August evenings and amid the dim flare of open windows, to the hum of domesticated insects. All but inexpressible the part played, in the young mind naturally even though perversely, even though inordinately, arranged as a stage for the procession and exhibition of appearances, by matters all of a usual cast, contacts and impressions not arriving at the dignity of shocks, but happening to be to the taste, as one may say, of the little intelligence, happening to be such as the fond fancy could assimilate. One's record becomes, under memories of this order—and that is the only trouble—a tale of assimilations small and fine; out of which refuse, directly interesting to the subject-victim only, the most branching vegetations may be conceived as having sprung. Such are the absurdities of the poor dear inward life—when translated, that is, and perhaps ineffectually translated, into terms of the outward and trying at all to flourish on the lines of the outward; a reflection that might stay me here weren't it that I somehow feel morally affiliated, tied as by knotted fibres, to the elements involved.

One of these was assuredly that my father had again, characteristically, suffered me to dangle; he having been called to Linwood by the dire trouble of his sister, Mrs. Temple, and brought me with him from Staten Island—I make the matter out as of the summer of '54. We had come up, he and I, to New York; but our doings there, with the journey following, are a blank to me; I recover but my sense, on our arrival, of being for the first time in the presence of tragedy, which the shining scene, roundabout, made more sinister—sharpened even to the point of my feeling abashed and irrelevant, wondering why I had come. My aunt, under her brother's roof, had left her husband, wasted with consumption, near death at Albany; gravely ill herself— she had taken the disease from him as it was taken in those days, and was in the event very scantly to survive him—she had been ordered away in her own interest, for which she cared no scrap, and my father, the person in all his family most justly appealed and most anxiously listened to, had been urged to come and support her in a separation that she passionately rejected. Vivid to me still, as floating across verandahs into the hot afternoon stillness, is the wail of her protest and her grief; I remember being scared and hushed by it and stealing away beyond its reach. I remember not less what resources of high control the whole case imputed, for my imagination, to my father; and how, creeping off to the edge of the eminence above the Hudson, I somehow felt the great bright harmonies of air and space becoming one with my rather proud assurance and confidence, that of my own connection, for life, for interest, with such sources of light. The great impression, however, the one that has brought me so far, was another matter: only that of the close, lamp-tempered, outer evening aforesaid, with my parent again, somewhere deep within, yet not too far to make us hold our breath for it, tenderly opposing his sister's purpose of flight, and the presence at my side of my young cousin Marie, youngest daughter of the house, exactly of my own age, and named in honour of her having been born in Paris, to the influence of which fact her shining black eyes, her small quickness and brownness, marking sharply her difference from her sisters, so oddly, so almost extravagantly testified. It had come home to me by some voice of the air that she was "spoiled," and it made her in the highest degree interesting; we ourselves had been so associated, at home, without being in the least spoiled (I think we even rather missed it:) so that I knew about these subjects of invidious reflection only by literature—mainly, no doubt, that of the nursery—in which they formed, quite by themselves, a romantic class; and, the fond fancy always predominant, I prized even while a little dreading the chance to see the condition at work. This chance was given me, it was clear—though I risk in my record of it a final anticlimax—by a remark from my uncle Augustus to his daughter: seated duskily in our group, which included two or three dim dependent forms, he expressed the strong opinion that Marie should go to bed—expressed it, that is, with the casual cursory humour that was to strike me as the main expressional resource of outstanding members of the family and that would perhaps have had under analysis the defect of making judgment very personal without quite making authority so. Authority they hadn't, of a truth, these all so human outstanding ones; they made shift but with light appreciation, sudden suggestion, a peculiar variety of happy remark in the air. It had been remarked but in the air, I feel sure, that Marie should seek her couch—a truth by the dark wing of which I ruefully felt myself brushed; and the words seemed therefore to fall with a certain ironic weight. What I have retained of their effect, at any rate, is the vague fact of some objection raised by my cousin and some sharper point to his sentence supplied by her father; promptly merged in a visible commotion, a flutter of my young companion across the gallery as for refuge in the maternal arms, a protest and an appeal in short which drew from my aunt the simple phrase that was from that moment so preposterously to "count" for me. "Come now, my dear; don't make a scene—I *insist* on your not making a scene!" That was all the witchcraft the occasion used, but the note was none the less epoch-making. The expression, so vivid, so portentous, was one I had never heard—it had never been addressed to us at home; and who should say now what a world one mightn't at once read into it? It seemed freighted to sail so far; it told me so much about life. Life at these intensities clearly became "scenes"; but the great thing, the immense illumination, was that we could make them or not as we chose. It was a long time of course before I began to distinguish between those within our compass more particularly as spoiled and those producible on a different basis and which should involve detachment, involve presence of mind; just the qualities in which Marie's possible output was apparently deficient. It didn't in the least matter accordingly whether or no a scene *was* then proceeded to—and I have lost all count of what immediately happened. The mark had been made for me and the door flung open; the passage, gathering up *all* the elements of the troubled time, had been itself a scene, quite enough of one, and I had become aware with it of a rich accession of possibilities.

XIV

It must have been after the Sing-Sing episode that Gussy came to us, in New York, for Sundays and holidays, from scarce further off than round the corner—his foreign Institution flourishing, I seem to remember, in West Tenth Street or wherever—and yet as floated by exotic airs and with the scent of the spice-islands hanging about him. He was being educated largely with Cubans and Mexicans, in those New York days more than half the little flock of the foreign Institutions in general; over whom his easy triumphs, while he wagged his little red head for them, were abundantly credible; reinforced as my special sense of them was moreover by the similar situation of his sister, older than he but also steeped in the exotic medium and also sometimes bringing us queer echoes of the tongues. I remember being deputed by my mother to go and converse with her, on some question of her coming to us, at the establishment of Madame Reichhardt (pronounced, à la française, Réchard,) where I felt that I had crossed, for the hour, the very threshold of "Europe"; it being impressed on me by my cousin, who was tall and handsome and happy, with a laugh of more beautiful sound than any laugh we were to know again, that French only was speakable on the premises. I sniffed it up aromatically, the superior language, in passage and parlour—it took the form of some strong savoury soup, an educational *potage Réchard* that must excellently have formed the taste: that was again, I felt as I came away, a part of the rich experience of being thrown in tender juvenile form upon the world. This genial girl, like her brother, was in the grand situation of having no home and of carrying on life, such a splendid kind of life, by successive visits to relations; though neither she nor Gussy quite achieved the range of their elder brother, "Bob" of that ilk, a handsome young man, a just blurred, attractive, illusive presence, who hovered a bit beyond our real reach and apparently displayed the undomesticated character at its highest. *He* seemed exposed, for his pleasure—if pleasure it was!—and my wonder, to every assault of experience; his very name took on, from these imputations, a browner glow; and it was all in the right key that, a few years later, he should, after "showing some talent for sculpture," have gone the hapless way of most of the Albany youth, have become a theme for sad vague headshakes (kind and very pitying in his case) and died prematurely and pointlessly, or in other words, by my conception, picturesquely. The headshakes were heavier and the sighs sharper for another slim shade, one of the younger and I believe quite the most hapless of those I have called the outstanding ones; he too, several years older than we again, a tormenting hoverer and vanisher; he too charmingly sister'd, though sister'd only, and succumbing to monstrous early trouble after having "shown some talent" for music. The ghostliness of these æsthetic manifestations, as I allude to them, is the thinnest conceivable chip of stray marble, the faintest far-off twang of old chords; I ask myself, for the odd obscurity of it, under what inspiration music and sculpture may have tinkled and glimmered to the Albany ear and eye (as we at least knew those organs) and with what queer and weak delusions our unfortunates may have played. Quite ineffably quaint and *falot* this proposition of *that* sort of resource for the battle of life as it then and there opened; and above all beautifully suggestive of our sudden collective disconnectedness (ours as the whole kinship's) from *the* American resource of those days, Albanian or other. That precious light was the light of "business" only; and we, by a common instinct, artlessly joining hands, went forth into the wilderness without so much as a twinkling taper.

Our consensus, on all this ground, was amazing—it brooked no exception; the word had been passed, all round, that we didn't, that we couldn't and shouldn't, understand these things, questions of arithmetic and of fond calculation, questions of the counting-house and the market; and we appear to have held to our agreement as loyally and to have accepted our doom as serenely as if our faith had been mutually pledged. The rupture with my grandfather's tradition and attitude was complete; we were never in a single case, I think, for two generations, guilty of a stroke of business; the most that could be said of us was that, though about equally wanting, all round, in any faculty of acquisition, we happened to pay for the amiable weakness less in some connections than in others. The point was that we moved so oddly and consistently—as it was our only form of consistency—over our limited pasture, never straying to nibble in the strange or the steep places. What was the matter with us under this spell, and what the moral might have been for our case, are issues of small moment, after all, in face of the fact of our mainly so brief duration. It was given to but few of us to be taught by the event, to be made to wonder with the last intensity what *had* been the matter. This it would be interesting to worry out, might I take the time; for the story wouldn't be told, I conceive, by any mere rueful glance at other avidities, the preference for ease, the play of the passions, the appetite for pleasure. These things have often accompanied the business imagination; just as the love of life and the love of other persons, and of many of the things of the world, just as quickness of soul and sense, have again and again not excluded it. However, it comes back, as I have already hinted, to the manner in which the "things of the world" could but present themselves; there were not enough of these, and they were not fine and fair enough, to engage happily so much unapplied, so much loose and crude attention. We hadn't doubtless at all a complete play of intelligence—if I may not so far discriminate as to say *they* hadn't; or our lack of the instinct of the market needn't have been so much worth speaking of: other curiosities, other sympathies might have redressed the balance. I make out our young cousin J. J. as dimly aware of this while composing the light melodies that preluded to his extinction, and which that catastrophe so tried to admonish us to think of as promising; but his image is more present to me still as the great incitement, during the few previous years, to our constant dream of "educational" relief, of some finer kind of social issue, through Europe.

It was to Europe J. J. had been committed; he was over there forging the small apologetic arms that were so little to avail him, but it was quite enough for us that he pointed the way to the Pension Sillig, at Vevey, which shone at us, from afar, as our own more particular solution. It was true that the Pension Sillig figured mainly as the solution in cases of recognised wildness; there long flourished among New York parents whose view of such resources had the proper range a faith in it for that complaint; and it was as an act of faith that, failing other remedies, our young wifeless uncle, conscious himself of no gift for control or for edification, had placed there his difficult son. He returned with delight from this judicious course and there was an hour when we invoked, to intensity, a similar one in our own interest and when the air of home did little but reflect from afar the glitter of blue Swiss lakes, the tinkle of cattle-bells in Alpine pastures, the rich *bonhomie* that M. Sillig, dispensing an education all of milk and honey and edelweiss and ranz-des-vaches, combined with his celebrated firmness for tough subjects. Poor J. J. came back, I fear, much the same subject that he went; but he had verily performed his scant office on earth, that of having brought our then prospect, our apparent possibility, a trifle nearer. He seemed to have been wild even beyond M. Sillig's measure—which was highly disappointing; but if we might on the other hand be open to the reproach of falling too short of it there were establishments adapted to every phase of the American predicament; so that our general direction could but gain in vividness. I think with compassion, altogether, of the comparative obscurity to which our eventual success in gathering the fruits, few and scant though they might be, thus relegates those to whom it was given but to toy so briefly with the flowers. They make collectively their tragic trio: J. J. the elder, most loved, most beautiful, most sacrificed of the Albany uncles; J. J. the younger—they were young together, they were luckless together, and the combination was as strange as the disaster was sweeping; and the daughter and sister, amplest of the "natural," easiest of the idle, who lived on to dress their memory with every thread and patch of her own perfect temper and then confirm the tradition, after all, by too early and woeful an end.

If it comes over me under the brush of multiplied memories that we might well have invoked the educational "relief" I just spoke of, I should doubtless as promptly add that my own case must have been intrinsically of the poorest, and indeed make the point once for all that I should be taken as having seen and felt much of the whole queerness through the medium of rare inaptitudes. I can only have been inapt, I make out, to have retained so positively joyless a sense of it all, to be aware of most of it now but as dim confusion, as bewildered anxiety. There was interest always, certainly—but it strikes me to-day as interest in everything that wasn't supposedly or prescriptively of the question at all, and in nothing that *was* so respectably involved and accredited. Without some sharpness of interest I shouldn't now have the memories; but these stick to me somehow with none of the hard glue of recovered "spirits," recovered vivacities, assurances, successes. I can't have had, through it all, I think, a throb of assurance or success; without which, at the same time, absurdly and indescribably, I lived and wriggled, floundered and failed, lost the clue of everything but a general lucid consciousness (lucid, that is, for my tender years;) which I clutched with a sense of its value. What happened all the while, I conceive, was that I imagined things—and as if quite on system—wholly other than as they were, and so carried on in the midst of the actual ones an existence that somehow floated and saved me even while cutting me off from any degree of direct performance, in fact from any degree of direct participation, at all. *There* presumably was the interest—in the intensity and plausibility and variety of the irrelevance: an irrelevance which, for instance, made all pastors and masters, and especially all fellow-occupants of benches and desks, all elbowing and kicking presences within touch or view, so many monsters and horrors, so many wonders and splendours and mysteries, but never, so far as I can recollect, realities of relation, dispensers either of knowledge or of fate, playmates, intimates, mere coævals and coequals. They were something better—better above all than the coequal or coæval; they were so thoroughly figures and characters, divinities or demons, and endowed in this light with a vividness that the mere reality of relation, a commoner directness of contact, would have made, I surmise, comparatively poor. This superior shade of interest was not, none the less, so beguiling that I recall without unmitigated horror, or something very like it, a winter passed with my brother at the Institution Vergnès; our sorry subjection to which argues to my present sense an unmitigated surrounding aridity. To a "French school" must have been earnestly imputed the virtue of keeping us in patience till easier days should come; infinitely touching our parents' view of that New York fetish of our young time, an "acquisition of the languages"—an acquisition reinforcing those opportunities which we enjoyed at home, so far as they mustered, and at which I have briefly glanced. Charming and amusing to me indeed certain faint echoes, wavering images, of this superstition as it played about our path: ladies and gentlemen, dimly foreign, mere broken syllables of whose names come back to me, attending there to converse in tongues and then giving way to others through failures of persistence—whether in pupils or preceptors I know not. There hovers even Count Adam Gurowski, Polish, patriotic, exiled, temporarily famous, with the vision of *his* being invoked for facility and then relinquished for difficulty; though I scarce guess on which of his battle-grounds—he was so polyglot that he even had a rich command of New Yorkese.

XV

It is to the Institution Vergnès that my earliest recovery of the sense of being in any degree "educated with" W. J. attaches itself; an establishment which occupied during the early 'fifties a site in the very middle of Broadway, of the lower, the real Broadway, where it could throb with the very pulse of the traffic in which we all innocently rejoiced—believing it, I surmise, the liveliest conceivable: a fact that is by itself, in the light of the present, an odd rococo note. The lower Broadway—I allude to the whole Fourth Street and Bond Street (where now *is* the Bond Street of that antiquity?)—was then a seat of education, since we had not done with it, as I shall presently show, even when we had done with the Institution, a prompt disillusionment; and I brood thus over a period which strikes me as long and during which my personal hours of diligence were somehow more than anything else hours of the pavement and the shopfront, or of such contemplative exercise as the very considerable distance, for small legs, between those regions and the westward Fourteenth Street might comprise. Pedestrian gaping having been in childhood, as I have noted, prevailingly my line, fate appeared to have kindly provided for it on no small scale; to the extent even that it must have been really my sole and single form of athletics. Vague heated competition and agitation in the then enclosed Union Square would seem to point a little, among us all, to nobler types of motion; but of any basis for recreation, anything in the nature of a playground or a breathing-space, the Institution itself was serenely innocent. This I take again for a note extraordinarily mediæval. It occupied the first and second floors, if I rightly remember, of a wide front that, overhanging the endless thoroughfare, looked out on bouncing, clattering "stages" and painfully dragged carts and the promiscuous human shuffle—the violence of repercussions from the New York pavement of those years to be further taken into account; and I win it back from every side as, in spite of these aspects of garish publicity, a dark and dreadful, and withal quite absurd, scene. I see places of that general time, even places of confinement, in a dusty golden light that special memories of small misery scarce in the least bedim, and this holds true of our next and quite neighbouring refuge; the establishment of M. Vergnès alone darkles and shrinks to me—a sordidly *black* interior is my main image for it; attenuated only by its having very soon afterwards, as a suffered ordeal, altogether lapsed and intermitted. Faintly, in the gloom, I distinguish M. Vergnès himself—quite "old," very old indeed as I supposed him, and highly irritated and markedly bristling; though of nothing in particular that happened to me at his or at anyone's else hands have I the scantest remembrance. What really most happened no doubt, was that my brother and I should both come away with a mind prepared for a perfect assimilation of Alphonse Daudet's chronicle of "Jack," years and years later on; to make the acquaintance in that work of the "petits pays chauds" among whom Jack learnt the first lessons of life was to see the Institution Vergnès at once revive, swarming as it did with small homesick Cubans and Mexicans; the complete failure of blondness that marks the memory is doubtless the cumulative effect of so many of the New York "petits pays chauds," preponderantly brown and black and conducing to a greasy gloom. Into this gloom I fear I should see all things recede together but for a certain salient note, the fact that the whole "staff" appears to have been constantly in a rage; from which naturally resulted the accent of shrillness (the only accent we could pick up, though we were supposed to be learning, for the extreme importance of it, quantities of French) and the sound of high vociferation. I remember infuriated ushers, of foreign speech and flushed complexion— the tearing across of hapless "exercises" and *dictées* and the hurtle through the air of dodged volumes; only never, despite this, the extremity of smiting. There can have been at the Institution no blows instructionally dealt—nor even from our hours of ease do any such echoes come back to me. Little Cubans and Mexicans, I make out, were not to be vulgarly whacked—in deference, presumably, to some latent relic or imputed survival of Castilian pride; which would impose withal considerations of quite practical prudence. Food for reflection and comparison might well have been so suggested; interesting at least the element of contrast between such opposed conceptions of tone, temper and manner as the passion without whacks, or with whacks only of inanimate objects, ruling the scene I have described, and the whacks without passion, the grim, impersonal, strictly penal applications of the rod, which then generally represented what was still involved in our English tradition. It was the two theories of sensibility, of personal dignity, that so diverged; but with such other divergences now on top of those that the old comparison falls away. We to-day go unwhacked altogether—though from a pride other than Castilian: it is difficult to say at least what ideal has thus triumphed. In the Vergnès air at any rate I seem myself to have sat unscathed and unterrified—not alarmed even by so much as a call to the blackboard; only protected by my insignificance, which yet covered such a sense of our dusky squalor. Queer for us the whole affair, assuredly; but how much queerer for the poor petits pays chauds who had come so far for their privilege. *We* had come, comparatively, but from round the corner—and that left the "state of education" and the range of selection all about as quaint enough. What could these things then have been in the various native climes of the petits pays chauds?

It was by some strong wave of reaction, clearly, that we were floated next into the quieter haven of Mr. Richard Pulling Jenks—where cleaner waters, as I feel their coolness still, must have filled a neater though, it was true, slightly more contracted trough. Yet the range of selection had been even on this higher plane none too strikingly exemplified; our jumping had scant compass—we still grubbed with a good conscience in Broadway and sidled about Fourth Street. But I think of the higher education as having there, from various causes, none the less begun to glimmer for us. A diffused brightness, a kind of high crosslight of conflicting windows, rests for me at all events on the little realm of Mr. Pulling Jenks and bathes it as with positively sweet limitations. Limited must it have been, I feel, with our couple of middling rooms, front and back, our close packing, our large unaccommodating stove, our grey and gritty oilcloth, and again our importunate Broadway; from the aggregation of which elements there distils itself, without my being able to account for it, a certain perversity of romance. I speak indeed here for myself in particular, and keen for romance must I have been in such conditions, I admit; since the sense of it had crept into a recreational desert even as utter as that of the Institution Vergnès. Up out of Broadway we still scrambled—I can smell the steep and cold and dusty wooden staircase; straight into Broadway we dropped—I feel again the generalised glare of liberation; and I scarce know what tenuity of spirit it argues that I should neither have enjoyed nor been aware of missing (speaking again for myself only) a space wider than the schoolroom floor to react and knock about in. I literally conclude that we must have knocked about in Broadway, and in Broadway alone, like perfect little men of the world; we must have been let loose there to stretch our legs and fill our lungs, without prejudice either to our earlier and later freedoms of going and coming. I as strictly infer, at the same time, that Broadway must have been then as one of the alleys of Eden, for any sinister contact or consequence involved for us; a circumstance that didn't in the least interfere, too, as I have noted, with its offer of an entrancing interest. The interest verily could have been a *calculated* thing on the part of our dear parents as little as on that of Mr. Jenks himself. Therefore let it be recorded as still most odd that we should all have assented to such deficiency of landscape, such exiguity of sport. I take the true inwardness of the matter to have been in our having such short hours, long as they may have appeared at the time, that the day left margin at the worst for private inventions. I think we found landscape, for ourselves—and wherever I at least found vision I found such sport as I was capable of—even between the front and back rooms and the conflicting windows; even by the stove which somehow scorched without warming, and yet round which Mr. Coe and Mr. Dolmidge, the drawing-master and the writing-master, arriving of a winter's day, used notedly, and in the case of Mr. Coe lamentedly, to draw out their delays. Is the dusty golden light of retrospect in this connection an effluence from Mr. Dolmidge and Mr. Coe, whose ministrations come back to me as the sole directly desired or invoked ones I was to know in my years, such as they were, of pupilage?

I see them in any case as old-world images, figures of an antique stamp; products, mustn't they have been, of an order in which some social relativity or matter-of-course adjustment, some transmitted form and pressure, were still at work? Mr. Dolmidge, inordinately lean, clean-shaved, as was comparatively uncommon then, and in a swallow-tailed coat and I think a black satin stock, was surely perfect in his absolutely functional way, a pure pen-holder of a man, melancholy and mild, who taught the most complicated flourishes—great scrolls of them met our view in the form of surging seas and beaked and beady-eyed eagles, the eagle being so calligraphic a bird—while he might just have taught resignation. He was not at all funny—no one out of our immediate family circle, in fact almost no one but W. J. himself, who flowered in every waste, seems to have struck me as funny in those years; but he was to remain with me a picture of somebody in Dickens, one of the Phiz if not the Cruikshank pictures. Mr. Coe was another affair, bristling with the question of the "hard," but somehow too with the revelation of the soft, the deeply attaching; a worthy of immense stature and presence, crowned as with the thick white hair of genius, wearing a great gathered or puckered cloak, with a vast velvet collar, and resembling, as he comes back to me, the General Winfield Scott who lived so much in our eyes then. The oddity may well even at that hour have been present to me of its taking so towering a person to produce such small "drawing-cards"; it was as if some mighty bird had laid diminutive eggs. Mr. Coe, of a truth, laid his all over the place, and though they were not of more than handy size—very small boys could set them up in state on very small desks—they had doubtless a great range of number and effect. They were scattered far abroad and I surmise celebrated; they represented crooked cottages, feathery trees, browsing and bristling beasts and other rural objects; all rendered, as I recall them, in little detached dashes that were like stories told in words of one syllable, or even more perhaps in short gasps of delight. It must have been a stammering art, but I admired its fluency, which swims for me moreover in richer though slightly vague associations. Mr. Coe practised on a larger scale, in colour, in oils, producing wondrous neat little boards that make me to this day think of them and more particularly smell them, when I hear of a "panel" picture: a glamour of greatness attends them as brought home by W. J. from the master's own place of instruction in that old University building which partly formed the east side of Washington Square and figures to memory, or to fond imagination, as throbbing with more offices and functions, a denser chiaroscuro, than any reared hugeness of to-day, where character is so lost in quantity. Is there any present structure that plays such a part in proportion to its size?—though even as I ask the question I feel how nothing on earth is proportioned to present sizes. These alone are proportioned—and to mere sky-space and mere amount, amount of steel and stone; which is comparatively uninteresting. Perhaps our needs and our elements were then absurdly, were then provincially few, and that the patches of character in that small grey granite compendium were all we had in general to exhibit. Let me add at any rate that some of them were exhibitional—even to my tender years, I mean; since I respond even yet to my privilege of presence at some Commencement or Commemoration, such as might be natural, doubtless, to any "university," where, as under a high rich roof, before a Chancellor in a gown and amid serried admirers and impressive applause, there was "speaking," of the finest sort, and where above all I gathered in as a dazzling example the rare assurance of young Winthrop Somebody or Somebody Winthrop, who, though still in jackets, held us spellbound by his rendering of Serjeant Buzfuz's exposure of Mr. Pickwick. Long was I to marvel at the high sufficiency of young Winthrop Somebody or Somebody Winthrop—in which romantic impression it is perhaps after all (though with the consecration of one or two of the novels of the once-admired Theodore of that name, which so remarkably insists, thrown in) the sense of the place is embalmed.

I must not forget indeed that I throw in also Mr. Coe—even if with less assured a hand; by way of a note on those higher flights of power and promise that I at this time began to see definitely determined in my brother. As I catch W. J.'s image, from far back, at its most characteristic, he sits drawing and drawing, always drawing, especially under the lamplight of the Fourteenth Street back parlour; and not as with a plodding patience, which I think would less have affected me, but easily, freely and, as who should say, infallibly: always at the stage of finishing off, his head dropped from side to side and his tongue rubbing his lower lip. I recover a period during which to see him at all was so to see him—the other flights and faculties removed him from my view. These were a matter of course—he recurred, he passed nearer, but in his moments of ease, and I clearly quite accepted the ease of his disappearances. Didn't he always when within my view light them up and justify them by renewed and enlarged vividness? so that my whole sense of him as formed for assimilations scarce conceivable made our gaps of contact too natural for me even to be lessons in humility. Humility had nothing to do with it—as little even as envy would have had; I was below humility, just as we were together outside of competition, mutually "hors concours." *His* competitions were with others—in which how wasn't he, how could he not be, successful? while mine were with nobody, or nobody's with me, which came to the same thing, as heaven knows I neither braved them nor missed them. That winter, as I recover it, represents him as sufficiently within view to make his position or whereabouts in the upper air definite—I must have taken it for granted before, but could now in a manner measure it; and the freshness of this sense, something serene in my complacency, had to do, I divine, with the effect of our moving, with the rest of our company, which was not numerous but practically, but appreciably "select," on a higher and fairer plane than ever yet. Predominantly of course we owed this benefit to Richard Pulling himself; of whom I recall my brother's saying to me, at a considerably later time, and with an authority that affected me as absolute, that he had been of all our masters the most truly genial, in fact the only one to whom the art of exciting an interest or inspiring a sympathy could be in any degree imputed. I take this to have meant that he would have adorned a higher sphere—and it may have been, to explain his so soon swimming out of our ken, that into a higher sphere he rapidly moved; I can account at least for our falling away from him the very next year and declining again upon baser things and a lower civilisation but by some probability of his flight, just thereafter effected, to a greater distance, to one of the far upper reaches of the town. Some years must have elapsed and some distinction have crowned him when, being briefly in New York together, W. J. and I called on him of a Sunday afternoon, to find—what I hadn't been at all sure of—that he still quite knew who we were, or handsomely pretended to; handsomely in spite of his markedly confirmed identity of appearance with the Punch, husband to Judy, of the funny papers and the street show. Bald, rotund, of ruddy complexion, with the nose, the chin, the arched eye, the paunch and the *barbiche*, to say nothing of the ferule nursed in his arms and with which, in the show, such free play is made, Mr. Jenks yet seems to me to have preserved a dignity as well as projected an image, and in fact have done other things besides. He whacked occasionally—he must have been one of the last of the whackers; but I don't remember it as ugly or dreadful or droll—don't remember, that is, either directly feeling or reflectively enjoying it: it fails somehow to break the spell of our civilisation; my share in which, however, comes back to me as merely contemplative. It is beyond measure odd, doubtless, that my main association with my "studies," whether of the infant or the adolescent order, should be with almost anything but the fact of learning—of learning, I mean, what I was supposed to learn. I could only have been busy, at the same time, with other pursuits—which must have borne some superficial likeness at least to the acquisition of knowledge of a free irresponsible sort; since I remember few either of the inward pangs or the outward pains of a merely graceless state. I recognise at the same time that it was perhaps a sorry business to be so interested in one didn't know what. Such are, whether at the worst or at the best, some of the aspects of that season as Mr. Jenks's image presides; in the light of which I *may* perhaps again rather wonder at my imputation to the general picture of so much amenity. Clearly the good man was a civiliser—whacks and all; and by some art not now to be detected. He was a complacent classic—which was what my brother's claim for him, I dare say, mostly represented; though that passed over the head of my tenth year. It was a good note for him in this particular that, deploring the facile text-books of Doctor Anthon of Columbia College, in which there was even more crib than text, and holding fast to the sterner discipline of Andrews and Stoddard and of that other more conservative commentator (he too doubtless long since superseded) whose name I blush to forget. I think in fine of Richard Pulling's small but sincere academy as a consistent little protest against its big and easy and quite out-distancing rival, the Columbia College school, apparently in those days quite the favourite of fortune.

XVI

I must in some degree have felt it a charm there that we were not, under his rule, inordinately prepared for "business," but were on the contrary to remember that the taste of Cornelius Nepos in the air, even rather stale though it may have been, had lacked the black bitterness marking our next ordeal and that I conceive to have proceeded from some rank predominance of the theory and practice of book-keeping. It had consorted with this that we found ourselves, by I know not what inconsequence, a pair of the "assets" of a firm; Messrs. Forest and Quackenboss, who carried on business at the northwest corner of Fourteenth Street and Sixth Avenue, having for the winter of 1854-5 taken our education in hand. As their establishment had the style, so I was conscious at the time of its having the general stamp and sense, of a shop—a shop of long standing, of numerous clients, of lively bustle and traffic. The structure itself was to my recent recognition still there and more than ever a shop, with improvements and extensions, but dealing in other wares than those anciently and as I suppose then quite freshly purveyed; so far at least as freshness was imputable to the senior member of the firm, who had come down to our generation from a legendary past and with a striking resemblance of head and general air to Benjamin Franklin. Mr. Forest, under whose more particular attention I languished, had lasted on from a plainer age and, having formed, by the legend, in their youth, the taste of two or three of our New York uncles—though for what it could have been goodness only knew—was still of a *trempe* to whack in the fine old way at their nephews and sons. I see him aloft, benevolent and hard, mildly massive, in a black dress coat and trousers and a white neckcloth that should have figured, if it didn't, a frill, and on the highest rostrum of our experience, whence he comes back to me as the dryest of all our founts of knowledge, though quite again as a link with far-off manners and forms and as the most "historic" figure we had ever had to do with. W. J., as I distinguish, had in truth scarcely to do with him—W. J. lost again on upper floors, in higher classes, in real pursuits, and connecting me, in an indirect and almost deprecated manner, with a strange, curly, glossy, an anointed and bearded, Mr. Quackenboss, the junior partner, who conducted the classical department and never whacked—only sent down his subjects, with every confidence, to his friend. I make out with clearness that Mr. Forest was awful and arid, and yet that somehow, by the same stroke, we didn't, under his sway, go in terror, only went exceedingly in want; even if in want indeed of I scarce (for myself) know what, since it might well have been enough for me, in so resounding an air, to escape with nothing worse than a failure of thrill. If I didn't feel that interest I must clearly not have inspired it, and I marvel afresh, under these memories, at the few points at which I appear to have touched constituted reality. That, however, is a different connection altogether, and I read back into the one I have been noting much of the chill, or at least the indifference, of a foreseen and foredoomed detachment: it was during that winter that I began to live by anticipation in another world and to feel our uneasy connection with New York loosen beyond recovery. I remember for how many months, when the rupture took place, we had been to my particular consciousness virtually in motion; though I regain at the same time the impression of more experience on the spot than had marked our small previous history: this, however, a branch of the matter that I must for the moment brush aside. For it would have been meanwhile odd enough to hold us in arrest a moment—that quality of our situation that could suffer such elements as those I have glanced at to take so considerably the place of education as more usually and conventionally understood, and by that understanding more earnestly mapped out; a deficiency, in the whole thing, that I fail at all consistently to deplore, however—struck as I am with the rare fashion after which, in any small victim of life, the inward perversity may work.

It works by converting to its uses things vain and unintended, to the great discomposure of their prepared opposites, which it by the same stroke so often reduces to naught; with the result indeed that one may most of all see it—so at least have I quite exclusively seen it, the little life out for its chance—as proceeding by the inveterate process of conversion. As I reconsider both my own and my brother's early start—even his too, made under stronger propulsions—it is quite for me as if the authors of our being and guardians of our youth had virtually said to us but one thing, directed our course but by one word, though constantly repeated: Convert, convert, convert! With which I have not even the sense of any needed appeal in us for further apprehension of the particular precious metal our chemistry was to have in view. I taste again in that pure air no ghost of a hint, for instance, that the precious metal was the refined gold of "success"—a reward of effort for which I remember to have heard at home no good word, nor any sort of word, ever faintly breathed. It was a case of the presumption that we should hear words enough abundantly elsewhere; so that any dignity the idea might claim was in the first place not worth insisting on, and in the second might well be overstated. We were to convert and convert, success—in the sense that was in the general air—or no success; and simply everything that should happen to us, every contact, every impression and every experience we should know, were to form our soluble stuff; with only ourselves to thank should we remain unaware, by the time our perceptions were decently developed, of the substance finally projected and most desirable. That substance might be just consummately Virtue, as a social grace and value—and as a matter furthermore on which pretexts for ambiguity of view and of measure were as little as possible called upon to flourish. This last luxury therefore quite failed us, and we understood no whit the less what was suggested and expected because of the highly liberal way in which the pill, if I may call it so, was gilded: it had been made up—to emphasise my image—in so bright an air of humanity and gaiety, of charity and humour. What I speak of is the medium itself, of course, that we were most immediately steeped in—I am glancing now at no particular turn of our young attitude in it, and I can scarce sufficiently express how little it could have conduced to the formation of prigs. Our father's prime horror was of *them*—he only cared for virtue that was more or less ashamed of itself; and nothing could have been of a happier whimsicality than the mixture in him, and in all his walk and conversation, of the strongest instinct for the human and the liveliest reaction from the literal. The literal played in our education as small a part as it perhaps ever played in any, and we wholesomely breathed inconsistency and ate and drank contradictions. The presence of paradox was so bright among us—though fluttering ever with as light a wing and as short a flight as need have been—that we fairly grew used to allow, from an early time, for the so many and odd declarations we heard launched, to the extent of happily "discounting" them; the moral of all of which was that we need never fear not to be good enough if we were only social enough: a splendid meaning indeed being attached to the latter term.

Thus we had ever the amusement, since I can really call it nothing less, of hearing morality, or moralism, as it was more invidiously worded, made hay of in the very interest of character and conduct; these things suffering much, it seemed, by their association with the conscience—that is the *conscious* conscience—the very home of the literal, the haunt of so many pedantries. Pedantries, on all this ground, were anathema; and if our dear parent had at all minded his not being consistent, and had entertained about us generally less passionate an optimism (not an easy but an arduous state in him moreover,) he might have found it difficult to apply to the promotion of our studies so free a suspicion of the inhumanity of Method. Method certainly never quite raged among us; but it was our fortune nevertheless that everything had its turn, and that such indifferences were no more pedantic than certain rigours might perhaps have been; of all of which odd notes of our situation there would, and possibly will, be more to say—my present aim is really but to testify to what most comes up for me to-day in the queer educative air I have been trying to breathe again. That definite reflection is that if we had not had in us to some degree the root of the matter no method, however confessedly or aggressively "pedantic," would much have availed for us; and that since we apparently did have it, deep down and inert in our small patches of virgin soil, the fashion after which it struggled forth was an experience as intense as any other and a record of as great a dignity. It may be asked me, I recognise, of the root of "what" matter I so complacently speak, and if I say "Why, of the matter of our having with considerable intensity *proved* educable, or, if you like better, teachable, that is accessible to experience," it may again be retorted: "That won't do for a decent account of a young consciousness; for think of all the things that the failure of method, of which you make so light, didn't put into yours; think of the splendid economy of a real—or at least of a planned and attempted education, a 'regular course of instruction'—and then think of the waste involved in the so inferior substitute of which the pair of you were evidently victims." An admonition this on which I brood, less, however, than on the still other sense, rising from the whole retrospect, of my now feeling sure, of my having mastered the particular history of just that waste—to the point of its actually affecting me as blooming with interest, to the point even of its making me ask myself how in the world, if the question is of the injection of more things into the consciousness (as would seem the case,) mine could have "done" with more: thanks to its small trick, perhaps vicious I admit, of having felt itself from an early time almost uncomfortably stuffed. I see my critic, by whom I mean my representative of method at any price, take in this plea only to crush it with his confidence—that without the signal effects of method one must have had by an inexorable law to resort to shifts and ingenuities, and can therefore only have been an artful dodger more or less successfully dodging. I take full account of the respectability of the prejudice against one or two of the uses to which the intelligence may at a pinch be put—the criminal use in particular of falsifying its history, of forging its records even, and of appearing greater than the traceable grounds warrant. One can but fall back, none the less, on the particular *un*traceability of grounds—when it comes to that: cases abound so in which, with the grounds all there, the intelligence itself is not to be identified. I contend for nothing moreover but the lively interest of the view, and above all of the measure, of almost any mental history after the fact. Of less interest, comparatively, is that sight of the mind *before*—before the demonstration of the fact, that is, and while still muffled in theories and presumptions (purple and fine linen, and as such highly becoming though these be) of what shall prove best for it.

Which doubtless too numerous remarks have been determined by my sense of the tenuity of some of my clues: I had begun to count our wavering steps from so very far back, and with a lively disposition, I confess, not to miss even the vaguest of them. I can scarce indeed overstate the vagueness that quite *had* to attend a great number in presence of the fact that our father, caring for our spiritual decency unspeakably more than for anything else, anything at all that might be or might become ours, would have seemed to regard this cultivation of it as profession and career enough for us, had he but betrayed more interest in our mastery of *any* art or craft. It was not certainly that the profession of virtue would have been anything less than abhorrent to him, but that, singular though the circumstance, there were times when he might have struck us as having after all more patience with it than with this, that or the other more technical thrifty scheme. Of the beauty of his dissimulated anxiety and tenderness on these and various other suchlike heads, however, other examples will arise; for I see him now as fairly afraid to recognise certain anxieties, fairly declining to dabble in the harshness of practical precautions or impositions. The effect of his attitude, so little thought out as shrewd or as vulgarly providential, but in spite of this so socially and affectionally founded, could only be to make life interesting to us at the worst, in default of making it extraordinarily "paying." He had a theory that it would somehow or other always be paying enough—and this much less by any poor conception of our wants (for he delighted in our wants and so sympathetically and sketchily and summarily wanted *for* us) than by a happy and friendly, though slightly nebulous, conception of our resources. Delighting ever in the truth while generously contemptuous of the facts, so far as we might make the difference—the facts having a way of being many and the truth remaining but one—he held that there would always be enough; since the truth, the true truth, was never ugly and dreadful, and we didn't and wouldn't depart from it by any cruelty or stupidity (for he wouldn't have had us stupid,) and might therefore depend on it for due abundance even of meat and drink and raiment, even of wisdom and wit and honour. It is too much to say that our so preponderantly humanised and socialised adolescence was to make us look out for these things with a subtle indirectness; but I return to my proposition that there may still be a charm in seeing such hazards at work through a given, even if not in a systematised, case. My cases are of course given, so that economy of observation after the fact, as I have called it, becomes inspiring, not less than the amusement, or whatever it may be, of the question of what might happen, of what in point of fact did happen, to several very towny and domesticated little persons, who were confirmed in their towniness and fairly enriched in their sensibility, instead of being chucked into a scramble or exposed on breezy uplands under the she-wolf of competition and discipline. Perhaps any success that attended the experiment—which was really, as I have hinted, no plotted thing at all, but only an accident of accidents—proceeded just from the fact that the small subjects, a defeated Romulus, a prematurely sacrificed Remus, had in their very sensibility an asset, as we have come to say, a principle of life and even of "fun." Perhaps on the other hand the success would have been greater with less of that particular complication or facilitation and more of some other which I shall be at a loss to identify. What I find in my path happens to be the fact of the sensibility, and from the light it sheds the curious, as also the common, things that did from occasion to occasion play into it seem each to borrow a separate and vivifying glow.

As at the Institution Vergnès and at Mr. Pulling Jenks's, however this might be, so at "Forest's," or in other words at the more numerous establishment of Messrs. Forest and Quackenboss, where we spent the winter of 1854, reality, in the form of multitudinous mates, was to have swarmed about me increasingly: at Forest's the prolonged roll-call in the morning, as I sit in the vast bright crowded smelly smoky room, in which rusty black stove-shafts were the nearest hint of architecture, bristles with names, Hoes and Havemeyers, Stokeses, Phelpses, Colgates and others, of a subsequently great New York salience. It was sociable and gay, it was sordidly spectacular, one was then, by an inch or two, a bigger boy—though with crushing superiorities in that line all round; and when I wonder why the scene was sterile (which was what I took it for at the worst) the reason glooms out again in the dreadful blight of arithmetic, which affected me at the time as filling all the air. The quantity imposed may not in fact have been positively gross, yet it is what I most definitely remember—not, I mean, that I have retained the dimmest notion of the science, but only of the dire image of our being in one way or another always supposedly addressed to it. I recall strange neighbours and deskfellows who, not otherwise too objectionable, were uncanny and monstrous through their possession, cultivation, imitation of ledgers, daybooks, double-entry, tall pages of figures, interspaces streaked with oblique ruled lines that weirdly "balanced," whatever that might mean, and other like horrors. Nothing in truth is more distinct to me than the tune to which they were, without exception, at their ease on such ground— unless it be my general dazzled, humiliated sense, through those years, of the common, the baffling, mastery, all round me, of a hundred handy arts and devices. Everyone did things and had things—everyone knew how, even when it was a question of the small animals, the dormice and grasshoppers,

211

or the hoards of food and stationery, that they kept in their desks, just as they kept in their heads such secrets for how to do sums—those secrets that I must even then have foreseen I should even so late in life as this have failed to discover. I may have known things, have by that time learnt a few, myself, but I didn't know *that*—what I did know; whereas those who surrounded me were all agog, to my vision, with the benefit of their knowledge. I see them, in this light, across the years, fairly grin and grimace with it; and the presumable vulgarity of some of them, certain scattered shades of baseness still discernible, comes to me as but one of the appearances of an abounding play of genius. Who was it I ever thought stupid?—even when knowing, or at least feeling, that sundry expressions of life or force, which I yet had no name for, represented somehow art without grace, or (what after a fashion came to the same thing) presence without type. All of which, I should add, didn't in the least prevent my moving on the plane of the remarkable; so that if, as I have noted, the general blank of consciousness, in the conditions of that winter, rather tended to spread, this could perhaps have but had for its best reason that I was fairly gorged with wonders. They were too much of the same kind; the result, that is, of everyone's seeming to know everything—to the effect, a little, that everything suffered by it. There was a boy called Simpson my juxtaposition to whom I recall as uninterruptedly close, and whose origin can only have been, I think, quite immediately Irish—and Simpson, I feel sure, was a friendly and helpful character. Yet even he reeked, to my sense, with strange accomplishment—no single show of which but was accompanied in him by a smart protrusion of the lower lip, a crude complacency of power, that almost crushed me to sadness. It is as if I had passed in that sadness most of those ostensibly animated months; an effect however doubtless in some degree proceeding, for later appreciation, from the more intelligible nearness of the time—it had brought me to the end of my twelfth year; which helps not a little to turn it to prose. How I gave to that state, in any case, such an air of occupation as to beguile not only myself but my instructors—which I infer I did from their so intensely letting me alone—I am quite at a loss to say; I have in truth mainly the remembrance of *being* consistently either ignored or exquisitely considered (I know not which to call it;) even if without the belief, which would explain it, that I passed for generally "wanting" any more than for naturally odious. It was strange, at all events—it could only have been—to be so stupid without being more brutish and so perceptive without being more keen. Here were a case and a problem to which no honest master with other and better cases could have felt justified in giving time; he would have had at least to be morbidly curious, and I recall from that sphere of rule no instance whatever of the least refinement of inquiry. I should even probably have missed one of these more flattering shades of attention had I missed attention at all; but I think I was never really aware of how little I got or how much I did without. I read back into the whole connection indeed the chill, or at least the indifference, of a foreseen and foredoomed detachment: I have noted how at this desperate juncture the mild forces making for our conscious relief, pushing the door to Europe definitely open, began at last to be effective. Nothing seemed to matter at all but that I should become personally and incredibly acquainted with Piccadilly and Richmond Park and Ham Common. I regain at the same time the impression of more experience on the spot than had marked our small previous history.

Pitiful as it looks to these ampler days the mere little fact that a small court for recreation was attached to our academy added something of a grace to life. We descended in relays, for "intermission," into a paved and walled yard of the scantest size; the only provision for any such privilege—not counting the street itself, of which, at the worst of other conditions, we must have had free range—that I recover from those years. The ground is built over now, but I could still figure, on a recent occasion, our small breathing-space; together with my then abject little sense that it richly sufficed—or rather, positively, that nothing could have been more romantic. For within our limit we freely conversed, and at nothing did I assist with more interest than at free conversation. Certain boys hover before me, the biggest, the fairest, the most worthy of freedom, dominating the scene and scattering upon fifty subjects the most surprising lights. One of these heroes, whose stature and complexion are still there for me to admire, did tricks of legerdemain, with the scant apparatus of a handkerchief, a key, a pocket-knife—as to some one of which it is as fresh as yesterday that I ingenuously invited him to show me how to do it, and then, on his treating me with scorn, renewed without dignity my fond solicitation. Fresher even than yesterday, fadelessly fresh for me at this hour, is the cutting remark thereupon of another boy, who certainly wasn't Simpson and whose identity is lost for me in his mere inspired authority: "Oh, oh, oh, I should think you'd be too proud—!" I had neither been too proud nor so much as conceived that one might be, but I remember well how it flashed on me with this that I had failed thereby of a high luxury or privilege—which the whole future, however, might help me to make up for. To what extent it *has* helped is another matter, but so fine was the force of the suggestion that I think I have never in all the years made certain returns upon my spirit without again feeling the pang from the cool little voice of the Fourteenth Street yard. Such was the moral exercise it at least allowed us room for. It also allowed us room, to be just, for an inordinate consumption of hot waffles retailed by a benevolent black "auntie" who presided, with her husband's aid as I remember, at a portable stove set up in a passage or recess opening from the court; to which we flocked and pushed, in a merciless squeeze, with all our coppers, and the products of which, the oblong farinaceous compound, faintly yet richly brown, stamped and smoking, not crisp nor brittle, but softly absorbent of the syrup dabbed upon it for a finish, revealed to me I for a long time, even for a very long time supposed, the highest pleasure of sense. We stamped about, we freely conversed, we ate sticky waffles by the hundred—I recall no worse acts of violence unless I count as such our intermissional rushes to Pynsent's of the Avenue, a few doors off, in the particular interest of a confection that ran the waffle close, as the phrase is, for popularity, while even surpassing it for stickiness. Pynsent's was higher up in the row in which Forest's had its front—other and dearer names have dropped from me, but Pynsent's adheres with all the force of the strong saccharine principle. This principle, at its highest, we conceived, was embodied in small amber-coloured mounds of chopped cocoanut or whatever other substance, if a finer there be; profusely, lusciously endued and distributed on small tin trays in the manner of haycocks in a field. We acquired, we appropriated, we transported, we enjoyed them, they fairly formed perhaps, after all, our highest enjoyment; but with consequences to our pockets—and I speak of those other than financial, with an intimacy, a reciprocity of contact at any, or at every, personal point, that I lose myself in the thought of.

XVII

I lose myself, of a truth, under the whole pressure of the spring of memory proceeding from recent revisitings and recognitions—the action of the fact that time until lately had spared hereabouts, and may still be sparing, in the most exceptional way, by an anomaly or a mercy of the rarest in New York, a whole cluster of landmarks, leaving me to "spot" and verify, right and left, the smallest preserved particulars. These things, at the pressure, flush together again, interweave their pattern and quite thrust it at me, the absurd little fusion of images, for a history or a picture of the time—the background of which I see after all so much less as the harsh Sixth Avenue corner than as many other matters. Those scant shades claimed us but briefly and superficially, and it comes back to me that oddly enough, in the light of autumn afternoons, our associates, the most animated or at any rate the best "put in" little figures of our landscape, were not our comparatively obscure schoolmates, who seem mostly to have swum out of our ken between any day and its morrow. Our other companions, those we practically knew "at home," ignored our school, having better or worse of their own, but peopled somehow for us the social scene, which, figuring there for me in documentary vividness, bristles with Van Burens, Van Winkles, De Peysters, Costers, Senters, Norcoms, Robinsons (these last composing round a stone-throwing "Eugene,") Wards, Hunts and *tutti quanti*—to whose ranks I must add our invariable Albert, before-mentioned, and who swarm from up and down and east and west, appearing to me surely to have formed a rich and various society. Our salon, it is true, was mainly the street, loose and rude and crude in those days at best—though with a rapid increase of redeeming features, to the extent to which the spread of micaceous brown stone could redeem: as exhibited especially in the ample face of the Scotch Presbyterian church promptly rising just opposite our own peculiar row and which it now marks for me somewhat grimly a span of life to have seen laboriously rear itself, continuously flourish and utterly disappear. While in construction it was only less interesting than the dancing-academy of Mr. Edward Ferrero, slightly west of it and forming with it, in their embryonic stage, a large and delightfully dangerous adjunct to our playground, though with the distinction of coming much to surpass it for interest in the final phase. While we clambered about on ladders and toyed with the peril of unfloored abysses, while we trespassed and pried and pervaded, snatching a scant impression from sorry material enough, clearly, the sacred edifice enjoyed a credit beyond that of the profane; but when both were finished and opened we flocked to the sound of the fiddle more freely, it need scarce be said, than to that of the psalm. "Freely" indeed, in our particular case, scarce expresses the latter relation; since our young liberty in respect to church-going was absolute and we might range at will, through the great city, from one place of worship and one form of faith to another, or might on occasion ignore them all equally, which was what we mainly did; whereas we rallied without a break to the halls of Ferrero, a view of the staringly and, as I supposed dazzlingly, frescoed walls, the internal economy, the high amenity, the general æsthetic and social appeal, of which still hangs in its wealth before me. Dr. McElroy, uplifting tight-closed eyes, strange long-drawn accents and gaunt scraggy chin, squirming and swaying and cushion-thumping in *his* only a shade more chastely adorned temple, is distinct enough too—just as we enjoyed this bleak intensity the more, to my personal vision, through the vague legend (and no legend was too vague for me to cherish) of his being the next pastor in succession to the one under whom our mother, thereto predirected by our good greatgrandfather, Alexander Robertson already named, who was nothing if not Scotch and Presbyterian and authoritative, as his brave old portrait by the elder Jarves attests, had "sat" before her marriage; the marriage so lamentedly diverting her indeed from this tradition that, to mark the rueful rupture, it had invoked, one evening, with the aid of India muslin and a wondrous gold headband, in the maternal, the Washington Square "parlours," but the secular nuptial consecration of the then Mayor of the city—I think Mr. Varick.

We progeny were of course after this mild convulsion not at all in the fold; yet it strikes me as the happy note of a simple age that we were practically, of a Sunday at least, wherever we might have chosen to enter: since, going forth hand in hand into the sunshine (and I connect myself here with my next younger, not with my elder, brother, whose orbit was other and larger) we sampled, in modern phrase, as small unprejudiced inquirers obeying their inspiration, any resort of any congregation detected by us; doing so, I make out moreover, with a sense of earnest provision for any contemporary challenge. "What church do you go to?"—the challenge took in childish circles that searching form; of the form it took among our elders my impression is more vague. To which I must add as well that our "fending" in this fashion for ourselves didn't so prepare us for invidious remark—remark I mean upon our pewless state, which involved, to my imagination, much the same discredit that a houseless or a cookless would have done—as to hush in my breast the appeal to our parents, not for religious instruction (of which we had plenty, and of the most charming and familiar) but simply for instruction (a very different thing) as to where we should say we "went," in our world, under cold scrutiny or derisive comment. It was colder than any criticism, I recall, to hear our father reply that we could plead nothing less than the whole privilege of Christendom and that there was no communion, even that of the Catholics, even that of the Jews, even that of the Swedenborgians, from which we need find ourselves excluded. With the freedom we enjoyed our dilemma clearly amused him: it would have been impossible, he affirmed, to be theologically more *en règle*. How as mere detached unaccompanied infants we enjoyed such impunity of range and confidence of welcome is beyond comprehension save by the light of the old manners and conditions, the old local bonhomie, the comparatively primal innocence, the absence of complications; with the several notes of which last beatitude my reminiscence surely shines. It was the theory of the time and place that the young, were they but young enough, could take publicly no harm; to which adds itself moreover, and touchingly enough, all the difference of the old importances. It wasn't doubtless that the social, or call it simply the human, position of the child was higher than to-day—a circumstance not conceivable; it was simply that other dignities and values and claims, other social and human positions, were less definite and settled, less prescriptive and absolute. A rich sophistication is after all a gradual growth, and it would have been sophisticated to fear for us, before such bright and vacant vistas, the perils of the way or to see us received anywhere even with the irony of patronage. We hadn't in fact seats of honour, but that justice was done us—that is that we were placed to our advantage—I infer from my having liked so to "go," even though my grounds may have been but the love of the *exhibition* in general, thanks to which figures, faces, furniture, sounds, smells and colours became for me, wherever enjoyed, and enjoyed most where most collected, a positive little orgy of the senses and riot of the mind. Let me at the same time make the point that— such may be the snobbery of extreme youth—I not only failed quite to rise to the parental reasoning, but made out in it rather a certain sophistry; such a prevarication for instance as if we had habitually said we kept the carriage we observably didn't keep, kept it because we sent when we wanted one to University Place, where Mr. Hathorn had his livery-stable: a connection, this last, promoted by my father's frequent need of the aid to circulate (his walks were limited through an injury received in youth) and promoting in turn and at a touch, to my consciousness, the stir of small, the smallest remembered things. I recall the adventure, no infrequent one, of being despatched to Mr. Hathorn to bespeak a conveyance, and the very air and odour, the genial warmth, at a fine steaming Irish pitch, of the stables and their stamping and backing beasts, their resounding boardedness, their chairs tipped up at such an angle for lifted heels, a pair of which latter seek the floor again, at my appeal, as those of big bearded Mr. Hathorn himself: an impression enriched by the drive home in lolling and bumping possession of the great vehicle and associated further with Sunday afternoons in spring, with the question of distant Harlem and remoter Bloomingdale, with the experience at one of these junctures of far-away Hoboken, if it wasn't Williamsburg, which fits in fancifully somewhere; when the carriage was reinforced by a ferry and the ferry by something, something to my present vision very dim and dusty and archaic, something quite ragged and graceless, in the nature of a public tea-garden and ices. The finest link here, however, is, for some reason, with the New York Hotel, and thereby with Albany uncles; thereby also with Mr. Hathorn in person waiting and waiting expensively on his box before the house and somehow felt as attuned to Albany uncles even as Mrs. Cannon had subtly struck me as being.

Intenser than these vague shades meanwhile is my vision of the halls of Ferrero—where the orgy of the senses and even the riot of the mind, of which I have just spoken, must quite literally have led me more of a dance than anywhere. Let this sketch of a lost order note withal that under so scant a general provision for infant exercise, as distinguished from infant ease, our hopping and sliding in tune had to be deemed urgent. It was the sense for this form of relief that clearly was general, superseding as the ampler Ferrero scene did previous limited exhibitions; even those, for that matter, coming back to me in the ancient person of M. Charriau—I guess at the writing of his name—whom I work in but confusedly as a professional visitor, a subject gaped at across a gulf of fear, in one of our huddled schools; all the more that I perfectly evoke him as resembling, with a difference or two, the portraits of the aged Voltaire, and that he had, fiddle in hand and *jarret tendu*, incited the young agility of our mother and aunt. Edward Ferrero was another matter; in the prime of life, good-looking, romantic and moustachio'd, he was suddenly to figure, on the outbreak of the Civil War, as a General of volunteers— very much as if he had been one of Bonaparte's improvised young marshals; in anticipation of which, however, he wasn't at all fierce or superior, to my remembrance, but most kind to sprawling youth, in a charming man of the world fashion and as if *we* wanted but a touch to become also men of the world. Remarkably good-looking, as I say, by the measure of that period, and extraordinarily agile—he could so gracefully leap and bound that his bounding into the military saddle, such occasion offering, had all the felicity, and only wanted the pink fleshings, of the circus—he was still more admired by the mothers, with whom he had to my eyes a most elegant relation, than by the pupils; among all of whom, at the frequent and delightful soirées, he caused trays laden with lucent syrups repeatedly to circulate. The scale of these entertainments, as I figured it, and the florid frescoes, just damp though they were with newness, and the free lemonade, and the freedom of remark, equally great, with the mothers, were the lavish note in him— just as the fact that he never himself fiddled, but was followed, over the shining parquet, by attendant fiddlers, represented doubtless a shadow the less on his later dignity, so far as that dignity was compassed. Dignity marked in full measure even at the time the presence of his sister Madame Dubreuil, a handsome authoritative person who instructed us equally, in fact preponderantly, and who, though comparatively not sympathetic, so engaged, physiognomically, my wondering interest, that I hear to this hour

219

her shrill Franco-American accent: "Don't look at *me*, little boy—look at my feet." I see them now, these somewhat fat members, beneath the uplifted skirt, encased in "bronzed" slippers, without heels but attached, by graceful cross-bands over her white stockings, to her solid ankles—an emphatic sign of the time; not less than I recover my surprised sense of their supporting her without loss of balance, substantial as she was, in the "first position"; her command of which, her ankles clapped close together and her body very erect, was so perfect that even with her toes, right and left, fairly turning the corner backward, she never fell prone on her face.

It consorted somehow with this wealth of resource in her that she appeared at the soirées, or at least at the great fancy-dress soirée in which the historic truth of my experience, free lemonade and all, is doubtless really shut up, as the "genius of California," a dazzling vision of white satin and golden flounces—her brother meanwhile maintaining that more distinctively European colour which I feel to have been for my young presumption the convincing essence of the scene in the character of a mousquetaire de Louis Quinze, highly consonant with his type. There hovered in the background a flushed, full-chested and tawnily short-bearded M. Dubreuil, who, as a singer of the heavy order, at the Opera, carried us off into larger things still—the Opera having at last about then, after dwelling for years, down town, in shifty tents and tabernacles, set up its own spacious pavilion and reared its head as the Academy of Music: all at the end, or what served for the end, of our very street, where, though it wasn't exactly near and Union Square bristled between, I could yet occasionally gape at the great bills beside the portal, in which M. Dubreuil always so serviceably came in at the bottom of the cast. A subordinate artist, a "grand utility" at the best, I believe, and presently to become, on that scene, slightly ragged I fear even in its freshness, permanent stage-manager or, as we say nowadays, producer, he had yet eminently, to my imagination, the richer, the "European" value; especially for instance when our air thrilled, in the sense that our attentive parents re-echoed, with the visit of the great Grisi and the great Mario, and I seemed, though the art of advertisement was then comparatively so young and so chaste, to see our personal acquaintance, as he could almost be called, thickly sandwiched between them. Such was one's strange sense for the connections of things that they drew out the halls of Ferrero till these too seemed fairly to resound with Norma and Lucrezia Borgia, as if opening straight upon the stage, and Europe, by the stroke, had come to us in such force that we had but to enjoy it on the spot. That could never have been more the case than on the occasion of my assuming, for the famous fancy-ball—not at the operatic Academy, but at the dancing-school, which came so nearly to the same thing—the dress of a débardeur, whatever that might be, which carried in its puckered folds of dark green relieved with scarlet and silver such an exotic fragrance and appealed to me by such a legend. The legend had come round to us, it was true, by way of Albany, whence we learned at the moment of our need, that one of the adventures, one of the least lamentable, of our cousin Johnny had been his figuring as a débardeur at some Parisian revel; the elegant evidence of which, neatly packed, though with but vague instructions for use, was helpfully sent on to us. The instructions for use were in fact so vague that I was afterward to become a bit ruefully conscious of having sadly dishonoured, or at least abbreviated, my model. I fell, that is I stood, short of my proper form by no less than half a leg; the essence of the débardeur being, it appeared, that he emerged at the knees, in white silk stockings and with neat calves, from the beribboned breeches which I artlessly suffered to flap at my ankles. The discovery, after the fact, was disconcerting—yet had been best made withal, too late; for it would have seemed, I conceive, a less monstrous act to attempt to lengthen my legs than to shorten Johnny's *culotte*. The trouble had been that we hadn't really known what a débardeur *was*, and I am not sure indeed that I know to this day. It had been more fatal still that even fond Albany couldn't tell us.

XVIII

I have nevertheless the memory of a restless relish of all that time—by which I mean of those final months of New York, even with so scant a record of other positive successes to console me. I had but one success, always—that of endlessly supposing, wondering, admiring: I was sunk in that luxury, which had never yet been so great, and it might well make up for anything. It made up perfectly, and more particularly as the stopgap as which I have already defined it, for the scantness of the period immediately round us; since how could I have wanted richer when the limits of reality, as I advanced upon them, seemed ever to recede and recede? It is true that but the other day, on the scene revisited, I was to be struck rather as by their weird immobility: there on the north side, still untenanted after sixty years, a tremendous span in the life of New York, was the vacant lot, undiminished, in which a friendly goat or two used to browse, whom we fed perversely with scraps of paper, just as perversely appreciated indeed, through the relaxed wooden palings. There hovers for me an impression of the glass roofs of a florist, a suffered squatter for a while; but florists and goats have alike disappeared and the barrenness of the place is as sordid as only untended gaps in great cities can seem. One of its boundaries, however, still breathes associations—the home of the Wards, the more eastward of a pair of houses then and still isolated has remained the same through all vicissitudes, only now quite shabbily mellow and, like everything else, much smaller than one had remembered it; yet this too without prejudice to the large, the lustrous part played in our prospect by that interesting family. I saddle their mild memory a bit "subjectively" perhaps with the burden of that character—making out that they were interesting really in spite of themselves and as unwittingly as M. Jourdain expressed himself in prose; owing their wild savour as they did to that New England stamp which we took to be strong upon them and no other exhibition of which we had yet enjoyed. It made them different, made them, in their homely grace, rather aridly romantic: I pored in those days over the freshness of the Franconia Stories of the brothers Abbott, then immediately sequent to the sweet Rollo series and even more admired; and there hung about the Wards, to my sense, that atmosphere of apples and nuts and cheese, of pies and jack-knives and "squrruls," of domestic Bible-reading and attendance at "evening lecture," of the fear of parental discipline and the cultivated art of dodging it, combined with great personal toughness and hardihood, an almost envied liability to warts on hard brown hands, a familiarity with garments domestically wrought, a brave rusticity in short that yet hadn't prevented the annexation of whole tracts of town life unexplored by ourselves and achieved by the brothers since their relatively recent migration from Connecticut—which State in general, with the city of Hartford in particular, hung as a hazy, fruity, rivery background, the very essence of Indian summer, in the rear of their discourse. Three in number, Johnny and Charley and Freddy, with castigating elders, even to the second and third generation back, dimly discerned through closed window-panes, they didn't at all haunt the halls of Ferrero—it was a part of their homely grace and their social tone, if not of their want of the latter, that this couldn't in the least be in question for them; on the other hand they frequented, Charley and Freddy at least, the Free School, which was round in Thirteenth Street—Johnny, the eldest, having entered the Free Academy, an institution that loomed large to us and that I see as towered or castellated or otherwise impressively embellished in vague vignettes, in stray representations, perhaps only of the grey schoolbook order, which are yet associated for me with those fond images of lovely ladies, "hand-painted," decorating at either end the interior of the old omnibusses. We must have been in relation with no other feeders at the public trough of learning—I can't account otherwise for the glamour as of envied privilege and strange experience that surrounded the Wards; they mixed, to the great sharpening of the edge of their wit, in the wild life *of* the people, beside which the life at Mr. Pulling Jenks's and even at the Institution Vergnès was colourless and commonplace. Somehow they were of the people, and still were full of family forms—which seemed, one dimly made out through the false perspective of all the cousinships, the stronger and clearer note of New England; the note that had already determined a shy yearning under perusal of the Rollo and Franconia chronicles. The special mark of these friends was perhaps however that of being socially young while they were annually old;

little Freddy in particular, very short, very inured and very popular, though less curiously wrinkled about eyes and mouth than Charley, confessed to monstrous birthdays even while crouching or hopping, even while racing or roaring, as a high superiority in the games of the street prescribed. It was to strike me later on, when reading or hearing of young Americans of those parts who had turned "hard" or reckless by reaction from excessive discipline, theologic and economic, and had gone to sea or to California or to the "bad," that Freddy and Charley were typical of the race, even if their fortunes had taken, as I hoped, a happier form. That, I said to myself for the interest of it, *that*, the stuff of the Wards, their homely grace, was all New England—so far at least as New England wasn't Emerson and Margaret Fuller and Mr. Channing and the "best Boston" families. Such, in small very plastic minds, is the intensity, if not the value, of early impressions.

And yet how can such visions not have paled in the southern glow of the Norcoms, who had lately arrived *en masse* from Louisville and had improvised a fine old Kentucky home in the last house of our row—the one to be occupied so differently, after their strange and precipitate flight, as I dimly make out, by the Ladies of the Sacred Heart; those who presently, if I mistake not, moved out to Bloomingdale, if they were not already in part established there. Next us westward were the Ogdens, three slim and fair sisters, who soared far above us in age and general amenity; then came the Van Winkles, two sisters, I think, and a brother—he much the most serious and judicious, as well as the most educated, of our friends; and so at last the Norcoms, during their brief but concentrated, most vivid and momentous, reign, a matter, as I recall it, of a couple of breathless winters. We were provided by their presence with as happy a foil as we could have wished to the plainness and dryness of the Wards; their homely grace was all their own and was also embodied in three brothers, Eugene, Reginald, Albert, whose ages would have corresponded, I surmise, with those of Johnny, Charley and Freddy if these latter hadn't, in their way, as I have hinted, defied any close notation. Elder sons—there were to my recollection no daughters—moved too as with their heads in the clouds; notably "Stiffy," eldest of all, whom we supposed gorgeous, who affected us as sublime and unapproachable and to whom we thus applied the term in use among us before we had acquired for reference to such types the notion of the *nuance*, the dandy, the dude, the masher. (Divided I was, I recall, between the dread and the glory of being so greeted, "Well, Stiffy—!" as a penalty of the least attempt at personal adornment.) The higher intensity for our sense of the Norcoms came from the large, the lavish, ease of their hospitality; whereas our intercourse with the Wards was mainly in the street or at most the "yard"—and it was a wonder how intimacy *could* to that degree consort with publicity. A glazed southern gallery, known to its occupants as the "poo'ch" and to the rake of which their innermost penetralia seemed ever to stand open, encompasses my other memories. Everything took place on the poo'ch, including the free, quite the profuse, consumption of hot cakes and molasses, including even the domestic manufacture of sausages, testified to by a strange machine that was worked like a handorgan and by the casual halves, when not the wholes, of stark stiff hogs fresh from Kentucky stores. We must have been for a time constantly engaged with this delightful group, who never ceased to welcome us or to feed us, and yet of the presence of whose members under other roofs than their own, by a return of hospitality received, I retain no image. They didn't count and didn't grudge—the sausage-mill kept turning and the molasses flowing for all who came; that was the expression of their southern grace, especially embodied in Albert, my exact contemporary and chosen friend (Reggie had but crushed my fingers under the hinge of a closing door, the mark of which act of inadvertence I was to carry through life,) who had profuse and tightly-crinkled hair, and the moral of whose queer little triangular brown teeth, casting verily a shade on my attachment to him, was pointed for me, not by himself, as the error of a Kentucky diet.

The great Kentucky error, however, had been the introduction into a free State of two pieces of precious property which our friends were to fail to preserve, the pair of affectionate black retainers whose presence contributed most to their exotic note. We revelled in the fact that Davy and Aunt Sylvia (pronounced An'silvy,) a light-brown lad with extraordinarily shining eyes and his straight, grave, deeper-coloured mother, not radiant as to anything but her vivid turban, had been born and kept in slavery of the most approved pattern and such as this intensity of their condition made them a joy, a joy to the curious mind, to consort with. Davy mingled in our sports and talk, he enriched, he adorned them with a personal, a pictorial lustre that none of us could emulate, and servitude in the absolute thus did more for him socially than we had ever seen done, above stairs or below, for victims of its lighter forms. What was not our dismay therefore when we suddenly learnt—it must have blown right up and down the street—that mother and son had fled, in the dead of night, from bondage? had taken advantage of their visit to the North simply to leave the house and not return, covering their tracks, successfully disappearing. They had never been for us so beautifully slaves as in this achievement of their freedom; for they did brilliantly achieve it—they escaped, on northern soil, beyond recall or recovery. I think we had already then, on the spot, the sense of some degree of presence at the making of history; the question of what persons of colour and of their condition might or mightn't do was intensely in the air; this was exactly the season of the freshness of Mrs. Stowe's great novel. It must have come out at the moment of our fondest acquaintance with our neighbours, though I have no recollection of hearing them remark upon it—any remark they made would have been sure to be so strong. I suspect they hadn't read it, as they certainly wouldn't have allowed it in the house; any more indeed than they had read or were likely ever to read any other work of fiction; I doubt whether the house contained a printed volume, unless its head had had in hand a law-book or so: I to some extent recover Mr. Norcom as a lawyer who had come north on important, difficult business, on contentious, precarious grounds—a large bald political-looking man, very loose and ungirt, just as his wife was a desiccated, depressed lady who mystified me by always wearing her nightcap, a feebly-frilled but tightly-tied and unmistakable one, and the compass of whose maternal figure beneath a large long collarless cape or mantle defined imperfectly for me of course its connection with the further increase of Albert's little brothers and sisters, there being already, by my impression, two or three of these in the background. Had Davy and An'silvy at least read Uncle Tom?—that question might well come up for us, with the certainty at any rate that they ignored him less than their owners were doing. These latter good people, who had been so fond of their humble dependents and supposed this affection returned, were shocked at such ingratitude, though I remember taking a vague little inward Northern comfort in their inability, in their discreet decision, not to raise the hue and cry. Wasn't one even just dimly aware of the heavy hush that, in the glazed gallery, among the sausages and the johnny-cakes, had followed the first gasp of resentment? I think the honest Norcoms were in any case astonished, let alone being much incommoded; just as *we* were, for that matter, when the genial family itself, installed so at its ease, failed us with an effect of abruptness, simply ceased, in their multitude, to be there. I don't remember their going, nor any pangs of parting; I remember only knowing with wonderment that they had gone, that obscurity had somehow engulfed them; and how afterwards, in the light of later things, memory and fancy attended them, figured their history as the public complication grew and the great intersectional plot thickened; felt even, absurdly and disproportionately, that they had helped one to "know Southerners." The slim, the sallow, the straight-haired and dark-eyed Eugene in particular haunted my imagination; he had not been my comrade of election—he was too much my senior; but I cherished the thought of the fine fearless young fire-eater he would have become and, when the War had broken out, I know not what dark but pitying vision of him stretched stark after a battle.

All of which sounds certainly like a meagre range—which heaven knows it was; but with a plea for the several attics, already glanced at, and the positive æsthetic reach that came to us through those dim resorts, quite worth making. They were scattered and they constituted on the part of such of our friends as had license to lead us up to them a ground of authority and glory proportioned exactly to the size of the field. This extent was at cousin Helen's, with a large house and few inmates, vast and free, so that no hospitality, under the eaves, might have matched that offered us by the young Albert—if only that heir of all the ages had had rather more imagination. He had, I think, as little as was possible—which would have counted in fact for an unmitigated blank had not W. J., among us, on that spot and elsewhere, supplied this motive force in any quantity required. He imagined—that was the point— the comprehensive comedies we were to prepare and to act; comprehensive by the fact that each one of us, even to the God-fearing but surreptitiously law-breaking Wards, was in fairness to be enabled to figure. Not one of us but was somehow to be provided with a part, though I recall my brother as the constant comic star. The attics were thus in a word our respective temples of the drama—temples in which the stage, the green-room and the wardrobe, however, strike me as having consumed most of our margin. I remember, that is, up and down the street—and the association is mainly with its far westward reaches—so much more preparation than performance, so much more conversation and costume than active rehearsal, and, on the part of some of us, especially doubtless on my own, so much more eager denudation, both of body and mind, than of achieved or inspired assumption. We shivered unclad and impatient both as to our persons and to our aims, waiting alike for ideas and for breeches; we were supposed to make our dresses no less than to create our characters, and our material was in each direction apt to run short. I remember how far ahead of us my brother seemed to keep, announcing a "motive," producing a figure, throwing off into space conceptions that I could stare at across the interval but couldn't appropriate; so that my vision of him in these connections is not so much of his coming toward me, or toward any of us, as of his moving rapidly away in fantastic garb and with his back turned, as if to perform to some other and more assured public. There were indeed other publics, publics downstairs, who glimmer before me seated at the open folding-doors of ancient parlours, but all from the point of view of an absolute supernumerary, more or less squashed into the wing but never coming on. Who were the copious Hunts?—whose ample house, on the north side, toward Seventh Avenue, still stands, next or near that of the De Peysters, so that I perhaps confound some of the attributes of each, though clear as to the blond Beekman, or "Beek," of the latter race, not less than to the robust George and the stout, the very stout, Henry of the former, whom I see bounding before a gathered audience for the execution of a *pas seul*, clad in a garment of "Turkey red" fashioned by his own hands and giving way at the seams, to a complete absence of *dessous*, under the strain of too fine a figure: this too though I make out in those connections, that is in the twilight of Hunt and De Peyster garrets, our command of a comparative welter of draperies; so that I am reduced to the surmise that Henry indeed had contours.

I recover, further, some sense of the high places of the Van Winkles, but think of them as pervaded for us by the upper air of the proprieties, the proprieties that were so numerous, it would appear, when once one had had a glimpse of them, rather than by the crude fruits of young improvisation.

Wonderful must it clearly have been still to fed amid laxities and vaguenesses such a difference of *milieux* and, as they used to say, of atmospheres. This was a word of those days—atmospheres were a thing to recognise and cultivate, for people really wanted them, gasped for them; which was why they took them, on the whole, on easy terms, never exposing them, under an apparent flush, to the last analysis. Did we at any rate really vibrate to one social tone after another, or are these adventures for me now but fond imaginations? No, we vibrated—or I'll be hanged, as I may say, if *I* didn't; little as I could tell it or may have known it, little as anyone else may have known. There were shades, after all, in our democratic order; in fact as I brood back to it I recognise oppositions the sharpest, contrasts the most intense. It wasn't given to us all to have a social tone, but the Costers surely had one and kept it in constant use; whereas the Wards, next door to them, were possessed of no approach to any, and indeed had the case been other, had they had such a consciousness, would never have employed it, would have put it away on a high shelf, as they put the last-baked pie, out of Freddy's and Charley's reach—heaven knows what *they* two would have done with it. The Van Winkles on the other hand were distinctly so provided, but with the special note that their provision was one, so to express it, with their educational, their informational, call it even their professional: Mr. Van Winkle, if I mistake not, was an eminent lawyer, and the note of our own house was the absence of any profession, to the quickening of our general as distinguished from our special sensibility. There was no Turkey red among those particular neighbours at all events, and if there had been it wouldn't have gaped at the seams. I didn't then know it, but I sipped at a fount of culture; in the sense, that is, that, our connection with the house being through Edgar, he knew about things—inordinately, as it struck me. So, for that matter, did little public Freddy Ward; but the things one of them knew about differed wholly from the objects of knowledge of the other: all of which was splendid for giving one exactly a sense of things. It intimated more and more how many such there would be altogether. And part of the interest was that while Freddy gathered his among the wild wastes Edgar walked in a regular maze of culture. I didn't then know about culture, but Edgar must promptly have known. This impression was promoted by his moving in a distant, a higher sphere of study, amid scenes vague to me; I dimly descry him as appearing at Jenks's and vanishing again, as if even that hadn't been good enough—though I may be here at fault, and indeed can scarce say on what arduous heights I supposed him, as a day-scholar, to dwell. I took the unknown always easily for the magnificent and was sure only of the limits of what I saw. It wasn't that the boys swarming for us at school were not often, to my vision, unlimited, but that those peopling our hours of ease, as I have already noted, were almost inveterately so—they seemed to describe always, out of view, so much larger circles. I linger thus on Edgar by reason of its having somehow seemed to us that he described—was it at Doctor Anthon's?—the largest of all. If there was a bigger place than Doctor Anthon's it was there he would have been. I break down, as to the detail of the matter, in any push toward vaster suppositions. But let me cease to stir this imponderable dust.

XIX

I try at least to recover here, however, some closer notation of W. J.'s aspects—yet only with the odd effect of my either quite losing him or but apprehending him again at seated play with his pencil under the lamp. When I see him he is intently, though summarily, rapidly drawing, his head critically balanced and his eyebrows working, and when I don't see him it is because I have resignedly relinquished him. I can't have been often for him a deprecated, still less an actively rebuffed suitor, because, as I say again, such aggressions were so little in order for me; but I remember that on my once offering him my company in conditions, those of some planned excursion, in which it wasn't desired, his putting the question of our difference at rest, with the minimum of explanation, by the responsible remark: "*I* play with boys who curse and swear!" I had sadly to recognise that I didn't, that I couldn't pretend to have come to that yet—and truly, as I look back, either the unadvisedness and inexpertness of my young contemporaries on all that ground must have been complete (an interesting note on our general manners after all,) or my personal failure to grasp must have been. Besides which I wonder scarce less now than I wondered then in just what company my brother's privilege was exercised; though if he had but richly wished to be discouraging he quite succeeded. It wasn't that I mightn't have been drawn to the boys in question, but that I simply wasn't qualified. All boys, I rather found, were difficult to play with—unless it was that they rather found *me*; but who would have been so difficult as these? They account but little, moreover, I make out, for W. J.'s eclipses; so that I take refuge easily enough in the memory of my own pursuits, absorbing enough at times to have excluded other views. I also plied the pencil, or to be more exact the pen—even if neither implement critically, rapidly or summarily. I was so often engaged at that period, it strikes me, in literary—or, to be more precise in dramatic, accompanied by pictorial composition—that I must again and again have delightfully lost myself. I had not on any occasion personally succeeded, amid our theatric strife, in reaching the footlights; but how could I have doubted, nevertheless, with our large theatrical experience, of the nature, and of my understanding, of the dramatic form? I sacrificed to it with devotion—by the aid of certain quarto sheets of ruled paper bought in Sixth Avenue for the purpose (my father's store, though I held him a great fancier of the article in general, supplied but the unruled;) grateful in particular for the happy provision by which each fourth page of the folded sheet was left blank. When the drama itself had covered three pages the last one, over which I most laboured, served for the illustration of what I had verbally presented. Every scene had thus its explanatory picture, and as each act—though I am not positively certain I arrived at acts—would have had its vivid climax. Addicted in that degree to fictive evocation, I yet recall, on my part, no practice whatever of narrative prose or any sort of verse. I cherished the "scene"—as I had so vibrated to the idea of it that evening at Linwood; I thought, I lisped, at any rate I composed, in scenes; though how much, or how far, the scenes "came" is another affair. Entrances, exits, the indication of "business," the animation of dialogue, the multiplication of designated characters, were things delightful in themselves—while I panted toward the canvas on which I should fling my figures; which it took me longer to fill than it had taken me to write what went with it, but which had on the other hand something of the interest of the dramatist's casting of his *personæ*, and must have helped me to believe in the validity of my subject.

From where on these occasions that subject can have dropped for me I am at a loss to say, and indeed have a strong impression that I didn't at any moment quite know what I was writing about: I am sure I couldn't otherwise have written so much. With scenes, when I think, what certitude did I want more?—scenes being the root of the matter, especially when they bristled with proper names and noted movements; especially, above all, when they flowered at every pretext into the very optic and perspective of the stage, where the boards diverged correctly, from a central point of vision, even as the lashes from an eyelid, straight down to the footlights. Let this reminiscence remind us of how rarely in those days the real stage was carpeted. The difficulty of composition was naught; the one difficulty was in so placing my figures on the fourth page that these radiations could be marked without making lines through them. The odd part of all of which was that whereas my cultivation of the picture was maintained my practice of the play, my addiction to scenes, presently quite dropped. I was capable of learning, though with inordinate slowness, to express ideas in scenes, and was not capable, with whatever patience, of making proper pictures; yet I aspired to this form of design to the prejudice of any other, and long after those primitive hours was still wasting time in attempts at it. I cared so much for nothing else, and that vaguely redressed, as to a point, my general failure of acuteness. I nursed the conviction, or at least I tried to, that if my clutch of the pencil or of the watercolour brush should once become intense enough it would make up for other weaknesses of grasp—much as that would certainly give it to do. This was a very false scent, which had however the excuse that my brother's example really couldn't but act upon me—the scent was apparently so true for *him*; from the moment my small "interest in art," that is my bent for gaping at illustrations and exhibitions, was absorbing and genuine. There were elements in the case that made it natural: the picture, the representative design, directly and strongly appealed to me, and was to appeal all my days, and I was only slow to recognise the *kind*, in this order, that appealed most. My face was turned from the first to the idea of representation—that of the gain of charm, interest, mystery, dignity, distinction, gain of importance in fine, on the part of the represented thing (over the thing of accident, of mere actuality, still unappropriated;) but in the house of representation there were many chambers, each with its own lock, and long was to be the business of sorting and trying the keys. When I at last found deep in my pocket the one I could more or less work, it was to feel, with reassurance, that the picture was still after all in essence one's aim. So there had been in a manner continuity, been not so much waste as one had sometimes ruefully figured; so many wastes are sweetened for memory as by the taste of the economy they have led to or imposed and from the vantage of which they could scarce look better if they had been current and blatant profit. Wasn't the very bareness of the field itself moreover a challenge, in a degree, to design?—not, I mean, that there seemed to one's infant eyes too few things to paint: as to that there were always plenty—but for the very reason that there were more than anyone noticed, and that a hunger was thus engendered which one cast about to gratify. The gratification nearest home was the imitative, the emulative—that is on my part: W. J., I see, needed no reasons, no consciousness other than that of being easily able. So he drew because he could, while I did so in the main only because he did; though I think we cast about, as I say, alike, making the most of every image within view. I doubt if he made more than I even then did, though earlier able to account for what he made. Afterwards, on other ground and in richer air, I admit, the challenge was in the fulness and not in the bareness of aspects, with their natural result of hunger appeased; exhibitions, illustrations abounded in Paris and London—the reflected image hung everywhere about; so that if there we daubed afresh and with more confidence it was not because no-one but because everyone did. In fact when I call our appetite appeased I speak less of our browsing vision, which was tethered and insatiable, than of our sense of the quite normal character of our own proceedings. In Europe we knew there was Art, just as there were soldiers and lodgings and concierges and little boys in the streets who stared at us, especially at our hats and boots, as at things of derision—just as, to put it negatively, there were practically no hot rolls and no iced water. Perhaps too, I should add, we didn't enjoy the works of Mr. Benjamin Haydon, then clustered at the Pantheon in Oxford Street, which in due course became our favourite haunt, so infinitely more, after all, than we had enjoyed those arrayed at the Düsseldorf collection in Broadway; whence the huge canvas of the Martyrdom of John Huss comes back to me in fact as a revelation of representational brightness and charm that pitched once for all in these matters my young sense of what should be.

Ineffable, unsurpassable those hours of initiation which the Broadway of the 'fifties had been, when all was said, so adequate to supply. If one wanted pictures there *were* pictures, as large, I seem to remember, as the side of a house, and of a bravery of colour and lustre of surface that I was never afterwards to see surpassed. We were shown without doubt, under our genial law here too, everything there was, and as I cast up the items I wonder, I confess, what ampler fare we could have dealt with. The Düsseldorf school commanded the market, and I think of its exhibition as firmly seated, going on from year to year—New York, judging now to such another tune, must have been a brave patron of that manufacture; I believe that scandal even was on occasion not evaded, rather was boldly invoked, though of what particular sacrifices to the pure plastic or undraped shocks to bourgeois prejudice the comfortable German genius of that period may have been capable history has kept no record. New accessions, at any rate, vividly new ones, in which the freshness and brightness of the paint, particularly lustrous in our copious light, enhanced from time to time the show, which I have the sense of our thus repeatedly and earnestly visiting and which comes back to me with some vagueness as installed in a disaffected church, where gothic excrescences and an ecclesiastical roof of a mild order helped the importance. No impression here, however, was half so momentous as that of the epoch-making masterpiece of Mr. Leutze, which showed us Washington crossing the Delaware in a wondrous flare of projected gaslight and with the effect of a revelation to my young sight of the capacity of accessories to "stand out." I live again in the thrill of that evening—which was the greater of course for my feeling it, in my parents' company, when I should otherwise have been in bed. We went down, after dinner, in the Fourteenth Street stage, quite as if going to the theatre; the scene of exhibition was near the Stuyvesant Institute (a circumstance stirring up somehow a swarm of associations, echoes probably of lectures discussed at home, yet at which my attendance had doubtless conveniently lapsed,) but Mr. Leutze's drama left behind any paler proscenium. We gaped responsive to every item, lost in the marvel of the wintry light, of the sharpness of the ice-blocks, of the sickness of the sick soldier, of the protrusion of the minor objects, that of the strands of the rope and the nails of the boots, that, I say, on the part of everything, of its determined purpose of standing out; but that, above all, of the profiled national hero's purpose, as might be said, of standing *up*, as much as possible, even indeed of doing it almost on one leg, in such difficulties, and successfully balancing. So memorable was that evening to remain for me that nothing could be more strange, in connection with it, than the illustration by the admired work, on its in after years again coming before me, of the cold cruelty with which time may turn and devour its children. The picture, more or less entombed in its relegation, was lividly dead—and that was bad enough. But half the substance of one's youth seemed buried with it. There were other pictorial evenings, I may add, not all of which had the thrill. Deep the disappointment, on my own part, I remember, at Bryan's Gallery of Christian Art, to which also, as for great emotions, we had taken the omnibus after dinner. It cast a chill, this collection of worm-eaten diptychs and triptychs, of angular saints and seraphs, of black Madonnas and obscure Bambinos, of such marked and approved "primitives" as had never yet been shipped to our shores. Mr. Bryan's shipment was presently to fall, I believe, under grave suspicion, was to undergo in fact fatal exposure; but it appealed at the moment in apparent good faith, and I have not forgotten how, conscious that it was fresh from Europe—"fresh" was beautiful in the connection!—I felt that my yearning should all have gone out to it. With that inconsequence to handle I doubt whether I proclaimed that it bored me—any more than I have ever noted till now that it made me begin badly with Christian art. I like to think that the collection consisted without abatement of frauds and "fakes" and that if these had been honest things my perception wouldn't so have slumbered; yet the principle of interest had been somehow compromised, and I think I have never since stood before a real Primitive, a primitive of the primitives, without having first to shake off the grey mantle of that night. The main disconcertment had been its ugly twist to the name of Italy, already sweet to me for all its dimness—even could dimness have prevailed in my felt measure of the pictorial testimony of home, testimony that dropped for us from the ample canvas of Mr. Cole, "the American Turner" which covered half a side of our front parlour, and in which, though not an object represented in it began to stand out after the manner of Mr. Leutze, I could always lose myself as soon as look. It depicted Florence from one of the neighbouring hills—I have often since wondered which, the picture being long ago lost to our sight; Florence with her domes and towers and old walls, the old walls Mr. Cole had engaged for, but which I was ruefully to miss on coming to know and love the place in after years. Then it was I felt how long before my attachment had started on its course— that closer vision was no beginning, it only took up the tale; just as it comes to me again to-day, at the end of time, that the contemplative monk seated on a terrace in the foreground, a constant friend of my childhood, must have been of the convent of San Miniato, which gives me the site from which the painter wrought. We had Italy again in the corresponding room behind—a great abundance of Italy I was free to think while I revolved between another large landscape over the sofa and the classic marble bust on a pedestal between the two back windows, the figure, a part of the figure, of a lady with her head crowned with vine-leaves and her hair disposed with a laxity that was emulated by the front of her dress, as my next younger brother exposed himself to my derision by calling the bit of brocade (simulated by the chisel) that, depending from a single shoulder-strap, so imperfectly covered her. This image was known and admired among us as the Bacchante; she had come to us straight from an American studio in Rome, and I see my horizon flush again with the first faint dawn of conscious appreciation, or in other words of the critical spirit, while two or three of the more restrictive friends of the house find our marble lady very "cold" for a Bacchante. Cold indeed she must have been— quite as of the tombstone temperament; but that objection would drop if she might only be called a Nymph, since nymphs were mild and moderate, and since discussion of a work of art mainly hung in those days on that issue of the producible *name*. I fondly recall, by the same token, that playing on a certain occasion over the landscape above the sofa, restrictive criticism, uttered in my indulged hearing, introduced me to what had probably been my very first chance, on such ground, for active participation. The picture, from the hand of a French painter, M. Lefèvre, and of but slightly scanter extent than the work of Mr. Cole, represented in frank rich colours and as a so-called "view in Tuscany" a rural scene of some exuberance, a broken and precipitous place, amid mountains and forests, where two or three bare-legged peasants or woodmen were engaged, with much emphasis of posture, in felling a badly gashed but spreading oak by means of a tense rope attached to an upper limb and at which they pulled together. "Tuscany?—are you sure it's Tuscany?" said the voice of restrictive criticism, that of the friend of the house who in the golden age of the precursors, though we were still pretty much precursors, had lived longest in Italy. And then on my father's challenge of this demur: "Oh in Tuscany, you know, the colours are much softer—there would be a certain haze in the atmosphere." "Why, of course," I can hear myself now blushingly but triumphantly intermingle—"the softness and the haze of our Florence there: isn't Florence in Tuscany?" It had to be parentally admitted that Florence was—besides which our friend had been there and knew; so that thereafter, within our walls, a certain *malaise* reigned, for if the Florence was "like it" then the Lefèvre couldn't be, and if the Lefèvre was like it then the Florence couldn't: a lapse from old convenience—as from the moment we couldn't name the Lefèvre where were we? All of which it might have been open to me to feel I had uncannily promoted.

XX

My own sense of the great matter, meanwhile—that is of our possibilities, still more than of our actualities, of Italy in general and of Florence in particular—was a perfectly recoverable little awareness, as I find, of certain mild soft irregular breathings thence on the part of an absent pair in whom our parents were closely interested and whose communications, whose Roman, Sorrentine, Florentine letters, letters in especial from the Baths of Lucca, kept open, in our air, more than any other sweet irritation, that "question of Europe" which was to have after all, in the immediate years, so limited, so shortened, a solution. Mary Temple the elder had, early in our Fourteenth Street period, married Edmund Tweedy, a haunter of that neighbourhood and of our house in it from the first, but never more than during a winter spent with us there by that quasi-relative, who, by an extension of interest and admiration—she was in those years quite exceedingly handsome—ranked for us with the Albany aunts, adding so a twist, as it were, to our tie with the Temple cousins, her own close kin. This couple must have been, putting real relatives aside, my parents' best friends in Europe, twitching thereby hardest the fine firm thread attached at one end to our general desire and at the other to their supposed felicity. The real relatives, those planted out in the same countries, are a chapter by themselves, whose effect on us, whose place in our vision, I should like to trace: that of the Kings, for instance, of my mother's kin, that of the Masons, of my father's—the Kings who cultivated, for years, the highest instructional, social and moral possibilities at Geneva, the Masons, above all, less strenuous but more sympathetic, who reported themselves to us hauntingly, during a considerable period, as enjoying every conceivable *agrément* at Tours and at the then undeveloped Trouville, even the winter Trouville, on the lowest possible terms. Fain would I, as for the "mere pleasure" of it, under the temptation to delineate, gather into my loose net the singularly sharp and rounded image of our cousin Charlotte of the former name, who figured for us, on the field of Europe, wherever we looked, and all the rest of time, as a character of characters and a marvel of placid consistency; through my vague remembrance of her return from China after the arrest of a commercial career there by her husband's death in the Red Sea—which somehow sounded like a dreadful form of death, and my scarce less faint recovery of some Christmas treat of our childhood under her roof in Gramercy Park, amid dim chinoiseries and, in that twilight of time, dimmer offspring, Vernon, Anne, Arthur, marked to us always, in the distincter years, as of all our young relatives the most intensely educated and most pointedly proper—an occasion followed by her permanent and invidious withdrawal from her own country. I would keep her in my eye through the Genevese age and on to the crisis of the Civil War, in which Vernon, unforgiven by her stiff conservatism for his Northern loyalty, laid down before Petersburg a young life of understanding and pain, uncommemorated as to the gallantry of its end—he had insistently returned to the front, after a recovery from first wounds, as under his mother's malediction—on the stone beneath which he lies in the old burial ground at Newport, the cradle of his father's family. I should further pursue my subject through other periods and places, other constantly "quiet" but vivid exhibitions, to the very end of the story—which for myself was the impression, first, of a little lonely, soft-voiced, gentle, relentless lady, in a dull Surrey garden of a summer afternoon, more than half blind and all dependent on the *dame de compagnie* who read aloud to her that Saturday Review which had ever been the prop and mirror of her opinions and to which she remained faithful, her children estranged and outworn, dead and ignored; and the vision, second and for a climax, of an old-world rez-de-chaussée at Versailles, goal of my final pilgrimage, almost in presence of the end (end of her very personal career, I mean, but not of her perfectly firm spirit or of her charmingly smooth address).

I confess myself embarrassed by my very ease of re-capture of my young consciousness; so that I perforce try to encourage lapses and keep my abundance down. The place for the lapse consents with difficulty, however, to be *any* particular point of the past at which I catch myself (easily caught as I am) looking about me; it has certainly nothing in common with that coign of vantage enjoyed by me one June afternoon of 1855 in the form of the minor share of the box of a carriage that conveyed us for the first time since our babyhood, W. J.'s and mine, through so much of a vast portentous London.

I was an item in the overflow of a vehicle completely occupied, and I thrilled with the spectacle my seat beside the coachman so amply commanded— without knowing at this moment why, amid other claims, I had been marked for such an eminence. I so far justify my privilege at least as still to feel that prime impression, of extreme intensity, underlie, deep down, the whole mass of later observation. There are London aspects which, so far as they still touch me, after all the years, touch me as just sensible reminders of this hour of early apprehension, so penetrated for me as to have kept its ineffaceable stamp. For at last we had come to Europe—we had disembarked at Liverpool, but a couple of days before, from that steamer Atlantic, of the Collins line, then active but so soon to be utterly undone, of which I had kept a romantic note ever since a certain evening of a winter or two before. I had on that occasion assisted with my parents at a varied theatrical exhibition—the theatre is distinct to me as Brougham's—one of the features of which was the at that time flourishing farce of Betsy Baker, a picture of some predicament, supposed droll, of its hero Mr. Mouser, whose wife, if I am correct, carries on a laundry and controls as she may a train of young assistants. A feature of the piece comes back to me as the pursuit of Mr. Mouser round and round the premises by the troop of laundresses, shouting his name in chorus, capture by them being abject, though whether through fear of their endearments or of their harsher violence I fail to remember. It was enough that the public nerve had at the moment been tried by the non-arrival of the Atlantic, several days overdue, to the pitch at last of extreme anxiety; so that, when after the fall of the curtain on the farce the distracted Mr. Mouser, still breathless, reappeared at the footlights, where I can see him now abate by his plight no jot of the dignity of his announcement, "Ladies and gentlemen, I rejoice to be able to tell you that the good ship Atlantic is safe!" the house broke into such plaudits, so huge and prolonged a roar of relief, as I had never heard the like of and which gave me my first measure of a great immediate public emotion—even as the incident itself to-day reminds me of the family-party smallness of the old New York, those happy limits that could make us all care, and care to fond vociferation, for the same thing at once. It was a moment of the golden age—representing too but a snatch of elation, since the wretched Arctic had gone down in mortal woe and her other companion, the Pacific, leaving England a few months later and under the interested eyes of our family group, then temporarily settled in London, was never heard of more. Let all of which show again what traps are laid about me for unguarded acute reminiscence.

I meet another of these, though I positively try to avoid it, in the sense of a day spent on the great fusty curtained bed, a mediæval four-poster such as I had never seen, of the hotel at the London and North-Western station, where it appeared, to our great inconvenience, that I had during the previous months somewhere perversely absorbed (probably on Staten Island upwards of a year before) the dull seed of malaria, which now suddenly broke out in chills and fever. This condition, of the intermittent order, hampered our movements but left alternate days on which we could travel, and as present to me as ever is the apprehended interest of my important and determinant state and of our complicated prospect while I lay, much at my ease—for I recall in particular certain short sweet times when I could be left alone—with the thick and heavy suggestions of the London room about me, the very smell of which was ancient, strange and impressive, a new revelation altogether, and the window open to the English June and the far off hum of a thousand possibilities. I consciously took them in, these last, and must then, I think, have first tasted the very greatest pleasure perhaps I was ever to know—that of almost holding my breath in presence of certain aspects to the end of so taking in. It was as if in those hours that precious fine art had been disclosed to me—scantly as the poor place and the small occasion might have seemed of an order to promote it. We seize our property by an avid instinct wherever we find it, and I must have kept seizing mine at the absurdest little rate, and all by this deeply dissimulative process of taking in, through the whole succession of those summer days. The next application of it that stands out for me, or the next that I make room for here, since I note after all so much less than I remember, is the intensity of a fond apprehension of Paris, a few days later, from the balcony of an hotel that hung, through the soft summer night, over the Rue de la Paix. I hung with the balcony, and doubtless with my brothers and my sister, though I recover what I felt as so much relation and response to the larger, the largest appeal only, that of the whole perfect Parisianism I seemed to myself always to have possessed mentally—even if

I had but just turned twelve!—and that now filled out its frame or case for me from every lighted window, up and down, as if each of these had been, for strength of sense, a word in some immortal quotation, the very breath of civilised lips. How I had anciently gathered such stores of preconception is more than I shall undertake an account of—though I believe I should be able to scrape one together; certain it is at any rate that half the beauty of the whole exposed second floor of a *modiste* just opposite, for instance, with the fittings and figurings, as well as the intent immobilities, of busy young women descried through frank, and, as it were, benignant apertures, and of such bright fine strain that they but asked to work far into the night, came from the effect on the part of these things of so exactly crowning and comforting I couldn't have said what momentous young dream. I might have been *right* to myself—as against some danger of being wrong, and if I had uttered my main comment on it all this must certainly have been "I told you so, I told you so!" What I had told myself was of course that the impression would be of the richest and at the same time of the most insinuating, and this after all didn't sail very close; but I had had before me from far back a picture (which might have been hung in the very sky,) and here was every touch in it repeated with a charm. Had I ever till then known what a charm *was?*—a large, a local, a social charm, leaving out that of a few individuals. It was at all events, this mystery, one's property—that of one's mind; and so, once for all, I helped myself to it from my balcony and tucked it away. It counted all immensely for practice in taking in.

I profited by that, no doubt, still a few days later, at an hour that has never ceased to recur to me all my life as crucial, as supremely determinant. The travelling-carriage had stopped at a village on the way from Lyons to Geneva, between which places there was then no railway; a village now nameless to me and which was not yet Nantua, in the Jura, where we were to spend the night. I was stretched at my ease on a couch formed by a plank laid from seat to seat and covered by a small mattress and other draperies; an indulgence founded on my visitation of fever, which, though not now checking our progress, assured me, in our little band, these invidious luxuries. It may have been that as my body was pampered so I was moved equally to pamper my spirit, for my appropriative instinct had neglected no item of our case from the first—by which I mean from the moment of our getting under way, that morning, with much elaboration, in the court of the old Hôtel de l'Univers at Lyons, where we had arrived two days before and awaited my good pleasure during forty-eight hours that overflowed for us perhaps somewhat less than any pair of days yet, but as regards which it was afterwards my complacent theory that my contemplative rest at the ancient inn, with all the voices and graces of the past, of the court, of the French scheme of manners in general and of ancient inns, as such, in particular, had prepared me not a little, when I should in due course hear of it, for what was meant by the *vie de province*—that expression which was to become later on so *toned*, as old fine colour and old fine opinion are toned. It was the romance of travel, and it was the *suggested* romance, flushed with suppositions and echoes, with implications and memories, memories of one's "reading," save the mark! all the more that our proper bestowal required two carriages, in which we were to "post," ineffable thought, and which bristled with every kind of contradiction of common experience. The postilion, in a costume rather recalling, from the halls of Ferrero, that of my débardeur, bobbed up and down, the Italian courier, Jean Nadali, black-whiskered and acquired in London, sat in the rumble along with Annette Godefroi of Metz, fresh-coloured, broad-faced and fair-braided, a "bonne Lorraine" if ever there was, acquired in New York: I enjoy the echo of their very names, neither unprecedented nor irreproducible, yet which melt together for me, to intensification, with all the rest; with the recovered moment, above all, of our pause at the inn-door in the cool sunshine—we had mounted and mounted—during which, in my absurdly cushioned state, I took in, as I have hinted, by a long slow swig that testified to some power of elbow, a larger draught of the wine of perception than any I had ever before owed to a single throb of that faculty. The village street, which was not as village streets hitherto known to me, opened out, beyond an interval, into a high place on which perched an object also a fresh revelation and that I recognised with a deep joy—though a joy that was doubtless partly the sense of fantastic ease, of abated illness and of cold chicken—as at once a castle and a ruin. The only castle within my ken had been, by my impression, the machicolated villa above us the previous summer at New Brighton, and as I had seen no structure rise beyond that majesty so I had seen none abased to the dignity of ruin. Loose boards were no expression of this latter phase, and I was already somehow aware of a deeper note in the crumbled castle than any note of the solid one—little experience as I had had either of solidity. At a point in the interval, at any rate, below the slope on which this memento stood, was a woman in a black bodice, a white shirt and a red petticoat, engaged in some sort of field labour, the effect of whose intervention just then is almost beyond my notation. I knew her for a peasant in sabots—the first peasant I had ever beheld, or beheld at least to such advantage. She had in the whole aspect an enormous value, emphasising with her petticoat's tonic strength the truth that sank in as I lay—the truth of one's embracing there, in all the presented character of the scene, an amount of character I had felt no scene present, not even the one I had raked from the Hôtel Westminster; the sort of thing that, even as mere fulness and mere weight, would sit most warmly in the mind. Supremely, in that ecstatic vision, was "Europe," sublime synthesis, expressed and guaranteed to me—as if by a mystic gage, which spread all through the summer air, that I should now, only now, never lose it, hold the whole consistency of it: up to that time it might have been but mockingly whisked before me. Europe mightn't have been flattered, it was true, at my finding her thus most signified and summarised in a sordid old woman scraping a mean living and an uninhabitable tower abandoned to the owls; that was but the momentary measure of a small sick boy, however, and the virtue of the impression was proportioned to my capacity. It made a bridge over to more things than I then knew.

XXI

How shall I render certain other impressions coming back to me from that summer, which were doubtless involved in my having still for a time, on the alternate days when my complaint was active, to lie up on various couches and, for my main comfort, consider the situation? I considered it best, I think, gathering in the fruits of a quickened sensibility to it, in certain umbrageous apartments in which my parents had settled themselves near Geneva; an old house, in ample grounds and among great spreading trees that pleasantly brushed our windows in the summer heats and airs, known, if I am not mistaken, as the Campagne Gerebsoff—which its mistress, an invalid Russian lady, had partly placed at our disposition while she reclined in her own quarter of the garden, on a chaise longue and under a mushroom hat with a green veil, and I, in the course of the mild excursions appointed as my limit, considered her from afar in the light of the legends supplied to me, as to her identity, history, general practices and proceedings, by my younger brother Wilky, who, according to his nature, or I may say to his genius, had made without loss of time great advances of acquaintance with her and quickened thereby my sense of his superior talent for life. Wilky's age followed closely on mine, and from that time on we conversed and consorted, though with lapses and disparities; I being on the whole, during the succession of those years, in the grateful, the really fortunate position of having one exposure, rather the northward, as it were, to the view of W. J., and the other, perhaps the more immediately sunned surface, to the genial glow of my junior. Of this I shall have more to say, but to meet in memory meanwhile even this early flicker of him is to know again something of the sense that I attached all along our boyhood to his successful sociability, his instinct for intercourse, his genius (as I have used the word) for making friends. It was the only genius he had, declaring itself from his tenderest years, never knowing the shadow of defeat, and giving me, above all, from as far back and by the very radiation of the fact, endlessly much to think of. For I had in a manner, thanks to the radiation, much of the benefit; his geniality was absolutely such that the friends he made were made almost less for himself, so to speak, than for other friends—of whom indeed we, his own adjuncts, were easily first—so far at least as he discriminated. At night all cats are grey, and in this brother's easy view all his acquaintance were his family. The trail of his sociability was over us all alike—though it here concerns me but to the effect, as I recover it, of its weight on my comparatively so indirect faculty for what is called taking life. I must have already at the Campagne Gerebsoff begun to see him take it with all his directness—begun in fact to be a trifle tormentedly aware that, though there might be many ways of so doing, we are condemned practically to a choice, not made free of them all; reduced to the use of but one, at the best, which it is to our interest to make the most of, since we may indeed sometimes make much. There was a small sad charm, I should doubtless add, in this operation of the contrast of the case before me with my own case; it was positively as if Wilky's were supplying me on occasion with the most immediate matter for my own. That was particularly marked after he had, with our elder brother, been placed at school, the Pensionnat Roediger, at Châtelaine, then much esteemed and where I was supposedly to join them on my complete recovery: I recall sociable, irrepressibly sociable *sorties* thence on the part of the pair as promptly breaking out, not less than I recall sociable afternoon visits to the establishment on the part of the rest of us: it was my brothers' first boarding school, but as we had in the New York conditions kept punctually rejoining our family, so in these pleasant Genevese ones our family returned the attention. Of this also more anon; my particular point is just the wealth of Wilky's contribution to my rich current consciousness—the consciousness fairly *made* rich by my taking in, as aforesaid, at reflective hours, hours when I was in a manner alone with it, our roomy and shadowy, our almost haunted interior.

Admirable the scale and solidity, in general, of the ancient villas planted about Geneva, and our house affected me as so massive and so spacious that even our own half of it seemed vast. I had never before lived so long in anything so old and, as I somehow felt, so deep; depth, depth upon depth, was what came out for me at certain times of my waiting above, in my immense room of thick embrasures and rather prompt obscurity, while the summer afternoon waned and my companions, often below at dinner, lingered and left me just perhaps a bit overwhelmed. That was the sense of it—the *character*, in the whole place, pressed upon me with a force I hadn't met and that was beyond my analysis—which is but another way of saying how directly notified I felt that such material conditions as I *had* known could have had no depth at all. My depth was a vague measure, no doubt, but it made space, in the twilight, for an occasional small sound of voice or step from the garden or the rooms of which the great homely, the opaque green shutters opened there softly to echo in—mixed with reverberations finer and more momentous, personal, experimental, if they might be called so; which I much encouraged (they borrowed such tone from our new surrounding medium) and half of which were reducible to Wilky's personalities and Wilky's experience: these latter, irrepressibly communicated, being ever, enviably, though a trifle bewilderingly and even formidably, *of* personalities. There was the difference and the opposition, as I really believe I was already aware— that one way of taking life was to go in for everything and everyone, which kept you abundantly occupied, and the other way was to be as occupied, quite as occupied, just with the sense and the image of it all, and on only a fifth of the actual immersion: a circumstance extremely strange. Life was taken almost equally both ways—that, I mean, seemed the strangeness; mere brute quantity and number being so much less in one case than the other. These latter were what I should have *liked* to go in for, had I but had the intrinsic faculties; that more than ever came home to me on those occasions when, as I could move further and stay out longer, I accompanied my parents on afternoon visits to Châtelaine and the Campagne Roediger, a scene that has remained with me as nobly placid and pastoral. The great trees stood about, casting afternoon shadows; the old thick-walled green-shuttered villa and its dépendances had the air of the happiest home; the big bearded bonhomie of M. Roediger among his little polyglot charges—no petits pays chauds these—appeared to justify, and more, the fond New York theory of Swiss education, the kind à la portée of young New Yorkers, as a beautifully genialised, humanised, civilised, even romanticised thing, in which, amid lawny mountain slopes, "the languages" flowed into so many beaming recipients on a stream of milk and honey, and "the relation," above all, the relation from master to pupil and back again, was of an amenity that wouldn't have been of this world save for the providential arrangement of a perfect pedagogic Switzerland. "Did you notice the relation—how charming it was?" our parents were apt to say to each other after these visits, in reference to some observed show of confidence between instructor and instructed; while, as for myself, I was lost in the wonder of *all* the relations—my younger brother seemed to live, and to his own ingenuous relish as well, in such a happy hum of them. The languages had reason to prosper—they were so copiously represented; the English jostled the American, the Russian the German, and there even trickled through a little funny French.

A great Geneva school of those days was the Institution Haccius, to which generations of our young countrymen had been dedicated and our own faces first turned—under correction, however, by the perceived truth that if the languages were in question the American reigned there almost unchallenged. The establishment chosen for our experiment must have appealed by some intimate and insinuating side, and as less patronised by the rich and the sophisticated—for even in those days some Americans were rich and several sophisticated; little indeed as it was all to matter in the event, so short a course had the experiment just then to run. What it mainly brings back to me is the fine old candour and queerness of the New York state of mind, begotten really not a little, I think, under our own roof, by the mere charmed perusal of Rodolphe Toeppfer's Voyages en Zigzag, the two goodly octavo volumes of which delightful work, an adorable book, taken with its illustrations, had come out early in the 'fifties and had engaged our fondest study. It is the copious chronicle, by a schoolmaster of endless humour and sympathy—of what degree and form of "authority" it never occurred to one even to ask—of his holiday excursions with his pupils, mainly on foot and with staff and knapsack, through the incomparable Switzerland of the time before the railways and the "rush," before the monster hotels, the desecrated summits, the vulgarised valleys, the circular tours, the perforating tubes, the funiculars, the hordes, the horrors. To turn back to Toeppfer's pages to-day is to get the sense of a lost paradise, and the effect for me even yet of having pored over them in my childhood is to steep in sweetness and quaintness some of the pictures—his own illustrations are of the pleasantest and drollest, and the association makes that faded Swiss master of landscape Calame, of the so-called calamités, a quite sufficient Ruysdael. It must have been conceived for us that we would lead in these conditions—always in pursuit of an education—a life not too dissimilar to that of the storied exiles in the forest of Arden; though one would fain not press, after all, upon ideals of culture so little organised, so little conscious, up to that moment, of our ferocities of comparison and competition, of imposed preparation. This particular loose ideal reached out from the desert—or what might under discouragement pass for such; it invoked the light, but a simplicity of view which was somehow one with the beauty of other convictions accompanied its effort; and though a glance at the social "psychology" of some of its cheerful estimates, its relative importances, assumed and acted upon, might here seem indicated, there are depths of the ancient serenity that nothing would induce me to sound.

I need linger the less, moreover, since we in fact, oddly enough, lingered so little; so very little, for reasons doubtless well known to ourselves at the time but which I at present fail to recapture, that what next stands vividly out for me is our renewed passage through Paris on the way to London for the winter; a turn of our situation invested at the time with nothing whatever of the wonderful, yet which would again half prompt me to soundings were I not to recognise in it that mark of the fitful, that accent of the improvised, that general quality of earnest and reasoned, yet at the same time almost passionate, impatience which was to devote us for some time to variety, almost to incoherency, of interest. We had fared across the sea under the glamour of the Swiss school in the abstract, but the Swiss school in the concrete soon turned stale on our hands; a fact over which I remember myself as no further critical than to feel, not without zest, that, since one was all eyes and the world decidedly, at such a pace, all images, it ministered to the panoramic. It ministered, to begin with, through our very early start for Lyons again in the October dawn—without Nadali or the carriages this time, but on the basis of the malle-poste, vast, yellow and rumbling, which we availed wholly to fill and of which the high haughtiness was such that it could stop, even for an instant, only at appointed and much dissevered places—to the effect, I recall, of its vainly attempted arrest by our cousin Charlotte King, beforementioned, whom I see now suddenly emerge, fresh, confident and pretty, from some rural retreat by the road, a scene of simple villeggiatura, "rien que pour saluer ces dames," as she pleaded to the conductor; whom she practically, if not permittedly, overmastered, leaving with me still the wonder of her happy fusion of opposites. The coach had not, in the event, paused, but so neither had she, and as it ignored flush and flurry quite as it defied delay, she was equally a match for it in these particulars, blandly achieving her visit to us while it rumbled on, making a perfect success and a perfect grace of her idea. She dropped as elegantly out as she had gymnastically floated in, and "ces dames" must much have wished they could emulate her art. Save for this my view of that migration has faded, though to shine out again to the sense of our early morning arrival in Paris a couple of days later, and our hunt there, vain at first, for an hotel that would put us numerously up; vain till we had sat awhile, in the Rue du Helder, I think, before that of an Albany uncle, luckily on the scene and finally invoked, who after some delay descended to us with a very foreign air, I fancied, and no possibility, to his regret, of placing us under his own roof; as if indeed, I remember reflecting, we could, such as we were, have been desired to share his foreign interests—such as *they* were. He espoused our cause, however, with gay goodnature—while I wondered, in my admiration for him and curiosity about him, how he really liked us, and (a bit doubtfully) whether I should have liked us had I been in his place; and after some further adventure installed us at the Hôtel de la Ville de Paris in the Rue de la Ville-l'Evêque, a resort now long since extinct, though it lingered on for some years, and which I think of as rather huddled and disappointingly private, to the abatement of spectacle, and standing obliquely beyond a wall, a high gateway and a more or less cobbled court.

XXII

Little else of that Parisian passage remains with me—it was probably of the briefest; I recover only a visit with my father to the Palais de l'Industrie, where the first of the great French Exhibitions, on the model, much reduced, of the English Crystal Palace of 1851, was still open, a fact explaining the crowded inns; and from that visit win back but the department of the English pictures and our stopping long before The Order of Release of a young English painter, J. E. Millais, who had just leaped into fame, and my impression of the rare treatment of whose baby's bare legs, pendent from its mother's arms, is still as vivid to me as if from yesterday. The vivid yields again to the vague—I scarce know why so utterly—till consciousness, waking up in London, renews itself, late one evening and very richly, at the Gloucester Hotel (or Coffee-House, as I think it was then still called,) which occupied that corner of Piccadilly and Berkeley Street where more modern establishments have since succeeded it, but where a fatigued and famished American family found on that occasion a fine old British virtue in cold roast beef and bread and cheese and ale; their expert acclamation of which echoes even now in my memory. It keeps company there with other matters equally British and, as we say now, early Victorian; the thick gloom of the inn rooms, the faintness of the glimmering tapers, the blest inexhaustibility of the fine joint, surpassed only by that of the grave waiter's reserve—plain, immutably plain fare all, but prompting in our elders an emphasis of relief and relish, the "There's nothing like it after all!" tone, which re-excited expectation, which in fact seemed this time to re-announce a basis for faith and joy.

That basis presently shrank to the scale of a small house hard by the hotel, at the entrance of Berkeley Square—expeditiously lighted on, it would thus appear, which again has been expensively superseded, but to the ancient little facts of which I fondly revert, since I owe them what I feel to have been, in the far past, the prime faint revelation, the small broken expression, of the London I was afterwards to know. The place wears on the spot, to this day, no very different face; the house that has risen on the site of ours is still immediately neighboured at the left by the bookseller, the circulating-librarian and news-agent, who modestly flourished in our time under the same name; the great establishment of Mr. Gunter, just further along, is as soberly and solidly seated; the mews behind the whole row, from the foot of Hay Hill at the right, wanders away to Bruton Street with the irregular grace that spoke to my young fancy; Hay Hill itself is somehow less sharply precipitous, besides being no longer paved, as I seem to recall its having been, with big boulders, and I was on the point of saying that its antique charm in some degree abides. Nothing, however, could be further from the truth; its antique charm quite succumbed, years ago, to that erection of lumpish "mansions" which followed the demolition of the old-world town-residence, as the house-agents say, standing, on the south side, between court and I suppose garden, where Dover Street gives way to Grafton; a house of many histories, of vague importances and cold reserves and deep suggestions, I used to think after scaling the steep quite on purpose to wonder about it. A whole chapter of life was condensed, for our young sensibility, I make out, into the couple of months—they can scarce have been more—spent by us in these quarters, which must have proved too narrow and too towny; but it can have had no passage so lively as the occurrences at once sequent to my father's having too candidly made known in some public print, probably The Times, that an American gentleman, at such an address, desired to arrange with a competent young man for the tuition at home of his three sons. The effect of his rash failure to invite application by letter only was the assault of an army of visitors who filled us with consternation; they hung about the door, cumbered the hall, choked the staircase and sat grimly individual in odd corners. How they were dealt with, given my father's precipitate and general charity, I can but feebly imagine; our own concern, in the event, was with a sole selected presence, that of Scotch Mr. Robert Thompson, who gave us his care from breakfast to luncheon each morning that winter, who afterwards carried on a school at Edinburgh, and whom, in years long subsequent, I happened to help R. L. Stevenson to recognise gaily as *his* early pedagogue. He was so deeply solicitous, yet withal so mild and kind and shy, with no harsher injunction to us ever than "Come now, be getting on!" that one could but think well of a world in which so gentle a spirit might flourish; while it is doubtless to the credit of his temper that remembrance is a blank in respect to his closer ministrations. I recall vividly his fresh complexion, his very round clear eyes, his tendency to trip over his own legs or feet while thoughtfully circling about us, and his constant dress-coat, worn with trousers of a lighter hue, which was perhaps the prescribed uniform of a daily tutor then; but I ask myself in vain what I can have "studied" with him, there remaining with me afterwards, to testify—this putting any scrap of stored learning aside—no single textbook save the Lambs' Tales from Shakespeare, which was given me as (of all things in the world) a reward. A reward for what I am again at a loss to say—not certainly for having "got on" to anything like the tune plaintively, for the most part, piped to me. It is a very odd and yet to myself very rich and full reminiscence, though I remember how, looking back at it from after days, W. J. denounced it to me, and with it the following year and more spent in Paris, as a poor and arid and lamentable time, in which, missing such larger chances and connections as we might have reached out to, we had done nothing, he and I, but walk about together, in a state of the direst propriety, little "high" black hats and inveterate gloves, the childish costume of the place and period, to stare at grey street-scenery (that of early Victorian London had tones of a neutrality!) dawdle at shop-windows and buy water-colours and brushes with which to bedaub eternal drawing-blocks. We might, I dare say, have felt higher impulses and carried out larger plans—though indeed present to me for this, on my brother's so expressing himself, is my then quick recognition of the deeper stirrings and braver needs he at least must have known, and my perfect if rueful sense of having myself had no such quarrel with our conditions: embalmed for me did they even to that shorter retrospect appear in a sort of fatalism of patience, spiritless in a manner, no doubt, yet with an inwardly active, productive and ingenious side.

It was just the fact of our having so walked and dawdled and dodged that made the charm of memory; in addition to which what could one have asked more than to be steeped in a medium so dense that whole elements of it, forms of amusement, interest and wonder, soaked through to some appreciative faculty and made one fail at the most of nothing but one's lessons? My brother was right in so far as that my question—the one I have just reproduced—could have been asked only by a person incorrigible in throwing himself back upon substitutes for lost causes, substitutes that might *temporarily* have appeared queer and small; a person so haunted, even from an early age, with visions of life, that aridities, for him, were half a terror and half an impossibility, and that the said substitutes, the economies and ingenuities that protested, in their dumb vague way, against weakness of situation or of direct and applied faculty, were in themselves really a revel of spirit and thought. It *had* indeed again an effect of almost pathetic incoherence that our brave quest of "the languages," suffering so prompt and for the time at least so accepted and now so inscrutably irrecoverable a check, should have contented itself with settling us by that Christmas in a house, more propitious to our development, in St. John's Wood, where we enjoyed a considerable garden and wistful view, though by that windowed privilege alone, of a large green expanse in which ladies and gentlemen practised archery. Just *that*—and not the art even, but the mere spectacle—might have been one of the substitutes in question; if not for the languages at least for one or another of the romantic connections we seemed a little to have missed: it was such a whiff of the old world of Robin Hood as we could never have looked up from the mere thumbed "story," in Fourteenth Street at any rate, to any soft confidence of. More than I can begin to say, that is by a greater number of queer small channels, did the world about us, thus continuous with the old world of Robin Hood, steal into my sense—a constant state of subjection to which fact is no bad instance of those refinements of surrender that I just named as my fond practice. I seem to see to-day that the London of the 'fifties was even to the weak perception of childhood a much less generalised, a much more eccentrically and variously characterised place, than the present great accommodated and accommodating city; it had fewer resources but it had many more features, scarce one of which failed to help the whole to bristle with what a little gaping American could take for an intensity of difference from *his* supposed order. It was extraordinarily the picture and the scene of Dickens, now so changed and superseded; it offered to my presumptuous vision still more the reflection of Thackeray—and where is the *detail* of the reflection of Thackeray now?—so that as I trod the vast length of Baker Street, the Thackerayan vista of other days, I throbbed with the pride of a vastly enlarged acquaintance.

I dare say our perambulations of Baker Street in our little "top" hats and other neatnesses must have been what W. J. meant by our poverty of life—whereas it was probably one of the very things most expressive to myself of the charm and the colour of history and (from the point of view of the picturesque) of society. We were often in Baker Street by reason of those stretched-out walks, at the remembered frequency and long-drawn push of which I am to-day amazed; recalling at the same time, however, that save for Robert Thompson's pitching ball with us in the garden they took for us the place of all other agilities. I can't but feel them to have been marked in their way by a rare curiosity and energy. Good Mr. Thompson had followed us in our move, occupying quarters, not far off, above a baker's shop on a Terrace—a group of objects still untouched by time—where we occasionally by way of change attended for our lessons and where not the least of our inspirations was the confidence, again and again justified, that our mid-morning "break" would determine the appearance of a self-conscious stale cake, straight from below, received by us all each time as if it had been a sudden happy thought, and ushered in by a little girl who might have been a Dickens foundling or "orfling." Our being reduced to mumble cake in a suburban lodging by way of reaction from the strain of study would have been perhaps a pathetic picture, but we had field-days too, when we accompanied our excellent friend to the Tower, the Thames Tunnel, St. Paul's and the Abbey, to say nothing of the Zoological Gardens, almost close at hand and with which we took in that age of lingering forms no liberty of abbreviation; to say nothing either of Madame Tussaud's, then in our interminable but so amiable Baker Street, the only shade on the amiability of which was just that gruesome association with the portal of the Bazaar—since Madame Tussaud had, of all her treasures, most vividly revealed to me the Mrs. Manning and the Burke and Hare of the Chamber of Horrors which lurked just within it; whom, for days after making their acquaintance (and prolonging it no further than our conscientious friend thought advisable) I half expected, when alone, to meet quite dreadfully on the staircase or on opening a door. All this experience was valuable, but it was not the languages—save in so far indeed as it was the English, which we hadn't in advance so much aimed at, yet which more or less, and very interestingly, came; it at any rate perhaps broke our fall a little that French, of a sort, continued to be with us in the remarkably erect person of Mademoiselle Cusin, the Swiss governess who had accompanied us from Geneva, whose quite sharply extrusive but on the whole exhilarating presence I associate with this winter, and who led in that longish procession of more or less similar domesticated presences which was to keep the torch, that is the accent, among us, fairly alight. The variety and frequency of the arrivals and departures of these ladies—whose ghostly names, again, so far as I recall them, I like piously to preserve, Augustine Danse, Amélie Fortin, Marie Guyard, Marie Bonningue, Félicie Bonningue, Clarisse Bader—mystifies me in much the same degree as our own academic vicissitudes in New York; I can no more imagine why, sociable and charitable, we so often changed governesses than I had contemporaneously grasped the principle of our succession of schools: the whole group of phenomena reflected, I gather, as a rule, much more the extreme promptitude of the parental optimism than any disproportionate habit of impatience. The optimism begot precipitation, and the precipitation had too often to confess itself. What is instructive, what is historic, is the probability that young persons offering themselves at that time as guides and communicators—the requirements of our small sister were for long modest enough—quite conceivably lacked preparedness, and were so thrown back on the extempore, which in turn lacked abundance. One of these figures, that of Mademoiselle Danse, the most Parisian, and prodigiously so, was afterwards to stand out for us quite luridly—a cloud of revelations succeeding her withdrawal; a cloud which, thick as it was, never obscured our impression of her genius and her charm. The daughter of a political proscript who had but just escaped, by the legend, being seized in his bed on the terrible night of the Deux-Décembre, and who wrote her micawberish letters from Gallipolis, Ohio, she subsequently figured to my imagination (in the light, that is, of the divined revelations, too dreadful for our young ears,) as the most brilliant and most genial of irregular characters, exhibiting the Parisian "mentality" at its highest, or perhaps rather its deepest, and more remarkable for nothing than for the consummate little art and grace with which she had for a whole year draped herself in the mantle of our innocent air. It was exciting, it was really valuable, to have to that extent rubbed shoulders with an "adventuress"; it showed one that for the adventuress there might on occasion be much to be said.

Those, however, were later things—extensions of view hampered for the present, as I have noted, by our mere London street-scenery, which had much to build out for us. I see again that we but endlessly walked and endlessly daubed, and that our walks, with an obsession of their own, constantly abetted our daubing. We knew no other boys at all, and we even saw no others, I seem to remember, save the essentially rude ones, rude with a kind of mediæval rudeness for which our clear New York experience had given us no precedent, and of which the great and constant sign was the artless, invidious wonder produced in them, on our public appearances, by the alien stamp in us that, for our comfort, we vainly sought to dissimulate. We conformed in each particular, so far as we could, to the prevailing fashion and standard, of a narrow range in those days, but in our very plumage—putting our *ramage* aside—our wood-note wild must have seemed to sound, so sharply we challenged, when abroad, the attention of our native contemporaries, and even sometimes of their elders, pulled up at sight of us in the from-head-to-foot stare, a curiosity void of sympathy and that attached itself for some reason especially to our feet, which were not abnormally large. The London people had for themselves, at the same time, an exuberance of type; we found it in particular a world of costume, often of very odd costume—the most intimate notes of which were the postmen in their frock-coats of military red and their black beaver hats; the milkwomen, in hats that often emulated these, in little shawls and strange short, full frocks, revealing enormous boots, with their pails swung from their shoulders on wooden yokes; the inveterate footmen hooked behind the coaches of the rich, frequently in pairs and carrying staves, together with the mounted and belted grooms without the attendance of whom riders, of whichever sex—and riders then were much more numerous— almost never went forth. The range of character, on the other hand, reached rather dreadfully down; there were embodied and exemplified "horrors" in the streets beside which any present exhibition is pale, and I well remember the almost terrified sense of their salience produced in me a couple of years later, on the occasion of a flying return from the Continent with my father, by a long, an interminable drive westward from the London Bridge railway-station. It was a soft June evening, with a lingering light and swarming crowds, as they then seemed to me, of figures reminding me of George Cruikshank's

Artful Dodger and his Bill Sikes and his Nancy, only with the bigger brutality of life, which pressed upon the cab, the early-Victorian fourwheeler, as we jogged over the Bridge, and cropped up in more and more gas-lit patches for all our course, culminating, somewhere far to the west, in the vivid picture, framed by the cab-window, of a woman reeling backward as a man felled her to the ground with a blow in the face. The London view at large had in fact more than a Cruikshank, there still survived in it quite a Hogarth, side—which I had of course then no name for, but which I was so sharply to recognise on coming back years later that it fixed for me the veracity of the great pictorial chronicler. Hogarth's mark is even yet not wholly overlaid; though time has *per contra* dealt with that stale servility of address which most expressed to our young minds the rich burden of a Past, the consequence of too much history. I liked for my own part a lot of history, but felt in face of certain queer old obsequiosities and appeals, whinings and sidlings and hand-rubbings and curtsey-droppings, the general play of apology and humility, behind which the great dim social complexity seemed to mass itself, that one didn't quite want so inordinate a quantity. Of that particular light and shade, however, the big broom of change has swept the scene bare; more history still has been after all what it wanted. Quite another order, in the whole connection, strikes me as reigning to-day—though not without the reminder from it that the relations in which manner, as a generalised thing, in which "tone," is *positively* pleasant, is really assured and sound, clear and interesting, are numerous and definite only when it has had in its past some strange phases and much misadventure.

XXIII

We were still being but vaguely "formed," yet it was a vagueness preferred apparently by our parents to the only definiteness in any degree open to us, that of the English school away from home (the London private school near home they would absolutely none of;) which they saw as a fearful and wonderful, though seemingly effective, preparation of the young for English life and an English career, but related to that situation only, so little related in fact to any other as to make it, in a differing case, an educational cul-de-sac, the worst of economies. They had doubtless heard claimed for it just that no other method for boys *was* so splendidly general, but they had, I judge, their own sense of the matter—which would have been that it all depended on what was meant by this. The truth was, above all, that to them the formative forces most closely bearing on us were not in the least vague, but very definite by *their* measure and intention; there were "advantages," generally much belauded, that appealed to them scantly, and other matters, conceptions of character and opportunity, ideals, values, importances, enjoying no great common credit but for which it was their belief that they, under whatever difficulties, more or less provided. In respect of which I further remind myself of the blest fewness, as yet, of our years; and I come back to my own sense, benighted though it may have been, of a highly-coloured and remarkably active life. I recognise our immediate, our practical ferment even in our decent perambulations, our discussions, W. J.'s and mine, of whether we had in a given case best apply for a renewal of our "artists' materials" to Messrs. Rowney or to Messrs. Windsor and Newton, and in our pious resort, on these determinations, to Rathbone Place, more beset by our steps, probably, than any other single corner of the town, and the short but charged vista of which lives for me again in the tempered light of those old winter afternoons. Of scarce less moment than these were our frequent visits, in the same general connection, to the old Pantheon of Oxford Street, now fallen from its high estate, but during that age a place of fine rococo traditions, a bazaar, an exhibition, an opportunity, at the end of long walks, for the consumption of buns and ginger-beer, and above all a monument to the genius of that wonderful painter B. R. Haydon. We must at one time quite have haunted the Pantheon, where we doubtless could better than elsewhere sink to contemplative, to ruminative rest: Haydon's huge canvases covered the walls—I wonder what has become now of The Banishment of Aristides, attended to the city gate by his wife and babe, every attitude and figure in which, especially that of the foreshortened boy picking up stones to shy at the all-too-just, stares out at me still. We found in these works remarkable interest and beauty, the reason of which was partly, no doubt, that we hung, to fascination, at home, over the three volumes of the hapless artist's Autobiography, then a new book, which our father, indulgent to our preoccupation, had provided us with; but I blush to risk the further surmise that the grand manner, the heroic and the classic, in Haydon, came home to us more warmly and humanly than in the masters commended as "old," who, at the National Gallery, seemed to meet us so little half-way, to hold out the hand of fellowship or suggest something that *we* could do, or could at least want to. The beauty of Haydon was just that he was new, shiningly new, and if he hinted that we might perhaps in some happy future emulate his big bravery there was nothing so impossible about it. If we adored daubing we preferred it *fresh*, and the genius of the Pantheon was fresh, whereas, strange to say, Rubens and Titian were not. Even the charm of the Pantheon yielded, however, to that of the English collection, the Vernon bequest to the nation, then arrayed at Marlborough House and to which the great plumed and draped and dusty funeral car of the Duke of Wellington formed an attractive adjunct. The ground-floor chambers there, none of them at that time royally inhabited, come back to me as altogether bleak and bare and as owing their only dignity to Maclise, Mulready and Landseer, to David Wilkie and Charles Leslie. *They* were, by some deep-seated English mystery, the real unattainable, just as they were none the less the directly inspiring and the endlessly delightful. I could never have enough of Maclise's Play-scene in Hamlet, which I supposed the finest composition in the world (though Ophelia did look a little as if cut in silhouette out of white paper and pasted on;) while as I gazed, and gazed again, at Leslie's Sancho Panza and his Duchess I pushed through the great hall of romance to the central or private apartments. Trafalgar Square had its straight message for us only in the May-time exhibition, the Royal Academy of those days having, without a home of its own, to borrow space from the National Gallery—space partly occupied, in the summer of 1856, by the first fresh fruits of the Pre-Raphaelite efflorescence, among which I distinguish Millais's Vale of Rest, his Autumn Leaves and, if I am not mistaken, his prodigious Blind Girl. The very word Pre-Raphaelite wore for us that intensity of meaning, not less than of mystery, that thrills us in its perfection but for one season, the prime hour of first initiations, and I may perhaps somewhat mix the order of our great little passages of perception. Momentous to us again was to be the Academy show of 1858, where there were, from the same wide source, still other challenges to wonder, Holman Hunt's Scapegoat most of all, which I remember finding so charged with the awful that I was glad I saw it in company—*it* in company and I the same: I believed, or tried to believe, I should have feared to face it all alone in a room. By that time moreover—I mean by 1858—we had been more fully indoctrinated, or such was the case at least with W. J., for whom, in Paris, during the winter of 1857, instruction at the atelier of M. Léon Coigniet, of a limited order and adapted to his years, had been candidly provided—that M. Léon Coigniet whose Marius meditating among the Ruins of Carthage impressed us the more, at the Luxembourg (even more haunted by us in due course than the Pantheon had been,) in consequence of this family connection.

Let me not, however, nip the present thread of our æsthetic evolution without a glance at that comparatively spare but deeply appreciated experience of the London theatric privilege which, so far as occasion favoured us, also pressed the easy spring. The New York familiarities had to drop; going to the play presented itself in London as a serious, ponderous business: a procession of two throbbing and heaving cabs over vast foggy tracts of the town, after much arrangement in advance and with a renewal of far peregrination, through twisting passages and catacombs, even after crossing the magic threshold. We sat in strange places, with still stranger ones behind or beside; we felt walls and partitions, in our rear, getting so hot that we wondered if the house was to burst into flame; I recall in especial our being arrayed, to the number of nine persons, all of our contingent, in a sort of rustic balcony or verandah which, simulating the outer gallery of a Swiss cottage framed in creepers, formed a feature of Mr. Albert Smith's once-famous representation of the Tour of Mont Blanc. Big, bearded, rattling, chattering, mimicking Albert Smith again charms my senses, though subject to the reflection that his type and presence, superficially so important, so ample, were somehow at odds with such ingratiations, with the reckless levity of his performance—a performance one of the great effects of which was, as I remember it, the very brief stop and re-departure of the train at Épernay, with the ringing of bells, the bawling of guards, the cries of travellers, the slamming of doors and the tremendous pop as of a colossal champagne-cork, made all simultaneous and vivid by Mr. Smith's mere personal resources and graces. But it is the publicity of our situation as a happy family that I best remember, and how, to our embarrassment, we seemed put forward in our illustrative châlet as part of the boisterous show and of what had been paid for by the house. Two other great evenings stand out for me as not less collectively enjoyed, one of these at the Princess's, then under the management of Charles Kean, the unprecedented (as he was held) Shakespearean revivalist, the other at the Olympic, where Alfred Wigan, the extraordinary and too short-lived Robson and the shrewd and handsome Mrs. Stirling were the high attraction. Our enjoyment of Charles Kean's presentation of Henry the Eighth figures to me as a momentous date in our lives: we did nothing for weeks afterwards but try to reproduce in water-colours Queen Katharine's dream-vision of the beckoning, consoling angels, a radiant group let down from the skies by machinery then thought marvellous—when indeed we were not parading across our schoolroom stage as the portentous Cardinal and impressively alternating his last speech to Cromwell with Buckingham's, that is with Mr. Ryder's, address on the way to the scaffold. The spectacle had seemed to us prodigious—as it was doubtless at its time the last word of costly scenic science; though as I look back from the high ground of an age that has mastered tone and fusion I seem to see it as comparatively garish and violent, after the manner of the complacently approved stained-glass church-windows of the same period. I was to have my impression of Charles Kean renewed later on—ten years later, in America—without a rag of scenic reinforcement; when I was struck with the fact that no actor so little graced by nature probably ever went so far toward repairing it by a kind of cold rage of endeavour. Were he and his wife really not *coercively* interesting on that Boston night of Macbeth in particular, hadn't their art a distinction that triumphed over battered age and sorry harshness, or was I but too easily beguiled by the old association? I have enjoyed and forgotten numberless rich hours of spectatorship, but somehow still find hooked to the wall of memory the picture of this hushed couple in the castle court, with the knocking at the gate, with Macbeth's stare of pitiful horror at his unused daggers and with the grand manner, up to the height of the argument, of Mrs. Kean's coldly portentous snatch of them. What I especially owe that lady is my sense of what she had in common, as a queer hooped and hook-nosed figure, of large circumference and archaic attire, strange tasteless toggery, with those performers of the past who are preserved for us on the small canvases of Hogarth and Zoffany; she helped one back at that time of her life to a vision of the Mrs. Cibbers and the Mrs. Pritchards— so affecting may often be such recovered links.

I see the evening at the Olympic as really itself partaking of that antiquity, even though Still Waters Run Deep, then in its flourishing freshness and as to which I remember my fine old friend Fanny Kemble's mentioning to me in the distant after-time that she had directed Tom Taylor to Charles de Bernard's novel of Un Gendre for the subject of it, passed at the moment for a highly modern "social study." It is perhaps in particular through the memory of our dismal approach to the theatre, the squalid slum of Wych Street, then incredibly brutal and barbarous as an avenue to joy, an avenue even sometimes for the muffled coach of Royalty, that the episode affects me as antedating some of the conditions of the mid-Victorian age; the general credit of which, I should add, was highly re-established for us by the consummately quiet and natural art, as we expertly pronounced it, of Alfred Wigan's John Mildmay and the breadth and sincerity of the representative of the rash mother-in-law whom he so imperturbably puts in her place. This was an exhibition supposed in its day to leave its spectators little to envy in the highest finish reached by the French theatre. At a remarkable height, in a different direction, moved the strange and vivid little genius of Robson, a master of fantastic intensity, unforgettable for us, we felt that night, in Planché's extravaganza of The Discreet Princess, a Christmas production preluding to the immemorial harlequinade. I still see Robson slide across the stage, in one sidelong wriggle, as the small black sinister Prince Richcraft of the fairy-tale, everything he did at once very dreadful and very droll, thoroughly true and yet none the less *macabre*, the great point of it all its parody of Charles Kean in The Corsican Brothers; a vision filled out a couple of years further on by his Daddy Hardacre in a two-acts version of a Parisian piece thriftily and coarsely extracted from Balzac's Eugénie Grandet. This occasion must have given the real and the finer measure of his highly original talent; so present to me, despite the interval, is the distinctiveness of his little concentrated rustic miser whose daughter helps herself from his money-box so that her cousin and lover shall save a desperate father, her paternal uncle, from bankruptcy; and the prodigious effect of Robson's appalled descent, from an upper floor, his literal headlong tumble and rattle of dismay down a steep staircase occupying the centre of the stage, on his discovery of the rifling of his chest. Long was I to have in my ears the repeated shriek of his alarm, followed by a panting babble of wonder and rage as his impetus hurled him, a prostrate scrap of despair (he was a tiny figure, yet "so held the stage" that in his company you could see nobody else) half way across the room. I associate a little uncertainly with the same night the sight of Charles Matthews in Sheridan's Critic and in a comedy botched from the French, like everything else in those days that was not either Sheridan or Shakespeare, called Married for Money; an example above all, this association, of the heaped measure of the old bills—vast and various enumerations as they were, of the size of but slightly reduced placards and with a strange and delightful greasy feel and redolence of printer's ink, intensely theatrical ink somehow, in their big black lettering. Charles Matthews must have been then in his mid-career, and him too, wasted and aged, infinitely "marked," I was to see again, ever so long after, in America; an impression reminding me, as I recover it, of how one took his talent so thoroughly for granted that he seemed somehow to get but half the credit of it: this at least in all save parts of mere farce and "patter," which were on a footing, and no very interesting one, of their own. The other effect, that of a naturalness so easy and immediate, so friendly and intimate, that one's relation with the artist lost itself in one's relation with the character, the artist thereby somehow positively suffering while the character gained, or at least while the spectator did—this comes back to me quite as a part even of my earlier experience and as attesting on behalf of the actor a remarkable genius; since there are no more charming artistic cases than those of the frank result, when it is frank *enough*, and the dissimulated process, when the dissimulation has been deep. To drop, or appear to drop, machinery and yet keep, or at least gain, intensity, the interesting intensity separated by a gulf from a mere unbought coincidence of aspect or organ, is really to do something. In spite of which, at the same time, what I perhaps most retain, by the light of the present, of the sense of that big and rather dusky night of Drury Lane is not so much the felt degree of anyone's talent as the fact that personality and artistry, *with* their intensity, could work their spell in such a material desert, in conditions intrinsically so charmless, so bleak and bare. The conditions gave nothing of what we regard to-day as most indispensable—since our present fine conception is but to reduce and fill in the material desert, to people and carpet and curtain it. We may be right, so far as that goes, but our predecessors were, with their eye on the essence, not wrong; thanks to which they wear the crown of our now thinking of them—if we do think of them—as in their way giants and heroes. What their successors were to become is another question; very much better dressed, beyond all doubt.

XXIV

Good Robert Thompson was followed by *fin* M. Lerambert—who was surely good too, in his different way; good at least for feigning an interest he could scarce have rejoicingly felt and that he yet somehow managed to give a due impression of: that artifice being, as we must dimly have divined at the time (in fact I make bold to say that I personally did divine it,) exactly a sign of his *finesse*. Of no such uncanny engine had Mr. Thompson, luckily, known a need—luckily since to what arsenal could he possibly have resorted for it? None capable of supplying it could ever have met his sight, and we ourselves should at a pinch have had to help him toward it. He was easily interested, or at least took an easy view, on such ground as we offered him, of what it was to be so; whereas his successor attached to the condition a different value—one recognising no secondary substitute. Perhaps this was why our connection with M. Lerambert can have lasted but four or five months—time even for his sharp subterfuge to have ceased entirely to serve him; though indeed even as I say this I vaguely recall that our separation was attended with friction, that it took him unaware and that he had been prepared (or so represented himself) for further sacrifices. It could have been no great one, assuredly, to deal with so intensely living a young mind as my elder brother's, it could have been but a happy impression constantly renewed; but we two juniors, Wilky and I, were a drag—Wilky's powers most displayed at that time in his preference for ingenuous talk over any other pursuit whatever, and my own aptitude showing for nil, according to our poor gentleman's report of me when a couple of months had sped, save as to rendering La Fontaine's fables into English with a certain corresponding felicity of idiom. I remember perfectly the parental communication to me of this fell judgment, I remember as well the interest with which its so quite definite character inspired me— that character had such beauty and distinctness; yet, and ever so strangely, I recover no sense of having been crushed, and this even though destitute, utterly, of any ground of appeal. The fact leaves me at a loss, since I also remember my not having myself thought particularly well, in the connection allowed, of my "rendering" faculty. "Oh," I seem inwardly to have said, "if it were to be, if it only could be, *really* a question of rendering—!" and so, without confusion, though in vague, very vague, mystification to have left it: as if so many things, intrinsic and extrinsic, would have to change and operate, so many would have to happen, so much water have to flow under the bridge, before I could give primary application to such a thought, much more finish such a sentence.

All of which is but a way of saying that we had since the beginning of the summer settled ourselves in Paris, and that M. Lerambert—by what agency invoked, by what revelation vouchsafed, I quite forget—was at this time attending us in a so-called pavilion, of middling size, that, between the Rond-Point and the Rue du Colisée, hung, at no great height, over the Avenue des Champs-Elysées; hung, that is, from the vantage of its own considerable terrace, surmounted as the parapet of the latter was with iron railings rising sufficiently to protect the place for familiar use and covert contemplation (we ever so fondly used it,) and yet not to the point of fencing out life. A blest little old-world refuge it must have seemed to us, with its protuberantly-paved and peculiarly resonant small court and idle *communs* beside it, accessible by a high grille where the jangle of the bell and the clatter of response across the stones might have figured a comprehensive echo of all old Paris. Old Paris then even there considerably lingered; I recapture much of its presence, for that matter, within our odd relic of a house, the property of an American southerner from whom our parents had briefly hired it and who appeared to divide his time, poor unadmonished gentleman of the eve of the Revolution, between Louisiana and France. What association could have breathed more from the queer graces and the queer incommodities alike, from the diffused glassy polish of floor and perilous staircase, from the redundancy of mirror and clock and ormolu vase, from the irrepressibility of the white and gold panel, from that merciless elegance of tense red damask, above all, which made the gilt-framed backs of sofa and chair as sumptuous, no doubt, but as sumptuously stiff, as the brocaded walls? It was amid these refinements that we presently resumed our studies—even explicitly far from arduous at first, as the Champs-Elysées were perforce that year our summer habitation and some deference was due to the place and the season, lessons of any sort being at best an infraction of the latter. M. Lerambert, who was spare and tightly black-coated, spectacled, pale and prominently intellectual, who lived in the Rue Jacob with his mother and sister, exactly as he should have done to accentuate prophetically his resemblance, save for the spectacles, to some hero of Victor Cherbuliez, and who, in fine, was conscious, not unimpressively, of his authorship of a volume of meditative verse sympathetically mentioned by the Sainte-Beuve of the Causeries in a review of the young poets of the hour ("M. Lerambert too has loved, M. Lerambert too has suffered, M. Lerambert too has sung!" or words to that effect:) this subtle personality, really a high form of sensibility I surmise, and as qualified for other and intenser relations as any Cherbuliez figure of them all, was naturally not to be counted on to lead us gapingly forth as good Mr. Thompson had done; so that my reminiscence of warm somniferous mornings by the windows that opened to the clattery, plashy court is quite, so far as my record goes, relievingly unbroken.

The afternoons, however, glimmer back to me shamelessly different, for our circle had promptly been joined by the all-knowing and all-imposing Mademoiselle Danse aforesaid, her of the so flexible *taille* and the so salient smiling eyes, than which even those of Miss Rebecca Sharp, that other epic governess, were not more pleasingly green; who provided with high efficiency for our immediate looser needs—mine and Wilky's and those of our small brother Bob (l'ingénieux petit Robertson as she was to dub him,) and of our still smaller sister at least—our first fine *flâneries* of curiosity. Her brave Vaudoise predecessor had been bequeathed by us in London to a higher sphere than service with mere earnest nomads could represent; but had left us clinging and weeping and was for a long time afterwards to write to us, faithfully, in the most beautiful copper-plate hand, out of the midst of her "rise"; with details that brought home to us as we had never known it brought the material and institutional difference between the nomadic and the solidly, the spreadingly seated. A couple of years later, on an occasion of our being again for a while in London, she hastened to call on us, and, on departing, amiably invited me to walk back with her, for a gossip—it was a bustling day of June—across a long stretch of the town; when I left her at a glittering portal with the impression of my having in our transit seen much of Society (the old London "season" filled the measure, had length and breadth and thickness, to an extent now foregone,) and, more particularly, achieved a small psychologic study, noted the action of the massive English machinery directed to its end, which had been in this case effectually to tame the presumptuous and "work over" the crude. I remember on that occasion retracing my steps from Eaton Square to Devonshire Street with a lively sense of observation exercised by the way, a perfect gleaning of golden straws. Our guide and philosopher of the summer days in Paris was no such character as that; she had arrived among us full-fledged and consummate, fortunately for the case altogether—as our mere candid humanity would otherwise have had scant practical pressure to bring. Thackeray's novel contains a plate from his own expressive hand representing Miss Sharp lost in a cynical day-dream while her neglected pupils are locked in a scrimmage on the floor; but the marvel of *our* exemplar of the Becky type was exactly that though her larger, her more interested and sophisticated views had a range that she not only permitted us to guess but agreeably invited us to follow almost to their furthest limits, we never for a moment ceased to be aware of her solicitude. We might, we must, so tremendously have bored her, but no ironic artist could have caught her at any juncture in the posture of disgust: really, I imagine, because her own ironies would have been too fine for him and too numerous and too mixed. And this remarkable creature vouchsafed us all information for the free enjoyment—on the terms proper to our tender years—of her beautiful city.

It was not by the common measure then so beautiful as now; the second Empire, too lately installed, was still more or less feeling its way, with the great free hand soon to be allowed to Baron Haussmann marked as yet but in the light preliminary flourish. Its connections with the past, however, still hung thickly on; its majesties and symmetries, comparatively vague and general, were subject to the happy accident, the charming lapse and the odd extrusion, a bonhomie of chance composition and colour now quite purged away. The whole region of the Champs-Elysées, where we must after all at first have principally prowled, was another world from the actual huge centre of repeated radiations; the splendid Avenue, as we of course already thought it, carried the eye from the Tuileries to the Arch, but pleasant old places abutted on it by the way, gardens and terraces and hôtels of another time, pavilions still braver than ours, cabarets and cafés of homely, almost of rural type, with a relative and doubtless rather dusty ruralism, spreading away to the River and the Wood. What was the Jardin d'Hiver, a place of entertainment standing quite over against us and that looped itself at night with little coloured oil-lamps, a mere twinkling grin upon the face of pleasure? Dim my impression of having been admitted—or rather, I suppose, conducted, though under conductorship now vague to me—to view it by colourless day, when it must have worn the stamp of an auction-room quite void of the "lots." More distinct on the other hand the image of the bustling barrière at the top of the Avenue, on the hither side of the Arch, where the old loose-girt *banlieue* began at once and the two matched lodges of the octroi, highly, that is expressly even if humbly, architectural, guarded the entrance, on either side, with such a suggestion of the generations and dynasties and armies, the revolutions and restorations they had seen come and go. But the Avenue of the Empress, now, so much more thinly, but of the Wood itself, had already been traced, as the Empress herself, young, more than young, attestedly and agreeably *new*, and fair and shining, was, up and down the vista, constantly on exhibition; with the thrill of that surpassed for us, however, by the incomparable passage, as we judged it, of the baby Prince Imperial borne forth for his airing or his progress to Saint-Cloud in the splendid coach that gave a glimpse of appointed and costumed nursing breasts and laps, and beside which the *cent-gardes*, all light-blue and silver and intensely erect quick jolt, rattled with pistols raised and cocked. Was a public holiday ever more splendid than that of the Prince's baptism at Notre Dame, the fête of Saint-Napoléon, or was any ever more immortalised, as we say, than this one was to be by the wonderfully ample and vivid picture of it in the Eugène Rougon of Emile Zola, who must have taken it in, on the spot, as a boy of about our own number of years, though of so much more implanted and predestined an evocatory gift? The sense of that interminable hot day, a day of hanging about and waiting and shuffling in dust, in crowds, in fatigue, amid booths and pedlars and performers and false alarms and expectations and renewed reactions and rushes, all transfigured at the last, withal, by the biggest and brightest illumination up to that time offered even the Parisians, the blinding glare of the new Empire effectually symbolised—the vision of the whole, I say, comes back to me quite in the form of a chapter from the Rougon-Macquart, with its effect of something long and dense and heavy, without shades or undertones, but immensely kept-up and done. I dare say that for those months our contemplations, our daily exercise in general, strayed little beyond the Champs-Elysées, though I recall confusedly as well certain excursions to Passy and Auteuil, where we foregathered with small resident compatriots the easy gutturalism of whose French, an unpremeditated art, was a revelation, an initiation, and whence we roamed, for purposes of picnic, into parts of the Bois de Boulogne that, oddly enough, figured to us the virgin forest better than anything at our own American door had done.

It was the social aspect of our situation that most appealed to me, none the less—for I detect myself, as I woo it all back, disengaging a social aspect again, and more than ever, from the phenomena disclosed to my reflective gape or to otherwise associated strolls; perceptive passages not wholly independent even of the occupancy of two-sous chairs within the charmed circle of Guignol and of Gringalet. I suppose I should have blushed to confess it, but Polichinelle and his puppets, in the afternoons, under an umbrage sparse till evening fell, had still their spell to cast—as part and parcel, that is, of the general intensity of animation and variety of feature. The "amusement," the æsthetic and human appeal, of Paris had in those days less the air of a great shining conspiracy to please, the machinery in movement confessed less to its huge purpose; but manners and types and traditions, the detail of the scene, its pointed particulars, went their way with a straighter effect, as well as often with a homelier grace—character, temper and tone had lost comparatively little of their emphasis. These scattered accents were matter for our eyes and ears—not a little even already for our respective imaginations; though it is only as the season waned and we set up our fireside afresh and for the winter that I connect my small revolution with a wider field and with the company of W. J. Again for that summer he was to be in eclipse to me; Guignol and Gringalet failed to claim his attention, and Mademoiselle Danse, I make out, deprecated his theory of exact knowledge, besides thinking him perhaps a little of an *ours*—which came to the same thing. We adjourned that autumn to quarters not far off, a wide-faced apartment in the street then bravely known as the Rue d'Angoulême-St.-Honoré and now, after other mutations, as the Rue La Boëtie; which we were again to exchange a year later for an abode in the Rue Montaigne, this last after a summer's absence at Boulogne-sur-Mer; the earlier migration setting up for me the frame of a considerably animated picture. Animated at best it was with the spirit and the modest facts of our family life, among which I number the cold finality of M. Lerambert, reflected in still other testimonies—that is till the date of our definite but respectful rupture with him, followed as the spring came on by our ineluctable phase at the Institution Fezandié in the Rue Balzac; of which latter there will be even more to say than I shall take freedom for. With the Rue d'Angoulême came extensions—even the mere immediate view of opposite intimacies and industries, the subdivided aspects and neat ingenuities of the applied Parisian genius counting as such: our many-windowed *premier*, above an entresol of no great height, hung over the narrow and, during the winter months, not a little dusky channel, with endless movement and interest in the vivid exhibition it supplied. What faced us was a series of subjects, with the baker, at the corner, for the first—the impeccable dispenser of the so softly-crusty crescent-rolls that we woke up each morning to hunger for afresh, with our weak café-au-lait, as for the one form of "European" breakfast-bread fit to be named even with the feeblest of our American forms. Then came the small crêmerie, white picked out with blue, which, by some secret of its own keeping, afforded, within the compass of a few feet square, prolonged savoury meals to working men, white-frocked or blue-frocked, to uniformed cabmen, stout or spare, but all more or less audibly *bavards* and discernibly critical; and next the compact embrasure of the écaillère or oyster-lady, she and her paraphernalia fitted into their interstice much as the mollusc itself into its shell; neighboured in turn by the marchand-de-bois, peeping from as narrow a cage, his neat faggots and chopped logs stacked beside him and above him in his sentry-box quite as the niches of saints, in early Italian pictures, are framed with tightly-packed fruits and flowers. Space and remembrance fail me for the rest of the series, the attaching note of which comes back as the note of diffused sociability and domestic, in fact more or less æsthetic, ingenuity, with the street a perpetual parlour or household centre for the flitting, pausing, conversing little bourgeoise or ouvrière to sport, on every pretext and in every errand, her fluted cap, her composed head, her neat ankles and her ready wit. Which is to say indeed but that life and manners were more pointedly and harmoniously expressed, under our noses there, than we had perhaps found them anywhere save in the most salient passages of "stories"; though I must in spite of it not write as if these trifles were all our fare.

XXV

That autumn renewed, I make out, our long and beguiled walks, my own with W. J. in especial; at the same time that I have somehow the sense of the whole more broken appeal on the part of Paris, the scanter confidence and ease it inspired in us, the perhaps more numerous and composite, but obscurer and more baffled intimations. Not indeed—for all my brother's later vision of an accepted flatness in it—that there was not some joy and some grasp; why else were we forever (as I seem to conceive we were) measuring the great space that separated us from the gallery of the Luxembourg, every step of which, either way we took it, fed us with some interesting, some admirable image, kept us in relation to something nobly intended? That particular walk was not prescribed us, yet we appear to have hugged it, across the Champs-Elysées to the river, and so over the nearest bridge and the quays of the left bank to the Rue de Seine, as if it somehow held the secret of our future; to the extent even of my more or less sneaking off on occasion to take it by myself, to taste of it with a due undiverted intensity and the throb as of the finest, which *could* only mean the most Parisian, adventure. The further quays, with their innumerable old bookshops and print-shops, the long cases of each of these commodities, exposed on the parapets in especial, must have come to know us almost as well as we knew them; with plot thickening and emotion deepening steadily, however, as we mounted the long, black Rue de Seine— *such* a stretch of perspective, *such* an intensity of tone as it offered in those days; where every low-browed vitrine waylaid us and we moved in a world of which the dark message, expressed in we couldn't have said what sinister way too, might have been "Art, art, art, don't you see? Learn, little gaping pilgrims, what *that* is!" Oh we learned, that is we tried to, as hard as ever we could, and were fairly well at it, I always felt, even by the time we had passed up into that comparatively short but wider and finer vista of the Rue de Tournon, which in those days more abruptly crowned the more compressed approach and served in a manner as a great outer vestibule to the Palace. Style, dimly described, looked down there, as with conscious encouragement, from the high grey-headed, clear-faced, straight-standing old houses—very much as if wishing to say "Yes, small staring jeune homme, we are dignity and memory and measure, we are conscience and proportion and taste, not to mention strong sense too: for all of which good things take us—you won't find one of them when you find (as you're going soon to begin to at such a rate) vulgarity." This, I admit, was an abundance of remark to such young ears; but it did all, I maintain, tremble in the air, with the sense that the Rue de Tournon, cobbled and a little grass-grown, might more or less have figured some fine old street *de province*: I cherished in short its very name and think I really hadn't to wait to prefer the then, the unmenaced, the inviolate Café Foyot of the left hand corner, the much-loved and so haunted Café Foyot of the old Paris, to its—well, to its roaring successor. The wide mouth of the present Boulevard Saint-Michel, a short way round the corner, had not yet been forced open to the exhibition of more or less glittering fangs; old Paris still pressed round the Palace and its gardens, which formed the right, the sober social antithesis to the "elegant" Tuileries, and which in fine, with these renewals of our young confidence, reinforced both in a general and in a particular way one of the fondest of our literary curiosities of that time, the conscientious study of Les Français Peints par Eux-Mêmes, rich in wood-cuts of Gavarni, of Grandville, of Henri-Monnier, which we held it rather our duty to admire and W. J. even a little his opportunity to copy in pen-and-ink. This gilt-edged and double-columned octavo it was that first disclosed to me, forestalling a better ground of acquaintance, the great name of Balzac, who, in common with every other "light" writer of his day, contributed to its pages: hadn't I pored over his exposition there of the contrasted types of L'Habituée des Tuileries and L'Habituée du Luxembourg?—finding it very *serré*, in fact what I didn't then know enough to call very stodgy, but flavoured withal and a trifle lubricated by Gavarni's two drawings, which had somehow so much, in general, to say.

Let me not however dally by the way, when nothing, at those hours, I make out, so much spoke to us as the animated pictured halls within the Palace, primarily those of the Senate of the Empire, but then also forming, as with extensions they still and much more copiously form, the great Paris museum of contemporary art. This array was at that stage a comparatively (though only comparatively) small affair; in spite of which fact we supposed it vast and final—so that it would have shocked us to foreknow how in many a case, and of the most cherished cases, the finality was to break down. Most of the works of the modern schools that we most admired are begging their bread, I fear, from door to door—that is from one provincial museum or dim back seat to another; though we were on much-subsequent returns to draw a long breath for the saved state of some of the great things as to which our faith had been clearest. It had been clearer for none, I recover, than for Couture's Romains de la Décadence, recently acclaimed, at that time, as the last word of the grand manner, but of the grand manner modernised, humanised, philosophised, redeemed from academic death; so that it was to this master's school that the young American contemporary flutter taught its wings to fly straightest, and that I could never, in the long aftertime, face his masterpiece and all its old meanings and marvels without a rush of memories and a stir of ghosts. William Hunt, the New Englander of genius, the "Boston painter" whose authority was greatest during the thirty years from 1857 or so, and with whom for a time in the early period W. J. was to work all devotedly, had prolonged his studies in Paris under the inspiration of Couture and of Edouard Frère; masters in a group completed by three or four of the so finely interesting landscapists of that and the directly previous age, Troyon, Rousseau, Daubigny, even Lambinet and others, and which summed up for the American collector and in the New York and Boston markets the idea of the modern in the masterly. It was a comfortable time—when appreciation could go so straight, could rise, and rise higher, without critical contortions; when we could, I mean, be both so intelligent and so "quiet." We were in our immediate circle to know Couture himself a little toward the end of his life, and I was somewhat to wonder then where he had picked up the æsthetic hint for the beautiful Page with a Falcon, if I have the designation right, his other great bid for style and capture of it—which we were long to continue to suppose perhaps the rarest of all modern pictures. The feasting Romans were conceivable enough, I mean *as* a conception; no mystery hung about them—in the sense of one's asking one's self whence they had come and by what romantic or roundabout or nobly-dangerous journey; which is that air of the poetic shaken out as from strong wings when great presences, in any one of the arts, appear to alight. What I remember, on the other hand, of the splendid fair youth in black velvet and satin or whatever who, while he mounts the marble staircase, shows off the great bird on his forefinger with a grace that shows *him* off, was that it failed to help us to divine, during that after-lapse of the glory of which I speak, by what rare chance, for the obscured old ex-celebrity we visited, the heavens had once opened. Poetry had swooped down, breathed on him for an hour and fled. Such at any rate are the see-saws of reputations—which it contributes to the interest of any observational lingering on this planet to have caught so repeatedly in their weird motion; the question of what may happen, under one's eyes, in particular cases, before that motion sinks to rest, whether at the up or at the down end, being really a bribe to one's own non-departure. Especially great the interest of having noted all the rises and falls and of being able to compare the final point—so far as any certainty may go as to that—either with the greatest or the least previous altitudes; since it is only when there have been exaltations (which is what is not commonest), that our attention is most rewarded.

If the see-saw was to have operated indeed for Eugène Delacroix, our next young admiration, though much more intelligently my brother's than mine, that had already taken place and settled, for we were to go on seeing him, and to the end, in firm possession of his crown, and to take even, I think, a harmless pleasure in our sense of having from so far back been sure of it. I was sure of it, I must properly add, but as an effect of my brother's sureness; since I must, by what I remember, have been as sure of Paul Delaroche—for whom the pendulum was at last to be arrested at a very different point. I could see in a manner, for all the queerness, what W. J. meant by that beauty and, above all, that living interest in La Barque du Dante, where the queerness, according to him, was perhaps what contributed most; see it doubtless in particular when he reproduced the work, at home, from a memory aided by a lithograph. Yet Les Enfants d'Edouard thrilled me to a different tune, and I couldn't doubt that the long-drawn odd face of the elder prince, sad and sore and sick, with his wide crimped side-locks of fair hair and his violet legs marked by the Garter and dangling from the bed, was a reconstitution of far-off history of the subtlest and most "last word" modern or psychologic kind. I had never heard of psychology in art or anywhere else—scarcely anyone then had; but I truly felt the nameless force at play. Thus if I also in my way "subtly" admired, one's noted practice of that virtue (mainly regarded indeed, I judge, as a vice) would appear to have at the time I refer to set in, under such encouragements, once for all; and I can surely have enjoyed up to then no formal exhibition of anything as I at one of those seasons enjoyed the commemorative show of Delaroche given, soon after his death, in one of the rather bleak salles of the École des Beaux-Arts to which access was had from the quay. *There* was reconstituted history if one would, in the straw-littered scaffold, the distracted ladies with three-cornered coifs and those immense hanging sleeves that made them look as if they had bath-towels over their arms; in the block, the headsman, the bandaged eyes and groping hands, of Lady Jane Grey—not less than in the noble indifference of Charles the First, compromised king but perfect gentleman, at his inscrutable ease in his chair and as if on his throne, while the Puritan soldiers insult and badger him: the thrill of which was all the greater from its pertaining to that English lore which the good Robert Thompson had, to my responsive delight, rubbed into us more than anything else and all from a fine old conservative and monarchical point of view. Yet of these things W. J. attempted no reproduction, though I remember his repeatedly laying his hand on Delacroix, whom he found always and everywhere interesting—to the point of trying effects, with charcoal and crayon, in his manner; and not less in the manner of Decamps, whom we regarded as more or less of a genius of the same rare family. They were touched with the ineffable, the inscrutable, and Delacroix in especial with the incalculable; categories these toward which we had even then, by a happy transition, begun to yearn and languish. We were not yet aware of style, though on the way to become so, but were aware of mystery, which indeed was one of its forms—while we saw all the others, without exception, exhibited at the Louvre, where at first they simply overwhelmed and bewildered me.

It was as if they had gathered there into a vast deafening chorus; I shall never forget how—speaking, that is, for my own sense—they filled those vast halls with the influence rather of some complicated sound, diffused and reverberant, than of such visibilities as one could directly deal with. To distinguish among these, in the charged and coloured and confounding air, was difficult—it discouraged and defied; which was doubtless why my impression originally best entertained was that of those magnificent parts of the great gallery simply not inviting us to distinguish. They only arched over us in the wonder of their endless golden riot and relief, figured and flourished in perpetual revolution, breaking into great high-hung circles and symmetries of squandered picture, opening into deep outward embrasures that threw off the rest of monumental Paris somehow as a told story, a sort of wrought effect or bold ambiguity for a vista, and yet held it there, at every point, as a vast bright gage, even at moments a felt adventure, of experience. This comes to saying that in those beginnings I felt myself most happily cross that bridge over to Style constituted by the wondrous Galerie d'Apollon, drawn out for me as a long but assured initiation and seeming to form with its supreme coved ceiling and inordinately shining parquet a prodigious tube or tunnel through which I inhaled little by little, that is again and again, a general sense of *glory*. The glory meant ever so many things at once, not only beauty and art and supreme design, but history and fame and power, the world in fine raised to the richest and noblest expression. The world there was at the same time, by an odd extension or intensification, the local present fact, to my small imagination, of the Second Empire, which was (for my notified consciousness) new and queer and perhaps even wrong, but on the spot so amply radiant and elegant that it took to itself, took under its protection with a splendour of insolence, the state and ancientry of the whole scene, profiting thus, to one's dim historic vision, confusedly though it might be, by the unparalleled luxury and variety of its heritage. But who shall count the sources at which an intense young fancy (when a young fancy *is* intense) capriciously, absurdly drinks?—so that the effect is, in twenty connections, that of a love-philtre or fear-philtre which fixes for the senses their supreme symbol of the fair or the strange. The Galerie d'Apollon became for years what I can only term a splendid scene of things, even of the quite irrelevant or, as might be, almost unworthy; and I recall to this hour, with the last vividness, what a precious part it played for me, and exactly by that continuity of honour, on my awaking, in a summer dawn many years later, to the fortunate, the instantaneous recovery and capture of the most appalling yet most admirable nightmare of my life. The climax of this extraordinary experience—which stands alone for me as a dream-adventure founded in the deepest, quickest, clearest act of cogitation and comparison, act indeed of life-saving energy, as well as in unutterable fear—was the sudden pursuit, through an open door, along a huge high saloon, of a just dimly-descried figure that retreated in terror before my rush and dash (a glare of inspired reaction from irresistible but shameful dread,) out of the room I had a moment before been desperately, and all the more abjectly, defending by the push of my shoulder against hard pressure on lock and bar from the other side. The lucidity, not to say the sublimity, of the crisis had consisted of the great thought that I, in my appalled state, was probably still more appalling than the awful agent, creature or presence, whatever he was, whom I had guessed, in the suddenest wild start from sleep, the sleep within my sleep, to be making for my place of rest. The triumph of my impulse, perceived in a flash as I acted on it by myself at a bound, forcing the door outward, was the grand thing, but the great point of the whole was the wonder of my final recognition. Routed, dismayed, the tables turned upon him by my so surpassing him for straight aggression and dire intention, my visitant was already but a diminished spot in the long perspective, the tremendous, glorious hall, as I say, over the far-gleaming floor of which, cleared for the occasion of its great line of priceless vitrines down the middle, he sped for *his* life, while a great storm of thunder and lightning played through the deep embrasures of high windows at the right. The lightning that revealed the retreat revealed also the wondrous place and, by the same amazing play, my young imaginative life in it of long before, the sense of which, deep within me, had kept it whole, preserved it to this thrilling use; for what in the world were the deep embrasures and the so polished floor but those of the Galerie d'Apollon of my childhood? The "scene of something" I had vaguely then felt it? Well I might, since it was to be the scene of that immense hallucination.

Of what, at the same time, in those years, were the great rooms of the Louvre almost equally, above and below, not the scene, from the moment they so wrought, stage by stage, upon our perceptions?—literally on almost all of these, in one way and another; quite in such a manner, I more and more see, as to have been educative, formative, fertilising, in a degree which no other "intellectual experience" our youth was to know could pretend, as a comprehensive, conducive thing, to rival. The sharp and strange, the quite heart-shaking little prevision had come to me, for myself, I make out, on the occasion of our very first visit of all, my brother's and mine, under conduct of the good Jean Nadali, before-mentioned, trustfully deputed by our parents, in the Rue de la Paix, on the morrow of our first arrival in Paris (July 1855) and while they were otherwise concerned. I hang again, appalled but uplifted, on brave Nadali's arm—his professional acquaintance with the splendours about us added for me on the spot to the charm of his "European" character: I cling to him while I gape at Géricault's Radeau de la Méduse, *the* sensation, for splendour and terror of interest, of that juncture to me, and ever afterwards to be associated, along with two or three other more or less contemporary products, Guérin's Burial of Atala, Prudhon's Cupid and Psyche, David's helmetted Romanisms, Madame Vigée-Lebrun's "ravishing" portrait of herself and her little girl, with how can I say what foretaste (as determined by that instant as if the hour had struck from a clock) of all the fun, confusedly speaking, that one was going to have, and the kind of life, always of the queer so-called inward sort, tremendously "sporting" in its way—though that description didn't then wait upon it, that one was going to lead. It came of itself, this almost awful apprehension in all the presences, under our courier's protection and in my brother's company—it came just there and so; there was alarm in it somehow as well as bliss. The bliss in fact I think scarce disengaged itself at all, but only the sense of a freedom of contact and appreciation really too big for one, and leaving such a mark on the very place, the pictures, the frames themselves, the figures within them, the particular parts and features of each, the look of the rich light, the smell of the massively enclosed air, that I have never since renewed the old exposure without renewing again the old emotion and taking up the small scared consciousness. *That*, with so many of the conditions repeated, is the charm—to feel afresh the beginning of so much that was to be. The beginning in short was with Géricault and David, but it went on and on and slowly spread; so that one's stretched, one's even strained, perceptions, one's discoveries and extensions piece by piece, come back, on the great premises, almost as so many explorations of the house of life, so many circlings and hoverings round the image of the world. I have dim reminiscences of permitted independent visits, uncorrectedly juvenile though I might still be, during which the house of life and the palace of art became so mixed and interchangeable—the Louvre being, under a general description, the most peopled of all scenes not less than the most hushed of all temples—that an excursion to look at pictures would have but half expressed my afternoon. I had looked at pictures, looked and looked again, at the vast Veronese, at Murillo's moon-borne Madonna, at Leonardo's almost unholy dame with the folded hands, treasures of the Salon Carré as that display was then composed; but I had also looked at France and looked at Europe, looked even at America as Europe itself might be conceived so to look, looked at history, as a still-felt past and a complacently personal future, at society, manners, types, characters, possibilities and prodigies and mysteries of fifty sorts; and all in the light of being splendidly "on my own," as I supposed it, though we hadn't then that perfection of slang, and of (in especial) going and coming along that interminable and incomparable Seine-side front of the Palace against which young sensibility felt itself almost rub, for endearment and consecration, as a cat invokes the friction of a protective piece of furniture. Such were at any rate some of the vague processes—I see for how utterly vague they must show—of picking up an education; and I was, in spite of the vagueness, so far from agreeing with my brother afterwards that we didn't pick one up and that that never *is* done, in any sense not negligible, and also that an education might, or should, in particular, have picked *us* up, and yet didn't—I was so far dissentient, I say, that I think I quite came to glorify such passages and see them as part of an order really fortunate. If we had been little asses, I seem to have reasoned, a higher intention driving us wouldn't have made us less so—to any point worth mentioning; and as we extracted such impressions, to put it at the worst, from redemptive accidents (to call Louvres and Luxembourgs nothing better) why we weren't little asses, but something wholly other: which appeared all I needed to contend for. Above all it would have been stupid and ignoble, an attested and lasting dishonour, not, with our chance, to have followed our straggling clues, as many as we could and disengaging as we happily did, I felt, the gold and the silver ones, whatever the others might have been—not to have followed them and not to have arrived by them, so far as we were to arrive. Instinctively, for any dim designs we might have nourished, we picked out the silver and the gold, attenuated threads though they must have been, and I positively feel that there were more of these, far more, casually interwoven, than will reward any present patience for my unravelling of the too fine tissue.

XXVI

I allude of course in particular here to the æsthetic clue in general, with which it was that we most (or that I at any rate most) fumbled, without our in the least having then, as I have already noted, any such rare name for it. There were sides on which it fairly dangled about us, involving our small steps and wits; though others too where I could, for my own part, but clutch at it in the void. Our experience of the theatre for instance, which had played such a part for us at home, almost wholly dropped in just the most propitious air: an anomaly indeed half explained by the fact that life in general, all round us, was perceptibly more theatrical. And there were other reasons, whether definitely set before us or not, which we grasped in proportion as we gathered, by depressing hearsay, that the French drama, great, strange and important, was as much out of relation to our time of life, our so little native strain and our cultivated innocence, as the American and English had been directly addressed to them. To the Cirque d'Été, the Cirque d'Hiver, the Théâtre du Cirque we were on occasion conducted—we had fallen so to the level of circuses, and that name appeared a safety; in addition to which the big theatre most bravely bearing it, the especial home at that time of the glittering and multitudinous *féerie*, did seem to lift the whole scenic possibility, for our eyes, into a higher sphere of light and grace than any previously disclosed. I recall Le Diable d'Argent as in particular a radiant revelation—kept before us a whole long evening and as an almost blinding glare; which was quite right for the *donnée*, the gradual shrinkage of the Shining One, the money-monster hugely inflated at first, to all the successive degrees of loose bagginess as he leads the reckless young man he has originally contracted with from dazzling pleasure to pleasure, till at last he is a mere shrivelled silver string such as you could almost draw through a keyhole. That was the striking moral, for the young man, however regaled, had been somehow "sold"; which *we* hadn't in the least been, who had had all his pleasures and none of his penalty, whatever this was to be. I was to repine a little, in these connections, at a much later time, on reflecting that had we only been "taken" in the Paris of that period as we had been taken in New York we might have come in for celebrities—supremely fine, perhaps supremely rank, flowers of the histrionic temperament, springing as they did from the soil of the richest romanticism and adding to its richness—who practised that braver art and finer finish which a comparatively homogenous public, forming a compact critical body, still left possible. Rachel was alive, but dying; the memory of Mademoiselle Mars, at her latest, was still in the air; Mademoiselle Georges, a massive, a monstrous antique, had withal returned for a season to the stage; but we missed her, as we missed Déjazet and Frédéric Lemâitre and Mélingue and Samson; to say nothing of others of the age before the flood—taking for the flood that actual high tide of the outer barbarian presence, the general alien and polyglot, in stalls and boxes, which I remember to have heard Gustave Flaubert lament as the ruin of the theatre through the assumption of judgeship by a bench to whom the very values of the speech of author and actor were virtually closed, or at the best uncertain.

I enjoyed but two snatches of the older representational art—no particular of either of which, however, has faded from me; the earlier and rarer of these an evening at the Gymnase for a *spectacle coupé*, with Mesdames Rose Chéri, Mélanie, Delaporte and Victoria (afterwards Victoria-Lafontaine). I squeeze again with my mother, my aunt and my brother into the stuffy baignoire, and I take to my memory in especial Madame de Girardin's Une Femme qui Déteste son Mari; the thrilling story, as I judged it, of an admirable lady who, to save her loyalist husband, during the Revolution, feigns the most Jacobin opinions, represents herself a citoyenne of citoyennes, in order to keep him the more safely concealed in her house. He flattens himself, to almost greater peril of life, behind a panel of the wainscot, which she has a secret for opening when he requires air and food and they may for a fearful fleeting instant be alone together; and the point of the picture is in the contrast between these melting moments and the heroine's *tenue* under the tremendous strain of receiving on the one side the invading, investigating Terrorist commissaries, sharply suspicious but successfully baffled, and on the other her noble relatives, her husband's mother and sister if I rightly remember, who are not in the secret and whom, for perfect prudence, she keeps out of it, though alone with her, and themselves in hourly danger, they might be trusted, and who, believing him concealed elsewhere and terribly tracked, treat her, in her republican rage, as lost to all honour and all duty. One's sense of such things after so long a time has of course scant authority for others; but I myself trust my vision of Rose Chéri's fine play just as I trust that of her *physique ingrat*, her at first extremely odd and positively osseous appearance; an emaciated woman with a high bulging forehead, somewhat of the form of Rachel's, for whom the triumphs of produced illusion, as in the second, third and fourth great dramas of the younger Dumas, had to be triumphs indeed. My one other reminiscence of this order connects itself, and quite three years later, with the old dingy Vaudeville of the Place de la Bourse, where I saw in my brother's company a rhymed domestic drama of the then still admired Ponsard, Ce qui Plaît aux Femmes; a piece that enjoyed, I believe, scant success, but that was to leave with me ineffaceable images. How was it possible, I wondered, to have more grace and talent, a rarer, cooler art, than Mademoiselle Fargeuil, the heroine?—the fine lady whom a pair of rival lovers, seeking to win her hand by offering her what will most please her, treat, in the one case, to a brilliant fête, a little play within a play, at which we assist, and in the other to the inside view of an attic of misery, into which the more cunning suitor introduces her just in time to save a poor girl, the tenant of the place, from being ruinously, that is successfully, tempted by a terrible old woman, a prowling *revendeuse*, who dangles before her the condition on which so pretty a person may enjoy every comfort. Her happier sister, the courted young widow, intervenes in time, reinforces her tottering virtue, opens for her an account with baker and butcher, and, doubting no longer which flame is to be crowned, charmingly shows us that what pleases women most is the exercise of charity.

Then it was I first beheld that extraordinary veteran of the stage, Mademoiselle Pierson, almost immemorially attached, for later generations, to the Théâtre Français, the span of whose career thus strikes me as fabulous, though she figured as a very juvenile beauty in the small *féerie* or allegory forming M. Ponsard's second act. She has been playing mothers and aunts this many and many a year—and still indeed much as a juvenile beauty. Not that light circumstance, however, pleads for commemoration, nor yet the further fact that I was to admire Mademoiselle Fargeuil, in the after-time, the time after she had given all Sardou's earlier successes the help of her shining firmness, when she had passed from interesting comedy and even from romantic drama—not less, perhaps still more, interesting, with Sardou's Patrie as a bridge—to the use of the bigger brush of the Ambigu and other homes of melodrama. The sense, such as it is, that I extract from the pair of modest memories in question is rather their value as a glimpse of the old order that spoke so much less of our hundred modern material resources, matters the stage of to-day appears mainly to live by, and such volumes more of the one thing that was then, and that, given various other things, had to be, of the essence. That one thing was the quality, to say nothing of the quantity, of the actor's personal resource, technical history, tested temper, proved experience; on which almost everything had to depend, and the thought of which makes the mere starved scene and medium of the period, the *rest* of the picture, a more confessed and more heroic battle-ground. They have been more and more eased off, the scene and medium, for our couple of generations, so much so in fact that the rest of the picture has become almost *all* the picture: the author and the producer, among us, lift the weight of the play from the performer—particularly of the play dealing with our immediate life and manners and aspects—after a fashion which does half the work, thus reducing the "personal equation," the demand for the maximum of individual doing, to a contribution mostly of the loosest and sparest. As a sop to historic curiosity at all events may even so short an impression serve; impression of the strenuous age and its fine old masterful *assouplissement* of its victims—who were not the expert spectators. The spectators were so expert, so broken in to material suffering for the sake of their passion, that, as the suffering was only material, they found the æsthetic reward, the critical relish of the essence, all adequate; a fact that seems in a sort to point a moral of large application. Everything but the "interpretation," the personal, in the French theatre of those days, had kinds and degrees of weakness and futility, say even falsity, of which our modern habit is wholly impatient—let alone other conditions still that were detestable even at the time, and some of which, forms of discomfort and annoyance, linger on to this day. The playhouse, in short, was almost a place of physical torture, and it is still rarely in Paris a place of physical ease. Add to this the old thinness of the school of Scribe and the old emptiness of the thousand vaudevillistes; which part of the exhibition, till modern comedy began, under the younger Dumas and Augier, had for its counterpart but the terrible dead weight, or at least the prodigious prolixity and absurdity, of much, not to say of most, of the romantic and melodramatic "output." It *paid* apparently, in the golden age of acting, to sit through interminable evenings in impossible places—since to assume that the age *was* in that particular respect golden (for which we have in fact a good deal of evidence) alone explains the patience of the public. With the public the *actors* were, according to their seasoned strength, almost exclusively appointed to deal, just as in the conditions most familiar to-day to ourselves this charge is laid on almost everyone concerned in the case save the representatives of the parts. And far more other people are now concerned than of old; not least those who have learned to make the playhouse endurable. All of which leaves us with this interesting vision of a possibly great truth, the truth that you can't have more than one kind of intensity—intensity worthy of the name—at once. The intensity of the golden age of the histrion was the intensity of *his* good faith. The intensity of our period is that of the "producer's" and machinist's, to which add even that of architect, author and critic. Between which derivative kind of that article, as we may call it, and the other, the immediate kind, it would appear that you have absolutely to choose.

XXVII

I see much of the rest of that particular Paris time in the light of the Institution Fezandié, and I see the Institution Fezandié, Rue Balzac, in the light, if not quite of Alphonse Daudet's lean asylum for the *petits pays chauds*, of which I have felt the previous institutions of New York sketchily remind me, at least in that of certain other of his studies in that field of the precarious, the ambiguous Paris over parts of which the great Arch at the top of the Champs-Elysées flings, at its hours, by its wide protective plausible shadow, a precious mantle of "tone." They gather, these chequered parts, into its vast paternal presence and enjoy at its expense a degree of reflected dignity. It was to the big square villa of the Rue Balzac that we turned, as pupils not unacquainted with vicissitudes, from a scene swept bare of M. Lerambert, an establishment that strikes me, at this distance of time, as of the oddest and most indescribable—or as describable at best in some of the finer turns and touches of Daudet's best method. The picture indeed should not be invidious—it so little needs that, I feel, for its due measure of the vivid, the queer, the droll, all coming back to me without prejudice to its air as of an equally futile felicity. I see it as bright and loose and vague, as confused and embarrassed and helpless; I see it, I fear, as quite ridiculous, but as wholly harmless to my brothers and me at least, and as having left us with a fund of human impressions; it played before us such a variety of figure and character and so relieved us of a sense of untoward discipline or of the pursuit of abstract knowledge. It was a recreational, or at least a social, rather than a tuitional house; which fact had, I really believe, weighed favourably with our parents, when, bereft of M. Lerambert, they asked themselves, with their considerable practice, how next to bestow us. Our father, like so many free spirits of that time in New York and Boston, had been much interested in the writings of Charles Fourier and in his scheme of the "phalanstery" as the solution of human troubles, and it comes to me that he must have met or in other words heard of M. Fezandié as an active and sympathetic ex-Fourierist (I think there were only ex-Fourierists by that time,) who was embarking, not far from us, on an experiment if not absolutely phalansteric at least inspired, or at any rate enriched, by a bold idealism. I like to think of the Institution as all but phalansteric—it so corrects any fear that such places might be dreary. I recall this one as positively gay—bristling and bustling and resonant, untouched by the strenuous note, for instance, of Hawthorne's co-operative Blithedale. I like to think that, in its then still almost suburban, its pleasantly heterogeneous quarter, now oppressively uniform, it was close to where Balzac had ended his life, though I question its identity—as for a while I tried not to—with the scene itself of the great man's catastrophe. Round its high-walled garden at all events he would have come and gone—a throb of inference that had for some years indeed to be postponed for me; though an association displacing to-day, over the whole spot, every other interest. I in any case can't pretend not to have been most appealed to by that especial phase of our education from which the pedagogic process as commonly understood was most fantastically absent. It excelled in this respect, the Fezandié phase, even others exceptionally appointed, heaven knows, for the supremacy; and yet its glory is that it was no poor blank, but that it fairly creaked and groaned, heatedly overflowed, with its wealth. We were *externes*, the three of us, but we remained in general to luncheon; coming home then, late in the afternoon, with an almost sore experience of multiplicity and vivacity of contact. For the beauty of it all was that the Institution was, speaking technically, not more a *pensionnat*, with prevailingly English and American pupils, than a *pension*, with mature beneficiaries of both sexes, and that our two categories were shaken up together to the liveliest effect. This had been M. Fezandié's grand conception; a son of the south, bald and slightly replete, with a delicate beard, a quick but anxious, rather melancholy eye and a slim, graceful, juvenile wife, who multiplied herself, though scarce knowing at moments, I think, where or how to turn; I see him as a Daudet *méridional*, but of the sensitive, not the sensual, type, as something of a rolling stone, rolling rather down hill—he had enjoyed some arrested, possibly blighted, connection in America—and as ready always again for some new application of faith and funds. If fondly failing in the least to see why the particular application in the Rue Balzac—the body of pensioners ranging from infancy to hoary eld—shouldn't have been a bright success could have made it one, it would have been a most original triumph.

I recover it as for ourselves a beautifully mixed adventure, a brave little seeing of the world on the happy pretext of "lessons." We *had* lessons from time to time, but had them in company with ladies and gentlemen, young men and young women of the Anglo-Saxon family, who sat at long boards of green cloth with us and with several of our contemporaries, English and American boys, taking *dictées* from the head of the house himself or from the aged and most remarkable M. Bonnefons, whom we believed to have been a superannuated actor (he above all such a model for Daudet!) and who interrupted our abashed readings aloud to him of the French classics older and newer by wondrous reminiscences and even imitations of Talma. He moved among us in a cloud of legend, the wigged and wrinkled, the impassioned, though I think alas underfed, M. Bonnefons: it was our belief that he "went back," beyond the first Empire, to the scenes of the Revolution—this perhaps partly by reason, in the first place, of his scorn of our pronunciation, when we met it, of the sovereign word *liberté*, the poverty of which, our deplorable "libbeté," without r's, he mimicked and derided, sounding the right, the revolutionary form out splendidly, with thirty r's, the prolonged beat of a drum. And then we believed him, if artistically conservative, politically obnoxious to the powers that then were, though knowing that those so marked had to walk, and even to breathe, cautiously for fear of the *mouchards* of the tyrant; we knew all about mouchards and talked of them as we do to-day of aviators or suffragettes—to remember which in an age so candidly unconscious of them is to feel how much history we have seen unrolled. There were times when he but paced up and down and round the long table—I see him as never seated, but always on the move, a weary Wandering Jew of the *classe*; but in particular I hear him recite to us the combat with the Moors from Le Cid and show us how Talma, describing it, seemed to crouch down on his haunches in order to spring up again terrifically to the height of "Nous nous levons alors!" which M. Bonnefons rendered as if on the carpet there fifty men at least had leaped to their feet. But he threw off these broken lights with a quick relapse to indifference; he didn't like the Anglo-Saxon—of the children of Albion at least his view was low; on his American specimens he had, I observed, more mercy; and this imperfection of sympathy (the question of Waterloo apart) rested, it was impossible not to feel, on his so resenting the dishonour suffered at our hands by his beautiful tongue, to which, as the great field of elocution, he was patriotically devoted. I think he fairly loathed our closed English vowels and confused consonants, our destitution of sounds that he recognised as sounds; though why in this connection he put up best with our own compatriots, embroiled at that time often in even stranger vocables than now, is more than I can say. I think that would be explained perhaps by his feeling in them as an old equalitarian certain accessibilities *quand même*. Besides, we of the younger persuasion at least must have done his ear less violence than those earnest ladies from beyond the sea and than those young Englishmen qualifying for examinations and careers who flocked with us both to the plausibly spread and the severely disgarnished table, and on whose part I seem to see it again an effort of anguish to "pick up" the happy idiom that we had unconsciously acquired. French, in the fine old formula of those days, so much diffused, "was the language of the family"; but I think it must have appeared to these students in general a family of which the youngest members were but scantly kept in their place. We piped with a greater facility and to a richer meed of recognition; which sounds as if we might have become, in these strange collocations, fairly offensive little prigs. That was none the less not the case, for there were, oddly enough, a few French boys as well, to whom on the lingual or the "family" ground, we felt ourselves feebly relative, and in comparison with whom, for that matter, or with one of whom, I remember an occasion of my having to sink to insignificance. There was at the Institution little of a staff—besides waiters and bonnes; but it embraced, such as it was, M. Mesnard as well as M. Bonnefons—M. Mesnard of the new generation, instructor in whatever it might be, among the arts, that didn't consist of our rolling our r's, and with them, to help us out, more or less our eyes. It is significant that this elegant branch is now quite vague to me; and I recall M. Mesnard, in fine, as no less modern and cheap than M. Bonnefons was rare and unappraiseable. He had nevertheless given me his attention, one morning, doubtless patiently enough, in some corner of the villa that we had for the moment practically to ourselves—I seem to see a small empty room looking on the garden; when there entered to us, benevolently ushered by Madame Fezandié, a small boy of very fair and romantic aspect, as it struck me, a pupil newly arrived. I remember of him mainly that he had a sort of nimbus of light curls, a face delicate and pale and that deeply hoarse voice with which French children used to excite our wonder. M. Mesnard asked of him at once, with interest, his name, and on his pronouncing it sought to know, with livelier attention, if he were then the son of M. Arsène Houssaye, lately director of the Théâtre Français. To this distinction the boy confessed—all to such intensification of our répétiteur's interest that I knew myself quite dropped, in comparison, from his scheme of things. Such an origin as our little visitor's affected him visibly as dazzling, and I felt justified after a while, in stealing away into the shade. The beautiful little boy was to live to be the late M. Henry Houssaye, the shining hellenist and historian. I have never forgotten the ecstasy of hope in M. Mesnard's question—as a light on the reverence then entertained for the institution M. Houssaye the elder had administered.

XXVIII

There comes to me, in spite of these memories of an extended connection, a sense as of some shrinkage or decline in the *beaux jours* of the Institution; which seems to have found its current run a bit thick and troubled, rather than with the pleasant plash in which we at first appeared all equally to bathe. I gather, as I try to reconstitute, that the general enterprise simply proved a fantasy not workable, and that at any rate the elders, and often such queer elders, tended to outnumber the candid *jeunesse*; so that I wonder by the same token on what theory of the Castalian spring, as taught there to trickle, if not to flow, M. Houssaye, holding his small son by the heel as it were, may have been moved to dip him into our well. Shall I blush to relate that my own impression of its virtue must have come exactly from this uncanny turn taken—and quite in spite of the high Fezandié ideals—by the *invraisemblable* house of entertainment where the assimilation of no form of innocence was doubted of by reason of the forms of experience that insisted somehow on cropping up, and no form of experience too directly deprecated by reason of the originally plotted tender growths of innocence. And some of these shapes were precisely those from which our good principal may well have first drawn his liveliest reassurance: I seem to remember such ancient American virgins in especial and such odd and either distinctively long-necked or more particularly long-haired and chinless compatriots, in black frock-coats of no type or "cut," no suggested application at all as garments—application, that is, to anything in the nature of character or circumstance, function or position—gathered about in the groups that M. Bonnefons almost terrorised by his refusal to recognise, among the barbarous races, any approach to his view of the great principle of Diction. I remember deeply and privately enjoying some of his shades of scorn and seeing how, given his own background, they were thoroughly founded; I remember above all as burnt in by the impression he gave me of the creature *wholly* animated and containing no waste expressional spaces, no imaginative flatnesses, the notion of the luxury of life, though indeed of the amount of trouble of it too, when *none* of the letters of the alphabet of sensibility might be dropped, involved in being a Frenchman. The liveliest lesson I must have drawn, however, from that source makes in any case, at the best, an odd educational connection, given the kind of concentration at which education, even such as ours, is supposed especially to aim: I speak of that direct promiscuity of insights which might easily have been pronounced profitless, with their attendant impressions and quickened sensibilities—yielding, as these last did, harvests of apparitions. I positively cherish at the present hour the fond fancy that we all soaked in some such sublime element as might still have hung about there—I mean on the very spot—from the vital presence, so lately extinct, of the prodigious Balzac; which had involved, as by its mere respiration, so dense a cloud of other presences, so arrayed an army of interrelated shades, that the air was still thick as with the fumes of witchcraft, with infinite seeing and supposing and creating, with a whole imaginative traffic. The Pension Vauquer, then but lately existent, according to Le Père Goriot, on the other side of the Seine, was still to be revealed to me; but the figures peopling it are not to-day essentially more intense (that is as a matter of the marked and featured, the terrible and the touching, as compared with the paleness of the conned page in general,) than I persuade myself, with so little difficulty, that I found the more numerous and more shifting, though properly doubtless less inspiring, constituents of the Pension Fezandié. Fantastic and all "subjective" that I should attribute a part of their interest, or that of the scene spreading round them, to any competent perception, in the small-boy mind, that the general or public moment had a rarity and a brevity, a sharp intensity, of its own; ruffling all things, as they came, with the morning breath of the Second Empire and making them twinkle back with a light of resigned acceptance, a freshness of cynicism, the force of a great grimacing example. The grimace might have been legibly there in the air, to the young apprehension, and could I but simplify this record enough I should represent everything as part of it. I seemed at any rate meanwhile to think of the Fezandié young men, young Englishmen mostly, who were getting up their French, in that many-coloured air, for what I supposed, in my candour, to be appointments and "posts," diplomatic, commercial, vaguely official, and who, as I now infer, though I didn't altogether embrace it at the time, must, under the loose rule of the establishment, have been amusing themselves not a little. It was as a side-wind of their free criticism, I take it, that I felt the first chill of an apprehended decline of the establishment, some pang of prevision of what might come, and come as with a crash, of the general fine fallacy on which it rested. Their criticism was for that matter free enough, causing me to admire it even while it terrified. They expressed themselves in terms of magnificent scorn—such as might naturally proceed, I think I felt, from a mightier race; they spoke of poor old Bonnefons, they spoke of our good Fezandié himself, they spoke more or less of everyone within view, as beggars and beasts, and I remember to have heard on their lips no qualification of any dish served to us at déjeuner (and still more at the later meal, of which my brothers and I didn't partake) but as rotten. These were expressions, absent from our domestic, our American air either of fonder discriminations or vaguer estimates, which fairly extended for me the range of intellectual, or at least of social resource; and as the general tone of them to-day comes back to me it floods somehow with light the image of the fine old insular confidence (so intellectually unregenerate then that such a name scarce covers it, though inward stirrings and the growth of a *comparative* sense of things have now begun unnaturally to agitate and disfigure it,) in which the general outward concussion of the English "abroad" with the fact of being abroad took place. The Fezandié young men were as much abroad as might be, and yet figured to me—largely by the upsetting force of that confidence, all but physically exercised—as the finest, handsomest, knowingest creatures; so that when I met them of an afternoon descending the Champs-Elysées with fine long strides and in the costume of the period, for which we can always refer to contemporary numbers of "Punch," the fact that I was for the most part walking sedately either with my mother or my aunt, or even with my sister and her governess, caused the spark of my vision that they were armed for conquest, or at the least for adventure, more expansively to glow. I am not sure whether as a general thing they honoured me at such instants with a sign of recognition; but I recover in especial the sense of an evening hour during which I had accompanied my mother to the Hôtel Meurice, where one of the New York cousins aforementioned, daughter of one of the Albany uncles—that is of the Rhinebeck member of the group—had perched for a time, so incongruously, one already seemed to feel, after the sorriest stroke of fate. I see again the gaslit glare of the Rue de Rivoli in the spring or the autumn evening (I forget which, for our year of the Rue d'Angoulême had been followed by a migration to the Rue Montaigne, with a period, or rather with two periods, of Boulogne-sur-mer interwoven, and we might have made our beguiled way from either domicile); and the whole impression seemed to hang too numerous lamps and too glittering *vitrines* about the poor Pendletons' bereavement, their loss of their only, their so sturdily handsome, little boy, and to suffuse their state with the warm rich exhalations of subterraneous cookery with which I find my recall of Paris from those years so disproportionately and so quite other than stomachically charged. The point of all of which is simply that just as we had issued from the hotel, my mother anxiously urging me through the cross currents and queer contacts, as it were, of the great bazaar (of which the Rue de Rivoli was then a much more bristling avenue than now) rather than depending on me for support and protection, there swung into view the most splendid, as I at least esteemed him, of my elders and betters in the Rue Balzac, who had left the questions there supposedly engaging us far behind, and, with his high hat a trifle askew and his cigar actively alight, revealed to me at a glance what it was to be in full possession of Paris. There was speed in his step, assurance in his air, he was visibly, impatiently on the way; and he gave me thereby my first full image of what it was exactly to *be* on the way. He gave it the more, doubtless, through the fact that, with a flourish of the aforesaid high hat (from which the Englishman of that age was so singularly inseparable) he testified to the act of recognition, and to deference to my companion, but with a grand big-boy good-humour that—as I remember from childhood the so frequent effect of an easy patronage, compared with a top-most overlooking, on the part of an admired senior—only gave an accent to the difference. As if he cared, or could have, that I but went forth through the Paris night in the hand of my mamma; while he had greeted us with a grace that was as a beat of the very wings of freedom! Of such shreds, at any rate, proves to be woven the stuff of young sensibility—when memory (if sensibility has at all existed for it) rummages over our old trunkful of spiritual duds and, drawing forth ever so tenderly this, that and the other tattered web, holds up the pattern to the light. I find myself in this connection so restlessly and tenderly rummage that the tatters, however thin, come out in handsful and every shred seems tangled with another.

Gertrude Pendleton's mere name, for instance, becomes, and very preferably, the frame of another and a better picture, drawing to it cognate associations, those of that element of the New York cousinship which had originally operated to place there in a shining and even, as it were, an economic light a "preference for Paris"—which preference, during the period of the Rue d'Angoulême and the Rue Montaigne, we wistfully saw at play, the very lightest and freest, on the part of the inimitable Masons. Their earlier days of Tours and Trouville were over; a period of relative rigour at the Florence of the still encircling walls, the still so existent abuses and felicities, was also, I seem to gather, a thing of the past; great accessions, consciously awaited during the previous leaner time, had beautifully befallen them, and my own whole consciousness of the general air—so insistently I discriminate for that alone—was coloured by a familiar view of their enjoyment of these on a tremendously draped and festooned *premier* of the Rue-St.-Honoré, bristling with ormolu and Pradier statuettes and looking almost straight across to the British Embassy; rather a low premier, after the manner of an entresol, as I remember it, and where the closed windows, which but scantly distinguished between our own sounds and those of the sociable, and yet the terrible, street of records and memories, seemed to maintain an air and a light thick with a mixture of every sort of queer old Parisian amenity and reference: as if to look or to listen or to touch were somehow at the same time to probe, to recover and communicate, to behold, to taste and even to smell—to one's greater assault by suggestion, no doubt, but also to the effect of some sweet and strange repletion, as from the continued consumption, say, out of flounced and puckered boxes, of serried rows of chocolate and other bonbons. I must have felt the whole thing as something for one's developed senses to live up to and make light of, and have been rather ashamed of my own for just a little sickishly staggering under it. This goes, however, with the fondest recall of our cousins' inbred ease, from far back, in all such assumable relations; and of how, four of the simplest, sweetest, best-natured girls as they were (with the eldest, a charming beauty, to settle on the general ground, after marriage and widowhood, and still to be blooming there), they were possessed of the scene and its great reaches and resources and possibilities in a degree that reduced us to small provincialism and a hanging on their lips when they told us, that is when the gentlest of mammas and the lovely daughter who was "out" did, of presentations at the Tuileries to the then all-wonderful, the ineffable Empress: reports touchingly qualified, on the part of our so exposed, yet after all so scantily indurated relatives, by the question of whether occasions so great didn't perhaps nevertheless profane the Sundays for which they were usually appointed. There was something of an implication in the air of those days, when young Americans were more numerously lovely than now, or at least more wide-eyed, it would fairly appear, that some account of the only tradition they had ever been rumoured to observe (that of the Lord's day) might have been taken even at the Tuileries.

But what most comes back to me as the very note and fragrance of the New York cousinship in this general connection is a time that I remember to have glanced at on a page distinct from these, when the particular cousins I now speak of had conceived, under the influence of I know not what unextinguished morning star, the liveliest taste for the earliest possible rambles and researches, in which they were so good as to allow me, when I was otherwise allowed, to participate: health-giving walks, of an extraordinarily *matinal* character, at the hour of the meticulous rag-pickers and exceptionally French polishers known to the Paris dawns of the Second Empire as at no time since; which made us all feel together, under the conduct of Honorine, bright child of the pavement herself, as if *we*, in our fresh curiosity and admiration, had also something to say to the great show presently to be opened, and were free, throughout the place, as those are free of a house who know its aspects of attic and cellar or how it looks from behind. I call our shepherdess Honorine even though perhaps not infallibly naming the sociable soubrette who might, with all her gay bold confidence, have been an official inspectress in person, and to whose easy care or, more particularly, expert sensibility and candour of sympathy and curiosity, our flock was freely confided. If she wasn't Honorine she was Clémentine or Augustine—which is a trifle; since what I thus recover, in any case, of these brushings of the strange Parisian dew, is those communities of contemplation that made us most hang about the jewellers' windows in the Palais Royal and the public playbills of the theatres on the Boulevard. The

Palais Royal, now so dishonoured and disavowed, was then the very Paris of Paris; the shutters of the shops seemed taken down, at that hour, for our especial benefit, and I remember well how, the "dressing" of so large a number of the compact and richly condensed fronts being more often than not a matter of diamonds and pearls, rubies and sapphires, that represented, in their ingenuities of combination and contortion, the highest taste of the time, I found open to me any amount of superior study of the fact that the spell of gems seemed for the feminine nature almost alarmingly boundless. I stared too, it comes back to me, at these exhibitions, and perhaps even thought it became a young man of the world to express as to this or that object a refined and intelligent preference; but what I really most had before me was the chorus of abjection, as I might well have called it, led, at the highest pitch, by Honorine and vaguely suggesting to me, by the crudity, so to say, of its wistfulness, a natural frankness of passion—goodness knew in fact (for my small intelligence really didn't) what depths of corruptibility. Droll enough, as I win them again, these queer dim plays of consciousness: my sense that my innocent companions, Honorine *en tête*, would have done anything or everything for the richest ruby, and that though one couldn't one's self be decently dead to that richness one didn't at all know what "anything" might be or in the least what "everything" was. The gushing cousins, at the same time, assuredly knew still less of that, and Honorine's brave gloss of a whole range alike of possibilities and actualities was in itself a true social grace.

They all enjoyed, in fine, while I somehow but wastefully mused—which was after all my form of enjoyment; I was shy for it, though it was a truth and perhaps odd enough withal, that I didn't really at all care for gems, that rubies and pearls, in no matter what collocations, left me comparatively cold; that I actually cared for them about as little as, monstrously, secretly, painfully, I cared for flowers. Later on I was to become aware that I "adored" trees and architectural marbles—that for a sufficient slab of a sufficiently rare, sufficiently bestreaked or empurpled marble in particular I would have given a bag of rubies; but by then the time had passed for my being troubled to make out what in that case would represent on a small boy's part the corruptibility, so to call it, proclaimed, before the *vitrines*, by the cousins. That hadn't, as a question, later on, its actuality; but it had so much at the time that if it had been frankly put to me I must have quite confessed my inability to say—and must, I gather, by the same stroke, have been ashamed of such inward penury; feeling that as a boy I showed more poorly than girls. There was a difference meanwhile for such puzzlements before the porticos of the theatres; all questions melted for me there into the single depth of envy—envy of the equal, the beatific command of the evening hour, in the *régime* of Honorine's young train, who were fresh for the early sparrow and the chiffonier even after shedding buckets of tears the night before, and not so much as for the first or the second time, over the beautiful story of La Dame aux Camélias. There indeed was another humiliation, but by my weakness of position much more than of nature: whatever doing of "everything" might have been revealed to me as a means to the end, I would certainly have done it for a sight of Madame Doche and Fechter in Dumas's triumphant idyll—now enjoying the fullest honours of innocuous classicism; with which, as with the merits of its interpreters, Honorine's happy charges had become perfectly and if not quite serenely, at least ever so responsively and feelingly, familiar. Of a wondrous mixed sweetness and sharpness and queerness of uneffaced reminiscence is all that aspect of the cousins and the rambles and the overlapping nights melting along the odorously bedamped and retouched streets and arcades; bright in the ineffable morning light, above all, of our peculiar young culture and candour!

All of which again has too easily led me to drop for a moment my more leading clue of that radiation of goodnature from Gertrude Pendleton and her headlong hospitalities in which we perhaps most complacently basked. The becraped passage at Meurice's alluded to a little back was of a later season, and the radiation, as I recall it, had been, that first winter, mainly from a *petit hôtel* somewhere "on the other side," as we used with a large sketchiness to say, of the Champs Elysées; a region at that time reduced to no regularity, but figuring to my fond fancy as a chaos of accidents and contrasts where *petits hôtels* of archaic type were elbowed by woodyards and cabarets, and pavilions ever so characteristic, yet ever so indefinable, snuggled between frank industries and vulgarities—all brightened these indeed by the sociable note of Paris, be it only that of chaffering or of other *bavardise*. The great consistencies of arch-refinement, now of so large a harmony, were still to come, so that it seemed rather original to live there; in spite of which the attraction of the hazard of it on the part of our then so uniformly natural young kinswoman, not so much ingeniously, or even expressively, as just gesticulatively and helplessly gay—since that earlier pitch of New York parlance scarce arrived at, or for that matter pretended to, enunciation—was quite in what I at least took to be the glitter of her very conventions and traditions themselves; exemplified for instance by a bright nocturnal christening-party in honour of the small son of all hopes whom she was so precipitately to lose: an occasion which, as we had, in our way, known the act of baptism but as so abbreviated and in fact so tacit a business, had the effect for us of one of the great "forms" of a society taking itself with typical seriousness. We were much more serious than the Pendletons, but, paradoxically enough, there was that weakness in our state of our being able to make no such attestation of it. The evening can have been but of the friendliest, easiest and least pompous nature, with small guests, in congruity with its small hero, as well as large; but I must have found myself more than ever yet in presence of a "rite," one of those round which as many kinds of circumstance as possible clustered—so that the more of these there were the more one might imagine a great social order observed. How shall I now pretend to say how many kinds of circumstance I supposed I recognised?—with the remarkable one, to begin with, and which led fancy so far afield, that the "religious ceremony" was at the same time a "party," of twinkling lustres and disposed flowers and ladies with bare shoulders (that platitudinous bareness of the period that suggested somehow the moral line, drawn as with a ruler and a firm pencil); with little English girls, daughters of a famous physician of that nationality then pursuing a Parisian career (he must have helped the little victim into the world), and whose emphasised type much impressed itself; with round glazed and beribboned boxes of multi-coloured sugared almonds, dragées de baptême above all, which we harvested, in their heaps, as we might have gathered apples from a shaken tree, and which symbolised as nothing else the ritual dignity. Perhaps this grand impression really came back but to the dragées de baptême, not strictly more immemorial to our young appreciation than the New Year's cake and the "Election" cake known to us in New York, yet immensely more official and of the nature of scattered largesse; partly through the days and days, as it seemed to me, that our life was to be furnished, reinforced and almost encumbered with them. It wasn't simply that they were so toothsome, but that they were somehow so important and so historic.

It was with no such frippery, however, that I connected the occasional presence among us of the young member of the cousinship (in this case of the maternal) who most moved me to wistfulness of wonder, though not at all, with his then marked difference of age, by inviting my free approach. Vernon King, to whom I have in another part of this record alluded, at that time doing his baccalauréat on the other side of the Seine and coming over to our world at scraps of moments (for I recall my awe of the tremendous nature, as I supposed it, of his toil), as to quite a make-believe and gingerbread place, the lightest of substitutes for the "Europe" in which he had been from the first so technically plunged. His mother and sister, also on an earlier page referred to, had, from their distance, committed him to the great city to be "finished," educationally, to the point that for our strenuous cousin Charlotte was the only proper one—and I feel sure he can have acquitted himself in this particular in a manner that would have passed for brilliant if such lights didn't, thanks to her stiff little standards, always tend to burn low in her presence. These ladies were to develop more and more the practice of living in odd places for abstract inhuman reasons—at Marseilles, at Düsseldorf (if I rightly recall their principal German sojourn), at Naples, above all, for a long stage; where, in particular, their grounds of residence were somehow not as those of others, even though I recollect, from a much later time, attending them there at the opera, an experience which, in their fashion, they succeeded in despoiling for me of every element of the concrete, or at least of the pleasantly vulgar. Later impressions, few but firm, were so to enhance one's tenderness for Vernon's own image, the most interesting surely in all the troop of our young kinsmen early baffled and gathered, that he glances at me out of the Paris period, fresh-coloured, just blond-bearded, always smiling and catching his breath a little as from a mixture of eagerness and shyness, with such an appeal to the right idealisation, or to belated justice, as makes of mere evocation a sort of exercise of loyalty. It seemed quite richly laid upon me at the time—I get it all back—that he, two or three years older than my elder brother and dipped more early, as well as held more firmly, in the deep, the refining waters the virtue of which we all together, though with our differences of consistency, recognised, was the positive and living proof of what the process, comparatively poor for ourselves, could do at its best and with clay originally and domestically kneaded to the right plasticity; besides which he shone, to my fancy, and all the more for its seeming so brightly and quietly in his very grain, with the vague, the supposititious, but the intensely accent-giving stamp of the Latin quarter, which we so thinly imagined and so superficially brushed on our pious walks to the Luxembourg and through the parts where the glamour might have hung thickest. We were to see him a little—but two or three times—three or four years later, when, just before our own return, he had come back to America for the purpose, if my memory serves, of entering the Harvard Law School; and to see him still always with the smile that was essentially as facial, as livingly and loosely fixed, somehow, as his fresh complexion itself; always too with the air of caring so little for what he had been put through that, under any appeal to give out, more or less wonderfully, some sample or echo of it, as who should say, he still mostly panted as from a laughing mental embarrassment: he had been put through too much; it was all stale to him, and he wouldn't have known where to begin. He did give out, a little, on occasion—speaking, that is, on my different plane, as it were, and by the roundabout report of my brother; he gave out, it appeared, as they walked together across shining Newport sands, some fragment, some beginning of a very youthful poem that "Europe" had, with other results, moved him to, and a faint thin shred of which was to stick in my remembrance for reasons independent of its quality:

"Harold, rememberest thou the day,

We rode along the Appian Way?

Neglected tomb and altar cast

Their lengthening shadow o'er the plain,

And while we talked the mighty past

Around us lived and breathed again!"

That was European enough, and yet he had returned to America really to find himself, even with every effort made immediately near him to defeat the discovery. He found himself, with the outbreak of the War, simply as the American soldier, and not under any bribe, however dim, of the epaulette or the girt sword; but just as the common enlisting native, which he smiled and gasped—to the increase of his happy shortness of breath, as from a repletion of culture, since it suggested no lack of personal soundness—at feeling himself so *like* to be. As strange, yet as still more touching than strange, I recall the sight, even at a distance, of the drop straight off him of all his layers of educational varnish, the possession of the "advantages," the tongues, the degrees, the diplomas, the reminiscences, a saturation too that had all sunk in—a sacrifice of precious attributes that might almost have been viewed as a wild bonfire. So his prodigious mother, whom I have perhaps sufficiently presented for my reader to understand, didn't fail to view it—judging it also, sharply hostile to the action of the North as the whole dreadful situation found her, with deep and resentful displeasure. I remember how I thought of Vernon himself, during the business, as at once so despoiled, so diverted, and above all so resistantly bright, as vaguely to suggest something more in him still, some deep-down reaction, some extremity of indifference and defiance, some exhibition of a young character too long pressed and impressed, too long prescribed to and with too much expected of it, and all under too firmer a will; so that the public pretext had given him a lift, or lent him wings, which without its greatness might have failed him. As the case was to turn nothing— that is nothing he most wanted and, remarkably, most enjoyed—did fail him at all. I forget with which of the possible States, New York, Massachusetts or Rhode Island (though I think the first) he had taken service; only seeming to remember that this all went on for him at the start in McClellan's and later on in Grant's army, and that, badly wounded in a Virginia battle, he came home to be nursed by his mother, recently restored to America for a brief stay. She held, I believe, in the event, that he had, under her care, given her his vow that, his term being up, he would not, should he get sufficiently well, re-engage. The question here was between them, but it was definite that, materially speaking, she was in no degree dependent on him. The old, the irrepressible adage, however, was to live again between them: when the devil was sick the devil a saint would be; when the devil was well the devil a saint was he!

The devil a saint, at all events, was Vernon, who denied that he had passed his word, and who, as soon as he had surmounted his first disablement, passionately and quite admirably re-enlisted. At once restored to the front and to what now gave life for him its indispensable relish, he was in the thick, again, of the great carnage roundabout Richmond, where, again gravely wounded, he (as I figure still incorrigibly smiling) succumbed. His mother had by this time indignantly returned to Europe, accompanied by her daughter and her younger son—the former of whom accepted, for our great pity, a little later on, the office of closing the story. Anne King, young and frail, but not less firm, under stress, than the others of her blood, came back, on her brother's death, and, quietest, most colourless Electra of a lucidest Orestes, making her difficult way amid massed armies and battle-drenched fields, got possession of his buried body and bore it for reinterment to Newport, the old habitation, as I have mentioned, of their father's people, both Vernons and Kings. It must have been to see my mother, as well as to sail again for Europe, that she afterwards came to Boston, where I remember going down with her, at the last, to the dock of the English steamer, some black and tub-like Cunarder, an archaic "Africa" or "Asia" sufficing to the Boston service of those days. I saw her off drearily and helplessly enough, I well remember, and even at that moment found for her another image: what was she most like, though in a still sparer and dryer form, but some low-toned, some employed little Brontë heroine?—though more indeed a Lucy Snowe than a Jane Eyre, and with no shade of a Brontë hero within sight. To this all the fine privilege and fine culture of all the fine countries (collective matter, from far back, of our intimated envy) had "amounted"; just as it had amounted for Vernon to the bare headstone on the Newport hillside where, by his mother's decree, as I have already noted, there figured no hint of the manner of his death. So grand, so finely personal a manner it appeared to me at the time, and has indeed appeared ever since, that this brief record irrepressibly springs from that. His mother, as I have equally noted, was however, with her views, to find no grace in it so long as she lived; and his sister went back to her, and to Marseille, as they always called it, but prematurely to die.

XXIX

I feel that much might be made of my memories of Boulogne-sur-Mer had I but here left room for the vast little subject; in which I should probably, once started, wander to and fro as exploringly, as perceivingly, as discoveringly, I am fairly tempted to call it, as might really give the measure of my small operations at the time. I was almost wholly reduced there to operations of that mere inward and superficially idle order at which we have already so freely assisted; reduced by a cause I shall presently mention, the production of a great blur, well-nigh after the fashion of some mild domestic but quite considerably spreading grease-spot, in respect to the world of action, such as it was, more or less immediately about me. I must personally have lived during this pale predicament almost only by seeing what I could, after my incorrigible ambulant fashion—a practice that may well have made me pass for bringing home nothing in the least exhibitional—rather than by pursuing the inquiries and interests that agitated, to whatever intensity, our on the whole widening little circle. The images I speak of as matter for more evocation that I can spare them were the fruit of two different periods at Boulogne, a shorter and a longer; this second appearing to us all, at the time, I gather, too endlessly and blightingly prolonged: so sharply, before it was over, did I at any rate come to yearn for the Rue Montaigne again, the Rue Montaigne "sublet" for a term under a flurry produced in my parents' breasts by a "financial crisis" of great violence to which the American world, as a matter now of recorded history, I believe, had tragically fallen victim, and which had imperilled or curtailed for some months our moderate means of existence. We were to recover, I make out, our disturbed balance, and were to pursue awhile further our chase of the alien, the somehow repeatedly postponed *real* opportunity; and the second, the comparatively cramped and depressed connection with the classic refuge, as it then was, of spasmodic thrift, when not of settled indigence, for the embarrassed of our race in the largest sense of this matter, was to be shuffled off at last with no scant relief and reaction. This is perhaps exactly why the whole picture of our existence at the Pas-de-Calais watering place pleads to me now for the full indulgence, what would be in other words every touch of tenderness workable, after all the years, over the lost and confused and above all, on their own side, poor ultimately rather vulgarised and violated little sources of impression: items and aspects these which while they in their degree and after their sort flourished we only asked to admire, or at least to appreciate, for their rewarding extreme queerness. The very centre of my particular consciousness of the place turned too soon to the fact of my coming in there for the gravest illness of my life, an all but mortal attack of the malignant typhus of old days; which, after laying me as low as I could well be laid for many weeks, condemned me to a convalescence so arduous that I saw my apparently scant possibilities, by the measure of them then taken, even as through a glass darkly, or through the expansive blur for which I found just above a homely image.

This experience was to become when I had emerged from it the great reminiscence or circumstance of old Boulogne for me, and I was to regard it, with much intelligence, I should have maintained, as the marked limit of my state of being a small boy. I took on, when I had decently, and all the more because I had so retardedly, recovered, the sense of being a boy of other dimensions somehow altogether, and even with a new dimension introduced and acquired; a dimension that I was eventually to think of as a stretch in the direction of essential change or of living straight into a part of myself previously quite unvisited and now made accessible as by the sharp forcing of a closed door. The blur of consciousness imaged by my grease-spot was not, I hasten to declare, without its relenting edges and even, during its major insistence, fainter thicknesses; short of which, I see, my picture, the picture I was always so incurably "after," would have failed of animation altogether—quite have failed to bristle with characteristics, with figures and objects and scenic facts, particular passages and moments, the stuff, in short, of that scrap of minor gain which I have spoken of as our multiplied memories. Wasn't I even at the time, and much more later on, to feel how we had been, through the thick and thin of the whole adventure, assaulted as never before in so concentrated a way by local and social character? Such was the fashion after which the Boulogne of long ago—I have known next to nothing of it since—could come forth, come more than half-way, as we say, to meet the imagination open to such advances. It was, taking one thing with another, so verily drenched in character that I see myself catching this fine flagrancy almost equally in everything; unless indeed I may have felt it rather smothered than presented on the comparatively sordid scene of the Collège Communal, not long afterwards to expand, I believe, into the local Lycée, to which the inimitable process of our education promptly introduced us. I was to have less of the Collège than my elder and my younger brother, thanks to the interrupting illness that placed me so long, with its trail of after-effects, half complacently, half ruefully apart; but I suffered for a few early weeks the mainly malodorous sense of the braver life, produced as this was by a deeply democratic institution from which no small son even of the most soapless home could possibly know exclusion. Odd, I recognise, that I should inhale the air of the place so particularly, so almost only, to that dismal effect; since character was there too, for whom it should concern, and my view of some of the material conditions, of the general collegiate presence toward the top of the steepish Grand' Rue, on the right and not much short, as it comes back to me, of the then closely clustered and inviolate haute ville, the more or less surviving old town, the idle grey rampart, the moated and towered citadel, the tree-shaded bastion for strolling and sitting "immortalised" by Thackeray, achieved the monumental, in its degree, after a fashion never yet associated for us with the pursuit of learning. Didn't the Campaigner, suffering indigence at the misapplied hands of Colonel Newcome, rage at that hushed victim supremely and dreadfully just thereabouts—by which I mean in the *haute ville*—over some question of a sacrificed sweetbread or a cold hacked joint that somebody had been "at"? Beside such builded approaches to an education as we had elsewhere known the Collège exhibited, with whatever reserves, the measure of style which almost any French accident of the administratively architectural order more easily rises to than fails of; even if the matter be but a question of the shyest similitude of a *cour d'honneur*, the court disconnecting the scene, by intention at least, from the basely bourgeois and giving value to the whole effect of opposed and windowed wall and important, or balanced and "placed," *perron*. These are many words for the dull precinct, as then presented, I admit, and they are perhaps half prompted by a special association, too ghostly now quite to catch again—the sense of certain Sundays, distinct from the grim, that is the flatly instructional, body of the week, when I seem to myself to have successfully flouted the whole constituted field by passing across it and from it to some quite ideally old-world little annexed *musée de province*, as inviolate in its way as the grey rampart and bare citadel, and very like them in unrelieved tone, where I repeatedly, and without another presence to hinder, looked about me at goodness knows what weird ancientries of stale academic art. Not one of these treasures, in its habit as it lived, do I recall; yet the sense and the "note" of them was at the time, none the less, not so elusive that I didn't somehow draw straight from them intimations of the interesting, that is revelations of the æsthetic, the historic, the critical mystery and charm of things (of such things taken altogether), that added to my small loose handful of the seed of culture.

That apprehension was, in its way, of our house of learning too, and yet I recall how, on the scant and simple terms I have glanced at, I quite revelled in it; whereas other impressions of my brief ordeal shrink, for anything in the nature of interest, but to three or four recovered marks of the social composition of the school. There were the sons of all the small shop-keepers and not less, by my remembrance, of certain of the mechanics and artisans; but there was also the English contingent, these predominantly *internes* and uniformed, blue-jacketed and brass-buttoned, even to an effect of odd redundancy, who by my conceit gave our association a lift. Vivid still to me is the summer morning on which, in the wide court—as wide, that is, as I liked to suppose it, and where we hung about helplessly enough for recreation—a brownish black-eyed youth, of about my own degree of youthfulness, mentioned to me with an air that comes back as that of the liveliest informational resource the outbreak, just heard of, of an awful Mutiny in India, where his military parents, who had not so long before sent him over thence, with such weakness of imagination, as I measured it, to the poor spot on which we stood, were in mortal danger of their lives; so that news of their having been killed would perhaps be already on the way. They might well have been military, these impressively exposed characters, since my friend's name was Napier, or Nappié as he was called at the school, and since, I may add also, there attached to him, in my eyes, the glamour of an altogether new emphasis of type. The English boys within our ken since our coming abroad had been of the fewest—the Fezandié youths, whether English or American, besides being but scantly boys, had been so lost, on that scene, in our heap of disparities; and it pressed upon me after a fashion of its own that those we had known in New York, and all aware of their varieties and "personalities" as one had supposed one's self, had in no case challenged the restless "placing" impulse with any such force as the finished little Nappié. They had not been, as he was by the very perversity of his finish, resultants of forces at all—or comparatively speaking; it was as if their producing elements had been simple and few, whereas behind this more mixed and, as we have learnt to say, evolved companion (his very simplicities, his gaps of possibility, being still evolved), there massed itself I couldn't have said what protective social order, what tangled creative complexity. Why I should have thought him almost Indian of stamp and hue because his English parents were of the so general Indian peril is more than I can say; yet I have his exotic and above all his bold, his imaginably even "bad," young face, finely unacquainted with law, before me at this hour quite undimmed—announcing, as I conceived it, and quite as a shock, any awful adventure one would, as well as something that I must even at the time have vaguely taken as the play of the "passions." He vanishes, and I dare say I but make him over, as I make everything; and he must have led his life, whatever it was to become, with the least possible waiting on the hour or the major consequence and no waste of energy at all in mooning, no patience with any substitute for his very own humour. We had another schoolmate, this one native to the soil, whose references were with the last vividness local and who was yet to escape with brilliancy in the aftertime the smallest shadow of effacement. His most direct reference at that season was to the principal pastry-cook's of the town, an establishment we then found supreme for little criss-crossed apple tartlets and melting *babas*— young Coquelin's home life amid which we the more acutely envied that the upward cock of his so all-important nose testified, for my fancy, to the largest range of free familiar sniffing. C.-B. Coquelin is personally most present to me, in the form of that hour, by the value, as we were to learn to put it, of this nose, the fine assurance and impudence of which fairly made it a trumpet for promises; yet in spite of that, the very gage, as it were, of his long career as the most interesting and many-sided comedian, or at least most unsurpassed dramatic *diseur* of his time, I failed to doubt that, with the rich recesses of the parental industry for his background, his subtlest identity was in his privilege, or perhaps even in his expertest trick, of helping himself well.

These images, however, were but drops in the bucket of my sense of catching character, roundabout us, as I say, at every turn and in every aspect; character that began even, as I was pleased to think, in our own habitation, the most spacious and pompous Europe had yet treated us to, in spite of its fronting on the Rue Neuve Chaussée, a street of lively shopping, by the measure of that innocent age, and with its own ground-floor occupied by a bristling exhibition of indescribably futile *articles de Paris*. Modern and commodious itself, it looked from its balcony at serried and mismatched and quaintly-named haunts of old provincial, of sedately passive rather than confidently eager, traffic; but this made, among us, for much harmless inquisitory life— while we were fairly assaulted, at home, by the scale and some of the striking notes of our fine modernity. The young, the agreeable (agreeable to anything), the apparently opulent M. Prosper Sauvage—wasn't it?—had not long before, unless I mistake, inherited the place as a monument of "family," quite modestly local yet propitious family, ambition; with an ample extension in the rear, and across the clearest prettiest court, for his own dwelling, which thus became elegant, *entre cour et jardin*, and showed all the happy symmetries and proper conventions. Here flourished, or rather, I surmise at this time of day, here languished, a domestic drama of which we enjoyed the murmurous overflow: frankly astounding to me, I confess, how I remain still in sensitive presence of our resigned proprietor's domestic drama, in and out of which I see a pair of figures quite up to the dramatic mark flit again with their air of the very rightest finish. I must but note these things, none the less, and pass; for scarce another item of the whole Boulogne concert of salient images failed, after all, of a significance either still more strangely social or more distinctively spectacular. These appearances indeed melt together for my interest, I once more feel, as, during the interminable stretch of the prescribed and for the most part solitary airings and outings involved in my slow convalescence from the extremity of fever, I approached that straitened and somewhat bedarkened issue of the Rue de l'Écu (was it?) toward the bright-coloured, strongly-peopled Port just where Merridew's English Library, solace of my vacuous hours and temple, in its degree too, of deep initiations, mounted guard at the right. Here, frankly, discrimination drops—every particular in the impression once so quick and fresh sits interlinked with every other in the large lap of the whole. The motley, sunny, breezy, bustling Port, with its classic, its admirable fisher-folk of both sexes, models of type and tone and of what might be handsomest in the thoroughly weathered condition, would have seemed the straightest appeal to curiosity had not the old Thackerayan side, as I may comprehensively call it, and the scattered wealth of illustration of *his* sharpest satiric range, not so constantly interposed and competed with it. The scene bristled, as I look back at it, with images from Men's Wives, from the society of Mr. Deuceace and that of fifty other figures of the same creation, with Bareacreses and Rawdon Crawleys and of course with Mrs. Macks, with Roseys of a more or less crumpled freshness and blighted bloom, with battered and bent, though doubtless never quite so fine, Colonel Newcomes not less; with more reminders in short than I can now gather in. Of those forms of the seedy, the subtly sinister, the vainly "genteel," the generally damaged and desperate, and in particular perhaps the invincibly impudent, all the marks, I feel sure, were stronger and straighter than such as we meet in generally like cases under our present levelling light. Such anointed and whiskered and eked-out, such brazen, bluffing, swaggering gentlemen, such floridly repaired ladies, their mates, all looking as hard as they could as if they were there for mere harmless amusement—it was as good, among them, as just *being* Arthur Pendennis to know so well, or at least to guess so fearfully, who and what they might be. They were floated on the tide of the manners then prevailing, I judge, with a rich processional effect that so many of our own grand lapses, when not of our mere final flatnesses, leave no material for; so that the living note of Boulogne was really, on a more sustained view, the opposition between a native race the most happily tempered, the most becomingly seasoned and salted and self-dependent, and a shifting colony—so far as the persons composing it *could* either urgently or speculatively shift—inimitably at odds with any active freshness. And the stale and the light, even though so scantly rebounding, the too densely socialised, group was the English, and the "positive" and hardy and steady and wind-washed the French; and it was all as flushed with colour and patched with costume and referable to record and picture, to literature and history, as a more easily amusing and less earnestly uniform age could make it. When I speak of this opposition indeed I see it again most take effect in an antithesis that, on one side and the other, swallowed all differences at a gulp. The general British show, as we had it there, in the artless mid-Victorian desert, had, I think, for its most sweeping sign the high assurance of its dowdiness; whereas one had only to glance about at the sea-faring and fisher-folk who were the real strength of the place to feel them shed at every step and by their every instinct of appearance the perfect lesson of taste. There it was to be learnt and taken home—with never a moral, none the less, drawn from it by the "higher types." I speak of course in particular of the tanned and trussed and kerchiefed, the active and productive women, all so short-skirted and free-limbed under stress; for as by the rule of the dowdy their sex is ever the finer example, so where the sense of the suitable, of the charmingly and harmoniously right prevails, they preserve the pitch even as a treasure committed to their piety. To hit that happy mean of rightness amid the mixed occupations of a home-mother and a fishwife, to be in especial both so bravely stripped below and so perfectly enveloped above as the deep-wading, far-striding, shrimp-netting, crab-gathering matrons or maidens who played, waist-high, with the tides and racily quickened the market, was to make grace thoroughly practical and discretion thoroughly vivid. These attributes had with them all, for the eye, however, a range too great for me to follow, since, as their professional undress was a turn-out positively self-consistent, so their household, or more responsibly public, or altogether festal, array played through the varied essentials of fluted coif and folded kerchief and sober skirt and tense, dark, displayed stocking and clicking wooden slipper, to say nothing of long gold ear-drop or solid short-hung pectoral cross, with a respect for the rigour of conventions that had the beauty of self-respect.

I owe to no season of the general period such a preserved sense of innumerable unaccompanied walks—at the reason of which luxury of freedom I have glanced; which as often as not were through the steep and low-browed and brightly-daubed *ruelles* of the fishing-town and either across and along the level sea-marge and sustained cliff beyond; this latter the site of the first Napoleon's so tremendously mustered camp of invasion, with a monument as futile, by my remembrance, as that enterprise itself had proved, to give it all the special accent I could ask for. Or I was as free for the *haute ville* and the ramparts and the scattered, battered benches of reverie—if I may so honour my use of them; they kept me not less complacently in touch with those of the so anciently odd and mainly contracted houses over which the stiff citadel and the ghost of Catherine de Médicis, who had dismally sojourned in it, struck me as throwing such a chill, and one of which precisely must have witnessed the never-to-be-forgotten Campaigner's passage in respect to her cold beef. Far from extinct for me is my small question of those hours, doubtless so mentally, so shamelessly wanton, as to what human life might be tucked away in such retreats, which expressed the last acceptance whether of desired or of imposed quiet; so absolutely appointed and obliged did I feel to make out, so far as I could, what, in so significant a world, they on their part *represented*. I think the force mainly sustaining me at that rather dreary time—as I see it can only show for—was this lively felt need that everything should represent something more than what immediately and all too blankly met the eye; I seem to myself to have carried it about everywhere and, though of course only without outward signs that might have betrayed my fatuity, and insistently, quite yearningly applied it. What I wanted, in my presumption, was that the object, the place, the person, the unreduced impression, often doubtless so difficult or so impossible to reduce, should give out to me something of a situation; living as I did in confused and confusing situations and thus hooking them on, however awkwardly, to almost any at all living surface I chanced to meet. My memory of Boulogne is that we had almost no society of any sort at home—there appearing to be about us but one sort, and that of far too great, or too fearful, an immediate bravery. Yet there were occasional figures that I recover from our scant circle and that I associate, whatever links I may miss, with the small still houses on the rampart; figures of the quaintest, quite perhaps the frowsiest, little English ladies in such mushroom hats, such extremely circular and bestriped scarlet petticoats, such perpetual tight gauntlets, such explicit claims to long descent, which showed them for everything that everyone else at Boulogne was not. These mid-Victorian samples of a perfect consistency "represented," by my measure, as hard as ever they could—and represented, of all things, literature and history and society. The literature was that of the three-volume novel, then, and for much after, enjoying its loosest and serenest spread; for they separately and anxiously and awfully "wrote"—and that must almost by itself have amounted in them to all the history I evoked.

The dreary months, as I am content that in their second phase especially they should be called, are subject, I repeat, to the perversion, quite perhaps to the obscuration, of my temporarily hindered health—which should keep me from being too sure of these small *proportions* of experience—I was to look back afterwards as over so grey a desert; through which, none the less, there flush as sharp little certainties, not to be disallowed, such matters as the general romance of Merridew, the English Librarian, before mentioned, at the mouth of the Port; a connection that thrusts itself upon me now as after all the truest centre of my perceptions—waylaying my steps at the time, as I came and went, more than any other object or impression. The question of what *that* spot represented, or could be encouraged, could be aided and abetted, to represent, may well have supremely engaged me—for depth within depth there could only open before me. The place "meant," on these terms, to begin with, frank and licensed fiction, licensed to my recordedly relaxed state; and what this particular luxury represented it might have taken me even more time than I had to give to make out. The blest novel in three volumes exercised through its form, to my sense, on grounds lying deeper for me to-day than my deepest sounding, an appeal that fairly made it do with me what it would. Possibly a drivelling confession, and the more drivelling perhaps the more development I should attempt for it; from which, however, the very difficulty of the case saves me. Too many associations, too much of the ferment of memory and fancy, are somehow stirred; they beset me again, they hover and whirl about me while I stand, as I used to stand, within the positively sanctified walls of the shop (so of the *vieux temps* now their aspect and fashion and worked system: by which I mean again of the frumpiest and civillest mid-Victorian), and surrender to the vision of the shelves packed with their rich individual trinities. Why should it have affected me so that my choice, so difficult in such a dazzle, could only be for a trinity? I am unable fully to say—such a magic dwelt in the mere rich fact of the trio.

When the novel of that age was "bad," as it so helplessly, so abjectly and prevailingly consented to be, the three volumes still did something for it, a something that was, all strangely, not an aggravation of its case. When it was "good" (our analysis, our terms of appreciation, had a simplicity that has lingered on) they made it copiously, opulently better; so that when, after the span of the years, my relation with them became, from that of comparatively artless reader, and to the effect of a superior fondness and acuteness, that of complacent author, the tradition of infatuated youth still flung over them its mantle: this at least till *all* relation, by one of the very rudest turns of life we of the profession were to have known, broke off, in clumsy interfering hands and with almost no notice given, in a day, in an hour. Besides connecting me with the lost but unforgotten note of waiting service and sympathy that quavered on the Merridew air, they represented just for intrinsic charm more than I could at any moment have given a plain account of; they fell, by their ineffable history, every trio I ever touched, into the category of such prized phenomena as my memory, for instance, of fairly hanging about the Rue des Vieillards, at the season I speak of, through the apprehension that something vague and sweet—if I shouldn't indeed rather say something of infinite future point and application—would come of it. This is a reminiscence that nothing would induce me to verify, as for example by any revisiting light; but it was going to be good for me, good, that is, for what I was pleased to regard as my intelligence or my imagination, in fine for my obscurely specific sense of things, that I *should* so have hung about. The name of the street was by itself of so gentle and intimate a persuasion that I must have been ashamed not to proceed, for the very grace of it, to some shade of active response. And there was always a place of particular arrest in the vista brief and blank, but inclusively blank, blank *after* ancient, settled, more and more subsiding things, blank almost, in short, with all Matthew Arnold's "ennui of the middle ages," rather than, poorly and meanly and emptily, before such states, which was previously what I had most known of blankness. This determined pause was at the window of a spare and solitary shop, a place of no amplitude at all, but as of an inveterate cheerful confidence, where, among a few artists' materials, an exhibited water-colour from some native and possibly then admired hand was changed but once in ever so long. That was perhaps after all the pivot of my revolution—the question of whether or no I should at a given moment find the old picture replaced. I made this, when I had the luck, pass for an event—yet an event which would *have* to have had for its scene the precious Rue des Vieillards, and pale though may be the recital of such pleasures I lose myself in depths of kindness for my strain of ingenuity.

All of which, and to that extent to be corrected, leaves small allowance for my service to good M. Ansiot, rendered while my elder and younger brothers—the younger completing our group of the ungovernessed—were continuously subject to collegial durance. Their ordeal was, I still blush to think, appreciably the heavier, as compared with mine, during our longer term of thrifty exile from Paris—the time of stress, as I find I recall it, when we had turned our backs on the Rue Montaigne and my privilege was so to roam on the winter and the spring afternoons. Mild M. Ansiot, "under" whom I for some three hours each forenoon sat sole and underided—and actually by himself too—was a curiosity, a benignity, a futility even, I gather; but save for a felt and remembered impulse in me to open the window of our scene of study as soon as he had gone was in no degree an ideal. He might rise here, could I do him justice, as the rarest of my poor evocations; for he it was, to be frank, who most literally smelt of the vieux temps—as to which I have noted myself as wondering and musing as much as might be, with recovered scraps and glimpses and other intimations, only never yet for such a triumph of that particular sense. To be still frank, he was little less than a monster—for mere unresisting or unresilient mass of personal presence I mean; so that I fairly think of him as a form of bland porpoise, violently blowing in an age not his own, as by having had to exchange deep water for thin air. Thus he impressed me as with an absolute ancientry of type, of tone, of responsible taste, above all; this last I mean in literature, since it was literature we sociably explored, to my at once charmed and shamed apprehension of the several firm traditions, the pure proprieties, the discussabilities, in the oddest way both so many and so few, of that field as they prevailed to his pious view. I must have had hold, in this mere sovereign sample of the accidentally, the quite unconsciously and unpretentiously, the all negligibly or superfluously handed-down, of a rare case of the provincial and academic *cuistre*; though even while I record it I see the good man as too helpless and unaggressive, too smothered in his poor facts of person and circumstance, of overgrown time of life alone, to incur with justness the harshness of classification. He rested with a weight I scarce even felt—such easy terms he made, without scruple, for both of us—on the cheerful innocence of my barbarism; and though our mornings were short and subject, I think, to quite drowsy lapses and other honest aridities, we did scumble together, I make out, by the aid of the collected extracts from the truly and academically great which formed his sole resource and which he had, in a small portable and pocketed library rather greasily preserved, some patch of picture of a saving as distinguished from a losing classicism. The point remains for me that when all was said—and even with everything that might directly have counted unsaid—he discharged for me such an office that I was to remain to this far-off hour in a state of possession of him that is the very opposite of a blank: quite after the fashion again in which I had all along and elsewhere suffered and resisted, and yet so perversely and intimately appropriated, tutoring; which was with as little as ever to show for my profit of his own express showings. The blank he fills out crowds itself with a wealth of value, since I shouldn't without him have been able to claim, for whatever it may be worth, a tenth (at that let me handsomely put it), of my "working" sense of the vieux temps. How can I allow then that we hadn't planted together, with a loose felicity, some of the seed of work?—even though the sprouting was so long put off. Everything, I have mentioned, had come at this time to be acceptedly, though far from braggingly, put off; and the ministrations of M. Ansiot really wash themselves over with the weak mixture that had begun to spread for me, to immensity, during that summer day or two of our earlier residence when, betraying strange pains and apprehensions, I was with all decision put to bed. Present to me still is the fact of my sharper sense, after an hour or two, of my being there in distress and, as happened for the moment, alone; present to me are the sounds of the soft afternoon, the mild animation of the Boulogne street through the half-open windows; present to me above all the strange sense that something had begun that would make more difference to me, directly and indirectly, than anything had ever yet made. I might verily, on the spot, have seen, as in a fading of day and a change to something suddenly queer, the whole large extent of it. I must thus, much impressed but half scared, have wanted to appeal; to which end I tumbled, all too weakly, out of bed and wavered toward the bell just across the room. The question of whether I really reached and rang it was to remain lost afterwards in the strong sick whirl of everything about me, under which I fell into a lapse of consciousness that I shall conveniently here treat as a considerable gap.

THE END

AN INTERNATIONAL
EPISODE

PART I

Four years ago—in 1874—two young Englishmen had occasion to go to the United States. They crossed the ocean at midsummer, and, arriving in New York on the first day of August, were much struck with the fervid temperature of that city. Disembarking upon the wharf, they climbed into one of those huge high-hung coaches which convey passengers to the hotels, and with a great deal of bouncing and bumping, took their course through Broadway. The midsummer aspect of New York is not, perhaps, the most favorable one; still, it is not without its picturesque and even brilliant side. Nothing could well resemble less a typical English street than the interminable avenue, rich in incongruities, through which our two travelers advanced—looking out on each side of them at the comfortable animation of the sidewalks, the high-colored, heterogeneous architecture, the huge white marble facades glittering in the strong, crude light, and bedizened with gilded lettering, the multifarious awnings, banners, and streamers, the extraordinary number of omnibuses, horsecars, and other democratic vehicles, the vendors of cooling fluids, the white trousers and big straw hats of the policemen, the tripping gait of the modish young persons on the pavement, the general brightness, newness, juvenility, both of people and things. The young men had exchanged few observations; but in crossing Union Square, in front of the monument to Washington—in the very shadow, indeed, projected by the image of the *pater patriae*—one of them remarked to the other, "It seems a rum-looking place."

"Ah, very odd, very odd," said the other, who was the clever man of the two.

"Pity it's so beastly hot," resumed the first speaker after a pause.

"You know we are in a low latitude," said his friend.

"I daresay," remarked the other.

"I wonder," said the second speaker presently, "if they can give one a bath?"

"I daresay not," rejoined the other.

"Oh, I say!" cried his comrade.

This animated discussion was checked by their arrival at the hotel, which had been recommended to them by an American gentleman whose acquaintance they made—with whom, indeed, they became very intimate—on the steamer, and who had proposed to accompany them to the inn and introduce them, in a friendly way, to the proprietor. This plan, however, had been defeated by their friend's finding that his "partner" was awaiting him on the wharf and that his commercial associate desired him instantly to come and give his attention to certain telegrams received from St. Louis. But the two Englishmen, with nothing but their national prestige and personal graces to recommend them, were very well received at the hotel, which had an air of capacious hospitality. They found that a bath was not unattainable, and were indeed struck with the facilities for prolonged and reiterated immersion with which their apartment was supplied. After bathing a good deal—more, indeed, than they had ever done before on a single occasion—they made their way into the dining room of the hotel, which was a spacious restaurant, with a fountain in the middle, a great many tall plants in ornamental tubs, and an array of French waiters. The first dinner on land, after a sea voyage, is, under any circumstances, a delightful occasion, and there was something particularly agreeable in the circumstances in which our young Englishmen found themselves. They were extremely good natured young men; they were more observant than they appeared; in a sort of inarticulate, accidentally dissimulative fashion, they were highly appreciative. This was, perhaps, especially the case with the elder, who was also, as I have said, the man of talent. They sat down at a little table, which was a very different affair from the great clattering seesaw in the saloon of the steamer. The wide doors and windows of the restaurant stood open, beneath large awnings, to a wide pavement, where there were other plants in tubs, and rows of spreading trees, and beyond which there was a large shady square, without any palings, and with marble-paved walks. And above the vivid verdure rose other facades of white marble and of pale chocolate-colored stone, squaring themselves against the deep blue sky. Here, outside, in the light and the shade and the heat, there was a great tinkling of the bells of innumerable streetcars, and a constant strolling and shuffling and rustling of many pedestrians, a large proportion of whom were young women in Pompadour-looking dresses. Within, the place was cool and vaguely lighted, with the plash of water, the odor of flowers, and the flitting of French waiters, as I have said, upon soundless carpets.

"It's rather like Paris, you know," said the younger of our two travelers.

"It's like Paris—only more so," his companion rejoined.

"I suppose it's the French waiters," said the first speaker. "Why don't they have French waiters in London?"

"Fancy a French waiter at a club," said his friend.

The young Englishman started a little, as if he could not fancy it. "In Paris I'm very apt to dine at a place where there's an English waiter. Don't you know what's-his-name's, close to the thingumbob? They always set an English waiter at me. I suppose they think I can't speak French."

"Well, you can't." And the elder of the young Englishmen unfolded his napkin.

His companion took no notice whatever of this declaration. "I say," he resumed in a moment, "I suppose we must learn to speak American. I suppose we must take lessons."

"I can't understand them," said the clever man.

"What the deuce is HE saying?" asked his comrade, appealing from the French waiter.

"He is recommending some soft-shell crabs," said the clever man.

And so, in desultory observation of the idiosyncrasies of the new society in which they found themselves, the young Englishmen proceeded to dine—going in largely, as the phrase is, for cooling draughts and dishes, of which their attendant offered them a very long list. After dinner they went out and slowly walked about the neighboring streets. The early dusk of waning summer was coming on, but the heat was still very great. The pavements were hot even to the stout boot soles of the British travelers, and the trees along the curbstone emitted strange exotic odors. The young men wandered through the adjoining square—that queer place without palings, and with marble walks arranged in black and white lozenges. There were a great many benches, crowded with shabby-looking people, and the travelers remarked, very justly, that it was not much like Belgrave Square. On one side was an enormous hotel, lifting up into the hot darkness an immense array of open, brightly lighted windows. At the base of this populous structure was an eternal jangle of horsecars, and all round it, in the upper dusk, was a sinister hum of mosquitoes. The ground floor of the hotel seemed to be a huge transparent cage, flinging a wide glare of gaslight into the street, of which it formed a sort of public adjunct, absorbing and emitting the passersby promiscuously. The young Englishmen went in with everyone else, from curiosity, and saw a couple of hundred men sitting on divans along a great marble-paved corridor, with their legs stretched out, together with several dozen more standing in a queue, as at the ticket office of a railway station, before a brilliantly illuminated counter of vast extent. These latter persons, who carried portmanteaus in their hands, had a dejected, exhausted look; their garments were not very fresh, and they seemed to be rendering some mysterious tribute to a magnificent young man with a waxed mustache, and a shirtfront adorned with diamond buttons, who every now and then dropped an absent glance over their multitudinous patience. They were American citizens doing homage to a hotel clerk.

"I'm glad he didn't tell us to go there," said one of our Englishmen, alluding to their friend on the steamer, who had told them so many things. They walked up the Fifth Avenue, where, for instance, he had told them that all the first families lived. But the first families were out of town, and our young travelers had only the satisfaction of seeing some of the second— or perhaps even the third—taking the evening air upon balconies and high flights of doorsteps, in the streets which radiate from the more ornamental thoroughfare. They went a little way down one of these side streets, and they saw young ladies in white dresses—charming-looking persons—seated in graceful attitudes on the chocolate-colored steps. In one or two places these young ladies were conversing across the street with other young ladies seated in similar postures and costumes in front of the opposite houses, and in the warm night air their colloquial tones sounded strange in the ears of the young Englishmen. One of our friends, nevertheless—the younger one—intimated that he felt a disposition to interrupt a few of these soft familiarities; but his companion observed, pertinently enough, that he had better be careful. "We must not begin with making mistakes," said his companion.

"But he told us, you know—he told us," urged the young man, alluding again to the friend on the steamer.

"Never mind what he told us!" answered his comrade, who, if he had greater talents, was also apparently more of a moralist.

By bedtime—in their impatience to taste of a terrestrial couch again our seafarers went to bed early—it was still insufferably hot, and the buzz of the mosquitoes at the open windows might have passed for an audible crepitation of the temperature. "We can't stand this, you know," the young Englishmen said to each other; and they tossed about all night more boisterously than they had tossed upon the Atlantic billows. On the morrow, their first thought was that they would re-embark that day for England; and then it occured to them that they might find an asylum nearer at hand. The cave of Aeolus became their ideal of comfort, and they wondered where the Americans went when they wished to cool off. They had not the least idea, and they determined to apply for information to Mr. J. L. Westgate. This was the name inscribed in a bold hand on the back of a letter carefully preserved in the pocketbook of our junior traveler. Beneath the address, in the left-hand corner of the envelope, were the words, "Introducing Lord Lambeth and Percy Beaumont, Esq." The letter had been given to the two Englishmen by a good friend of theirs in London, who had been in America two years previously, and had singled out Mr. J. L. Westgate from the many friends he had left there as the consignee, as it were, of his compatriots. "He is a capital fellow," the Englishman in London had said, "and he has got an awfully pretty wife. He's tremendously hospitable—he will do everything in the world for you; and as he knows everyone over there, it is quite needless I should give you any other introduction. He will make you see everyone; trust to him for putting you into circulation. He has got a tremendously pretty wife." It was natural that in the hour of tribulation Lord Lambeth and Mr. Percy Beaumont should have bethought themselves of a gentleman whose attractions had been thus vividly depicted; all the more so that he lived in the Fifth Avenue, and that the Fifth Avenue, as they had ascertained the night before, was contiguous to their hotel. "Ten to one he'll be out of town," said Percy Beaumont; "but we can at least find out where he has gone, and we can immediately start in pursuit. He can't possibly have gone to a hotter place, you know."

"Oh, there's only one hotter place," said Lord Lambeth, "and I hope he hasn't gone there."

They strolled along the shady side of the street to the number indicated upon the precious letter. The house presented an imposing chocolate-colored expanse, relieved by facings and window cornices of florid sculpture, and by a couple of dusty rose trees which clambered over the balconies and the portico. This last-mentioned feature was approached by a monumental flight of steps.

"Rather better than a London house," said Lord Lambeth, looking down from this altitude, after they had rung the bell.

"It depends upon what London house you mean," replied his companion. "You have a tremendous chance to get wet between the house door and your carriage."

"Well," said Lord Lambeth, glancing at the burning heavens, "I 'guess' it doesn't rain so much here!"

The door was opened by a long Negro in a white jacket, who grinned familiarly when Lord Lambeth asked for Mr. Westgate.

"He ain't at home, sah; he's downtown at his o'fice."

"Oh, at his office?" said the visitors. "And when will he be at home?"

"Well, sah, when he goes out dis way in de mo'ning, he ain't liable to come home all day."

This was discouraging; but the address of Mr. Westgate's office was freely imparted by the intelligent black and was taken down by Percy Beaumont in his pocketbook. The two gentlemen then returned, languidly, to their hotel, and sent for a hackney coach, and in this commodious vehicle they rolled comfortably downtown. They measured the whole length of Broadway again and found it a path of fire; and then, deflecting to the left, they were deposited by their conductor before a fresh, light, ornamental structure, ten stories high, in a street crowded with keen-faced, light-limbed young men, who were running about very quickly and stopping each other eagerly at corners and in doorways. Passing into this brilliant building, they were introduced by one of the keen-faced young men—he was a charming fellow, in wonderful cream-colored garments and a hat with a blue ribbon, who had evidently perceived them to be aliens and helpless—to a very snug hydraulic elevator, in which they took their place with many other persons, and which, shooting upward in its vertical socket, presently projected them into the seventh horizontal compartment of the edifice. Here, after brief delay, they found themselves face to face with the friend of their friend in London. His office was composed of several different rooms, and they waited very silently in one of them after they had sent in their letter and their cards. The letter was not one which it would take Mr. Westgate very long to read, but he came out to speak to them more instantly than they could have expected; he had evidently jumped up from his work. He was a tall, lean personage and was dressed all in fresh white linen; he had a thin, sharp, familiar face, with an expression that was at one and the same time sociable and businesslike, a quick, intelligent eye, and a large brown mustache, which concealed his mouth and made his chin, beneath it, look small. Lord Lambeth thought he looked tremendously clever.

"How do you do, Lord Lambeth—how do you do, sir?" he said, holding the open letter in his hand. "I'm very glad to see you; I hope you're very well. You had better come in here; I think it's cooler," and he led the way into another room, where there were law books and papers, and windows wide open beneath striped awning. Just opposite one of the windows, on a line with his eyes, Lord Lambeth observed the weathervane of a church steeple. The uproar of the street sounded infinitely far below, and Lord Lambeth felt very high in the air. "I say it's cooler," pursued their host, "but everything is relative. How do you stand the heat?"

"I can't say we like it," said Lord Lambeth; "but Beaumont likes it better than I."

"Well, it won't last," Mr. Westgate very cheerfully declared; "nothing unpleasant lasts over here. It was very hot when Captain Littledale was here; he did nothing but drink sherry cobblers. He expressed some doubt in his letter whether I will remember him—as if I didn't remember making six sherry cobblers for him one day in about twenty minutes. I hope you left him well, two years having elapsed since then."

"Oh, yes, he's all right," said Lord Lambeth.

"I am always very glad to see your countrymen," Mr. Westgate pursued. "I thought it would be time some of you should be coming along. A friend of mine was saying to me only a day or two ago, 'It's time for the watermelons and the Englishmen.'"

"The Englishmen and the watermelons just now are about the same thing," Percy Beaumont observed, wiping his dripping forehead.

"Ah, well, we'll put you on ice, as we do the melons. You must go down to Newport."

"We'll go anywhere," said Lord Lambeth.

"Yes, you want to go to Newport; that's what you want to do," Mr. Westgate affirmed. "But let's see—when did you get here?"

"Only yesterday," said Percy Beaumont.

"Ah, yes, by the Russia. Where are you staying?"

"At the Hanover, I think they call it."

"Pretty comfortable?" inquired Mr. Westgate.

"It seems a capital place, but I can't say we like the gnats," said Lord Lambeth.

Mr. Westgate stared and laughed. "Oh, no, of course you don't like the gnats. We shall expect you to like a good many things over here, but we shan't

332

insist upon your liking the gnats; though certainly you'll admit that, as gnats, they are fine, eh? But you oughtn't to remain in the city."

"So we think," said Lord Lambeth. "If you would kindly suggest something—"

"Suggest something, my dear sir?" and Mr. Westgate looked at him, narrowing his eyelids. "Open your mouth and shut your eyes! Leave it to me, and I'll put you through. It's a matter of national pride with me that all Englishmen should have a good time; and as I have had considerable practice, I have learned to minister to their wants. I find they generally want the right thing. So just please to consider yourselves my property; and if anyone should try to appropriate you, please to say, 'Hands off; too late for the market.' But let's see," continued the American, in his slow, humorous voice, with a distinctness of utterance which appeared to his visitors to be part of a humorous intention—a strangely leisurely, speculative voice for a man evidently so busy and, as they felt, so professional—"let's see; are you going to make something of a stay, Lord Lambeth?"

"Oh, dear, no," said the young Englishman; "my cousin was coming over on some business, so I just came across, at an hour's notice, for the lark."

"Is it your first visit to the United States?"

"Oh, dear, yes."

"I was obliged to come on some business," said Percy Beaumont, "and I brought Lambeth along."

"And *you* have been here before, sir?"

"Never—never."

"I thought, from your referring to business—" said Mr. Westgate.

"Oh, you see I'm by way of being a barrister," Percy Beaumont answered. "I know some people that think of bringing a suit against one of your railways, and they asked me to come over and take measures accordingly."

"What's your railroad?" he asked.

"The Tennessee Central."

The American tilted back his chair a little and poised it an instant. "Well, I'm sorry you want to attack one of our institutions," he said, smiling. "But I guess you had better enjoy yourself *first*!"

"I'm certainly rather afraid I can't work in this weather," the young barrister confessed.

"Leave that to the natives," said Mr. Westgate. "Leave the Tennessee Central to me, Mr. Beaumont. Some day we'll talk it over, and I guess I can make it square. But I didn't know you Englishmen ever did any work, in the upper classes."

"Oh, we do a lot of work; don't we, Lambeth?" asked Percy Beaumont.

"I must certainly be at home by the 19th of September," said the younger Englishman, irrelevantly but gently.

"For the shooting, eh? or is it the hunting, or the fishing?" inquired his entertainer.

"Oh, I must be in Scotland," said Lord Lambeth, blushing a little.

"Well, then," rejoined Mr. Westgate, "you had better amuse yourself first, also. You must go down and see Mrs. Westgate."

"We should be so happy, if you would kindly tell us the train," said Percy Beaumont.

"It isn't a train—it's a boat."

"Oh, I see. And what is the name of—a—the—a—town?"

"It isn't a town," said Mr. Westgate, laughing. "It's a—well, what shall I call it? It's a watering place. In short, it's Newport. You'll see what it is. It's cool; that's the principal thing. You will greatly oblige me by going down there and putting yourself into the hands of Mrs. Westgate. It isn't perhaps for me to say it, but you couldn't be in better hands. Also in those of her sister, who is staying with her. She is very fond of Englishmen. She thinks there is nothing like them."

"Mrs. Westgate or—a—her sister?" asked Percy Beaumont modestly, yet in the tone of an inquiring traveler.

"Oh, I mean my wife," said Mr. Westgate. "I don't suppose my sister-in-law knows much about them. She has always led a very quiet life; she has lived in Boston."

Percy Beaumont listened with interest. "That, I believe," he said, "is the most—a—intellectual town?"

"I believe it is very intellectual. I don't go there much," responded his host.

"I say, we ought to go there," said Lord Lambeth to his companion.

"Oh, Lord Lambeth, wait till the great heat is over," Mr. Westgate interposed. "Boston in this weather would be very trying; it's not the temperature for intellectual exertion. At Boston, you know, you have to pass an examination at the city limits; and when you come away they give you a kind of degree."

Lord Lambeth stared, blushing a little; and Percy Beaumont stared a little also—but only with his fine natural complexion—glancing aside after a moment to see that his companion was not looking too credulous, for he had heard a great deal of American humor. "I daresay it is very jolly," said the younger gentleman.

"I daresay it is," said Mr. Westgate. "Only I must impress upon you that at present—tomorrow morning, at an early hour—you will be expected at Newport. We have a house there; half the people in New York go there for the summer. I am not sure that at this very moment my wife can take you in; she has got a lot of people staying with her; I don't know who they all are; only she may have no room. But you can begin with the hotel, and meanwhile you can live at my house. In that way—simply sleeping at the hotel—you will find it tolerable. For the rest, you must make yourself at home at my place. You mustn't be shy, you know; if you are only here for a month that will be a great waste of time. Mrs. Westgate won't neglect you, and you had better not try to resist her. I know something about that. I expect you'll find some pretty girls on the premises. I shall write to my wife by this afternoon's mail, and tomorrow morning she and Miss Alden will look out for you. Just walk right in and make yourself comfortable. Your steamer leaves from this part of the city, and I will immediately send out and get you a cabin. Then, at half past four o'clock, just call for me here, and I will go with you and put you on board. It's a big boat; you might get lost. A few days hence, at the end of the week, I will come down to Newport and see how you are getting on."

The two young Englishmen inaugurated the policy of not resisting Mrs. Westgate by submitting, with great docility and thankfulness, to her husband. He was evidently a very good fellow, and he made an impression upon his visitors; his hospitality seemed to recommend itself consciously—with a friendly wink, as it were—as if it hinted, judicially, that you could not possibly make a better bargain. Lord Lambeth and his cousin left their entertainer to his labors and returned to their hotel, where they spent three or four hours in their respective shower baths. Percy Beaumont had suggested that they ought to see something of the town; but "Oh, damn the town!" his noble kinsman had rejoined. They returned to Mr. Westgate's office in a carriage, with their luggage, very punctually; but it must be reluctantly recorded that, this time, he kept them waiting so long that they felt themselves missing the steamer, and were deterred only by an amiable modesty from dispensing with his attendance and starting on a hasty scramble to the wharf. But when at last he appeared, and the carriage plunged into the purlieus of Broadway, they jolted and jostled to such good purpose that they reached the huge white vessel while the bell for departure was still ringing and the absorption of passengers still active. It was indeed, as Mr. Westgate had said, a big boat, and his leadership in the innumerable and interminable corridors and cabins, with which he seemed perfectly acquainted, and of which anyone and everyone appeared to have the entree, was very grateful to the slightly bewildered voyagers. He showed them their stateroom—a spacious apartment, embellished with gas lamps, mirrors en pied, and sculptured furniture—and then, long after they had been intimately convinced that the steamer was in motion and launched upon the unknown stream that they were about to navigate, he bade them a sociable farewell.

"Well, goodbye, Lord Lambeth," he said; "goodbye, Mr. Percy Beaumont. I hope you'll have a good time. Just let them do what they want with you. I'll come down by-and-by and look after you."

The young Englishmen emerged from their cabin and amused themselves with wandering about the immense labyrinthine steamer, which struck them as an extraordinary mixture of a ship and a hotel. It was densely crowded with passengers, the larger number of whom appeared to be ladies and very young children; and in the big saloons, ornamented in white and gold, which followed each other in surprising succession, beneath the swinging gaslight, and among the small side passages where the Negro domestics of both sexes assembled with an air of philosophic leisure, everyone was moving to and fro and exchanging loud and familiar observations. Eventually, at the instance of a discriminating black, our young men went and had some "supper" in a wonderful place arranged like a theater, where, in a gilded gallery, upon which little boxes appeared to open, a large orchestra was playing operatic selections, and, below, people were handing about bills of fare, as if they had been programs. All this was sufficiently curious; but the agreeable thing, later, was to sit out on one of the great white decks of the steamer, in the warm breezy darkness, and, in the vague starlight, to make out the line of low, mysterious coast. The young Englishmen tried American cigars—those of Mr. Westgate—and talked together as they usually talked, with many odd silences, lapses of logic, and incongruities of transition; like people who have grown old together and learned to supply each other's missing phrases; or, more especially, like people thoroughly conscious of a common point of view, so that a style of conversation superficially lacking in finish might suffice for reference to a fund of associations in the light of which everything was all right.

"We really seem to be going out to sea," Percy Beaumont observed. "Upon my word, we are going back to England. He has shipped us off again. I call that 'real mean.'"

"I suppose it's all right," said Lord Lambeth. "I want to see those pretty girls at Newport. You know, he told us the place was an island; and aren't all islands in the sea?"

"Well," resumed the elder traveler after a while, "if his house is as good as his cigars, we shall do very well."

"He seems a very good fellow," said Lord Lambeth, as if this idea had just occurred to him.

"I say, we had better remain at the inn," rejoined his companion presently. "I don't think I like the way he spoke of his house. I don't like stopping in the house with such a tremendous lot of women."

"Oh, I don't mind," said Lord Lambeth. And then they smoked a while in silence. "Fancy his thinking we do no work in England!" the young man resumed.

"I daresay he didn't really think so," said Percy Beaumont.

"Well, I guess they don't know much about England over here!" declared Lord Lambeth humorously. And then there was another long pause. "He was devilish civil," observed the young nobleman.

"Nothing, certainly, could have been more civil," rejoined his companion.

"Littledale said his wife was great fun," said Lord Lambeth.

"Whose wife—Littledale's?"

"This American's—Mrs. Westgate. What's his name? J.L."

Beaumont was silent a moment. "What was fun to Littledale," he said at last, rather sententiously, "may be death to us."

"What do you mean by that?" asked his kinsman. "I am as good a man as Littledale."

"My dear boy, I hope you won't begin to flirt," said Percy Beaumont.

"I don't care. I daresay I shan't begin."

"With a married woman, if she's bent upon it, it's all very well," Beaumont expounded. "But our friend mentioned a young lady—a sister, a sister-in-law. For God's sake, don't get entangled with her!"

"How do you mean entangled?"

"Depend upon it she will try to hook you."

"Oh, bother!" said Lord Lambeth.

"American girls are very clever," urged his companion.

"So much the better," the young man declared.

"I fancy they are always up to some game of that sort," Beaumont continued.

"They can't be worse than they are in England," said Lord Lambeth judicially.

"Ah, but in England," replied Beaumont, "you have got your natural protectors. You have got your mother and sisters."

"My mother and sisters—" began the young nobleman with a certain energy. But he stopped in time, puffing at his cigar.

"Your mother spoke to me about it, with tears in her eyes," said Percy Beaumont. "She said she felt very nervous. I promised to keep you out of mischief."

"You had better take care of yourself," said the object of maternal and ducal solicitude.

"Ah," rejoined the young barrister, "I haven't the expectation of a hundred thousand a year, not to mention other attractions."

"Well," said Lord Lambeth, "don't cry out before you're hurt!"

It was certainly very much cooler at Newport, where our travelers found themselves assigned to a couple of diminutive bedrooms in a faraway angle of an immense hotel. They had gone ashore in the early summer twilight and had very promptly put themselves to bed; thanks to which circumstance and to their having, during the previous hours, in their commodious cabin, slept the sleep of youth and health, they began to feel, toward eleven o'clock, very alert and inquisitive. They looked out of their windows across a row of small green fields, bordered with low stone walls of rude construction, and saw a deep blue ocean lying beneath a deep blue sky, and flecked now and then with scintillating patches of foam. A strong, fresh breeze came in through the curtainless casements and prompted our young men to observe, generally, that it didn't seem half a bad climate. They made other observations after they had emerged from their rooms in pursuit of breakfast—a meal of which they partook in a huge bare hall, where a hundred Negroes, in white jackets, were shuffling about upon an uncarpeted floor; where the flies were superabundant, and the tables and dishes covered over with a strange, voluminous integument of coarse blue gauze; and where several little boys and girls, who had risen late, were seated in fastidious solitude at the morning repast. These young persons had not the morning paper before them, but they were engaged in languid perusal of the bill of fare.

This latter document was a great puzzle to our friends, who, on reflecting that its bewildering categories had relation to breakfast alone, had an uneasy prevision of an encyclopedic dinner list. They found a great deal of entertainment at the hotel, an enormous wooden structure, for the erection of which it seemed to them that the virgin forests of the West must have been terribly deflowered. It was perforated from end to end with immense bare corridors, through which a strong draught was blowing—bearing along wonderful figures of ladies in white morning dresses and clouds of Valenciennes lace, who seemed to float down the long vistas with expanded furbelows, like angels spreading their wings. In front was a gigantic veranda, upon which an army might have encamped—a vast wooden terrace, with a roof as lofty as the nave of a cathedral. Here our young Englishmen enjoyed, as they supposed, a glimpse of American society, which was distributed over the measureless expanse in a variety of sedentary attitudes, and appeared to consist largely of pretty young girls, dressed as if for a fete champetre, swaying to and fro in rocking chairs, fanning themselves with large straw fans, and enjoying an enviable exemption from social cares. Lord Lambeth had a theory, which it might be interesting to trace to its origin, that it would be not only agreeable, but easily possible, to enter into relations with one of these young ladies; and his companion (as he had done a couple of days before) found occasion to check the young nobleman's colloquial impulses.

"You had better take care," said Percy Beaumont, "or you will have an offended father or brother pulling out a bowie knife."

"I assure you it is all right," Lord Lambeth replied. "You know the Americans come to these big hotels to make acquaintances."

"I know nothing about it, and neither do you," said his kinsman, who, like a clever man, had begun to perceive that the observation of American society demanded a readjustment of one's standard.

"Hang it, then let's find out!" cried Lord Lambeth with some impatience. "You know I don't want to miss anything."

"We will find out," said Percy Beaumont very reasonably. "We will go and see Mrs. Westgate and make all proper inquiries."

And so the two inquiring Englishmen, who had this lady's address inscribed in her husband's hand upon a card, descended from the veranda of the big hotel and took their way, according to direction, along a large straight road, past a series of fresh-looking villas embosomed in shrubs and flowers and enclosed in an ingenious variety of wooden palings. The morning was brilliant and cool, the villas were smart and snug, and the walk of the young travelers was very entertaining. Everything looked as if it had received a coat of fresh paint the day before—the red roofs, the green shutters, the clean, bright browns and buffs of the housefronts. The flower beds on the little lawns seemed to sparkle in the radiant air, and the gravel in the short carriage sweeps to flash and twinkle. Along the road came a hundred little basket phaetons, in which, almost always, a couple of ladies were sitting—ladies in white dresses and long white gloves, holding the reins and looking at the two Englishmen, whose nationality was not elusive, through thick blue veils tied tightly about their faces as if to guard their complexions. At last the young men came within sight of the sea again, and then, having interrogated a gardener over the paling of a villa, they turned into an open gate. Here they found themselves face to face with the ocean and with a very picturesque structure, resembling a magnified chalet, which was perched upon a green embankment just above it. The house had a veranda of extraordinary width all around it and a great many doors and windows standing open to the veranda. These various apertures had, in common, such an accessible, hospitable air, such a breezy flutter within of light curtains, such expansive thresholds and reassuring interiors, that our friends hardly knew which was the regular entrance, and, after hesitating a moment, presented themselves at one of the windows. The room within was dark, but in a moment a graceful figure vaguely shaped itself in the rich-looking gloom, and a lady came to meet them. Then they saw that she had been seated at a table writing, and that she had heard them and had got up. She stepped out into the light; she wore a frank, charming smile, with which she held out her hand to Percy Beaumont.

"Oh, you must be Lord Lambeth and Mr. Beaumont," she said. "I have heard from my husband that you would come. I am extremely glad to see you." And she shook hands with each of her visitors. Her visitors were a little shy, but they had very good manners; they responded with smiles and exclamations, and they apologized for not knowing the front door. The lady rejoined, with vivacity, that when she wanted to see people very much she did not insist upon those distinctions, and that Mr. Westgate had written to her of his English friends in terms that made her really anxious. "He said you were so terribly prostrated," said Mrs. Westgate.

"Oh, you mean by the heat?" replied Percy Beaumont. "We were rather knocked up, but we feel wonderfully better. We had such a jolly—a—voyage down here. It's so very good of you to mind."

"Yes, it's so very kind of you," murmured Lord Lambeth.

Mrs. Westgate stood smiling; she was extremely pretty. "Well, I did mind," she said; "and I thought of sending for you this morning to the Ocean House. I am very glad you are better, and I am charmed you have arrived. You must come round to the other side of the piazza." And she led the way, with a light, smooth step, looking back at the young men and smiling.

The other side of the piazza was, as Lord Lambeth presently remarked, a very jolly place. It was of the most liberal proportions, and with its awnings, its fanciful chairs, its cushions and rugs, its view of the ocean, close at hand, tumbling along the base of the low cliffs whose level tops intervened in lawnlike smoothness, it formed a charming complement to the drawing room. As such it was in course of use at the present moment; it was occupied by a social circle. There were several ladies and two or three gentlemen, to whom Mrs. Westgate proceeded to introduce the distinguished strangers. She mentioned a great many names very freely and distinctly; the young Englishmen, shuffling about and bowing, were rather bewildered. But at last they were provided with chairs—low, wicker chairs, gilded, and tied with a great many ribbons—and one of the ladies (a very young person, with a little snub nose and several dimples) offered Percy Beaumont a fan. The fan was also adorned with pink love knots; but Percy Beaumont declined it, although he was very hot. Presently, however, it became cooler; the breeze from the sea was delicious, the view was charming, and the people sitting there looked exceedingly fresh and comfortable. Several of the ladies seemed to be young girls, and the gentlemen were slim, fair youths, such as our friends had seen the day before in New York. The ladies were working upon bands of tapestry, and one of the young men had an open book in his lap. Beaumont afterward learned from one of the ladies that this young man had been reading aloud, that he was from Boston and was very fond of reading aloud. Beaumont said it was a great pity that they had interrupted him; he should like so much (from all he had heard) to hear a Bostonian read. Couldn't the young man be induced to go on?

"Oh no," said his informant very freely; "he wouldn't be able to get the young ladies to attend to him now."

There was something very friendly, Beaumont perceived, in the attitude of the company; they looked at the young Englishmen with an air of animated sympathy and interest; they smiled, brightly and unanimously, at everything either of the visitors said. Lord Lambeth and his companion felt that they were being made very welcome. Mrs. Westgate seated herself between them, and, talking a great deal to each, they had occasion to observe that she was as pretty as their friend Littledale had promised. She was thirty years old, with the eyes and the smile of a girl of seventeen, and she was extremely light and graceful, elegant, exquisite. Mrs. Westgate was extremely spontaneous. She was very frank and demonstrative and appeared always—while she looked at you delightedly with her beautiful young eyes—to be making sudden confessions and concessions, after momentary hesitations.

"We shall expect to see a great deal of you," she said to Lord Lambeth with a kind of joyous earnestness. "We are very fond of Englishmen here; that is, there are a great many we have been fond of. After a day or two you must come and stay with us; we hope you will stay a long time. Newport's a very nice place when you come really to know it, when you know plenty of people. Of course you and Mr. Beaumont will have no difficulty about that. Englishmen are very well received here; there are almost always two or three of them about. I think they always like it, and I must say I should think they would. They receive ever so much attention. I must say I think they sometimes get spoiled; but I am sure you and Mr. Beaumont are proof against that. My husband tells me you are a friend of Captain Littledale; he was such a charming man. He made himself most agreeable here, and I am sure I wonder he didn't stay. It couldn't have been pleasanter for him in his own country, though, I suppose, it is very pleasant in England, for English people. I don't know myself; I have been there very little. I have been a great deal abroad, but I am always on the Continent. I must say I'm extremely fond of Paris; you know we Americans always are; we go there when we die. Did you ever hear that before? That was said by a great wit, I mean the good Americans; but we are all good; you'll see that for yourself. All I know of England is London, and all I know of London is that place on that little corner, you know, where you buy jackets—jackets with that coarse braid and those big buttons. They make very good jackets in London, I will do you the justice to say that. And some people like the hats; but about the hats I was always a heretic; I always got my hats in Paris. You can't wear an English hat—at least I never could—unless you dress your hair a l'Anglaise; and I must say that is a talent I have never possessed. In Paris they will make things to suit your peculiarities; but in England I think you like much more to have—how shall I say it?—one thing for everybody. I mean as regards dress. I don't know about other things; but I have always supposed that in other things everything was different. I mean according to the people—according to the classes, and all that. I am afraid you will think that I don't take a very favorable view; but you know you can't take a very favorable view in Dover Street in the month of November. That has always been my fate. Do you know Jones's Hotel in Dover Street? That's all I know of England. Of course everyone admits that the English hotels are your weak point. There was always the most frightful fog; I couldn't see to try my things on. When I got over to America—into the light—I usually found they were twice too big. The next time I mean to go in the season; I think I shall go next year. I want very much to take my sister; she has never been to England. I don't know whether you know what I mean by saying that the Englishmen who come here sometimes get spoiled. I mean that they take things as a matter of course—things that are done for them. Now, naturally, they are only a matter of course when the Englishmen are very nice. But, of course, they are almost always very nice. Of course this isn't nearly such an interesting country as England; there are not nearly so many things to see, and we haven't your country life. I have never seen anything of your country life; when I am in Europe I am always on the Continent. But I have heard a great deal about it; I know that when you are among yourselves in the country you have the most beautiful time. Of course we have nothing of that sort, we have nothing on that scale. I don't apologize, Lord Lambeth; some Americans are always apologizing; you must have noticed that. We have the reputation of always boasting and bragging and waving the American flag; but I must say that what strikes me is that we are perpetually making excuses and trying to smooth things over. The American flag has quite gone out of fashion; it's very carefully folded up, like an old tablecloth. Why should we apologize? The English never apologize—do they? No; I must say I never apologize. You must take us as we come—with all our imperfections on our heads. Of course we haven't your country life, and your old ruins, and your great estates, and your leisure class, and all that. But if we haven't, I should think you might find it a pleasant change—I think any country is pleasant where they have pleasant manners. Captain Littledale told me he had never seen such pleasant manners as at Newport, and he had been a great deal in European society. Hadn't he been in the diplomatic service? He told me the dream of his life was to get appointed to a diplomatic post in Washington. But he doesn't seem to have succeeded. I suppose that in England promotion—and all that sort of thing—is fearfully slow. With us, you know, it's a great deal too fast. You see, I admit our drawbacks. But I must confess I think Newport is an ideal place. I don't know anything like it anywhere. Captain Littledale told me he didn't know anything like it anywhere. It's entirely different from most watering places; it's a most charming life. I must say I think that when one goes to a foreign country one ought to enjoy the differences. Of course there are differences, otherwise what did one come abroad for? Look for your pleasure in the differences, Lord Lambeth; that's the way to do it; and then I am sure you will find American society—at least Newport society—most charming and most interesting. I wish very much my husband were here; but he's dreadfully confined to New York. I suppose you think that is very strange—for a gentleman. But you see we haven't any leisure class."

Mrs. Westgate's discourse, delivered in a soft, sweet voice, flowed on like a miniature torrent, and was interrupted by a hundred little smiles, glances, and gestures, which might have figured the irregularities and obstructions of such a stream. Lord Lambeth listened to her with, it must be confessed, a rather ineffectual attention, although he indulged in a good many little murmurs and ejaculations of assent and deprecation. He had no great faculty for apprehending generalizations. There were some three or four indeed which, in the play of his own intelligence, he had originated, and which had seemed convenient at the moment; but at the present time he could hardly have been said to follow Mrs. Westgate as she darted gracefully about in the sea of speculation. Fortunately she asked for no especial rejoinder, for she looked about at the rest of the company as well, and smiled at Percy Beaumont, on the other side of her, as if he too much understand her and agree with her. He was rather more successful than his companion; for besides being, as we know, cleverer, his attention was not vaguely distracted by close vicinity to a remarkably interesting young girl, with dark hair and blue eyes. This was the case with Lord Lambeth, to whom it occurred after a while that the young girl with blue eyes and dark hair was the pretty sister of whom Mrs. Westgate had spoken. She presently turned to him with a remark which established her identity.

"It's a great pity you couldn't have brought my brother-in-law with you. It's a great shame he should be in New York in these days."

"Oh, yes; it's so very hot," said Lord Lambeth.

"It must be dreadful," said the young girl.

"I daresay he is very busy," Lord Lambeth observed.

"The gentlemen in America work too much," the young girl went on.

"Oh, do they? I daresay they like it," said her interlocutor.

"I don't like it. One never sees them."

"Don't you, really?" asked Lord Lambeth. "I shouldn't have fancied that."

"Have you come to study American manners?" asked the young girl.

"Oh, I don't know. I just came over for a lark. I haven't got long." Here there was a pause, and Lord Lambeth began again. "But Mr. Westgate will come down here, will not he?"

"I certainly hope he will. He must help to entertain you and Mr. Beaumont."

Lord Lambeth looked at her a little with his handsome brown eyes. "Do you suppose he would have come down with us if we had urged him?"

Mr. Westgate's sister-in-law was silent a moment, and then, "I daresay he would," she answered.

"Really!" said the young Englishman. "He was immensely civil to Beaumont and me," he added.

"He is a dear good fellow," the young lady rejoined, "and he is a perfect husband. But all Americans are that," she continued, smiling.

"Really!" Lord Lambeth exclaimed again and wondered whether all American ladies had such a passion for generalizing as these two.

He sat there a good while: there was a great deal of talk; it was all very friendly and lively and jolly. Everyone present, sooner or later, said something to him, and seemed to make a particular point of addressing him by name. Two or three other persons came in, and there was a shifting of seats and changing of places; the gentlemen all entered into intimate conversation with the two Englishmen, made them urgent offers of hospitality, and hoped they might frequently be of service to them. They were afraid Lord Lambeth and Mr. Beaumont were not very comfortable at their hotel; that it was not, as one of them said, "so private as those dear little English inns of yours." This last gentleman went on to say that unfortunately, as yet, perhaps, privacy was not quite so easily obtained in America as might be desired; still, he continued, you could generally get it by paying for it; in fact, you could get everything in America nowadays by paying for it. American life was certainly growing a great deal more private; it was growing very much like England. Everything at Newport, for instance, was thoroughly private; Lord Lambeth would probably be struck with that. It was also represented to the strangers that it mattered very little whether their hotel was agreeable, as everyone would want them to make visits; they would stay with other people, and, in any case, they would be a great deal at Mrs. Westgate's. They would find that very charming; it was the pleasantest house in Newport. It was a pity Mr. Westgate was always away; he was a man of the highest ability—very acute, very acute. He worked like a horse, and he left his wife—well, to do about as she liked. He liked her to enjoy herself, and she seemed to know how. She was extremely brilliant and a splendid talker. Some people preferred her sister; but Miss Alden was very different; she was in a different style altogether. Some people even thought her prettier, and, certainly, she was not so sharp. She was more in the Boston style; she had lived a great deal in Boston, and she was very highly educated. Boston girls, it was propounded, were more like English young ladies.

Lord Lambeth had presently a chance to test the truth of this proposition, for on the company rising in compliance with a suggestion from their hostess that they should walk down to the rocks and look at the sea, the young Englishman again found himself, as they strolled across the grass, in proximity to Mrs. Westgate's sister. Though she was but a girl of twenty, she appeared to feel the obligation to exert an active hospitality; and this was, perhaps, the more to be noticed as she seemed by nature a reserved and retiring person, and had little of her sister's fraternizing quality. She was perhaps rather too thin, and she was a little pale; but as she moved slowly over the grass, with her arms hanging at her sides, looking gravely for a moment at the sea and then brightly, for all her gravity, at him, Lord Lambeth thought her at least as pretty as Mrs. Westgate, and reflected that if this was the Boston style the Boston style was very charming. He thought she looked very clever; he could imagine that she was highly educated; but at the same time she seemed gentle and graceful. For all her cleverness, however, he felt that she had to think a little what to say; she didn't say the first thing that came into her head; he had come from a different part of the world and from a different society, and she was trying to adapt her conversation. The others were scattering themselves near the rocks; Mrs. Westgate had charge of Percy Beaumont.

"Very jolly place, isn't it?" said Lord Lambeth. "It's a very jolly place to sit."

"Very charming," said the young girl. "I often sit here; there are all kinds of cozy corners—as if they had been made on purpose."

"Ah! I suppose you have had some of them made," said the young man.

Miss Alden looked at him a moment. "Oh no, we have had nothing made. It's pure nature."

"I should think you would have a few little benches—rustic seats and that sort of thing. It might be so jolly to sit here, you know," Lord Lambeth went on.

"I am afraid we haven't so many of those things as you," said the young girl thoughtfully.

"I daresay you go in for pure nature, as you were saying. Nature over here must be so grand, you know." And Lord Lambeth looked about him.

The little coast line hereabouts was very pretty, but it was not at all grand, and Miss Alden appeared to rise to a perception of this fact. "I am afraid it seems to you very rough," she said. "It's not like the coast scenery in Kingsley's novels."

"Ah, the novels always overdo it, you know," Lord Lambeth rejoined. "You must not go by the novels."

They were wandering about a little on the rocks, and they stopped and looked down into a narrow chasm where the rising tide made a curious bellowing sound. It was loud enough to prevent their hearing each other, and they stood there for some moments in silence. The young girl looked at her companion, observing him attentively, but covertly, as women, even when very young, know how to do. Lord Lambeth repaid observation; tall, straight, and strong, he was handsome as certain young Englishmen, and certain young Englishmen almost alone, are handsome; with a perfect finish of feature and a look of intellectual repose and gentle good temper which seemed somehow to be consequent upon his well-cut nose and chin. And to speak of Lord Lambeth's expression of intellectual repose is not simply a civil way of saying that he looked stupid. He was evidently not a young man of an irritable imagination; he was not, as he would himself have said, tremendously clever; but though there was a kind of appealing dullness in his eye, he looked thoroughly reasonable and competent, and his appearance proclaimed that to be a nobleman, an athlete, and an excellent fellow was a sufficiently brilliant combination of qualities. The young girl beside him, it may be attested without further delay, thought him the handsomest young man she had ever seen; and Bessie Alden's imagination, unlike that of her companion, was irritable. He, however, was also making up his mind that she was uncommonly pretty.

"I daresay it's very gay here, that you have lots of balls and parties," he said; for, if he was not tremendously clever, he rather prided himself on having, with women, a sufficiency of conversation.

"Oh, yes, there is a great deal going on," Bessie Alden replied. "There are not so many balls, but there are a good many other things. You will see for yourself; we live rather in the midst of it."

"It's very kind of you to say that. But I thought you Americans were always dancing."

"I suppose we dance a good deal; but I have never seen much of it. We don't do it much, at any rate, in summer. And I am sure," said Bessie Alden, "that we don't have so many balls as you have in England."

"Really!" exclaimed Lord Lambeth. "Ah, in England it all depends, you know."

"You will not think much of our gaieties," said the young girl, looking at him with a little mixture of interrogation and decision which was peculiar to her. The interrogation seemed earnest and the decision seemed arch; but the mixture, at any rate, was charming. "Those things, with us, are much less splendid than in England."

"I fancy you don't mean that," said Lord Lambeth, laughing.

"I assure you I mean everything I say," the young girl declared. "Certainly, from what I have read about English society, it is very different."

"Ah well, you know," said her companion, "those things are often described by fellows who know nothing about them. You mustn't mind what you read."

"Oh, I *shall* mind what I read!" Bessie Alden rejoined. "When I read Thackeray and George Eliot, how can I help minding them?"

"Ah well, Thackeray, and George Eliot," said the young nobleman; "I haven't read much of them."

"Don't you suppose they know about society?" asked Bessie Alden.

"Oh, I daresay they know; they were so very clever. But these fashionable novels," said Lord Lambeth, "they are awful rot, you know."

His companion looked at him a moment with her dark blue eyes, and then she looked down in the chasm where the water was tumbling about. "Do you mean Mrs. Gore, for instance?" she said presently, raising her eyes.

"I am afraid I haven't read that, either," was the young man's rejoinder, laughing a little and blushing. "I am afraid you'll think I am not very intellectual."

"Reading Mrs. Gore is no proof of intellect. But I like reading everything about English life—even poor books. I am so curious about it."

"Aren't ladies always curious?" asked the young man jestingly.

But Bessie Alden appeared to desire to answer his question seriously. "I don't think so—I don't think we are enough so—that we care about many things. So it's all the more of a compliment," she added, "that I should want to know so much about England."

The logic here seemed a little close; but Lord Lambeth, made conscious of a compliment, found his natural modesty just at hand. "I am sure you know a great deal more than I do."

"I really think I know a great deal—for a person who has never been there."

"Have you really never been there?" cried Lord Lambeth. "Fancy!"

"Never—except in imagination," said the young girl.

"Fancy!" repeated her companion. "But I daresay you'll go soon, won't you?"

"It's the dream of my life!" declared Bessie Alden, smiling.

"But your sister seems to know a tremendous lot about London," Lord Lambeth went on.

The young girl was silent a moment. "My sister and I are two very different persons," she presently said. "She has been a great deal in Europe. She has been in England several times. She has known a great many English people."

"But you must have known some, too," said Lord Lambeth.

"I don't think that I have ever spoken to one before. You are the first Englishman that—to my knowledge—I have ever talked with."

Bessie Alden made this statement with a certain gravity—almost, as it seemed to Lord Lambeth, an impressiveness. Attempts at impressiveness always made him feel awkward, and he now began to laugh and swing his stick. "Ah, you would have been sure to know!" he said. And then he added, after an instant, "I'm sorry I am not a better specimen."

The young girl looked away; but she smiled, laying aside her impressiveness. "You must remember that you are only a beginning," she said. Then she retraced her steps, leading the way back to the lawn, where they saw Mrs. Westgate come toward them with Percy Beaumont still at her side. "Perhaps I shall go to England next year," Miss Alden continued; "I want to, immensely. My sister is going to Europe, and she has asked me to go with her. If we go, I shall make her stay as long as possible in London."

"Ah, you must come in July," said Lord Lambeth. "That's the time when there is most going on."

"I don't think I can wait till July," the young girl rejoined. "By the first of May I shall be very impatient." They had gone further, and Mrs. Westgate and her companion were near them. "Kitty," said Miss Alden, "I have given out that we are going to London next May. So please to conduct yourself accordingly."

Percy Beaumont wore a somewhat animated—even a slightly irritated—air. He was by no means so handsome a man as his cousin, although in his cousin's absence he might have passed for a striking specimen of the tall, muscular, fair-bearded, clear-eyed Englishman. Just now Beaumont's clear eyes, which were small and of a pale gray color, had a rather troubled light, and, after glancing at Bessie Alden while she spoke, he rested them upon his kinsman. Mrs. Westgate meanwhile, with her superfluously pretty gaze, looked at everyone alike.

"You had better wait till the time comes," she said to her sister. "Perhaps next May you won't care so much about London. Mr. Beaumont and I," she went on, smiling at her companion, "have had a tremendous discussion. We don't agree about anything. It's perfectly delightful."

"Oh, I say, Percy!" exclaimed Lord Lambeth.

"I disagree," said Beaumont, stroking down his back hair, "even to the point of not thinking it delightful."

"Oh, I say!" cried Lord Lambeth again.

"I don't see anything delightful in my disagreeing with Mrs. Westgate," said Percy Beaumont.

"Well, I do!" Mrs. Westgate declared; and she turned to her sister. "You know you have to go to town. The phaeton is there. You had better take Lord Lambeth."

At this point Percy Beaumont certainly looked straight at his kinsman; he tried to catch his eye. But Lord Lambeth would not look at him; his own eyes were better occupied. "I shall be very happy," cried Bessie Alden. "I am only going to some shops. But I will drive you about and show you the place."

"An American woman who respects herself," said Mrs. Westgate, turning to Beaumont with her bright expository air, "must buy something every day of her life. If she can not do it herself, she must send out some member of her family for the purpose. So Bessie goes forth to fulfill my mission."

The young girl had walked away, with Lord Lambeth by her side, to whom she was talking still; and Percy Beaumont watched them as they passed toward the house. "She fulfills her own mission," he presently said; "that of being a very attractive young lady."

"I don't know that I should say very attractive," Mrs. Westgate rejoined. "She is not so much that as she is charming when you really know her. She is very shy."

"Oh, indeed!" said Percy Beaumont.

"Extremely shy," Mrs. Westgate repeated. "But she is a dear good girl; she is a charming species of girl. She is not in the least a flirt; that isn't at all her line; she doesn't know the alphabet of that sort of thing. She is very simple, very serious. She has lived a great deal in Boston, with another sister of mine—the eldest of us—who married a Bostonian. She is very cultivated, not at all like me; I am not in the least cultivated. She has studied immensely and read everything; she is what they call in Boston 'thoughtful.'"

"A rum sort of girl for Lambeth to get hold of!" his lordship's kinsman privately reflected.

"I really believe," Mrs. Westgate continued, "that the most charming girl in the world is a Boston superstructure upon a New York fonds; or perhaps a New York superstructure upon a Boston fonds. At any rate, it's the mixture," said Mrs. Westgate, who continued to give Percy Beaumont a great deal of information.

Lord Lambeth got into a little basket phaeton with Bessie Alden, and she drove him down the long avenue, whose extent he had measured on foot a couple of hours before, into the ancient town, as it was called in that part of the world, of Newport. The ancient town was a curious affair—a collection of fresh-looking little wooden houses, painted white, scattered over a hillside and clustered about a long straight street paved with enormous cobblestones. There were plenty of shops—a large proportion of which appeared to be those of fruit vendors, with piles of huge watermelons and pumpkins stacked in front of them; and, drawn up before the shops, or bumping about on the cobblestones, were innumerable other basket phaetons freighted with ladies of high fashion, who greeted each other from vehicle to vehicle and conversed on the edge of the pavement in a manner that struck Lord Lambeth as demonstrative, with a great many "Oh, my dears," and little quick exclamations and caresses. His companion went into seventeen shops—he amused himself with counting them—and accumulated at the bottom of the phaeton a pile of bundles that hardly left the young Englishman a place for his feet. As she had no groom nor footman, he sat in the phaeton to hold the ponies, where, although he was not a particularly acute observer, he saw much to entertain him—especially the ladies just mentioned, who wandered up and down with the appearance of a kind of aimless intentness, as if they were looking for something to buy, and who, tripping in and out of their vehicles, displayed remarkably pretty feet. It all seemed to Lord Lambeth very odd, and bright, and gay. Of course, before they got back to the villa, he had had a great deal of desultory conversation with Bessie Alden.

The young Englishmen spent the whole of that day and the whole of many successive days in what the French call the intimite of their new friends. They agreed that it was extremely jolly, that they had never known anything more agreeable. It is not proposed to narrate minutely the incidents of their sojourn on this charming shore; though if it were convenient I might present a record of impressions nonetheless delectable that they were not exhaustively analyzed. Many of them still linger in the minds of our travelers, attended by a train of harmonious images—images of brilliant mornings on lawns and piazzas that overlooked the sea; of innumerable pretty girls; of infinite lounging and talking and laughing and flirting and lunching and dining; of universal friendliness and frankness; of occasions on which they knew everyone and everything and had an extraordinary sense of ease; of drives and rides in the late afternoon over gleaming beaches, on long sea roads, beneath a sky lighted up by marvelous sunsets; of suppers, on the return, informal, irregular, agreeable; of evenings at open windows or on the perpetual verandas, in the summer starlight, above the warm Atlantic. The young Englishmen were introduced to everybody, entertained by everybody, intimate with everybody. At the end of three days they had removed their luggage from the hotel and had gone to stay with Mrs. Westgate—a step to which Percy Beaumont at first offered some conscientious opposition. I call his opposition conscientious, because it was founded upon some talk that he had had, on the second day, with Bessie Alden. He had indeed had a good deal of talk with her, for she was not literally always in conversation with Lord Lambeth. He had meditated upon Mrs. Westgate's account of her sister, and he discovered for himself that the young lady was clever, and appeared to have read a great deal. She seemed very nice, though he could not make out, as Mrs. Westgate had said, she was shy. If she was shy, she carried it off very well.

"Mr. Beaumont," she had said, "please tell me something about Lord Lambeth's family. How would you say it in England—his position?"

"His position?" Percy Beaumont repeated.

"His rank, or whatever you call it. Unfortunately we haven't got a *peerage*, like the people in Thackeray."

"That's a great pity," said Beaumont. "You would find it all set forth there so much better than I can do it."

"He is a peer, then?"

"Oh, yes, he is a peer."

"And has he any other title than Lord Lambeth?"

"His title is the Marquis of Lambeth," said Beaumont; and then he was silent. Bessie Alden appeared to be looking at him with interest. "He is the son of the Duke of Bayswater," he added presently.

"The eldest son?"

"The only son."

"And are his parents living?"

"Oh yes; if his father were not living he would be a duke."

"So that when his father dies," pursued Bessie Alden with more simplicity than might have been expected in a clever girl, "he will become Duke of Bayswater?"

"Of course," said Percy Beaumont. "But his father is in excellent health."

"And his mother?"

Beaumont smiled a little. "The duchess is uncommonly robust."

"And has he any sisters?"

"Yes, there are two."

"And what are they called?"

"One of them is married. She is the Countess of Pimlico."

"And the other?"

"The other is unmarried; she is plain Lady Julia."

Bessie Alden looked at him a moment. "Is she very plain?"

Beaumont began to laugh again. "You would not find her so handsome as her brother," he said; and it was after this that he attempted to dissuade the heir of the Duke of Bayswater from accepting Mrs. Westgate's invitation. "Depend upon it," he said, "that girl means to try for you."

"It seems to me you are doing your best to make a fool of me," the modest young nobleman answered.

"She has been asking me," said Beaumont, "all about your people and your possessions."

"I am sure it is very good of her!" Lord Lambeth rejoined.

"Well, then," observed his companion, "if you go, you go with your eyes open."

"Damn my eyes!" exclaimed Lord Lambeth. "If one is to be a dozen times a day at the house, it is a great deal more convenient to sleep there. I am sick of traveling up and down this beastly avenue."

Since he had determined to go, Percy Beaumont would, of course, have been very sorry to allow him to go alone; he was a man of conscience, and he remembered his promise to the duchess. It was obviously the memory of this promise that made him say to his companion a couple of days later that he rather wondered he should be so fond of that girl.

"In the first place, how do you know how fond I am of her?" asked Lord Lambeth. "And, in the second place, why shouldn't I be fond of her?"

"I shouldn't think she would be in your line."

"What do you call my 'line'? You don't set her down as 'fast'?"

"Exactly so. Mrs. Westgate tells me that there is no such thing as the 'fast girl' in America; that it's an English invention, and that the term has no meaning here."

"All the better. It's an animal I detest."

"You prefer a bluestocking."

"Is that what you call Miss Alden?"

"Her sister tells me," said Percy Beaumont, "that she is tremendously literary."

"I don't know anything about that. She is certainly very clever."

"Well," said Beaumont, "I should have supposed you would have found that sort of thing awfully slow."

"In point of fact," Lord Lambeth rejoined, "I find it uncommonly lively."

After this, Percy Beaumont held his tongue; but on the 10th of August he wrote to the Duchess of Bayswater. He was, as I have said, a man of conscience, and he had a strong, incorruptible sense of the proprieties of life. His kinsman, meanwhile, was having a great deal of talk with Bessie Alden—on the red sea rocks beyond the lawn; in the course of long island rides, with a slow return in the glowing twilight; on the deep veranda late in the evening. Lord Lambeth, who had stayed at many houses, had never stayed at a house in which it was possible for a young man to converse so frequently with a young lady. This young lady no longer applied to Percy Beaumont for information concerning his lordship. She addressed herself directly to the young nobleman. She asked him a great many questions, some of which bored him a little; for he took no pleasure in talking about himself.

"Lord Lambeth," said Bessie Alden, "are you a hereditary legislator?"

"Oh, I say!" cried Lord Lambeth, "don't make me call myself such names as that."

"But you are a member of Parliament," said the young girl.

"I don't like the sound of that, either."

"Don't you sit in the House of Lords?" Bessie Alden went on.

"Very seldom," said Lord Lambeth.

"Is it an important position?" she asked.

"Oh, dear, no," said Lord Lambeth.

"I should think it would be very grand," said Bessie Alden, "to possess, simply by an accident of birth, the right to make laws for a great nation."

"Ah, but one doesn't make laws. It's a great humbug."

"I don't believe that," the young girl declared. "It must be a great privilege, and I should think that if one thought of it in the right way—from a high point of view—it would be very inspiring."

"The less one thinks of it, the better," Lord Lambeth affirmed.

"I think it's tremendous," said Bessie Alden; and on another occasion she asked him if he had any tenantry. Hereupon it was that, as I have said, he was a little bored.

"Do you want to buy up their leases?" he asked.

"Well, have you got any livings?" she demanded.

"Oh, I say!" he cried. "Have you got a clergyman that is looking out?" But she made him tell her that he had a castle; he confessed to but one. It was the place in which he had been born and brought up, and, as he had an old-time liking for it, he was beguiled into describing it a little and saying it was really very jolly. Bessie Alden listened with great interest and declared that she would give the world to see such a place. Whereupon—"It would be awfully kind of you to come and stay there," said Lord Lambeth. He took a vague satisfaction in the circumstance that Percy Beaumont had not heard him make the remark I have just recorded.

Mr. Westgate all this time had not, as they said at Newport, "come on." His wife more than once announced that she expected him on the morrow; but on the morrow she wandered about a little, with a telegram in her jeweled fingers, declaring it was very tiresome that his business detained him in New York; that he could only hope the Englishmen were having a good time. "I must say," said Mrs. Westgate, "that it is no thanks to him if you are." And she went on to explain, while she continued that slow-paced promenade which enabled her well-adjusted skirts to display themselves so advantageously, that unfortunately in America there was no leisure class. It was Lord Lambeth's theory, freely propounded when the young men were together, that Percy Beaumont was having a very good time with Mrs. Westgate, and that, under the pretext of meeting for the purpose of animated discussion, they were indulging in practices that imparted a shade of hypocrisy to the lady's regret for her husband's absence.

"I assure you we are always discussing and differing," said Percy Beaumont. "She is awfully argumentative. American ladies certainly don't mind contradicting you. Upon my word I don't think I was ever treated so by a woman before. She's so devilish positive."

Mrs. Westgate's positive quality, however, evidently had its attractions, for Beaumont was constantly at his hostess's side. He detached himself one day to the extent of going to New York to talk over the Tennessee Central with Mr. Westgate; but he was absent only forty-eight hours, during which, with Mr. Westgate's assistance, he completely settled this piece of business. "They certainly do things quickly in New York," he observed to his cousin; and he added that Mr. Westgate had seemed very uneasy lest his wife should miss her visitor—he had been in such an awful hurry to send him back to her. "I'm afraid you'll never come up to an American husband, if that's what the wives expect," he said to Lord Lambeth.

Mrs. Westgate, however, was not to enjoy much longer the entertainment with which an indulgent husband had desired to keep her provided. On the 21st of August Lord Lambeth received a telegram from his mother, requesting him to return immediately to England; his father had been taken ill, and it was his filial duty to come to him.

The young Englishman was visibly annoyed. "What the deuce does it mean?" he asked of his kinsman. "What am I to do?"

Percy Beaumont was annoyed as well; he had deemed it his duty, as I have narrated, to write to the duchess, but he had not expected that this distinguished woman would act so promptly upon his hint. "It means," he said, "that your father is laid up. I don't suppose it's anything serious; but you have no option. Take the first steamer; but don't be alarmed."

Lord Lambeth made his farewells; but the few last words that he exchanged with Bessie Alden are the only ones that have a place in our record. "Of course I needn't assure you," he said, "that if you should come to England next year, I expect to be the first person that you inform of it."

Bessie Alden looked at him a little, and she smiled. "Oh, if we come to London," she answered, "I should think you would hear of it."

Percy Beaumont returned with his cousin, and his sense of duty compelled him, one windless afternoon, in mid-Atlantic, to say to Lord Lambeth that he suspected that the duchess's telegram was in part the result of something he himself had written to her. "I wrote to her—as I explicitly notified you I had promised to do—that you were extremely interested in a little American girl."

Lord Lambeth was extremely angry, and he indulged for some moments in the simple language of indignation. But I have said that he was a reasonable young man, and I can give no better proof of it than the fact that he remarked to his companion at the end of half an hour, "You were quite right, after all. I am very much interested in her. Only, to be fair," he added, "you should have told my mother also that she is not—seriously—interested in me."

Percy Beaumont gave a little laugh. "There is nothing so charming as modesty in a young man in your position. That speech is a capital proof that you are sweet on her."

"She is not interested—she is not!" Lord Lambeth repeated.

"My dear fellow," said his companion, "you are very far gone."

PART II

In point of fact, as Percy Beaumont would have said, Mrs. Westgate disembarked on the 18th of May on the British coast. She was accompanied by her sister, but she was not attended by any other member of her family. To the deprivation of her husband's society Mrs. Westgate was, however, habituated; she had made half a dozen journeys to Europe without him, and she now accounted for his absence, to interrogative friends on this side of the Atlantic, by allusion to the regrettable but conspicuous fact that in America there was no leisure class. The two ladies came up to London and alighted at Jones's Hotel, where Mrs. Westgate, who had made on former occasions the most agreeable impression at this establishment, received an obsequious greeting. Bessie Alden had felt much excited about coming to England; she had expected the "associations" would be very charming, that it would be an infinite pleasure to rest her eyes upon the things she had read about in the poets and historians. She was very fond of the poets and historians, of the picturesque, of the past, of retrospect, of mementos and reverberations of greatness; so that on coming into the English world, where strangeness and familiarity would go hand in hand, she was prepared for a multitude of fresh emotions. They began very promptly—these tender, fluttering sensations; they began with the sight of the beautiful English landscape, whose dark richness was quickened and brightened by the season; with the carpeted fields and flowering hedgerows, as she looked at them from the window of the train; with the spires of the rural churches peeping above the rook-haunted treetops; with the oak-studded parks, the ancient homes, the cloudy light, the speech, the manners, the thousand differences. Mrs. Westgate's impressions had, of course, much less novelty and keenness, and she gave but a wandering attention to her sister's ejaculations and rhapsodies.

"You know my enjoyment of England is not so intellectual as Bessie's," she said to several of her friends in the course of her visit to this country. "And yet if it is not intellectual, I can't say it is physical. I don't think I can quite say what it is, my enjoyment of England." When once it was settled that the two ladies should come abroad and should spend a few weeks in England on their way to the Continent, they of course exchanged a good many allusions to their London acquaintance.

"It will certainly be much nicer having friends there," Bessie Alden had said one day as she sat on the sunny deck of the steamer at her sister's feet on a large blue rug.

"Whom do you mean by friends?" Mrs. Westgate asked.

"All those English gentlemen whom you have known and entertained. Captain Littledale, for instance. And Lord Lambeth and Mr. Beaumont," added Bessie Alden.

"Do you expect them to give us a very grand reception?"

Bessie reflected a moment; she was addicted, as we know, to reflection. "Well, yes."

"My poor, sweet child," murmured her sister.

"What have I said that is so silly?" asked Bessie.

"You are a little too simple; just a little. It is very becoming, but it pleases people at your expense."

"I am certainly too simple to understand you," said Bessie.

"Shall I tell you a story?" asked her sister.

"If you would be so good. That is what they do to amuse simple people."

Mrs. Westgate consulted her memory, while her companion sat gazing at the shining sea. "Did you ever hear of the Duke of Green-Erin?"

"I think not," said Bessie.

"Well, it's no matter," her sister went on.

"It's a proof of my simplicity."

"My story is meant to illustrate that of some other people," said Mrs. Westgate. "The Duke of Green-Erin is what they call in England a great swell, and some five years ago he came to America. He spent most of his time in New York, and in New York he spent his days and his nights at the Butterworths'. You have heard, at least, of the Butterworths. *Bien.* They did everything in the world for him—they turned themselves inside out. They gave him a dozen dinner parties and balls and were the means of his being invited to fifty more. At first he used to come into Mrs. Butterworth's box at the opera in a tweed traveling suit; but someone stopped that. At any rate, he had a beautiful time, and they parted the best friends in the world. Two years elapse, and the Butterworths come abroad and go to London. The first thing they see in all the papers—in England those things are in the most prominent place—is that the Duke of Green-Erin has arrived in town for the Season. They wait a little, and then Mr. Butterworth—as polite as ever—goes and leaves a card. They wait a little more; the visit is not returned; they wait three weeks—silence de mort—the Duke gives no sign. The Butterworths see a lot of other people, put down the Duke of Green-Erin as a rude, ungrateful man, and forget all about him. One fine day they go to Ascot Races, and there they meet him face to face. He stares a moment and then comes up to Mr. Butterworth, taking something from his pocketbook—something which proves to be a banknote. 'I'm glad to see you, Mr. Butterworth,' he says, 'so that I can pay you that ten pounds I lost to you in New York. I saw the other day you remembered our bet; here are the ten pounds, Mr. Butterworth. Goodbye, Mr. Butterworth.' And off he goes, and that's the last they see of the Duke of Green-Erin."

"Is that your story?" asked Bessie Alden.

"Don't you think it's interesting?" her sister replied.

"I don't believe it," said the young girl.

"Ah," cried Mrs. Westgate, "you are not so simple after all! Believe it or not, as you please; there is no smoke without fire."

"Is that the way," asked Bessie after a moment, "that you expect your friends to treat you?"

"I defy them to treat me very ill, because I shall not give them the opportunity. With the best will in the world, in that case they can't be very offensive."

Bessie Alden was silent a moment. "I don't see what makes you talk that way," she said. "The English are a great people."

"Exactly; and that is just the way they have grown great—by dropping you when you have ceased to be useful. People say they are not clever; but I think they are very clever."

"You know you have liked them—all the Englishmen you have seen," said Bessie.

"They have liked me," her sister rejoined; "it would be more correct to say that. And, of course, one likes that."

Bessie Alden resumed for some moments her studies in sea green. "Well," she said, "whether they like me or not, I mean to like them. And happily," she added, "Lord Lambeth does not owe me ten pounds."

During the first few days after their arrival at Jones's Hotel our charming Americans were much occupied with what they would have called looking about them. They found occasion to make a large number of purchases, and their opportunities for conversation were such only as were offered by the deferential London shopmen. Bessie Alden, even in driving from the station, took an immense fancy to the British metropolis, and at the risk of exhibiting her as a young woman of vulgar tastes it must be recorded that for a considerable period she desired no higher pleasure than to drive about the crowded streets in a hansom cab. To her attentive eyes they were full of a strange picturesque life, and it is at least beneath the dignity of our historic muse to enumerate the trivial objects and incidents which this simple young lady from Boston found so entertaining. It may be freely mentioned, however, that whenever, after a round of visits in Bond Street and Regent Street, she was about to return with her sister to Jones's Hotel, she made an earnest request that they should be driven home by way of Westminster Abbey. She had begun by asking whether it would not be possible to take the Tower on the way to their lodgings; but it happened that at a more primitive stage of her culture Mrs. Westgate had paid a visit to this venerable monument, which she spoke of ever afterward vaguely as a dreadful disappointment; so that she expressed the liveliest disapproval of any attempt to combine historical researches with the purchase of hairbrushes and notepaper. The most she would consent to do in this line was to spend half an hour at Madame Tussaud's, where she saw several dusty wax effigies of members of the royal family. She told Bessie that if she wished to go to the Tower she must get someone else to take her. Bessie expressed hereupon an earnest disposition to go alone; but upon this proposal as well Mrs. Westgate sprinkled cold water.

"Remember," she said, "that you are not in your innocent little Boston. It is not a question of walking up and down Beacon Street." Then she went on to explain that there were two classes of American girls in Europe—those that walked about alone and those that did not. "You happen to belong, my dear," she said to her sister, "to the class that does not."

"It is only," answered Bessie, laughing, "because you happen to prevent me." And she devoted much private meditation to this question of effecting a visit to the Tower of London.

Suddenly it seemed as if the problem might be solved; the two ladies at Jones's Hotel received a visit from Willie Woodley. Such was the social appellation of a young American who had sailed from New York a few days after their own departure, and who, having the privilege of intimacy with them in that city, had lost no time, on his arrival in London, in coming to pay them his respects. He had, in fact, gone to see them directly after going to see his tailor, than which there can be no greater exhibition of promptitude on the part of a young American who has just alighted at the Charing Cross Hotel. He was a slim, pale youth, of the most amiable disposition, famous for the skill with which he led the "German" in New York. Indeed, by the young ladies who habitually figured in this Terpsichorean revel he was believed to be "the best dancer in the world"; it was in these terms that he was always spoken of, and that his identity was indicated. He was the gentlest, softest young man it was possible to meet; he was beautifully dressed—"in the English style"—and he knew an immense deal about London. He had been at

Newport during the previous summer, at the time of our young Englishmen's visit, and he took extreme pleasure in the society of Bessie Alden, whom he always addressed as "Miss Bessie." She immediately arranged with him, in the presence of her sister, that he should conduct her to the scene of Anne Boleyn's execution.

"You may do as you please," said Mrs. Westgate. "Only—if you desire the information—it is not the custom here for young ladies to knock about London with young men."

"Miss Bessie has waltzed with me so often," observed Willie Woodley; "she can surely go out with me in a hansom."

"I consider waltzing," said Mrs. Westgate, "the most innocent pleasure of our time."

"It's a compliment to our time!" exclaimed the young man with a little laugh, in spite of himself.

"I don't see why I should regard what is done here," said Bessie Alden. "Why should I suffer the restrictions of a society of which I enjoy none of the privileges?"

"That's very good—very good," murmured Willie Woodley.

"Oh, go to the Tower, and feel the ax, if you like," said Mrs. Westgate. "I consent to your going with Mr. Woodley; but I should not let you go with an Englishman."

"Miss Bessie wouldn't care to go with an Englishman!" Mr. Woodley declared with a faint asperity that was, perhaps, not unnatural in a young man, who, dressing in the manner that I have indicated and knowing a great deal, as I have said, about London, saw no reason for drawing these sharp distinctions. He agreed upon a day with Miss Bessie—a day of that same week.

An ingenious mind might, perhaps, trace a connection between the young girl's allusion to her destitution of social privileges and a question she asked on the morrow as she sat with her sister at lunch.

"Don't you mean to write to—to anyone?" said Bessie.

"I wrote this morning to Captain Littledale," Mrs. Westgate replied.

"But Mr. Woodley said that Captain Littledale had gone to India."

"He said he thought he had heard so; he knew nothing about it."

For a moment Bessie Alden said nothing more; then, at last, "And don't you intend to write to—to Mr. Beaumont?" she inquired.

"You mean to Lord Lambeth," said her sister.

"I said Mr. Beaumont because he was so good a friend of yours."

Mrs. Westgate looked at the young girl with sisterly candor. "I don't care two straws for Mr. Beaumont."

"You were certainly very nice to him."

"I am nice to everyone," said Mrs. Westgate simply.

"To everyone but me," rejoined Bessie, smiling.

Her sister continued to look at her; then, at last, "Are you in love with Lord Lambeth?" she asked.

The young girl stared a moment, and the question was apparently too humorous even to make her blush. "Not that I know of," she answered.

"Because if you are," Mrs. Westgate went on, "I shall certainly not send for him."

"That proves what I said," declared Bessie, smiling—"that you are not nice to me."

"It would be a poor service, my dear child," said her sister.

"In what sense? There is nothing against Lord Lambeth that I know of."

Mrs. Westgate was silent a moment. "You *are* in love with him then?"

Bessie stared again; but this time she blushed a little. "Ah! if you won't be serious," she answered, "we will not mention him again."

For some moments Lord Lambeth was not mentioned again, and it was Mrs. Westgate who, at the end of this period, reverted to him. "Of course I will let him know we are here, because I think he would be hurt—justly enough—if we should go away without seeing him. It is fair to give him a chance to come and thank me for the kindness we showed him. But I don't want to seem eager."

"Neither do I," said Bessie with a little laugh.

"Though I confess," added her sister, "that I am curious to see how he will behave."

"He behaved very well at Newport."

"Newport is not London. At Newport he could do as he liked; but here it is another affair. He has to have an eye to consequences."

"If he had more freedom, then, at Newport," argued Bessie, "it is the more to his credit that he behaved well; and if he has to be so careful here, it is possible he will behave even better."

"Better—better," repeated her sister. "My dear child, what is your point of view?"

"How do you mean—my point of view?"

"Don't you care for Lord Lambeth—a little?"

This time Bessie Alden was displeased; she slowly got up from the table, turning her face away from her sister. "You will oblige me by not talking so," she said.

Mrs. Westgate sat watching her for some moments as she moved slowly about the room and went and stood at the window. "I will write to him this afternoon," she said at last.

"Do as you please!" Bessie answered; and presently she turned round. "I am not afraid to say that I like Lord Lambeth. I like him very much."

"He is not clever," Mrs. Westgate declared.

"Well, there have been clever people whom I have disliked," said Bessie Alden; "so that I suppose I may like a stupid one. Besides, Lord Lambeth is not stupid."

"Not so stupid as he looks!" exclaimed her sister, smiling.

"If I were in love with Lord Lambeth, as you said just now, it would be bad policy on your part to abuse him."

"My dear child, don't give me lessons in policy!" cried Mrs. Westgate. "The policy I mean to follow is very deep."

The young girl began to walk about the room again; then she stopped before her sister. "I have never heard in the course of five minutes," she said, "so many hints and innuendoes. I wish you would tell me in plain English what you mean."

"I mean that you may be much annoyed."

"That is still only a hint," said Bessie.

Her sister looked at her, hesitating an instant. "It will be said of you that you have come after Lord Lambeth—that you followed him."

Bessie Alden threw back her pretty head like a startled hind, and a look flashed into her face that made Mrs. Westgate rise from her chair. "Who says such things as that?" she demanded.

"People here."

"I don't believe it," said Bessie.

"You have a very convenient faculty of doubt. But my policy will be, as I say, very deep. I shall leave you to find out this kind of thing for yourself."

Bessie fixed her eyes upon her sister, and Mrs. Westgate thought for a moment there were tears in them. "Do they talk that way here?" she asked.

"You will see. I shall leave you alone."

"Don't leave me alone," said Bessie Alden. "Take me away."

"No; I want to see what you make of it," her sister continued.

"I don't understand."

"You will understand after Lord Lambeth has come," said Mrs. Westgate with a little laugh.

The two ladies had arranged that on this afternoon Willie Woodley should go with them to Hyde Park, where Bessie Alden expected to derive much entertainment from sitting on a little green chair, under the great trees, beside Rotten Row. The want of a suitable escort had hitherto rendered this pleasure inaccessible; but no escort now, for such an expedition, could have been more suitable than their devoted young countryman, whose mission in life, it might almost be said, was to find chairs for ladies, and who appeared on the stroke of half-past five with a white camellia in his buttonhole.

"I have written to Lord Lambeth, my dear," said Mrs. Westgate to her sister, on coming into the room where Bessie Alden, drawing on her long gray gloves, was entertaining their visitor.

Bessie said nothing, but Willie Woodley exclaimed that his lordship was in town; he had seen his name in the Morning Post.

"Do you read the Morning Post?" asked Mrs. Westgate.

"Oh, yes; it's great fun," Willie Woodley affirmed.

"I want so to see it," said Bessie; "there is so much about it in Thackeray."

"I will send it to you every morning," said Willie Woodley.

He found them what Bessie Alden thought excellent places, under the great trees, beside the famous avenue whose humors had been made familiar to the young girl's childhood by the pictures in Punch. The day was bright and warm, and the crowd of riders and spectators, and the great procession of carriages, were proportionately dense and brilliant. The scene bore the stamp of the London Season at its height, and Bessie Alden found more entertainment in it than she was able to express to her companions. She sat silent, under her parasol, and her imagination, according to its wont, let itself loose into the great changing assemblage of striking and suggestive figures. They stirred up a host of old impressions and preconceptions, and she found herself fitting a history to this person and a theory to that, and making a place for them all in her little private museum of types. But if she said little, her sister on one side and Willie Woodley on the other expressed themselves in lively alternation.

"Look at that green dress with blue flounces," said Mrs. Westgate. "Quelle toilette!"

"That's the Marquis of Blackborough," said the young man—"the one in the white coat. I heard him speak the other night in the House of Lords; it was something about ramrods; he called them 'wamwods.' He's an awful swell."

"Did you ever see anything like the way they are pinned back?" Mrs. Westgate resumed. "They never know where to stop."

"They do nothing but stop," said Willie Woodley. "It prevents them from walking. Here comes a great celebrity—Lady Beatrice Bellevue. She's awfully fast; see what little steps she takes."

"Well, my dear," Mrs. Westgate pursued, "I hope you are getting some ideas for your couturiere?"

"I am getting plenty of ideas," said Bessie, "but I don't know that my couturiere would appreciate them."

Willie Woodley presently perceived a friend on horseback, who drove up beside the barrier of the Row and beckoned to him. He went forward, and the crowd of pedestrians closed about him, so that for some ten minutes he was hidden from sight. At last he reappeared, bringing a gentleman with him—a gentleman whom Bessie at first supposed to be his friend dismounted. But at a second glance she found herself looking at Lord Lambeth, who was shaking hands with her sister.

"I found him over there," said Willie Woodley, "and I told him you were here."

And then Lord Lambeth, touching his hat a little, shook hands with Bessie. "Fancy your being here!" he said. He was blushing and smiling; he looked very handsome, and he had a kind of splendor that he had not had in America. Bessie Alden's imagination, as we know, was just then in exercise; so that the tall young Englishman, as he stood there looking down at her, had the benefit of it. "He is handsomer and more splendid than anything I have ever seen," she said to herself. And then she remembered that he was a marquis, and she thought he looked like a marquis.

"I say, you know," he cried, "you ought to have let a man know you were here!"

"I wrote to you an hour ago," said Mrs. Westgate.

"Doesn't all the world know it?" asked Bessie, smiling.

"I assure you I didn't know it!" cried Lord Lambeth. "Upon my honor I hadn't heard of it. Ask Woodley now; had I, Woodley?"

"Well, I think you are rather a humbug," said Willie Woodley.

"You don't believe that—do you, Miss Alden?" asked his lordship. "You don't believe I'm a humbug, eh?"

"No," said Bessie, "I don't."

"You are too tall to stand up, Lord Lambeth," Mrs. Westgate observed. "You are only tolerable when you sit down. Be so good as to get a chair."

He found a chair and placed it sidewise, close to the two ladies. "If I hadn't met Woodley I should never have found you," he went on. "Should I, Woodley?"

"Well, I guess not," said the young American.

"Not even with my letter?" asked Mrs. Westgate.

"Ah, well, I haven't got your letter yet; I suppose I shall get it this evening. It was awfully kind of you to write."

"So I said to Bessie," observed Mrs. Westgate.

"Did she say so, Miss Alden?" Lord Lambeth inquired. "I daresay you have been here a month."

"We have been here three," said Mrs. Westgate.

"Have you been here three months?" the young man asked again of Bessie.

"It seems a long time," Bessie answered.

"I say, after that you had better not call me a humbug!" cried Lord Lambeth. "I have only been in town three weeks; but you must have been hiding away; I haven't seen you anywhere."

"Where should you have seen us—where should we have gone?" asked Mrs. Westgate.

"You should have gone to Hurlingham," said Willie Woodley.

"No; let Lord Lambeth tell us," Mrs. Westgate insisted.

"There are plenty of places to go to," said Lord Lambeth; "each one stupider than the other. I mean people's houses; they send you cards."

"No one has sent us cards," said Bessie.

"We are very quiet," her sister declared. "We are here as travelers."

"We have been to Madame Tussaud's," Bessie pursued.

"Oh, I say!" cried Lord Lambeth.

"We thought we should find your image there," said Mrs. Westgate—"yours and Mr. Beaumont's."

"In the Chamber of Horrors?" laughed the young man.

"It did duty very well for a party," said Mrs. Westgate. "All the women were decolletes, and many of the figures looked as if they could speak if they tried."

"Upon my word," Lord Lambeth rejoined, "you see people at London parties that look as if they couldn't speak if they tried."

"Do you think Mr. Woodley could find us Mr. Beaumont?" asked Mrs. Westgate.

Lord Lambeth stared and looked round him. "I daresay he could. Beaumont often comes here. Don't you think you could find him, Woodley? Make a dive into the crowd."

"Thank you; I have had enough diving," said Willie Woodley. "I will wait till Mr. Beaumont comes to the surface."

"I will bring him to see you," said Lord Lambeth; "where are you staying?"

"You will find the address in my letter—Jones's Hotel."

"Oh, one of those places just out of Piccadilly? Beastly hole, isn't it?" Lord Lambeth inquired.

"I believe it's the best hotel in London," said Mrs. Westgate.

"But they give you awful rubbish to eat, don't they?" his lordship went on.

"Yes," said Mrs. Westgate.

"I always feel so sorry for the people that come up to town and go to live in those places," continued the young man. "They eat nothing but filth."

"Oh, I say!" cried Willie Woodley.

"Well, how do you like London, Miss Alden?" Lord Lambeth asked, unperturbed by this ejaculation.

"I think it's grand," said Bessie Alden.

"My sister likes it, in spite of the 'filth'!" Mrs. Westgate exclaimed.

"I hope you are going to stay a long time."

"As long as I can," said Bessie.

"And where is Mr. Westgate?" asked Lord Lambeth of this gentleman's wife.

"He's where he always is—in that tiresome New York."

"He must be tremendously clever," said the young man.

"I suppose he is," said Mrs. Westgate.

Lord Lambeth sat for nearly an hour with his American friends; but it is not our purpose to relate their conversation in full. He addressed a great many remarks to Bessie Alden, and finally turned toward her altogether, while Willie Woodley entertained Mrs. Westgate. Bessie herself said very little; she was on her guard, thinking of what her sister had said to her at lunch. Little by little, however, she interested herself in Lord Lambeth again, as she had done at Newport; only it seemed to her that here he might become more interesting. He would be an unconscious part of the antiquity, the impressiveness, the picturesqueness, of England; and poor Bessie Alden, like many a Yankee maiden, was terribly at the mercy of picturesqueness.

"I have often wished I were at Newport again," said the young man. "Those days I spent at your sister's were awfully jolly."

"We enjoyed them very much; I hope your father is better."

"Oh, dear, yes. When I got to England, he was out grouse shooting. It was what you call in America a gigantic fraud. My mother had got nervous. My three weeks at Newport seemed like a happy dream."

"America certainly is very different from England," said Bessie.

"I hope you like England better, eh?" Lord Lambeth rejoined almost persuasively.

"No Englishman can ask that seriously of a person of another country."

Her companion looked at her for a moment. "You mean it's a matter of course?"

"If I were English," said Bessie, "it would certainly seem to me a matter of course that everyone should be a good patriot."

"Oh, dear, yes, patriotism is everything," said Lord Lambeth, not quite following, but very contented. "Now, what are you going to do here?"

"On Thursday I am going to the Tower."

"The Tower?"

"The Tower of London. Did you never hear of it?"

"Oh, yes, I have been there," said Lord Lambeth. "I was taken there by my governess when I was six years old. It's a rum idea, your going there."

"Do give me a few more rum ideas," said Bessie. "I want to see everything of that sort. I am going to Hampton Court, and to Windsor, and to the Dulwich Gallery."

Lord Lambeth seemed greatly amused. "I wonder you don't go to the Rosherville Gardens."

"Are they interesting?" asked Bessie.

"Oh, wonderful."

"Are they very old? That's all I care for," said Bessie.

"They are tremendously old; they are all falling to ruins."

"I think there is nothing so charming as an old ruinous garden," said the young girl. "We must certainly go there."

Lord Lambeth broke out into merriment. "I say, Woodley," he cried, "here's Miss Alden wants to go to the Rosherville Gardens!"

Willie Woodley looked a little blank; he was caught in the fact of ignorance of an apparently conspicuous feature of London life. But in a moment he turned it off. "Very well," he said, "I'll write for a permit."

Lord Lambeth's exhilaration increased. "Gad, I believe you Americans would go anywhere!" he cried.

"We wish to go to Parliament," said Bessie. "That's one of the first things."

"Oh, it would bore you to death!" cried the young man.

"We wish to hear you speak."

"I never speak—except to young ladies," said Lord Lambeth, smiling.

Bessie Alden looked at him a while, smiling, too, in the shadow of her parasol. "You are very strange," she murmured. "I don't think I approve of you."

"Ah, now, don't be severe, Miss Alden," said Lord Lambeth, smiling still more. "Please don't be severe. I want you to like me—awfully."

"To like you awfully? You must not laugh at me, then, when I make mistakes. I consider it my right—as a freeborn American—to make as many mistakes as I choose."

"Upon my word, I didn't laugh at you," said Lord Lambeth.

"And not only that," Bessie went on; "but I hold that all my mistakes shall be set down to my credit. You must think the better of me for them."

"I can't think better of you than I do," the young man declared.

Bessie Alden looked at him a moment again. "You certainly speak very well to young ladies. But why don't you address the House?—isn't that what they call it?"

"Because I have nothing to say," said Lord Lambeth.

"Haven't you a great position?" asked Bessie Alden.

He looked a moment at the back of his glove. "I'll set that down," he said, "as one of your mistakes—to your credit." And as if he disliked talking about his position, he changed the subject. "I wish you would let me go with you to the Tower, and to Hampton Court, and to all those other places."

"We shall be most happy," said Bessie.

"And of course I shall be delighted to show you the House of Lords—some day that suits you. There are a lot of things I want to do for you. I want to make you have a good time. And I should like very much to present some of my friends to you, if it wouldn't bore you. Then it would be awfully kind of you to come down to Branches."

"We are much obliged to you, Lord Lambeth," said Bessie. "What is Branches?"

"It's a house in the country. I think you might like it."

Willie Woodley and Mrs. Westgate at this moment were sitting in silence, and the young man's ear caught these last words of Lord Lambeth's. "He's inviting Miss Bessie to one of his castles," he murmured to his companion.

Mrs. Westgate, foreseeing what she mentally called "complications," immediately got up; and the two ladies, taking leave of Lord Lambeth, returned, under Mr. Woodley's conduct, to Jones's Hotel.

Lord Lambeth came to see them on the morrow, bringing Percy Beaumont with him—the latter having instantly declared his intention of neglecting none of the usual offices of civility. This declaration, however, when his kinsman informed him of the advent of their American friends, had been preceded by another remark.

"Here they are, then, and you are in for it."

"What am I in for?" demanded Lord Lambeth.

"I will let your mother give it a name. With all respect to whom," added Percy Beaumont, "I must decline on this occasion to do any more police duty. Her Grace must look after you herself."

"I will give her a chance," said her Grace's son, a trifle grimly. "I shall make her go and see them."

"She won't do it, my boy."

"We'll see if she doesn't," said Lord Lambeth.

But if Percy Beaumont took a somber view of the arrival of the two ladies at Jones's Hotel, he was sufficiently a man of the world to offer them a smiling countenance. He fell into animated conversation—conversation, at least, that was animated on her side—with Mrs. Westgate, while his companion made himself agreeable to the younger lady. Mrs. Westgate began confessing and protesting, declaring and expounding.

"I must say London is a great deal brighter and prettier just now than it was when I was here last—in the month of November. There is evidently a great deal going on, and you seem to have a good many flowers. I have no doubt it is very charming for all you people, and that you amuse yourselves immensely. It is very good of you to let Bessie and me come and sit and look at you. I suppose you will think I am very satirical, but I must confess that that's the feeling I have in London."

"I am afraid I don't quite understand to what feeling you allude," said Percy Beaumont.

"The feeling that it's all very well for you English people. Everything is beautifully arranged for you."

"It seems to me it is very well for some Americans, sometimes," rejoined Beaumont.

"For some of them, yes—if they like to be patronized. But I must say I don't like to be patronized. I may be very eccentric, and undisciplined, and outrageous, but I confess I never was fond of patronage. I like to associate with people on the same terms as I do in my own country; that's a peculiar taste that I have. But here people seem to expect something else—Heaven knows what! I am afraid you will think I am very ungrateful, for I certainly have received a great deal of attention. The last time I was here, a lady sent me a message that I was at liberty to come and see her."

"Dear me! I hope you didn't go," observed Percy Beaumont.

"You are deliciously naive, I must say that for you!" Mrs. Westgate exclaimed. "It must be a great advantage to you here in London. I suppose that if I myself had a little more naivete, I should enjoy it more. I should be content to sit on a chair in the park, and see the people pass, and be told that this is the Duchess of Suffolk, and that is the Lord Chamberlain, and that I must be thankful for the privilege of beholding them. I daresay it is very wicked and critical of me to ask for anything else. But I was always critical, and I freely confess to the sin of being fastidious. I am told there is some remarkably superior second-rate society provided here for strangers. *Merci!*

I don't want any superior second-rate society. I want the society that I have been accustomed to."

"I hope you don't call Lambeth and me second rate," Beaumont interposed.

"Oh, I am accustomed to you," said Mrs. Westgate. "Do you know that you English sometimes make the most wonderful speeches? The first time I came to London I went out to dine—as I told you, I have received a great deal of attention. After dinner, in the drawing room, I had some conversation with an old lady; I assure you I had. I forget what we talked about, but she presently said, in allusion to something we were discussing, 'Oh, you know, the aristocracy do so-and-so; but in one's own class of life it is very different.' In one's own class of life! What is a poor unprotected American woman to do in a country where she is liable to have that sort of thing said to her?"

"You seem to get hold of some very queer old ladies; I compliment you on your acquaintance!" Percy Beaumont exclaimed. "If you are trying to bring me to admit that London is an odious place, you'll not succeed. I'm extremely fond of it, and I think it the jolliest place in the world."

"*Pour vous autres.* I never said the contrary," Mrs. Westgate retorted. I make use of this expression, because both interlocutors had begun to raise their voices. Percy Beaumont naturally did not like to hear his country abused, and Mrs. Westgate, no less naturally, did not like a stubborn debater.

"Hallo!" said Lord Lambeth; "what are they up to now?" And he came away from the window, where he had been standing with Bessie Alden.

"I quite agree with a very clever countrywoman of mine," Mrs. Westgate continued with charming ardor, though with imperfect relevancy. She smiled at the two gentlemen for a moment with terrible brightness, as if to toss at their feet—upon their native heath—the gauntlet of defiance. "For me, there are only two social positions worth speaking of—that of an American lady and that of the Emperor of Russia."

"And what do you do with the American gentlemen?" asked Lord Lambeth.

"She leaves them in America!" said Percy Beaumont.

On the departure of their visitors, Bessie Alden told her sister that Lord Lambeth would come the next day, to go with them to the Tower, and that he had kindly offered to bring his "trap" and drive them thither. Mrs. Westgate listened in silence to this communication, and for some time afterward she said nothing. But at last, "If you had not requested me the other day not to mention it," she began, "there is something I should venture to ask you." Bessie frowned a little; her dark blue eyes were more dark than blue. But her sister went on. "As it is, I will take the risk. You are not in love with Lord Lambeth: I believe it, perfectly. Very good. But is there, by chance, any danger of your becoming so? It's a very simple question; don't take offense. I have a particular reason," said Mrs. Westgate, "for wanting to know."

Bessie Alden for some moments said nothing; she only looked displeased. "No; there is no danger," she answered at last, curtly.

"Then I should like to frighten them," declared Mrs. Westgate, clasping her jeweled hands.

"To frighten whom?"

"All these people; Lord Lambeth's family and friends."

"How should you frighten them?" asked the young girl.

"It wouldn't be I—it would be you. It would frighten them to think that you should absorb his lordship's young affections."

Bessie Alden, with her clear eyes still overshadowed by her dark brows, continued to interrogate. "Why should that frighten them?"

Mrs. Westgate poised her answer with a smile before delivering it. "Because they think you are not good enough. You are a charming girl, beautiful and amiable, intelligent and clever, and as bien-elevee as it is possible to be; but you are not a fit match for Lord Lambeth."

Bessie Alden was decidedly disgusted. "Where do you get such extraordinary ideas?" she asked. "You have said some such strange things lately. My dear Kitty, where do you collect them?"

Kitty was evidently enamored of her idea. "Yes, it would put them on pins and needles, and it wouldn't hurt you. Mr. Beaumont is already most uneasy; I could soon see that."

The young girl meditated a moment. "Do you mean that they spy upon him—that they interfere with him?"

"I don't know what power they have to interfere, but I know that a British mama may worry her son's life out."

It has been intimated that, as regards certain disagreeable things, Bessie Alden had a fund of skepticism. She abstained on the present occasion from expressing disbelief, for she wished not to irritate her sister. But she said to herself that Kitty had been misinformed—that this was a traveler's tale. Though she was a girl of a lively imagination, there could in the nature of things be, to her sense, no reality in the idea of her belonging to a vulgar category. What she said aloud was, "I must say that in that case I am very sorry for Lord Lambeth."

Mrs. Westgate, more and more exhilarated by her scheme, was smiling at her again. "If I could only believe it was safe!" she exclaimed. "When you begin to pity him, I, on my side, am afraid."

"Afraid of what?"

"Of your pitying him too much."

Bessie Alden turned away impatiently; but at the end of a minute she turned back. "What if I should pity him too much?" she asked.

Mrs. Westgate hereupon turned away, but after a moment's reflection she also faced her sister again. "It would come, after all, to the same thing," she said.

Lord Lambeth came the next day with his trap, and the two ladies, attended by Willie Woodley, placed themselves under his guidance, and were conveyed eastward, through some of the duskier portions of the metropolis, to the great turreted donjon which overlooks the London shipping. They all descended from their vehicle and entered the famous inclosure; and they secured the services of a venerable beefeater, who, though there were many other claimants for legendary information, made a fine exclusive party of them and marched them through courts and corridors, through armories and prisons. He delivered his usual peripatetic discourse, and they stopped and stared, and peeped and stooped, according to the official admonitions. Bessie Alden asked the old man in the crimson doublet a great many questions; she thought it a most fascinating place. Lord Lambeth was in high good humor; he was constantly laughing; he enjoyed what he would have called the lark. Willie Woodley kept looking at the ceilings and tapping the walls with the knuckle of a pearl-gray glove; and Mrs. Westgate, asking at frequent intervals to be allowed to sit down and wait till they came back, was as frequently informed that they would never come back. To a great many of Bessie's questions—chiefly on collateral points of English history—the ancient warder was naturally unable to reply; whereupon she always appealed to Lord Lambeth. But his lordship was very ignorant. He declared that he knew nothing about that sort of thing, and he seemed greatly diverted at being treated as an authority.

"You can't expect everyone to know as much as you," he said.

"I should expect you to know a great deal more," declared Bessie Alden.

"Women always know more than men about names and dates and that sort of thing," Lord Lambeth rejoined. "There was Lady Jane Grey we have just been hearing about, who went in for Latin and Greek and all the learning of her age."

"*you* have no right to be ignorant, at all events," said Bessie.

"Why haven't I as good a right as anyone else?"

"Because you have lived in the midst of all these things."

"What things do you mean? Axes, and blocks, and thumbscrews?"

"All these historical things. You belong to a historical family."

"Bessie is really too historical," said Mrs. Westgate, catching a word of this dialogue.

"Yes, you are too historical," said Lord Lambeth, laughing, but thankful for a formula. "Upon my honor, you are too historical!"

He went with the ladies a couple of days later to Hampton Court, Willie Woodley being also of the party. The afternoon was charming, the famous horse chestnuts were in blossom, and Lord Lambeth, who quite entered into the spirit of the cockney excursionist, declared that it was a jolly old place. Bessie Alden was in ecstasies; she went about murmuring and exclaiming.

"It's too lovely," said the young girl; "it's too enchanting; it's too exactly what it ought to be!"

At Hampton Court the little flocks of visitors are not provided with an official bellwether, but are left to browse at discretion upon the local antiquities. It happened in this manner that, in default of another informant, Bessie Alden, who on doubtful questions was able to suggest a great many alternatives, found herself again applying for intellectual assistance to Lord Lambeth. But he again assured her that he was utterly helpless in such matters—that his education had been sadly neglected.

"And I am sorry it makes you unhappy," he added in a moment.

"You are very disappointing, Lord Lambeth," she said.

"Ah, now don't say that," he cried. "That's the worst thing you could possibly say."

"No," she rejoined, "it is not so bad as to say that I had expected nothing of you."

"I don't know. Give me a notion of the sort of thing you expected."

"Well," said Bessie Alden, "that you would be more what I should like to be—what I should try to be—in your place."

"Ah, my place!" exclaimed Lord Lambeth. "You are always talking about my place!"

The young girl looked at him; he thought she colored a little; and for a moment she made no rejoinder.

"Does it strike you that I am always talking about your place?" she asked.

"I am sure you do it a great honor," he said, fearing he had been uncivil.

"I have often thought about it," she went on after a moment. "I have often thought about your being a hereditary legislator. A hereditary legislator ought to know a great many things."

"Not if he doesn't legislate."

"But you do legislate; it's absurd your saying you don't. You are very much looked up to here—I am assured of that."

"I don't know that I ever noticed it."

"It is because you are used to it, then. You ought to fill the place."

"How do you mean to fill it?" asked Lord Lambeth.

"You ought to be very clever and brilliant, and to know almost everything."

Lord Lambeth looked at her a moment. "Shall I tell you something?" he asked. "A young man in my position, as you call it—"

"I didn't invent the term," interposed Bessie Alden. "I have seen it in a great many books."

"Hang it! you are always at your books. A fellow in my position, then, does very well whatever he does. That's about what I mean to say."

"Well, if your own people are content with you," said Bessie Alden, laughing, "it is not for me to complain. But I shall always think that, properly, you should have been a great mind—a great character."

"Ah, that's very theoretic," Lord Lambeth declared. "Depend upon it, that's a Yankee prejudice."

"Happy the country," said Bessie Alden, "where even people's prejudices are so elevated!"

"Well, after all," observed Lord Lambeth, "I don't know that I am such a fool as you are trying to make me out."

"I said nothing so rude as that; but I must repeat that you are disappointing."

"My dear Miss Alden," exclaimed the young man, "I am the best fellow in the world!"

"Ah, if it were not for that!" said Bessie Alden with a smile.

Mrs. Westgate had a good many more friends in London than she pretended, and before long she had renewed acquaintance with most of them. Their hospitality was extreme, so that, one thing leading to another, she began, as the phrase is, to go out. Bessie Alden, in this way, saw something of what she found it a great satisfaction to call to herself English society. She went to balls and danced, she went to dinners and talked, she went to concerts and listened (at concerts Bessie always listened), she went to exhibitions and wondered. Her enjoyment was keen and her curiosity insatiable, and, grateful in general for all her opportunities, she especially prized the privilege of meeting certain celebrated persons—authors and artists, philosophers and statesmen—of whose renown she had been a humble and distant beholder, and who now, as a part of the habitual furniture of London drawing rooms, struck her as stars fallen from the firmament and become palpable—revealing also sometimes, on contact, qualities not to have been predicted of sidereal bodies. Bessie, who knew so many of her contemporaries by reputation, had a good many personal disappointments; but, on the other hand, she had innumerable satisfactions and enthusiasms, and she communicated the emotions of either class to a dear friend, of her own sex, in Boston, with whom she was in voluminous correspondence. Some of her reflections, indeed, she attempted to impart to Lord Lambeth, who came almost every day to Jones's Hotel, and whom Mrs. Westgate admitted to be really devoted. Captain Littledale, it appeared, had gone to India; and of several others of Mrs. Westgate's ex-pensioners—gentlemen who, as she said, had made, in New York, a clubhouse of her drawing room—no tidings were to be obtained; but Lord Lambeth was certainly attentive enough to make up for the accidental absences, the short memories, all the other irregularities of everyone else. He drove them in the park, he took them to visit private collections of pictures, and, having a house of his own, invited them to dinner. Mrs. Westgate, following the fashion of many of her compatriots, caused herself and her sister to be presented at the English court by her diplomatic representative—for it was in this manner that she alluded to the American minister to England, inquiring what on earth he was put there for, if not to make the proper arrangements for one's going to a Drawing Room.

Lord Lambeth declared that he hated Drawing Rooms, but he participated in the ceremony on the day on which the two ladies at Jones's Hotel repaired to Buckingham Palace in a remarkable coach which his lordship had sent to fetch them. He had on a gorgeous uniform, and Bessie Alden was particularly struck with his appearance—especially when on her asking him, rather foolishly as she felt, if he were a loyal subject, he replied that he was a loyal subject to *her*. This declaration was emphasized by his dancing with her at a royal ball to which the two ladies afterward went, and was not impaired by the fact that she thought he danced very ill. He seemed to her wonderfully kind; she asked herself, with growing vivacity, why he should be so kind. It was his disposition—that seemed the natural answer. She had told her sister that she liked him very much, and now that she liked him more she wondered why. She liked him for his disposition; to this question as well that seemed the natural answer. When once the impressions of London life began to crowd thickly upon her, she completely forgot her sister's warning about the cynicism of public opinion. It had given her great pain at the moment, but there was no particular reason why she should remember it; it corresponded too little with any sensible reality; and it was disagreeable to Bessie to remember disagreeable things. So she was not haunted with the sense of a vulgar imputation. She was not in love with Lord Lambeth— she assured herself of that. It will immediately be observed that when such assurances become necessary the state of a young lady's affections is already ambiguous; and, indeed, Bessie Alden made no attempt to dissimulate—to herself, of course—a certain tenderness that she felt for the young nobleman. She said to herself that she liked the type to which he belonged—the simple, candid, manly, healthy English temperament. She spoke to herself of him as women speak of young men they like—alluded to his bravery (which she had never in the least seen tested), to his honesty and gentlemanliness, and was not silent upon the subject of his good looks. She was perfectly conscious, moreover, that she liked to think of his more adventitious merits; that her imagination was excited and gratified by the sight of a handsome young man endowed with such large opportunities—opportunities she hardly knew for what, but, as she supposed, for doing great things—for setting an example, for exerting an influence, for conferring happiness, for encouraging the arts. She had a kind of ideal of conduct for a young man who should find himself in this magnificent position, and she tried to adapt it to Lord Lambeth's deportment as you might attempt to fit a silhouette in cut paper upon a shadow projected upon a wall. But Bessie Alden's silhouette refused to coincide with his lordship's image, and this want of harmony sometimes vexed her more than she thought reasonable. When he was absent it was, of course, less striking; then he seemed to her a sufficiently graceful combination of high responsibilities and amiable qualities. But when he sat there within sight, laughing and talking with his customary good humor and simplicity, she measured it more accurately, and she felt acutely that if Lord Lambeth's position was heroic, there was but little of the hero in the young man himself. Then her imagination wandered away from him—very far away; for it was an incontestable fact that at such moments he seemed distinctly dull. I am afraid that while Bessie's imagination was thus invidiously roaming, she cannot have been herself a very lively companion; but it may well have been that these occasional fits of indifference seemed to Lord Lambeth a part of the young girl's personal charm. It had been a part of this charm from the first that he felt that she judged him and measured him more freely and irresponsibly— more at her ease and her leisure, as it were—than several young ladies with whom he had been on the whole about as intimate. To feel this, and yet to feel that she also liked him, was very agreeable to Lord Lambeth. He fancied he had compassed that gratification so desirable to young men of title and fortune—being liked for himself. It is true that a cynical counselor might have whispered to him, "Liked for yourself? Yes; but not so very much!" He had, at any rate, the constant hope of being liked more.

It may seem, perhaps, a trifle singular—but it is nevertheless true—that Bessie Alden, when he struck her as dull, devoted some time, on grounds of conscience, to trying to like him more. I say on grounds of conscience because she felt that he had been extremely "nice" to her sister, and because she reflected that it was no more than fair that she should think as well of him as he thought of her. This effort was possibly sometimes not so successful as it might have been, for the result of it was occasionally a vague irritation, which expressed itself in hostile criticism of several British institutions. Bessie Alden went to some entertainments at which she met Lord Lambeth; but she went to others at which his lordship was neither actually nor potentially present; and it was chiefly on these latter occasions that she encountered those literary and artistic celebrities of whom mention has been made. After a while she reduced the matter to a principle. If Lord Lambeth should appear anywhere, it was a symbol that there would be no poets and philosophers; and in consequence—for it was almost a strict consequence—she used to enumerate to the young man these objects of her admiration.

"You seem to be awfully fond of those sort of people," said Lord Lambeth one day, as if the idea had just occurred to him.

"They are the people in England I am most curious to see," Bessie Alden replied.

"I suppose that's because you have read so much," said Lord Lambeth gallantly.

"I have not read so much. It is because we think so much of them at home."

"Oh, I see," observed the young nobleman. "In Boston."

"Not only in Boston; everywhere," said Bessie. "We hold them in great honor; they go to the best dinner parties."

"I daresay you are right. I can't say I know many of them."

"It's a pity you don't," Bessie Alden declared. "It would do you good."

"I daresay it would," said Lord Lambeth very humbly. "But I must say I don't like the looks of some of them."

"Neither do I—of some of them. But there are all kinds, and many of them are charming."

"I have talked with two or three of them," the young man went on, "and I thought they had a kind of fawning manner."

"Why should they fawn?" Bessie Alden demanded.

"I'm sure I don't know. Why, indeed?"

"Perhaps you only thought so," said Bessie.

"Well, of course," rejoined her companion, "that's a kind of thing that can't be proved."

"In America they don't fawn," said Bessie.

"Ah, well, then, they must be better company."

Bessie was silent a moment. "That is one of the things I don't like about England," she said; "your keeping the distinguished people apart."

"How do you mean apart?"

"Why, letting them come only to certain places. You never see them."

Lord Lambeth looked at her a moment. "What people do you mean?"

"The eminent people—the authors and artists—the clever people."

"Oh, there are other eminent people besides those," said Lord Lambeth.

"Well, you certainly keep them apart," repeated the young girl.

"And there are other clever people," added Lord Lambeth simply.

Bessie Alden looked at him, and she gave a light laugh. "Not many," she said.

On another occasion—just after a dinner party—she told him that there was something else in England she did not like.

"Oh, I say!" he cried, "haven't you abused us enough?"

"I have never abused you at all," said Bessie; "but I don't like your *precedence.*"

"It isn't my precedence!" Lord Lambeth declared, laughing.

"Yes, it is yours—just exactly yours; and I think it's odious," said Bessie.

"I never saw such a young lady for discussing things! Has someone had the impudence to go before you?" asked his lordship.

"It is not the going before me that I object to," said Bessie; "it is their thinking that they have a right to do it—*a right that I recognize.*"

"I never saw such a young lady as you are for not 'recognizing.' I have no doubt the thing is *beastly,* but it saves a lot of trouble."

"It makes a lot of trouble. It's horrid," said Bessie.

"But how would you have the first people go?" asked Lord Lambeth. "They can't go last."

"Whom do you mean by the first people?"

"Ah, if you mean to question first principles!" said Lord Lambeth.

"If those are your first principles, no wonder some of your arrangements are horrid," observed Bessie Alden with a very pretty ferocity. "I am a young girl, so of course I go last; but imagine what Kitty must feel on being informed that she is not at liberty to budge until certain other ladies have passed out."

"Oh, I say, she is not 'informed!'" cried Lord Lambeth. "No one would do such a thing as that."

"She is made to feel it," the young girl insisted—"as if they were afraid she would make a rush for the door. No; you have a lovely country," said Bessie Alden, "but your precedence is horrid."

"I certainly shouldn't think your sister would like it," rejoined Lord Lambeth with even exaggerated gravity. But Bessie Alden could induce him to enter no formal protest against this repulsive custom, which he seemed to think an extreme convenience.

Percy Beaumont all this time had been a very much less frequent visitor at Jones's Hotel than his noble kinsman; he had, in fact, called but twice upon the two American ladies. Lord Lambeth, who often saw him, reproached him with his neglect and declared that, although Mrs. Westgate had said nothing about it, he was sure that she was secretly wounded by it. "She suffers too much to speak," said Lord Lambeth.

"That's all gammon," said Percy Beaumont; "there's a limit to what people can suffer!" And, though sending no apologies to Jones's Hotel, he undertook in a manner to explain his absence. "You are always there," he said, "and that's reason enough for my not going."

"I don't see why. There is enough for both of us."

"I don't care to be a witness of your—your reckless passion," said Percy Beaumont.

Lord Lambeth looked at him with a cold eye and for a moment said nothing. "It's not so obvious as you might suppose," he rejoined dryly, "considering what a demonstrative beggar I am."

"I don't want to know anything about it—nothing whatever," said Beaumont. "Your mother asks me everytime she sees me whether I believe you are really lost—and Lady Pimlico does the same. I prefer to be able to answer that I know nothing about it—that I never go there. I stay away for consistency's sake. As I said the other day, they must look after you themselves."

"You are devilish considerate," said Lord Lambeth. "They never question me."

"They are afraid of you. They are afraid of irritating you and making you worse. So they go to work very cautiously, and, somewhere or other, they get their information. They know a great deal about you. They know that you have been with those ladies to the dome of St. Paul's and—where was the other place?—to the Thames Tunnel."

"If all their knowledge is as accurate as that, it must be very valuable," said Lord Lambeth.

"Well, at any rate, they know that you have been visiting the 'sights of the metropolis.' They think—very naturally, as it seems to me—that when you take to visiting the sights of the metropolis with a little American girl, there is serious cause for alarm." Lord Lambeth responded to this intimation by scornful laughter, and his companion continued, after a pause: "I said just now I didn't want to know anything about the affair; but I will confess that I am curious to learn whether you propose to marry Miss Bessie Alden."

On this point Lord Lambeth gave his interlocutor no immediate satisfaction; he was musing, with a frown. "By Jove," he said, "they go rather too far. They *shall* find me dangerous—I promise them."

Percy Beaumont began to laugh. "You don't redeem your promises. You said the other day you would make your mother call."

Lord Lambeth continued to meditate. "I asked her to call," he said simply.

"And she declined?"

"Yes; but she shall do it yet."

"Upon my word," said Percy Beaumont, "if she gets much more frightened I believe she will." Lord Lambeth looked at him, and he went on. "She will go to the girl herself."

"How do you mean she will go to her?"

"She will beg her off, or she will bribe her. She will take strong measures."

Lord Lambeth turned away in silence, and his companion watched him take twenty steps and then slowly return. "I have invited Mrs. Westgate and Miss Alden to Branches," he said, "and this evening I shall name a day."

"And shall you invite your mother and your sisters to meet them?"

"Explicitly!"

"That will set the duchess off," said Percy Beaumont. "I suspect she will come."

"She may do as she pleases."

Beaumont looked at Lord Lambeth. "You do really propose to marry the little sister, then?"

"I like the way you talk about it!" cried the young man. "She won't gobble me down; don't be afraid."

"She won't leave you on your knees," said Percy Beaumont. "What IS the inducement?"

"You talk about proposing: wait till I *have* proposed," Lord Lambeth went on.

"That's right, my dear fellow; think about it," said Percy Beaumont.

"She's a charming girl," pursued his lordship.

"Of course she's a charming girl. I don't know a girl more charming, intrinsically. But there are other charming girls nearer home."

"I like her spirit," observed Lord Lambeth, almost as if he were trying to torment his cousin.

"What's the peculiarity of her spirit?"

"She's not afraid, and she says things out, and she thinks herself as good as anyone. She is the only girl I have ever seen that was not dying to marry me."

"How do you know that, if you haven't asked her?"

"I don't know how; but I know it."

"I am sure she asked me questions enough about your property and your titles," said Beaumont.

"She has asked me questions, too; no end of them," Lord Lambeth admitted. "But she asked for information, don't you know."

"Information? Aye, I'll warrant she wanted it. Depend upon it that she is dying to marry you just as much and just as little as all the rest of them."

"I shouldn't like her to refuse me—I shouldn't like that."

"If the thing would be so disagreeable, then, both to you and to her, in Heaven's name leave it alone," said Percy Beaumont.

Mrs. Westgate, on her side, had plenty to say to her sister about the rarity of Mr. Beaumont's visits and the nonappearance of the Duchess of Bayswater. She professed, however, to derive more satisfaction from this latter circumstance than she could have done from the most lavish attentions on the part of this great lady. "It is most marked," she said—"most marked. It is a delicious proof that we have made them miserable. The day we dined with Lord Lambeth I was really sorry for the poor fellow." It will have been gathered that the entertainment offered by Lord Lambeth to his American friends had not been graced by the presence of his anxious mother. He had invited several choice spirits to meet them; but the ladies of his immediate family were to Mrs. Westgate's sense—a sense possibly morbidly acute—conspicuous by their absence.

"I don't want to express myself in a manner that you dislike," said Bessie Alden; "but I don't know why you should have so many theories about Lord Lambeth's poor mother. You know a great many young men in New York without knowing their mothers."

Mrs. Westgate looked at her sister and then turned away. "My dear Bessie, you are superb!" she said.

"One thing is certain," the young girl continued. "If I believed I were a cause of annoyance—however unwitting—to Lord Lambeth's family, I should insist—"

"Insist upon my leaving England," said Mrs. Westgate.

"No, not that. I want to go to the National Gallery again; I want to see Stratford-on-Avon and Canterbury Cathedral. But I should insist upon his coming to see us no more."

"That would be very modest and very pretty of you; but you wouldn't do it now."

"Why do you say 'now'?" asked Bessie Alden. "Have I ceased to be modest?"

"You care for him too much. A month ago, when you said you didn't, I believe it was quite true. But at present, my dear child," said Mrs. Westgate, "you wouldn't find it quite so simple a matter never to see Lord Lambeth again. I have seen it coming on."

"You are mistaken," said Bessie. "You don't understand."

"My dear child, don't be perverse," rejoined her sister.

"I know him better, certainly, if you mean that," said Bessie. "And I like him very much. But I don't like him enough to make trouble for him with his family. However, I don't believe in that."

"I like the way you say 'however,'" Mrs. Westgate exclaimed. "Come; you would not marry him?"

"Oh, no," said the young girl.

Mrs. Westgate for a moment seemed vexed. "Why not, pray?" she demanded.

"Because I don't care to," said Bessie Alden.

The morning after Lord Lambeth had had, with Percy Beaumont, that exchange of ideas which has just been narrated, the ladies at Jones's Hotel received from his lordship a written invitation to pay their projected visit to Branches Castle on the following Tuesday. "I think I have made up a very pleasant party," the young nobleman said. "Several people whom you know, and my mother and sisters, who have so long been regrettably prevented from making your acquaintance." Bessie Alden lost no time in calling her sister's attention to the injustice she had done the Duchess of Bayswater, whose hostility was now proved to be a vain illusion.

"Wait till you see if she comes," said Mrs. Westgate. "And if she is to meet us at her son's house the obligation was all the greater for her to call upon us."

Bessie had not to wait long, and it appeared that Lord Lambeth's mother now accepted Mrs. Westgate's view of her duties. On the morrow, early in the afternoon, two cards were brought to the apartment of the American ladies—one of them bearing the name of the Duchess of Bayswater and the other that of the Countess of Pimlico. Mrs. Westgate glanced at the clock. "It is not yet four," she said; "they have come early; they wish to see us. We will receive them." And she gave orders that her visitors should be admitted. A few moments later they were introduced, and there was a solemn exchange of amenities. The duchess was a large lady, with a fine fresh color; the Countess of Pimlico was very pretty and elegant.

The duchess looked about her as she sat down—looked not especially at Mrs. Westgate. "I daresay my son has told you that I have been wanting to come and see you," she observed.

"You are very kind," said Mrs. Westgate, vaguely—her conscience not allowing her to assent to this proposition—and, indeed, not permitting her to enunciate her own with any appreciable emphasis.

"He says you were so kind to him in America," said the duchess.

"We are very glad," Mrs. Westgate replied, "to have been able to make him a little more—a little less—a little more comfortable."

"I think he stayed at your house," remarked the Duchess of Bayswater, looking at Bessie Alden.

"A very short time," said Mrs. Westgate.

"Oh!" said the duchess; and she continued to look at Bessie, who was engaged in conversation with her daughter.

"Do you like London?" Lady Pimlico had asked of Bessie, after looking at her a good deal—at her face and her hands, her dress and her hair.

"Very much indeed," said Bessie.

"Do you like this hotel?"

"It is very comfortable," said Bessie.

"Do you like stopping at hotels?" inquired Lady Pimlico after a pause.

"I am very fond of traveling," Bessie answered, "and I suppose hotels are a necessary part of it. But they are not the part I am fondest of."

"Oh, I hate traveling," said the Countess of Pimlico and transferred her attention to Mrs. Westgate.

"My son tells me you are going to Branches," the duchess presently resumed.

"Lord Lambeth has been so good as to ask us," said Mrs. Westgate, who perceived that her visitor had now begun to look at her, and who had her customary happy consciousness of a distinguished appearance. The only mitigation of her felicity on this point was that, having inspected her visitor's own costume, she said to herself, "She won't know how well I am dressed!"

"He has asked me to go, but I am not sure I shall be able," murmured the duchess.

"He had offered us the p—prospect of meeting you," said Mrs. Westgate.

"I hate the country at this season," responded the duchess.

Mrs. Westgate gave a little shrug. "I think it is pleasanter than London."

But the duchess's eyes were absent again; she was looking very fixedly at Bessie. In a moment she slowly rose, walked to a chair that stood empty at the young girl's right hand, and silently seated herself. As she was a majestic, voluminous woman, this little transaction had, inevitably, an air of somewhat impressive intention. It diffused a certain awkwardness, which Lady Pimlico, as a sympathetic daughter, perhaps desired to rectify in turning to Mrs. Westgate.

"I daresay you go out a great deal," she observed.

"No, very little. We are strangers, and we didn't come here for society."

"I see," said Lady Pimlico. "It's rather nice in town just now."

"It's charming," said Mrs. Westgate. "But we only go to see a few people—whom we like."

"Of course one can't like everyone," said Lady Pimlico.

"It depends upon one's society," Mrs. Westgate rejoined.

The Duchess meanwhile had addressed herself to Bessie. "My son tells me the young ladies in America are so clever."

"I am glad they made so good an impression on him," said Bessie, smiling.

The Duchess was not smiling; her large fresh face was very tranquil. "He is very susceptible," she said. "He thinks everyone clever, and sometimes they are."

"Sometimes," Bessie assented, smiling still.

The duchess looked at her a little and then went on; "Lambeth is very susceptible, but he is very volatile, too."

"Volatile?" asked Bessie.

"He is very inconstant. It won't do to depend on him."

"Ah," said Bessie, "I don't recognize that description. We have depended on him greatly—my sister and I—and he has never disappointed us."

"He will disappoint you yet," said the duchess.

Bessie gave a little laugh, as if she were amused at the duchess's persistency. "I suppose it will depend on what we expect of him."

"The less you expect, the better," Lord Lambeth's mother declared.

"Well," said Bessie, "we expect nothing unreasonable."

The duchess for a moment was silent, though she appeared to have more to say. "Lambeth says he has seen so much of you," she presently began.

"He has been to see us very often; he has been very kind," said Bessie Alden.

"I daresay you are used to that. I am told there is a great deal of that in America."

"A great deal of kindness?" the young girl inquired, smiling.

"Is that what you call it? I know you have different expressions."

"We certainly don't always understand each other," said Mrs. Westgate, the termination of whose interview with Lady Pimlico allowed her to give her attention to their elder visitor.

"I am speaking of the young men calling so much upon the young ladies," the duchess explained.

"But surely in England," said Mrs. Westgate, "the young ladies don't call upon the young men?"

"Some of them do—almost!" Lady Pimlico declared. "What the young men are a great *parti*."

"Bessie, you must make a note of that," said Mrs. Westgate. "My sister," she added, "is a model traveler. She writes down all the curious facts she hears in a little book she keeps for the purpose."

The duchess was a little flushed; she looked all about the room, while her daughter turned to Bessie. "My brother told us you were wonderfully clever," said Lady Pimlico.

"He should have said my sister," Bessie answered—"when she says such things as that."

"Shall you be long at Branches?" the duchess asked, abruptly, of the young girl.

"Lord Lambeth has asked us for three days," said Bessie.

"I shall go," the duchess declared, "and my daughter, too."

"That will be charming!" Bessie rejoined.

"Delightful!" murmured Mrs. Westgate.

"I shall expect to see a great deal of you," the duchess continued. "When I go to Branches I monopolize my son's guests."

"They must be most happy," said Mrs. Westgate very graciously.

"I want immensely to see it—to see the castle," said Bessie to the duchess. "I have never seen one—in England, at least; and you know we have none in America."

"Ah, you are fond of castles?" inquired her Grace.

"Immensely!" replied the young girl. "It has been the dream of my life to live in one."

The duchess looked at her a moment, as if she hardly knew how to take this assurance, which, from her Grace's point of view, was either very artless or very audacious. "Well," she said, rising, "I will show you Branches myself." And upon this the two great ladies took their departure.

"What did they mean by it?" asked Mrs. Westgate, when they were gone.

"They meant to be polite," said Bessie, "because we are going to meet them."

"It is too late to be polite," Mrs. Westgate replied almost grimly. "They meant to overawe us by their fine manners and their grandeur, and to make you *lacher prise*."

"*Lacher prise*? What strange things you say!" murmured Bessie Alden.

"They meant to snub us, so that we shouldn't dare to go to Branches," Mrs. Westgate continued.

"On the contrary," said Bessie, "the duchess offered to show me the place herself."

"Yes, you may depend upon it she won't let you out of her sight. She will show you the place from morning till night."

"You have a theory for everything," said Bessie.

"And you apparently have none for anything."

"I saw no attempt to 'overawe' us," said the young girl. "Their manners were not fine."

"They were not even good!" Mrs. Westgate declared.

Bessie was silent a while, but in a few moments she observed that she had a very good theory. "They came to look at me," she said, as if this had been a very ingenious hypothesis. Mrs. Westgate did it justice; she greeted it with a smile and pronounced it most brilliant, while, in reality, she felt that the young girl's skepticism, or her charity, or, as she had sometimes called it appropriately, her idealism, was proof against irony. Bessie, however, remained meditative all the rest of that day and well on into the morrow.

On the morrow, before lunch, Mrs. Westgate had occasion to go out for an hour, and left her sister writing a letter. When she came back she met Lord Lambeth at the door of the hotel, coming away. She thought he looked slightly embarrassed; he was certainly very grave. "I am sorry to have missed you. Won't you come back?" she asked.

"No," said the young man, "I can't. I have seen your sister. I can never come back." Then he looked at her a moment and took her hand. "Goodbye, Mrs. Westgate," he said. "You have been very kind to me." And with what she thought a strange, sad look in his handsome young face, he turned away.

She went in, and she found Bessie still writing her letter; that is, Mrs. Westgate perceived she was sitting at the table with the pen in her hand and not writing. "Lord Lambeth has been here," said the elder lady at last.

Then Bessie got up and showed her a pale, serious face. She bent this face upon her sister for some time, confessing silently and a little pleading. "I told him," she said at last, "that we could not go to Branches."

Mrs. Westgate displayed just a spark of irritation. "He might have waited," she said with a smile, "till one had seen the castle." Later, an hour afterward, she said, "Dear Bessie, I wish you might have accepted him."

"I couldn't," said Bessie gently.

"He is an excellent fellow," said Mrs. Westgate.

"I couldn't," Bessie repeated.

"If it is only," her sister added, "because those women will think that they succeeded—that they paralyzed us!"

Bessie Alden turned away; but presently she added, "They were interesting; I should have liked to see them again."

"So should I!" cried Mrs. Westgate significantly.

"And I should have liked to see the castle," said Bessie. "But now we must leave England," she added.

Her sister looked at her. "You will not wait to go to the National Gallery?"

"Not now."

"Nor to Canterbury Cathedral?"

Bessie reflected a moment. "We can stop there on our way to Paris," she said.

Lord Lambeth did not tell Percy Beaumont that the contingency he was not prepared at all to like had occurred; but Percy Beaumont, on hearing that the two ladies had left London, wondered with some intensity what had happened; wondered, that is, until the Duchess of Bayswater came a little to his assistance. The two ladies went to Paris, and Mrs. Westgate beguiled the journey to that city by repeating several times—"That's what I regret; they will think they petrified us." But Bessie Alden seemed to regret nothing.

About Author

Henry James OM (15 April 1843 – 28 February 1916) was an American-British author regarded as a key transitional figure between literary realism and literary modernism, and is considered by many to be among the greatest novelists in the English language. He was the son of Henry James Sr. and the brother of renowned philosopher and psychologist William James and diarist Alice James.

He is best known for a number of novels dealing with the social and marital interplay between émigré Americans, English people, and continental Europeans. Examples of such novels include The Portrait of a Lady, The Ambassadors, and The Wings of the Dove. His later works were increasingly experimental. In describing the internal states of mind and social dynamics of his characters, James often made use of a style in which ambiguous or contradictory motives and impressions were overlaid or juxtaposed in the discussion of a character's psyche. For their unique ambiguity, as well as for other aspects of their composition, his late works have been compared to impressionist painting.

His novella The Turn of the Screw has garnered a reputation as the most analysed and ambiguous ghost story in the English language and remains his most widely adapted work in other media. He also wrote a number of other highly regarded ghost stories and is considered one of the greatest masters of the field.

James published articles and books of criticism, travel, biography, autobiography, and plays. Born in the United States, James largely relocated to Europe as a young man and eventually settled in England, becoming a British subject in 1915, one year before his death. James was nominated for the Nobel Prize in Literature in 1911, 1912 and 1916.

Life

Early years, 1843–1883

James was born at 2 Washington Place in New York City on 15 April 1843. His parents were Mary Walsh and Henry James Sr. His father was intelligent and steadfastly congenial. He was a lecturer and philosopher who had inherited independent means from his father, an Albany banker and investor. Mary came from a wealthy family long settled in New York City. Her sister Katherine lived with her adult family for an extended period of time. Henry Jr. had three brothers, William, who was one year his senior, and younger brothers Wilkinson (Wilkie) and Robertson. His younger sister was Alice. Both of his parents were of Irish and Scottish descent.

The family first lived in Albany, at 70 N. Pearl St., and then moved to Fourteenth Street in New York City when James was still a young boy. His education was calculated by his father to expose him to many influences, primarily scientific and philosophical; it was described by Percy Lubbock, the editor of his selected letters, as "extraordinarily haphazard and promiscuous." James did not share the usual education in Latin and Greek classics. Between 1855 and 1860, the James' household traveled to London, Paris, Geneva, Boulogne-sur-Mer and Newport, Rhode Island, according to the father's current interests and publishing ventures, retreating to the United States when funds were low. Henry studied primarily with tutors and briefly attended schools while the family traveled in Europe. Their longest stays were in France, where Henry began to feel at home and became fluent in French. He was afflicted with a stutter, which seems to have manifested itself only when he spoke English; in French, he did not stutter.

In 1860 the family returned to Newport. There Henry became a friend of the painter John La Farge, who introduced him to French literature, and in particular, to Balzac. James later called Balzac his "greatest master," and said that he had learned more about the craft of fiction from him than from anyone else.

In the autumn of 1861 Henry received an injury, probably to his back, while fighting a fire. This injury, which resurfaced at times throughout his life, made him unfit for military service in the American Civil War.

In 1864 the James family moved to Boston, Massachusetts to be near William, who had enrolled first in the Lawrence Scientific School at Harvard and then in the medical school. In 1862 Henry attended Harvard Law School, but realised that he was not interested in studying law. He pursued his interest in literature and associated with authors and critics William Dean Howells and Charles Eliot Norton in Boston and Cambridge, formed lifelong friendships with Oliver Wendell Holmes Jr., the future Supreme Court Justice, and with James and Annie Fields, his first professional mentors.

His first published work was a review of a stage performance, "Miss Maggie Mitchell in Fanchon the Cricket," published in 1863. About a year later, A Tragedy of Error, his first short story, was published anonymously. James's first payment was for an appreciation of Sir Walter Scott's novels, written for the North American Review. He wrote fiction and non-fiction pieces for The Nation and Atlantic Monthly, where Fields was editor. In 1871 he published his first novel, Watch and Ward, in serial form in the Atlantic Monthly. The novel was later published in book form in 1878.

During a 14-month trip through Europe in 1869–70 he met Ruskin, Dickens, Matthew Arnold, William Morris, and George Eliot. Rome impressed him profoundly. "Here I am then in the Eternal City," he wrote to his brother William. "At last—for the first time—I live!" He attempted to support himself as a freelance writer in Rome, then secured a position as Paris correspondent for the New York Tribune, through the influence of its editor John Hay. When these efforts failed he returned to New York City. During 1874 and 1875 he published Transatlantic Sketches, A Passionate Pilgrim, and Roderick Hudson. During this early period in his career he was influenced by Nathaniel Hawthorne.

In 1869 he settled in London. There he established relationships with Macmillan and other publishers, who paid for serial installments that they would later publish in book form. The audience for these serialized novels was largely made up of middle-class women, and James struggled to fashion serious literary work within the strictures imposed by editors' and publishers' notions of what was suitable for young women to read. He lived in rented rooms but was able to join gentlemen's clubs that had libraries and where he could entertain male friends. He was introduced to English society by Henry Adams and Charles Milnes Gaskell, the latter introducing him to the Travellers' and the Reform Clubs.

In the fall of 1875 he moved to the Latin Quarter of Paris. Aside from two trips to America, he spent the next three decades—the rest of his life—in Europe. In Paris he met Zola, Alphonse Daudet, Maupassant, Turgenev, and others. He stayed in Paris only a year before moving to London.

In England he met the leading figures of politics and culture. He continued to be a prolific writer, producing The American (1877), The Europeans (1878), a revision of Watch and Ward (1878), French Poets and Novelists (1878), Hawthorne (1879), and several shorter works of fiction. In 1878 Daisy Miller established his fame on both sides of the Atlantic. It drew notice perhaps mostly because it depicted a woman whose behavior is outside the social norms of Europe. He also began his first masterpiece, The Portrait of a Lady, which would appear in 1881.

In 1877 he first visited Wenlock Abbey in Shropshire, home of his friend Charles Milnes Gaskell whom he had met through Henry Adams. He was much inspired by the darkly romantic Abbey and the surrounding countryside, which features in his essay Abbeys and Castles. In particular the gloomy monastic fishponds behind the Abbey are said to have inspired the lake in The Turn of the Screw.

While living in London, James continued to follow the careers of the "French realists", Émile Zola in particular. Their stylistic methods influenced his own work in the years to come. Hawthorne's influence on him faded during this period, replaced by George Eliot and Ivan Turgenev. 1879–1882 saw the publication of The Europeans, Washington Square, Confidence, and The Portrait of a Lady. He visited America in 1882–1883, then returned to London.

The period from 1881 to 1883 was marked by several losses. His mother died in 1881, followed by his father a few months later, and then by his brother Wilkie. Emerson, an old family friend, died in 1882. His friend Turgenev died in 1883.

Middle years, 1884–1897

In 1884 James made another visit to Paris. There he met again with Zola, Daudet, and Goncourt. He had been following the careers of the French "realist" or "naturalist" writers, and was increasingly influenced by them. In 1886, he published The Bostonians and The Princess Casamassima, both influenced by the French writers he'd studied assiduously. Critical reaction and sales were poor. He wrote to Howells that the books had hurt his career rather than helped because they had "reduced the desire, and demand, for my productions to zero". During this time he became friends with Robert Louis Stevenson, John Singer Sargent, Edmund Gosse, George du Maurier, Paul Bourget, and Constance Fenimore Woolson. His third novel from the 1880s was The Tragic Muse. Although he was following the precepts of Zola in his novels of the '80s, their tone and attitude are closer to the fiction of Alphonse Daudet. The lack of critical and financial success for his novels during this period led him to try writing for the theatre. (His dramatic works and his experiences with theatre are discussed below.)

In the last quarter of 1889, he started translating "for pure and copious lucre" Port Tarascon, the third volume of Alphonse Daudet adventures of Tartarin de Tarascon. Serialized in Harper's Monthly Magazine from June 1890, this translation praised as "clever" by The Spectator was published in January 1891 by Sampson Low, Marston, Searle & Rivington.

After the stage failure of Guy Domville in 1895, James was near despair and thoughts of death plagued him. The years spent on dramatic works were not entirely a loss. As he moved into the last phase of his career he found ways to adapt dramatic techniques into the novel form.

In the late 1880s and throughout the 1890s James made several trips through Europe. He spent a long stay in Italy in 1887. In that year the short novel The Aspern Papers and The Reverberator were published.

Late years, 1898–1916

In 1897–1898 he moved to Rye, Sussex, and wrote The Turn of the Screw. 1899–1900 saw the publication of The Awkward Age and The Sacred

411

Fount. During 1902–1904 he wrote The Ambassadors, The Wings of the Dove, and The Golden Bowl.

In 1904 he revisited America and lectured on Balzac. In 1906–1910 he published The American Scene and edited the "New York Edition", a 24-volume collection of his works. In 1910 his brother William died; Henry had just joined William from an unsuccessful search for relief in Europe on what then turned out to be his (Henry's) last visit to the United States (from summer 1910 to July 1911), and was near him, according to a letter he wrote, when he died.

In 1913 he wrote his autobiographies, A Small Boy and Others, and Notes of a Son and Brother. After the outbreak of the First World War in 1914 he did war work. In 1915 he became a British subject and was awarded the Order of Merit the following year. He died on 28 February 1916, in Chelsea, London. As he requested, his ashes were buried in Cambridge Cemetery in Massachusetts.

Biographers

James regularly rejected suggestions that he should marry, and after settling in London proclaimed himself "a bachelor". F. W. Dupee, in several volumes on the James family, originated the theory that he had been in love with his cousin Mary ("Minnie") Temple, but that a neurotic fear of sex kept him from admitting such affections: "James's invalidism ... was itself the symptom of some fear of or scruple against sexual love on his part." Dupee used an episode from James's memoir A Small Boy and Others, recounting a dream of a Napoleonic image in the Louvre, to exemplify James's romanticism about Europe, a Napoleonic fantasy into which he fled.

Dupee had not had access to the James family papers and worked principally from James's published memoir of his older brother, William, and the limited collection of letters edited by Percy Lubbock, heavily weighted toward James's last years. His account therefore moved directly from James's childhood, when he trailed after his older brother, to elderly invalidism. As more material became available to scholars, including the diaries of contemporaries and hundreds of affectionate and sometimes erotic letters

412

written by James to younger men, the picture of neurotic celibacy gave way to a portrait of a closeted homosexual.

Between 1953 and 1972, Leon Edel authored a major five-volume biography of James, which accessed unpublished letters and documents after Edel gained the permission of James's family. Edel's portrayal of James included the suggestion he was celibate. It was a view first propounded by critic Saul Rosenzweig in 1943. In 1996 Sheldon M. Novick published Henry James: The Young Master, followed by Henry James: The Mature Master (2007). The first book "caused something of an uproar in Jamesian circles" as it challenged the previous received notion of celibacy, a once-familiar paradigm in biographies of homosexuals when direct evidence was non-existent. Novick also criticised Edel for following the discounted Freudian interpretation of homosexuality "as a kind of failure." The difference of opinion erupted in a series of exchanges between Edel and Novick which were published by the online magazine Slate, with the latter arguing that even the suggestion of celibacy went against James's own injunction "live!"—not "fantasize!"

A letter James wrote in old age to Hugh Walpole has been cited as an explicit statement of this. Walpole confessed to him of indulging in "high jinks", and James wrote a reply endorsing it: "We must know, as much as possible, in our beautiful art, yours & mine, what we are talking about — & the only way to know it is to have lived & loved & cursed & floundered & enjoyed & suffered — I don't think I regret a single 'excess' of my responsive youth".

The interpretation of James as living a less austere emotional life has been subsequently explored by other scholars. The often intense politics of Jamesian scholarship has also been the subject of studies. Author Colm Tóibín has said that Eve Kosofsky Sedgwick's Epistemology of the Closet made a landmark difference to Jamesian scholarship by arguing that he be read as a homosexual writer whose desire to keep his sexuality a secret shaped his layered style and dramatic artistry. According to Tóibín such a reading "removed James from the realm of dead white males who wrote about posh people. He became our contemporary."

James's letters to expatriate American sculptor Hendrik Christian Andersen have attracted particular attention. James met the 27-year-old Andersen in Rome in 1899, when James was 56, and wrote letters to Andersen that are intensely emotional: "I hold you, dearest boy, in my innermost love, & count on your feeling me—in every throb of your soul". In a letter of 6 May 1904, to his brother William, James referred to himself as "always your hopelessly celibate even though sexagenarian Henry". How accurate that description might have been is the subject of contention among James's biographers,   but the letters to Andersen were occasionally quasi-erotic: "I put, my dear boy, my arm around you, & feel the pulsation, thereby, as it were, of our excellent future & your admirable endowment." To his homosexual friend Howard Sturgis, James could write: "I repeat, almost to indiscretion, that I could live with you. Meanwhile I can only try to live without you."

His numerous letters to the many young gay men among his close male friends are more forthcoming. In a letter to Howard Sturgis, following a long visit, James refers jocularly to their "happy little congress of two" and in letters to Hugh Walpole he pursues convoluted jokes and puns about their relationship, referring to himself as an elephant who "paws you oh so benevolently" and winds about Walpole his "well meaning old trunk". His letters to Walter Berry printed by the Black Sun Press have long been celebrated for their lightly veiled eroticism.

He corresponded in almost equally extravagant language with his many female friends, writing, for example, to fellow novelist Lucy Clifford: "Dearest Lucy! What shall I say? when I love you so very, very much, and see you nine times for once that I see Others! Therefore I think that—if you want it made clear to the meanest intelligence—I love you more than I love Others." To his New York friend Mary Cadwalader Jones: "Dearest Mary Cadwalader. I yearn over you, but I yearn in vain; & your long silence really breaks my heart, mystifies, depresses, almost alarms me, to the point even of making me wonder if poor unconscious & doting old Célimare [Jones's pet name for James] has 'done' anything, in some dark somnambulism of the spirit, which has ... given you a bad moment, or a wrong impression, or a 'colourable pretext' ... However these things may be, he loves you as tenderly as ever;

414

nothing, to the end of time, will ever detach him from you, & he remembers those Eleventh St. matutinal intimes hours, those telephonic matinées, as the most romantic of his life ..." His long friendship with American novelist Constance Fenimore Woolson, in whose house he lived for a number of weeks in Italy in 1887, and his shock and grief over her suicide in 1894, are discussed in detail in Edel's biography and play a central role in a study by Lyndall Gordon. (Edel conjectured that Woolson was in love with James and killed herself in part because of his coldness, but Woolson's biographers have objected to Edel's account.)

Works

Style and themes

James is one of the major figures of trans-Atlantic literature. His works frequently juxtapose characters from the Old World (Europe), embodying a feudal civilisation that is beautiful, often corrupt, and alluring, and from the New World (United States), where people are often brash, open, and assertive and embody the virtues—freedom and a more highly evolved moral character—of the new American society. James explores this clash of personalities and cultures, in stories of personal relationships in which power is exercised well or badly. His protagonists were often young American women facing oppression or abuse, and as his secretary Theodora Bosanquet remarked in her monograph Henry James at Work:

> When he walked out of the refuge of his study and into the world and looked around him, he saw a place of torment, where creatures of prey perpetually thrust their claws into the quivering flesh of doomed, defenseless children of light ... His novels are a repeated exposure of this wickedness, a reiterated and passionate plea for the fullest freedom of development, unimperiled by reckless and barbarous stupidity.

Critics have jokingly described three phases in the development of James's prose: "James I, James II, and The Old Pretender." He wrote short stories and plays. Finally, in his third and last period he returned to the long, serialised novel. Beginning in the second period, but most noticeably in the third, he increasingly abandoned direct statement in favour of frequent double negatives, and complex descriptive imagery. Single paragraphs began to run for page after page, in which an initial noun would be succeeded by pronouns surrounded by clouds of adjectives and prepositional clauses, far from their original referents, and verbs would be deferred and then preceded by a series of adverbs. The overall effect could be a vivid evocation of a scene as perceived by a sensitive observer. It has been debated whether this change of style was engendered by James's shifting from writing to dictating to a typist, a change made during the composition of What Maisie Knew.

In its intense focus on the consciousness of his major characters, James's later work foreshadows extensive developments in 20th century fiction. Indeed, he might have influenced stream-of-consciousness writers such as Virginia Woolf, who not only read some of his novels but also wrote essays about them. Both contemporary and modern readers have found the late style difficult and unnecessary; his friend Edith Wharton, who admired him greatly, said that there were passages in his work that were all but incomprehensible. James was harshly portrayed by H. G. Wells as a hippopotamus laboriously attempting to pick up a pea that had got into a corner of its cage. The "late James" style was ably parodied by Max Beerbohm in "The Mote in the Middle Distance".

More important for his work overall may have been his position as an expatriate, and in other ways an outsider, living in Europe. While he came from middle-class and provincial beginnings (seen from the perspective of European polite society) he worked very hard to gain access to all levels of society, and the settings of his fiction range from working class to aristocratic, and often describe the efforts of middle-class Americans to make their way in European capitals. He confessed he got some of his best story ideas from gossip at the dinner table or at country house weekends. He worked for a living, however, and lacked the experiences of select schools, university, and army service, the common bonds of masculine society. He was furthermore a man whose tastes and interests were, according to the prevailing standards of Victorian era Anglo-American culture, rather feminine, and who was shadowed by the cloud of prejudice that then and later accompanied suspicions of his homosexuality. Edmund Wilson famously compared James's objectivity to Shakespeare's:

One would be in a position to appreciate James better if one compared him with the dramatists of the seventeenth century—Racine and Molière, whom he resembles in form as well as in point of view, and even Shakespeare, when allowances are made for the most extreme differences in subject and form. These poets are not, like Dickens and Hardy, writers of melodrama—either humorous or pessimistic, nor secretaries of society like Balzac, nor prophets like Tolstoy: they are occupied simply with the presentation of conflicts of moral character, which they do not concern themselves about softening or averting. They do not indict society for these situations: they regard them as universal and inevitable. They do not even blame God for allowing them: they accept them as the conditions of life.

It is also possible to see many of James's stories as psychological thought-experiments. In his preface to the New York edition of The American he describes the development of the story in his mind as exactly such: the "situation" of an American, "some robust but insidiously beguiled and betrayed, some cruelly wronged, compatriot..." with the focus of the story being on the response of this wronged man. The Portrait of a Lady may be an experiment to see what happens when an idealistic young woman suddenly becomes very rich. In many of his tales, characters seem to exemplify alternative futures and possibilities, as most markedly in "The Jolly Corner", in which the protagonist and a ghost-doppelganger live alternative American and European lives; and in others, like The Ambassadors, an older James seems fondly to regard his own younger self facing a crucial moment.

Major novels

The first period of James's fiction, usually considered to have culminated in The Portrait of a Lady, concentrated on the contrast between Europe and America. The style of these novels is generally straightforward and, though personally characteristic, well within the norms of 19th-century fiction. Roderick Hudson (1875) is a Künstlerroman that traces the development of the title character, an extremely talented sculptor. Although the book shows some signs of immaturity—this was James's first serious attempt at a full-length novel—it has attracted favourable comment due to the vivid realisation of the three major characters: Roderick Hudson, superbly gifted but unstable and unreliable; Rowland Mallet, Roderick's limited but much more mature friend and patron; and Christina Light, one of James's most enchanting and maddening femmes fatales. The pair of Hudson and Mallet has been seen as representing the two sides of James's own nature: the wildly imaginative artist and the brooding conscientious mentor.

In The Portrait of a Lady (1881) James concluded the first phase of his career with a novel that remains his most popular piece of long fiction. The story is of a spirited young American woman, Isabel Archer, who "affronts her destiny" and finds it overwhelming. She inherits a large amount of money and subsequently becomes the victim of Machiavellian scheming by two American expatriates. The narrative is set mainly in Europe, especially in England and Italy. Generally regarded as the masterpiece of his early phase, The Portrait of a Lady is described as a psychological novel, exploring the minds of his characters, and almost a work of social science, exploring the differences between Europeans and Americans, the old and the new worlds.

The second period of James's career, which extends from the publication of The Portrait of a Lady through the end of the nineteenth century, features less popular novels including The Princess Casamassima, published serially in The Atlantic Monthly in 1885–1886, and The Bostonians, published serially in The Century Magazine during the same period. This period also featured James's celebrated Gothic novella, The Turn of the Screw.

The third period of James's career reached its most significant achievement in three novels published just around the start of the 20th century: The Wings of the Dove (1902), The Ambassadors (1903), and The Golden Bowl (1904). Critic F. O. Matthiessen called this "trilogy" James's major phase, and these novels have certainly received intense critical study. It was the second-written of the books, The Wings of the Dove (1902) that was the first published because it attracted no serialization. This novel tells the story of Milly Theale, an American heiress stricken with a serious disease, and her impact on the people around her. Some of these people befriend Milly with honourable motives, while others are more self-interested. James stated in his autobiographical books that Milly was based on Minny Temple, his beloved cousin who died at an early age of tuberculosis. He said that he attempted in the novel to wrap her memory in the "beauty and dignity of art".

Shorter narratives

James was particularly interested in what he called the "beautiful and blest nouvelle", or the longer form of short narrative. Still, he produced a number of very short stories in which he achieved notable compression of sometimes complex subjects. The following narratives are representative of James's achievement in the shorter forms of fiction.

- "A Tragedy of Error" (1864), short story
- "The Story of a Year" (1865), short story
- A Passionate Pilgrim (1871), novella
- Madame de Mauves (1874), novella
- Daisy Miller (1878), novella
- The Aspern Papers (1888), novella
- The Lesson of the Master (1888), novella
- The Pupil (1891), short story
- "The Figure in the Carpet" (1896), short story
- The Beast in the Jungle (1903), novella
- An International Episode (1878)
- Picture and Text
- Four Meetings (1885)
- A London Life, and Other Tales (1889)
- The Spoils of Poynton (1896)

- Embarrassments (1896)

- The Two Magics: The Turn of the Screw, Covering End (1898)

- A Little Tour of France (1900)

- The Sacred Fount (1901)

- Views and Reviews (1908)

- The Wings of the Dove, Volume I (1902)

- The Wings of the Dove, Volume II (1909)

- The Finer Grain (1910)

- The Outcry (1911)

- Lady Barbarina: The Siege of London, An International Episode and Other Tales (1922)

- The Birthplace (1922)

Plays

At several points in his career James wrote plays, beginning with one-act plays written for periodicals in 1869 and 1871 and a dramatisation of his popular novella Daisy Miller in 1882. From 1890 to 1892, having received a bequest that freed him from magazine publication, he made a strenuous effort to succeed on the London stage, writing a half-dozen plays of which only one, a dramatisation of his novel The American, was produced. This play was performed for several years by a touring repertory company and had a respectable run in London, but did not earn very much money for James. His other plays written at this time were not produced.

In 1893, however, he responded to a request from actor-manager George Alexander for a serious play for the opening of his renovated St. James's Theatre, and wrote a long drama, Guy Domville, which Alexander produced. There was a noisy uproar on the opening night, 5 January 1895, with hissing from the gallery when James took his bow after the final curtain, and the author was upset. The play received moderately good reviews and had a modest run of four weeks before being taken off to make way for Oscar Wilde's The Importance of Being Earnest, which Alexander thought would have better prospects for the coming season.

After the stresses and disappointment of these efforts James insisted that he would write no more for the theatre, but within weeks had agreed to write a curtain-raiser for Ellen Terry. This became the one-act "Summersoft", which he later rewrote into a short story, "Covering End", and then expanded into a full-length play, The High Bid, which had a brief run in London in 1907, when James made another concerted effort to write for the stage. He wrote three new plays, two of which were in production when the death of Edward VII on 6 May 1910 plunged London into mourning and theatres closed. Discouraged by failing health and the stresses of theatrical work, James did not renew his efforts in the theatre, but recycled his plays as successful novels. The Outcry was a best-seller in the United States when it was published in 1911. During the years 1890–1893 when he was most engaged with the theatre, James wrote a good deal of theatrical criticism and assisted Elizabeth Robins and others in translating and producing Henrik Ibsen for the first time in London.

Leon Edel argued in his psychoanalytic biography that James was traumatised by the opening night uproar that greeted Guy Domville, and that it plunged him into a prolonged depression. The successful later novels, in Edel's view, were the result of a kind of self-analysis, expressed in fiction, which partly freed him from his fears. Other biographers and scholars have not accepted this account, however; the more common view being that of F.O. Matthiessen, who wrote: "Instead of being crushed by the collapse of his hopes [for the theatre]... he felt a resurgence of new energy."

Non-fiction

Beyond his fiction, James was one of the more important literary critics in the history of the novel. In his classic essay The Art of Fiction (1884), he argued against rigid prescriptions on the novelist's choice of subject and method of treatment. He maintained that the widest possible freedom in content and approach would help ensure narrative fiction's continued vitality.

421

James wrote many valuable critical articles on other novelists; typical is his book-length study of Nathaniel Hawthorne, which has been the subject of critical debate. Richard Brodhead has suggested that the study was emblematic of James's struggle with Hawthorne's influence, and constituted an effort to place the elder writer "at a disadvantage." Gordon Fraser, meanwhile, has suggested that the study was part of a more commercial effort by James to introduce himself to British readers as Hawthorne's natural successor.

When James assembled the New York Edition of his fiction in his final years, he wrote a series of prefaces that subjected his own work to searching, occasionally harsh criticism.

At 22 James wrote The Noble School of Fiction for The Nation's first issue in 1865. He would write, in all, over 200 essays and book, art, and theatre reviews for the magazine.

For most of his life James harboured ambitions for success as a playwright. He converted his novel The American into a play that enjoyed modest returns in the early 1890s. In all he wrote about a dozen plays, most of which went unproduced. His costume drama Guy Domville failed disastrously on its opening night in 1895. James then largely abandoned his efforts to conquer the stage and returned to his fiction. In his Notebooks he maintained that his theatrical experiment benefited his novels and tales by helping him dramatise his characters' thoughts and emotions. James produced a small but valuable amount of theatrical criticism, including perceptive appreciations of Henrik Ibsen.

With his wide-ranging artistic interests, James occasionally wrote on the visual arts. Perhaps his most valuable contribution was his favourable assessment of fellow expatriate John Singer Sargent, a painter whose critical status has improved markedly in recent decades. James also wrote sometimes charming, sometimes brooding articles about various places he visited and lived in. His most famous books of travel writing include Italian Hours (an example of the charming approach) and The American Scene (most definitely on the brooding side).

James was one of the great letter-writers of any era. More than ten thousand of his personal letters are extant, and over three thousand have been published in a large number of collections. A complete edition of James's letters began publication in 2006, edited by Pierre Walker and Greg Zacharias. As of 2014, eight volumes have been published, covering the period from 1855 to 1880. James's correspondents included celebrated contemporaries like Robert Louis Stevenson, Edith Wharton and Joseph Conrad, along with many others in his wide circle of friends and acquaintances. The letters range from the "mere twaddle of graciousness" to serious discussions of artistic, social and personal issues.

Very late in life James began a series of autobiographical works: A Small Boy and Others, Notes of a Son and Brother, and the unfinished The Middle Years. These books portray the development of a classic observer who was passionately interested in artistic creation but was somewhat reticent about participating fully in the life around him.

Reception

Criticism, biographies and fictional treatments

James's work has remained steadily popular with the limited audience of educated readers to whom he spoke during his lifetime, and has remained firmly in the canon, but, after his death, some American critics, such as Van Wyck Brooks, expressed hostility towards James for his long expatriation and eventual naturalisation as a British subject. Other critics such as E. M. Forster complained about what they saw as James's squeamishness in the treatment of sex and other possibly controversial material, or dismissed his late style as difficult and obscure, relying heavily on extremely long sentences and excessively latinate language. Similarly Oscar Wilde criticised him for writing "fiction as if it were a painful duty". Vernon Parrington, composing a canon of American literature, condemned James for having cut himself off from America. Jorge Luis Borges wrote about him, "Despite the scruples and delicate complexities of James, his work suffers from a major defect: the absence of life." And Virginia Woolf, writing to Lytton Strachey, asked, "Please tell me what you find in Henry James. ... we have his works here, and

I read, and I can't find anything but faintly tinged rose water, urbane and sleek, but vulgar and pale as Walter Lamb. Is there really any sense in it?" The novelist W. Somerset Maugham wrote, "He did not know the English as an Englishman instinctively knows them and so his English characters never to my mind quite ring true," and argued "The great novelists, even in seclusion, have lived life passionately. Henry James was content to observe it from a window." Maugham nevertheless wrote, "The fact remains that those last novels of his, notwithstanding their unreality, make all other novels, except the very best, unreadable." Colm Tóibín observed that James "never really wrote about the English very well. His English characters don't work for me."

Despite these criticisms, James is now valued for his psychological and moral realism, his masterful creation of character, his low-key but playful humour, and his assured command of the language. In his 1983 book, The Novels of Henry James, Edward Wagenknecht offers an assessment that echoes Theodora Bosanquet's:

> "To be completely great," Henry James wrote in an early review, "a work of art must lift up the heart," and his own novels do this to an outstanding degree ... More than sixty years after his death, the great novelist who sometimes professed to have no opinions stands foursquare in the great Christian humanistic and democratic tradition. The men and women who, at the height of World War II, raided the secondhand shops for his out-of-print books knew what they were about. For no writer ever raised a braver banner to which all who love freedom might adhere.

William Dean Howells saw James as a representative of a new realist school of literary art which broke with the English romantic tradition epitomised by the works of Charles Dickens and William Makepeace Thackeray. Howells wrote that realism found "its chief exemplar in Mr. James... A novelist he is not, after the old fashion, or after any fashion but his own." F.R. Leavis championed Henry James as a novelist of "established pre-eminence" in The Great Tradition (1948), asserting that The Portrait of a Lady and The Bostonians were "the two most brilliant novels in the language." James is now prized as a master of point of view who moved literary fiction forward by insisting in showing, not telling, his stories to the reader. (Source: Wikipedia)

424

NOTABLE WORKS

NOVELS

Watch and Ward (1871)

Roderick Hudson (1875)

The American (1877)

The Europeans (1878)

Confidence (1879)

Washington Square (1880)

The Portrait of a Lady (1881)

The Bostonians (1886)

The Princess Casamassima (1886)

The Reverberator (1888)

The Tragic Muse (1890)

The Other House (1896)

The Spoils of Poynton (1897)

What Maisie Knew (1897)

The Awkward Age (1899)

The Sacred Fount (1901)

The Wings of the Dove (1902)

The Ambassadors (1903)

The Golden Bowl (1904)

The Whole Family (collaborative novel with eleven other authors, 1908)

The Outcry (1911)

The Ivory Tower (unfinished, published posthumously 1917)

The Sense of the Past (unfinished, published posthumously 1917)

SHORT STORIES AND NOVELLAS

A Tragedy of Error (1864)

The Story of a Year (1865)

A Landscape Painter (1866)

A Day of Days (1866)

My Friend Bingham (1867)

Poor Richard (1867)

The Story of a Masterpiece (1868)

A Most Extraordinary Case (1868)

A Problem (1868)

De Grey: A Romance (1868)

Osborne's Revenge (1868)

The Romance of Certain Old Clothes (1868)

A Light Man (1869)

Gabrielle de Bergerac (1869)

Travelling Companions (1870)

A Passionate Pilgrim (1871)

At Isella (1871)

Master Eustace (1871)

Guest's Confession (1872)

The Madonna of the Future (1873)

The Sweetheart of M. Briseux (1873)

The Last of the Valerii (1874)

Madame de Mauves (1874)

Adina (1874)

Professor Fargo (1874)

Eugene Pickering (1874)

Benvolio (1875)

Crawford's Consistency (1876)

The Ghostly Rental (1876)

Four Meetings (1877)

Rose-Agathe (1878, as Théodolinde)

Daisy Miller (1878)

Longstaff's Marriage (1878)

An International Episode (1878)

The Pension Beaurepas (1879)

A Diary of a Man of Fifty (1879)

A Bundle of Letters (1879)

The Point of View (1882)

The Siege of London (1883)

Impressions of a Cousin (1883)

Lady Barberina (1884)

Pandora (1884)

The Author of Beltraffio (1884)

Georgina's Reasons (1884)

A New England Winter (1884)

The Path of Duty (1884)

Mrs. Temperly (1887)

Louisa Pallant (1888)

The Aspern Papers (1888)

The Liar (1888)

The Modern Warning (1888, originally published as The Two Countries)

A London Life (1888)

The Patagonia (1888)

The Lesson of the Master (1888)

The Solution (1888)

The Pupil (1891)

Brooksmith (1891)

The Marriages (1891)

The Chaperon (1891)

Sir Edmund Orme (1891)

Nona Vincent (1892)

The Real Thing (1892)

The Private Life (1892)

Lord Beaupré (1892)

The Visits (1892)

Sir Dominick Ferrand (1892)

Greville Fane (1892)

Collaboration (1892)

Owen Wingrave (1892)

The Wheel of Time (1892)

The Middle Years (1893)

The Death of the Lion (1894)

The Coxon Fund (1894)

The Next Time (1895)

Glasses (1896)

The Altar of the Dead (1895)

The Figure in the Carpet (1896)

The Way It Came (1896, also published as The Friends of the Friends)

The Turn of the Screw (1898)

Covering End (1898)

In the Cage (1898)

John Delavoy (1898)

The Given Case (1898)

Europe (1899)

The Great Condition (1899)

The Real Right Thing (1899)

Paste (1899)

The Great Good Place (1900)

Maud-Evelyn (1900)

Miss Gunton of Poughkeepsie (1900)

The Tree of Knowledge (1900)

The Abasement of the Northmores (1900)

The Third Person (1900)

The Special Type (1900)

The Tone of Time (1900)

Broken Wings (1900)

The Two Faces (1900)

Mrs. Medwin (1901)

The Beldonald Holbein (1901)

The Story in It (1902)

Flickerbridge (1902)

The Birthplace (1903)

The Beast in the Jungle (1903)

The Papers (1903)

Fordham Castle (1904)

Julia Bride (1908)

The Jolly Corner (1908)

The Velvet Glove (1909)

Mora Montravers (1909)

Crapy Cornelia (1909)

The Bench of Desolation (1909)

A Round of Visits (1910)

OTHER

Transatlantic Sketches (1875)

French Poets and Novelists (1878)

Hawthorne (1879)

Portraits of Places (1883)

A Little Tour in France (1884)

Partial Portraits (1888)

Essays in London and Elsewhere (1893)

Picture and Text (1893)

Terminations (1893)

Theatricals (1894)

Theatricals: Second Series (1895)

Guy Domville (1895)

The Soft Side (1900)

William Wetmore Story and His Friends (1903)

The Better Sort (1903)

English Hours (1905)

The Question of our Speech; The Lesson of Balzac. Two Lectures (1905)

The American Scene (1907)

Views and Reviews (1908)

Italian Hours (1909)

A Small Boy and Others (1913)

Notes on Novelists (1914)

Notes of a Son and Brother (1914)

Within the Rim (1918)

Travelling Companions (1919)

Notebooks (various, published posthumously)

The Middle Years (unfinished, published posthumously 1917)

A Most Unholy Trade (1925, published posthumously)

The Art of the Novel : Critical Prefaces (1934)